Storm Constantine's Wraeththu Mythos

Para Spectral

Hauntings of Wraeththu

Para Spectral

Hauntings of Wraeththu

Edited by Storm Constantine
and Wendy Darling

IMMANION PRESS
Stafford, England

Cover art and Wraeththu Mythos logo: Ruby
Interior layout: Storm Constantine
Interior illustrations: Storm Constantine
Map of Alba Sulh by Maria J. Leel and Gordon Leel, based upon an original illustration by Andy Bigwood.

Set in Garamond

IP0147
ISBN 978-1-907737-96-1

First edition by Immanion Press, 2018
An Immanion Press Edition
http://www.immanion-press.com
info@immanion-press.com

Contents

Introduction

Storm Constantine

I adore ghost stories, so am delighted to present this fifth volume in the 'Para' series of Wraeththu anthologies, which comprises stories of the supernatural. The book was immense fun to compile, edit and contribute to.

Before talking about the stories, and for those who might not have read any Wraeththu books before, this volume in your hands is a shared world project, based upon my novels in the three science fantasy trilogies 'The Wraeththu Chronicles', 'The Wraeththu Histories' and 'The Alba Sulh Sequence'. The first of these, (*The Enchantments of Flesh and Spirit*), was published in the late 1980s – Immanion Press has recently released the fourth edition of the trilogy, with lavish new covers by official Wraeththu artist, Ruby.

The world of Wraeththu had been my constant companion – and continues to be – since long before my first book was published. Although I write across genres, and have created other worlds with rich histories, Wraeththu remains my first love. These characters originally made themselves known to my imagination way back when I was a young teenager – they were androgynous beings with heightened physical, mental and spiritual powers, who rose from the ashes of a shattered human civilisation to create a new and hopefully better world. Conflict arose from the fact they struggled to live up to their potential, and in most cases were so traumatised by their transformation from human to har they were – at least initially – incapable of healthy evolution.

I've included a brief explanation of the Wraeththu and their world after this introduction, and you'll also find a glossary of terms at the end of the book.

Previous anthologies in the series have covered the origins of Wraeththu, then stories set in their far future, followed by musings on how strange mutations might have evolved in various hara, and also a collection on their spiritual relationship with animals. This book focuses upon the supernatural – hara's experience of the unseen, the uncanny.

My piece, 'The Emptiness Next Door' is an adaptation of a story by the American writer Mary Wilkins Freeman, which was written in 1902. It was called 'The Vacant Lot' and appeared in *Everybody's Magazine* and more recently in an eBook collection of her stories. There was an abundance of accomplished, female ghost story writers in those times, some of them famous mainstream authors, such as Edith Wharton and Mrs Gaskell, who wrote supernatural stories for magazines and newspapers. I devour voraciously the often long-forgotten ghost tales of these superb authors, thanks to the new collections that have appeared – and continue to appear – in eBook. (More people should read them now because a lot of these women certainly knew how to spook!)

When I read 'The Vacant Lot' it intrigued me immensely and also gave me an idea for this anthology. Freeman wrote it with a light touch – it has some comedic elements amid the weirdness – whereas my story has a darker tone. I knew what the Blue Leopard would be in a Wraeththu tale, and how the story would differ from the original. The only thing I've retained is the rough outline – the basic manifestations of the haunting – but the characters, the explanation for and expansion of the plot are entirely mine.

In 'The Vacant Lot', Freeman never explains exactly what the haunting is, and why it takes the forms it does. One of the protagonists gets *some* idea of why his family might have encountered these odd appearances, but never learns why they manifest in the forms his people witness. I give more explanation in my story, but then, at the end of writing it, I realised I had at the very least a much longer novella on my hands, if not a full-length novel. I knew I'd have to expand the tale and reveal much more. 'The Emptiness Next Door' can be read as the first few chapters of a book. I'm already working on it.

Wendy Darling also found her inspiration in an old Victorian ghost story and adapted one for this anthology. 'When Storm suggested the theme of ghosts, my mind immediately went to Victorian Gothic stories of haunted manors, spectres on the moors, that sort of thing. Looking for inspiration, I searched the Internet for examples and not long into it, stumbled onto 'The Old Nurse's

Story' by Elizabeth Gaskell, dating to 1852. It has all the classic elements of a Victorian scare story and some even of *Jane Eyre* – orphan, big house full of family secrets, a ghost organ, mysterious forces luring a child to their doom. I was so inspired I decided to do a full-on adaptation of the story, drastically changing the style of the original – long paragraphs without a great deal of dialog and rather poor pacing – into something more up to modern taste. I think I must've always wanted to write about a big, old house like that, because I persisted on with what proved to be a more difficult than usual writing process. Fortunately, I did have the benefit of many visits to historic homes, from Edith Wharton's home *The Mount* in western Massachusetts to *Waddesdon Manor* in Buckinghamshire. For the purpose of the story, *Leven Manor* is actually located in Scotland, which in the story is called Alba Caledon.

Martina Bellovičová tells us: "The original premise of my story was pretty simple: a har's chesnari dies and, courtesy of a near-death experience, he's able to access his beloved in the spiritual plane, while engaging in aruna with others. I wanted to explore the influence this would have on his life, but it took me some time to decide about the plot and setting. One of the things I love about Wraeththu is the diversity – you can use inspiration from almost any mythology or cultural background and implant it on a tribe inhabiting the corresponding part of the world. My interest in Scandinavian lore, fond memories of the year I lived in Finland during my studies, and binge-watching of the show *Vikings* all contributed to the Freyhellan revenge tale I ultimately chose to go with. I like to believe that the ominous nature of northern mythology enhanced the paranormal feel of the story."

Nerine Dorman found her inspiration in the sea: "'A Handful of Sea Coins' is born out of my long association with the ocean. As a child, I often spent hours in the tidal pools in and around the Cape Peninsula in South Africa, poking at sea anemones, and collecting alikreukel shells (or rather their disc-like 'doors' or sea coins, as I called them) – often making up stories for the microcosms I explored. There's a particular magic in the relentless wash of the cold Atlantic – and I have always been drawn to wonder about what lies beneath the surface, hidden in the depths. Invariably in the stories or songs I write, there is often reference to the ocean in some shape or form. The sea is in my blood, and in this particular story, I tell about a har's connection to a deeper mystery.'

Amanda Kear had done volunteering behind the scenes in the natural history collections of her local museum and was struck by the idea that if all those specimens are invaluable for conservation efforts now, then that is doubly so when you add hara magic and animal ghosts into the equation. It seemed logical to her that there would be hara who wanted to use the museum collections to restore Earth's ecosystems to what they had once been before the impact of humanity, including resurrecting extinct species. She says: 'The Natural History Museum in London was an obvious and iconic location to set the story and has the added bonus that Lund is a very, very dangerous place, which makes it fun to write about. The scholars and Shadow let me channel my inner science geek. Drey, the sarcastic scavenger, is the descendant of many roleplaying characters who have exclaimed: *They want to hire us to do WHAT? Are they insane?*'

Zane Marc Gentis found his inspiration in the rituals of ascension to adulthood. He explains: 'Many cultures around the world have a tradition of rite of passage, marking the moment children officially become adults in the eyes of their community. A ritual of this nature felt ideally suited to the telling of a story with ghosts both literal and metaphorical. Every choice we make is a simultaneous affirmation and rejection, creating ghosts of who we were and who we could have been.'

Christiane Gertz is involved in the music business through organising rock concerts. This enthusiasm provided the inspiration for her story 'The Strangest Ghost of Apaley'. In the town of Apaley, the 'spirit subsessor' Zeboah is called to a new client. This is a famous singer, who's haunted by a mysterious entity. Together with his young, enthusiastic assistant Altavi, Zeboah tries to solve the case — why can't they communicate with this strange ghost? Even their usual rituals don't seem to work. But could music be the key?

Fiona Lane tells us her story was inspired by a line from the poem 'Leda and the Swan' by W B Yeats, which itself is based on ancient

Greek mythology.

'In the myth, Zeus, the king of the Olympian gods takes on the form of a swan in order to rape Leda, daughter of King Thestius (as you do). The law of unintended consequences applies, and Leda duly gives birth to Helen of Troy, thereby setting in motion the whole chain of events which lead to the Trojan War. The poem draws a direct and sudden connection between the conception and later, tragic events:

A shudder in the loins engenders there
The broken wall, the burning roof and tower
And Agamemnon dead.

'Perhaps Zeus would have kept his beak to himself* if he'd been aware of the chain of events he was about to set in motion, but no-one knows how the past and the present will affect the future.

'But suppose you did know….?

'Observant readers will notice that I stole and har-ified Leda's name for one of the characters in my story.

(* or perhaps not, he was that sort of god.)'

Maria J. Leel says that being a fan of Wraeththu back in the late 1980s could be a lonely old business… but then in the late 1990s a most wondrous invention went mainstream – The Internet – and a disparate group of isolated Wraeththu fans from all over the world discovered each other and began to 'meet' on a regular basis. Their meeting place was a chat room called 'The Stone Inn'. Here they used to discuss the trilogy, (now the Wraeththu Chronicles), their favourite characters and an awful lot of 'what ifs'. On occasion I joined them myself and had great fun chatting with like-minded people about my beloved creations. Inevitably, a great deal of fan fiction came out of 'The Stone Inn' gatherings, much of which is still housed on the 'Forever' website, presided over for many years by Wendy Darling.

Maria's story for this anthology, 'Recalled to Life', had its origin as a piece of collaborative fan fiction from the days before Immanion Press entitled 'Tales from Fallsend' (also known as the 'Serious Round Robin'). Two such humorous collaborations, 'From Har to Maternity' and 'A Day at the Races', were completed and made it into the Forever fiction archive, but the more serious 'Tales from Fallsend' foundered and was never completed.

Maria says she always wondered how the character Toban's

story would pan out and in *Para Spectral*, she's glad to have been able to explore that. Her original plans for Toban were quite different, however. She'd been intrigued by something Opalexian said in the later part of *The Fulfilments of Fate and Desire*. All along she'd had a Roselane posted in Fallsend to keep an eye out for Cal during his time there but, thanks to Panthera, his input wasn't needed. The Roselane '...had his own karmic debts to sort out; Cal was part of it'. Maria wondered about this har but, ultimately, Toban wasn't him and Toban's story became his own. Maria muses that perhaps one day she'll revisit the poor abandoned Roselane and see what tale he has to tell...

E. S. Wynn reveals that the inspiration for 'The Hardest Hue to Hold' was, strangely enough, personal experience. He grew up in a haunted house in the Gold Country of California and encountered many spirits during the first 20 years of his life out there. Stories of paranormal phenomena are common fodder for conversation with his family, and this no doubt provided a firm foundation early on for all that he experienced on the long, lonely nights way out in the hills. The house from the story is the house he grew up in, and to this day he still dreams about it almost every night. He says that a part of him will always be there, even though the house is an abandoned ruin now. For him, 'The Hardest Hue to Hold' is a story of farewell, of letting go, of moving on and growing into something better. It was written at a time when he was finally starting to let go of the deep pain of the nasty divorce he'd recently gone through, so in a way, it's a farewell not just to the house and life of his youth, but also to all of the lives he's lived before, all of the people he's been, both in this body and in those he may have inhabited in centuries past.

As usual, I'm delighted that another Para anthology includes authors from around the world – Scotland, England, America, Germany, Czech Republic and South Africa – expanding upon the Wraeththu Mythos. So now, sit back, preferably in a darkened room lit only by candlelight, and discover the ghosts that walk these pages.

Storm Constantine,
May 2018

The Wraeththu

A Brief Definition of Their Origin

Humanity is in decline, ravaged by insanity, natural disasters, conflict, disease and infertility. A mysterious new race has risen from the ghettos and ruins of the decaying, dying cities. The young are evolving into a new species, which is stronger, sharper and more beautiful than their forerunners. Androgynous beings, they transcend gender and race. They possess keen psychic abilities and the means, through a process called inception, to transform humans into creatures like themselves. But they are wild in their rebirth and must strive to overcome all that is human within them in order to create society anew. They are the Wraeththu...

A Word on Pronouns

Within the Wraeththu Mythos, hara are referred to as 'he', since back in the 1980s when I first started writing within the mythos, this pronoun seemed to me less gender specific than 'she'. A lot has changed in both culture and language since then, (which necessitates the inclusion of this clarification), but to glue a new pronoun over all the stories would feel at best clunky and contrived. I ask readers to look beyond the loaded meaning of the male pronoun, and to read it as non-gender specific.

Storm Constantine

Recalled to Life

Maria J. Leel

That particular night seemed no different from any other. I don't recall doing anything exceptionally stupid. It had been such an ordinary evening, a steady stream of customers through the etched glass doors of *The Topaz Crown*. The seafood and wild mushroom risotto proved most popular that night, especially served with the crisp Santha wine. After closing, the usual crowd hung around the kitchen door, hungry for leftovers.

'Are you alright to close up, Toban?' Surkka called from his chair by the cash till. My employer knew he was onto a good thing. I'm one of the best waiters in Fallsend and he was content for me to run the place. *The Topaz Crown* is a favoured haunt of many a musenda owner and well-heeled trader, and Surkka enjoys lounging around in such company and feeling important. On a typical evening, he will settle himself in his chair and not move until closing time. Typically, a bottle of something fine and a plate of sweetmeats will be at his elbow. Without his harish constitution I'm sure he would be the size of a house.

'Of course,' I replied as he heaved himself upright and headed up to his opulent apartment on the second floor. I shouldn't mock him. He indulged me and overlooked the scraps I fed to the destitute. He laughed for a week when I planted a herb garden at the back of the inn. Although later he did have to concede that the improved cuisine resulting from those herbs had been good for business. 'All right, all right... you win this one.'

It amused him greatly that most of my wages were spent sending home the crazy kids who come to Fallsend in search of adventure. Next time Surkka needed a good laugh, I planned to tell him about the trailing vines and hanging baskets I had planned for the front of *The Crown*.

I heard the stair creak as I went to tend to the quiet, hungry huddle of hara who had collected, hopeful and out of sight, at the back. Once the food was distributed and wounds tended to, I went to bed myself, hoping to get a few hours' sleep before my usual dawn constitutional.

But that night, sleep was elusive. Up in my monastic little attic, the bed felt like a slab of granite and no matter how I punched or adjusted the pillow, I just couldn't get comfortable. But it wasn't the physical discomforts that kept me wakeful; it was the machinations of my mind. You know those nights – all too frequent for me – when the body is weary beyond description, but the brain wants to up and party? That night my grey matter chose to delight me with its best selection of visions from my Varrish past...

The young Unneah I surprised slaking his thirst at a woodland stream. I slit his throat and stained the waters red. We would have met in battle the next day, so I had only killed him a little earlier than necessary; besides, his horse was better than mine.

The grizzled war veteran, his tunic stained with the blood of so many, who had seen enough fighting and thanked me as I slid my blade into his belly.

The inadequately-armed messenger, barely past inception, sent for reinforcements that, thanks to me, would never arrive. I remember the sickening crunch of bone and sinew when I broke his neck.

On and on the memories came. After about an hour I couldn't take it anymore. I slipped down the stairs, through the kitchen and went out to prowl the streets. Walking helps keep the memories at bay. Perhaps this was my mistake, but how could I have known?

Perhaps I should say a word or two about Fallsend? You will almost certainly have heard of it – as a place to avoid. A place of reputation but not repute. A cold town in a cold country in an overlooked northerly corner of Thaine. In the low town, among the mud and rotting timbers of the canal district and the valley floor, the Garridan ply their trade, dealing in toxins and venoms. Farther up the hill the more salubrious 'up town' area is formed of high Gothic houses mainly run as musendas – that's whorehouses to the uninitiated. A veritable nest of vipers, and this is where I've chosen to make my home.

I turned my collar up against the icy wind as I left the inn. It's never warm in Fallsend, not even in high summer. Not far from *The Topaz Crown*, I came across two young hara, not yet ready to go home, who gladly took the food I had with me. Then there was a striking Ferike, disillusioned with his muddy kerb stone pillow, who consented to take the money I offered and head back to Jaddayoth. And so I came to the seedy alleys that led to the canal. Here, thick mist clings to the crumbling buildings and water gathers in foetid pools that never drain away. The stench of rot and decay rose up to greet me. After seven years you would think I'd have become used to the stink, but it still made me gag every time.

I'd been taking these night-time walks for so long that my senses were honed like talons. I knew who to help and who to avoid. That is... until that night. That is... I thought I did...

He was huddled at the top of a flight of stone steps. Paying customer at *The Crown* or destitute down and out, the greeting is always the same.

I laid my hand on his shoulder. 'Tiahaar, may I help you?'

I have never seen anything like it. The benign, huddled figure turned quickly. His aura shattered, fragmented, and screamed away from him in dagger-like shards. It is rare to meet one of our kind who is truly ugly. This one was. Thickened features. Twisted lips. As I met his eyes, I saw a flash of insanity, a raging cold hatred.

Almost at the same time the knife flashed in the greasy light of a street lamp.

His intention was to kill me, of that I was absolutely certain; only my past warrior training saved me from instant death. He pushed me away and fled towards the canal path.

I collapsed in a shop doorway, blood pouring from a dirty great hole in my guts. There was a lot of blood... a hell of a lot of blood. I'd seen blood before. Almost got blasé about it... But it's always more disturbing when it's your own, isn't it? And damnation it hurt...

I tried to get a grip.

'Breathe.
Still the mind.
Slow the heart.
Calm.
All will be well.'

My thoughts started to race, 'Surkka's going to be mad as a snake. His best waiter out of action.' But Surkka's anger was the least of my problems.

'Breathe.
Still the mind.
Slow the heart.
Calm.
All will be well.'

It wasn't working but still I tried.

'Breathe.
Still the mind.
Slow the heart.
Calm.
All will be well.'

An icy tide ran through my limbs, and before me the world began to blur.

I visualised a cloak of white light surrounding me, protecting me. In this safe little bubble, I hoped to restore the balance, give myself a chance. I had to get help. From somewhere, I summoned a little strength – my skills were atrophied but not dead – and sent out a mind touch to anyone who might aid me. Shortly after that I blacked out.

I was surprised when I woke. Surprised, mainly, that I'd woken at all. I was lying in a bed of some considerable comfort, in a cosy room where firelight made pretty patterns on the ceiling. From somewhere came the homely aroma of stewing vegetables. Only the dull blatter of rain against the window suggested I was still in Fallsend and not in some Nirvana. I tried to sit up and get a better look at my surroundings, but a vicious stabbing in my side made me lie back down and convinced me still further that I was very much alive.

The room swam for a moment as the pain subsided, and then a face loomed over me. It was a kindly face, not the sort you often see in Fallsend, and I thought I recognised it.

'You dine at *The Topaz Crown*,' I said, surprised how weak my own voice sounded.

He smiled. 'You recognise me?'

'A good waiter knows his patrons,' I whispered, but in truth the har before me had only been to the inn a handful of times during the past few weeks. Quiet, dined alone, no trouble, and had a preference for simple, unadorned, well-cooked food.

He sat gently on the bed, so as not to disturb me. 'My name is Alessi. And you are?'

'Toban,' I replied. 'You heard my mind touch?'

'I did, but I was almost too late getting to you. You had lost a great deal of blood.'

I looked around the room. 'Where am I?'

'My apartments in Upper Clay Street.'

Upper Clay Street... One of the better neighbourhoods in Fallsend.

Then I remembered. 'I was attacked... I don't know by who. Look, you've been very kind. Not many around here would take the trouble.'

He smiled a little. 'I saw in you... a kindred spirit? Forgive my directness, but you are Varr, aren't you?'

Well, that caught me out of left field. For a moment I hesitated, as this was not a subject I normally discussed with anyhar. But then, I had just nearly died and this har had saved my life.

'I was,' I replied carefully.

'So was I.'

A dawning of recognition. 'You fought in Ponclast's army?'

Alessi grimaced. 'Who didn't? Did we have much choice?'

'No,' I quietly agreed, exhaling slowly, expecting to be assailed by the usual array of guilt-fuelled images... but none were forthcoming.

Alessi shifted a little and asked in a voice that was little more than a whisper, 'Were you at Gebaddon?'

I blanched. I'd heard the rumours... *Gebaddon*. Thiede's enchanted forest... neither this world nor the next; a marriage of the realms of Hell. Those who did return from there came back on rafts like funeral barques, their bodies wasted, minds irreparably damaged, with eyes that had looked into the abyss.

I shivered as I shook my head. 'No, I'd escaped some time before that.'

'With the Zigane?'

I nodded, 'Yes, that's right.' Then I frowned. 'Were you at Gebaddon?'

'I was.'

'But I thought...'

Alessi sighed. 'The Gelaming allowed some of us to slip the net. Those they thought had the potential for redemption. Like you, I escaped with the Zigane and then spent some time in the healing houses at Shilalama.'

I was silent for a while. It was a lot to take in. My Varrish past was something that for years I'd taken great pains to hide, and to have it suddenly brought into the open like this was beyond disconcerting, maybe even frightening. But yet there was also a sense of relief, a release of pressure, similar to that when a boil is lanced.

Alessi got to his feet. 'I'm tiring you. I should let you rest.'

'No,' I replied. 'I'm interested. I want to know more.'

'There's plenty of time. Do you think you could manage something to eat? I could bring you some soup.'

'I think so'.

The soup was, like the har who brought it to me, unadorned and nourishing, and I wanted more.

'Sleep now,' Alessi advised as I finished the last spoonful. 'We'll talk later.'

I think I slept for a long while. A deep sleep, unbroken by dreams; the sweetest sleep I'd known in years. When I awoke this time, unusually for Fallsend, a little weak sunlight was streaming in through the window. I turned onto my side and my injured flesh gave a little yelp but was nothing compared to the pain of before. I allowed my eyes to travel the room. Pale drapes hung at the windows, a shade or two lighter than the oyster-coloured walls, a thick pile carpet in hues to rival the deepest forests of Ferike, and a general air of restrained elegance. Along the length of one wall stood a sagging wooden bookcase, crammed full of weighty tomes and bundles of papers. Some of the volumes looked archaic, bound in leather and heavily embossed with gold. Alessi, himself, was sitting by the fire reading. I watched a strand of his dark hair fall across his delicate face as he bent over the page. Affection stirred in a part of me I had believed long dead. He was intriguing, and I wanted to know more.

'Why did you help me?' I asked.

Alessi looked up, not a bit startled by my sudden question. He put down his book and moved his chair closer to my bed. 'Perhaps it's easier to explain if I'm the one asking the questions. Tell me why you help the forlorn and the destitute? I've been watching you for weeks... feeding the starving, helping the helpless. Why do you do that?

I drew in a long breath and found I was shaking. 'Atonement? For my crimes in Megalithica? For all the deaths?'

Alessi put his head on one side. 'Is that your only reason?'

I pondered for a moment and my hands became still. 'No, it's... just what I do. And I'm good at it.'

'It's the same for me.' Alessi said, softly.

'So you just wait around for someone to get attacked and then rescue them? That seems a bit random.'

He laughed at that. 'No, no... That's not what I do. I was looking for an opportunity to approach you and offer my services before all this happened. But... well... events rather precipitated things.'

'Your services?'

Alessi gazed into the middle distance for a moment, as if searching for the right words. 'Forgive me, but you are, I think, someone who is haunted by the past?' He looked at me and I nodded, then he continued. 'When I look at you and hara like you, I see a golden light at your heart, but at the same time, you're constantly followed by a dark shadow, a black miasma that coils about you like smoke.'

'You see this?'

'It is my gift and my curse. You are driven to serve and succour the needy, I am driven to aid those who are tortured by things past.'

Before I could question him further, an impatient fist hammered on the door. Only one har knocked like that.

'Surkka,' I said as Alessi led him to my bedside.

Somewhat flushed in the face, my employer tossed his mud-coloured hair out of his eyes and plonked himself down heavily upon the chair, which creaked its displeasure. He placed a weighty box of sweetmeats beside me and waved a bunch of hothouse flowers in my direction.

'So this is when you've been hiding yourself!'

'Hardly hiding, Surkka.'

The flowers joined the sweetmeats on the bed. 'The entire town is outraged. We've had hara scouring the streets for your attacker.'

Surkka nodded his thanks as Alessi handed him a glass of herbal tea. 'You're missed at *The Crown*, you know. You must hurry up and get well. I can't do without you.' All the while he was speaking, Surkka's pale eyes roamed around Alessi's apartment, taking in every detail.

My employer was tactful enough not to stay too long; he didn't want to tire me. He thanked Alessi for aiding me and complimented him on his rooms. 'Upper Clay Street, eh? I've always wanted to see inside one of these houses. And I do like these drapes,' he said, indicating the ivory silk at the window. Quietly I shook my head. Trust Surkka to be impressed.

After my employer had gone I opened the box of sweetmeats. Crystallised pineapple and candied plums glistened inside. I offered the box to Alessi and popped a sugared nugget into my own mouth.

In unison we spat them out.

'Too sweet!' Alessi grimaced, throwing the confection into the bin and hurrying to brew another herbal infusion to take away the taste.

'Surkka means well,' I said as I sipped my tea. 'He may tend to indolence, but when he gets his mind set on something, he usually succeeds. Do you think they'll find him?'

'Find who?'

'The har who attacked me. Surkka seemed quite determined.'

Alessi studied the contents of his cup for too long. 'No... I don't think they will.'

'Why not?' I burst out.

Alessi set down his cup and took one of my hands in both of his.

'They will not find the har who attacked you because... that har... was *you*.'

'Impossible! That creature was real! As flesh and blood as you and I!'

'I don't deny that.'

I shook my head. 'You're going to have to explain.'

Without letting go of my hand, Alessi moved from his chair to sit on the bed. 'Perhaps, as before, I can better explain by asking questions?'

'Ask away.'

'Tell me, how do you usually sleep? Prior to this business, I mean.'

'Poorly.' I answered him. 'A few hours at best.'

'Nightmares?'

I nodded. 'Yes, every night.'

'And since the attack?'

I paused for a moment. 'Not a one.'

'And you've slept the clock around.'

'I have...' I faltered, thinking about it. 'My guilt has gone!' A sudden hope flared within me. 'I'm free of it!'

Alessi held up a hand. 'Not free. Not just yet...'

Bewildered, I could only repeat myself. 'But my guilt has gone! I'm sleeping well now.'

Alessi spoke urgently. 'Your guilt has manifested as a physical being. It's no longer a part of you, but it's not gone. It is tethered to you and will find you again. It will attack you again unless you confront it.'

I sat there dumbfounded. 'I don't understand...' I said feebly.

Alessi permitted himself a small smile. 'I'm not surprised,' he said kindly. 'I suspect I am at the forefront of research into this field.' He indicated the overstuffed bookcase behind him, 'And I'm still working on the terminology, let alone anything else.'

I nodded, encouraging him to continue.

'You have, perhaps, heard of an entity called a *poltergeist?*'

'I have,' I affirmed. 'Er... a ghost or a supernatural being supposedly responsible for physical disturbances, such as making loud noises and throwing objects about? They were often associated with the psychic energy produced by adolescent humans?'

'Yes, that's right,' Alessi encouraged. 'And have you come across the term *tulpa?*'

Here I shook my head. This was new to me.

'No? A *tulpa* is a being or an object, usually benign, which is created through sheer spiritual or mental discipline alone... But such a being is always created with full awareness.'

'Okay,' I said, 'So what am I dealing with here?'

Alessi pulled a thoughtful face. 'Sort of a combination of the two, I think. Wraeththu spiritual and psychic energies are known to be far more powerful and advanced than that of humans. Hara who have experienced great trauma often unconsciously expel their most painful emotions... guilt, rage, despair... in the form of... what I call... a *gestalt*. A physical entity that encompasses that emotion.'

'But why did it attack me?'

'It requires release.'

'And how do I do that?'

The smile Alessi gave me was of such shining power and certainty it fairly took my breath away.

'That is what I am here to teach you.'

The next day, Alessi permitted me to get out of bed, and my training began.

We spent many hours meditating, sitting together on the thick pile carpet. Just a few minutes at first, but gradually building to longer sessions. I grew stronger each day. Alessi also honed my dormant visualisation skills. I spent days recreating the calming image of a forest clearing high on the hills above Fallsend in my head. I had often visited this place on days when I wasn't needed at *The Crown*. I enjoyed the solitude. The trees there are somewhat twisted by the tortuous winter winds and the bushes rather scrubby, but in spring the wild flowers transform the place and it looks almost beautiful.

Alessi also coached me in spiritual defence. 'You will need to make your confession,' he told me and, seeing me blanch, continued 'Not the guilt-fuelled prostrations of the old religions, but the clear and determined declaration of your soul's true urge... Like the pharaohs of ancient Egypt...'

This last was lost on me.

Surkka visited daily, bringing with him notes of condolence and "get well" cards from our many patrons.

'You see,' Alessi told me later. 'You are well-respected and well-loved. Believe it. You'll need to tap into that when you face your *gestalt*.'

One letter I found particularly touching. Alessi came upon me sitting on the floor clutching the missive and on the point of tears.

'What is it?'

'I can't believe it. News of my attack has spread as far as Kalamah...'

'For that I suspect we have to thank Surkka,' Alessi said with wry humour.

'It's from a har named Tian...'

Alessi settled himself beside me. 'Tell me about Tian.'

'It was about five years ago. Tian was a regular at *The Crown*. He was very young and had, unwisely, followed his Garridan lover,

Dask, to Fallsend and was utterly besotted with him. Dask didn't share Tian's feelings and treated him rather poorly. One night, Tian returned home from work and found Dask in the arms of another har. Tian was devastated.'

Alessi shook his head and sighed. 'It's an old story...'

'It is... but back then it was all new to Tian.'

Alessi rubbed his face. 'I wonder at Dask. The Kalamah are not noted for their tolerance and forbearance when slighted. Did Dask have some kind of death wish? The Kalamah are famed for taking rather extreme revenge, aren't they?'

'They are... but I think Tian is rather the exception that proves the rule. His Kalamah rage turned inward and he came to *The Crown* that night fully intent on destroying himself.'

'And this is where you stepped in?'

I nodded. 'I did. I built up the fire after closing, poured endless glasses of spiced milk down his throat, wrapped him in a blanket, and talked with him until he fell asleep. He awoke the next morning a different har. He packed his bags and left Dask and Fallsend for good.'

'And now he writes to you?'

'He's back in Kalamah.' I held up a little square of painted card, a water colour image of a street of rose and cream-coloured stone buildings. On the back were the words "Zaltana City" and "Come and Visit" underlined three times.

'He works as a painter and has a harling of his own... says he couldn't be happier and... that... it's all down to me.'

Alessi looked at me steadily. 'You'll want to pay attention to that.'

Later Alessi and I took our usual positions on the carpet for more meditation. I quickly settled into posture and slowed my breathing, calling up the forest glade in my mind and painting it with flowers. I was just enjoying the sensation of sunshine on my back and adding bird song to the imagery when a vicious wind blew up that was none of my making. The icy vortex tore through the clearing, ripping trees from their roots and scattering leaves and branches far and wide.

'Toban! Quickly! Take control!' Alessi's voice sounded strained and far away.

But I could not. All I could do was cover my face with my hands to keep my hair from whipping into my eyes. Even so a flying twig sliced into my cheek, making the blood run.

There was a rustle of movement to the side of me and I risked a peek. Alessi, dressed in a robe of pure white, a globe of light held high in his left hand, approached the vortex. For a moment they seemed locked together, and then we were back in the room in Upper Clay Street and all was still.

'What the hell happened?' I choked out, my hand held tight to my bleeding face.

Alessi hesitated for a moment. 'Your *gestalt* is stronger than I had anticipated... and it is impatient.'

Although he was trying to hide it, I could see the anxiety in his eyes.

'What does that mean?'

Alessi looked at me steadily. 'You are going to have to face it sooner than I had hoped.'

My insides turned to ice. 'How soon?'

Alessi paused. 'Tomorrow.'

'And am I ready for that?'

'You're going to have to be.'

Alessi tended to my wound, applying a healing paste, but it continued to throb for hours. However, it was not the pain from my face that kept me awake that night. My old friend insomnia had returned with a vengeance, playing not the usual stream of guilt-filled images but instead every shade of fear and anxiety.

At around two, Alessi got up from his own bed and brought me a sleeping draught. It was bitter and chalky but did the trick. I choked it down and knew nothing more until around mid-morning, when I awoke feeling groggy and lethargic with a foul taste in my mouth.

We breakfasted in silence. I really wasn't hungry but ate and drank what was before me just to take the bitter taste from my mouth. My face remained a little swollen. The pain had faded to a dull ache but was still sufficient to remind me how vulnerable and helpless I had felt in the face of my *gestalt*.

I spent the morning oscillating between complete terror and a fractious desire to just get on with it and get it over with.

Come on, I chided myself. *You were a warrior once. This fear is completely irrational.*

Alessi seemed to pick up on my thoughts. 'Take it easy, Toban. You fought in Ponclast's army, remember? You've got this.'

'I know,' I said through gritted teeth. 'I know... but then I had a sword in my hand... or a knife... or even just my bare hands. But this? This is just... mental!' And then I laughed at the double-meaning of my words and it was easier after that.

We had a light lunch and Alessi gave me a nerve tonic to purge the rest of the sleeping draught from my system. It tasted surprisingly sweet and refreshing.

'Are you ready?' Alessi asked a short while later.

I merely nodded. I just wanted it over – one way or another.

Alessi had me make myself comfortable on the couch and set a small basin of smouldering herbs by my side. 'Rosemary for a clear mind, clary sage for inner strength, and frankincense for truth,' he murmured, as if to himself.

He had a few last words of advice. 'Your *gestalt* will assail you with anything it can in an attempt to break you. Hold fast to your own truth. You can deny any reality it presents you with, but remember... if you die in there... you die here too. There is no going back.'

The cut on my face gave a vicious stab. I didn't need reminding. I nodded. It was time.

Alessi brought in a steel lamp of simple clean lines. It had been constantly lit all the time I had been in Alessi's rooms.

'What is that?'

'A lamp of protection. I undertook some caste training with the Sahale and I was fortunate to be gifted this by their Lyris. It is very powerful and it's helping to keep your *gestalt* at bay. When I extinguish it... your guilt will come for you...'

Alessi paused, waiting for my signal to proceed.

'Do it.' I said and closed my eyes.

When next I looked I was out in the open, the sky, blood red, above me. It felt as if I were lying upon rocks and, gingerly, I got to my feet. Before me lay a scorched plain, devoid of all life, battle-scarred and wretched.

Slowly I turned a full circle to get my bearings, but I already knew where I was... the acrid stench, blood and burning, all too familiar... Fulminir. Ponclast's citadel rose before me, its walls thick, black and imposing. This was Fulminir as I had last seen it, not Fulminir as I now knew it to be; razed to the ground, its poison purged.

'I deny this reality!' I shouted to the skies.

The image of Fulminir shimmered for a moment and, briefly, I stood in my woodland clearing, but then the desolation crashed back and Fulminir locked solidly into place.

I heard a voice then, my own, but hollow somehow and mocking. 'You are in my domain. I rule here. It shall be my pleasure to destroy you.'

He appeared before me. *My Guilt.* Cast in a hellish parody of Justice, he was clad in silken black robes, his face, apart from his mouth, hidden by a cruelly carved iron mask. His right hand clenched a sword of flames, and in his left dangled the scales of justice, tarnished, rusted and broken.

'I am ready,' I said, marvelling that I had kept the tremor from my voice.

He assailed me then, vision after vision.

The dead, the dying, the fallen, all at my hand. I withstood them, allowing them to wash over me as Alessi had taught me. The pale-eyed youth, the battle-weary har, the Unneah, the Uigenna... I had seen them all before in my dreams and night terrors.

With each image the skies darkened, and lightning flitted from cloud to cloud. Far off, the thunder rumbled, and a heavy rain began to fall.

'I do not deny my culpability,' I said steadily, and the rain pounded down upon me. 'I accept my responsibility. It is a part of me and of my past, but this is not all that I am.'

The stream of images ceased. My Guilt swung his sword around in a slow arc, narrowly missing me, a movement purely for show, not to maim. He was demonstrating the power he had over me.

'Show me your mitigation, then,' he mocked, thrusting his masked face towards mine. 'Show me how you have atoned.'

As Alessi had trained me, I began to transmit images of my own. I took My Guilt on a walk around Fallsend, showing him the desperate poverty and the depravity of those desolate streets. He trailed behind me as I gave blankets to the shivering, food to the starving, and coins to those frantic to escape. With each image, the rain fell a little less heavily, then slowed, then ceased, and above the sky faded to pale blue.

'Is this all you have to offer?' he sneered, and we were back in Fulminir. 'Is this the best you can do?' The rain started to fall once more, and I began to shiver.

I offered up scenes from the cosy interior of *The Topaz Crown*. The care I gave to every patron who stepped through the door. The disputes I had helped settle. The maudlin drunks I had cleaned up and put to bed in the back room. My Guilt threw back his head and laughed.

'Pitiful!'

In desperation, I sent an image of the mother cat I fed one Fallsend spring when winter wouldn't relinquish its grip on the land. I had fed her so she could feed her kittens and later wean them. When spring arrived, she moved on with her brood, leaving me a dead mouse as a gift.

He screeched with laughter at this.

'*Pitiful!*' he screamed and with no warning he swung his sword again. I leapt back. This time it was not for show. The blade crackled through the air and would have severed my head. He took another step towards me, and I backed up again.

'What of the images you deny?' he shrieked. 'What of the images you deny even to yourself?'

'What images? I don't know what you're talking about.'

He spat at me, a full gobbet of blood-tinged saliva. The viscous mass landed on my cheek and I wiped it away angrily.

'Show me, then!' I yelled at him. 'Show me your worst.'

The rain intensified, but now it was hot... now it was *blood*. It ran through my hair, into my eyes and into my mouth. I was nearly blinded by it. The blood wormed its way into the wound on my face and made me bleed afresh.

'I deny this reality!' I screamed. '*I deny this reality!*'

But the blood rain did not stop. Choking and nauseated, I scrubbed at my face.

'How can I see anything in all of this?' I asked him more quietly. 'How can I understand if I can't see?'

The rain fell a little less heavily, but it was still blood. It ran down my face and arms, congealing along my jaw and at my fingertips.

My Guilt tossed the broken scales to the ground and pointed an accusing finger. Now we were within the walls of Ponclast's citadel, and I watched myself, wretched as I was then, picking my way through the streets. I watched myself turn into a blind alley and... and... suddenly I knew what was coming. *How could I have forgotten this?* I must have buried this memory so deeply...

My former self stumbled over a stinking pile of rags, and some creature growled at me. I looked down... into the blank, glassy stare of a harling gone mad. Filthy and naked, he held his prize close to his breast. His small teeth were tearing at the flesh of a severed limb, harish or human I couldn't tell; the fingers, one with a ring on, dangled uselessly. The harling growled again and lashed out a grimy foot. I watched myself turn and run, stumbling away. My own meagre breakfast I lost at the next corner, a dry biscuit with the maggots picked out. The harling was not the only one who was starving. That was when I fled, fled Fulminir, fled Ponclast's army. I slept under hedges and scavenged in fields and farms until the Zigane found me and took me eventually to Roselane.

The blood-rain ran down my face along with my tears as I watched myself flee.

My Guilt turned to me, sword trailing in the mud. 'How can you possibly atone for that?' he cried hoarsely. 'No matter how many you feed, how many you help... you walked away... you walked away from that child!'

My head was reeling. I had no answer for him. What could I say? Phrases like... *'It was war... There was nothing I could do...'* All hollow, meaningless and trite.

'There's nothing I can say or do to atone for this,' I replied. I stood before him ready. 'Kill me if you must.'

The sword clattered to the ground. My Guilt sank to his knees. 'How can I kill you? You're already dead.'

On impulse I reached out my hand and tore away the mask. My own face stared back at me. The sallow skin, thin as paper, drawn tightly over razor-edged bone; wretched and wasted from years of torment. Slowly I knelt by the side of My Guilt.

'I deny this reality,' I said, softly. Again the image of Fulminir shimmered. This time, instead of the forest clearing, the interior of *The Topaz Crown* stood before us, solid and homely, all wood panelling and heavily felted rugs. The blood-rain ceased, and I found myself clean.

The inn was quiet, save for myself, and Tian seated at the bar. The fire crackled in the ornamented grate and the sweet smell of spiced milk reached towards me. It was the night I had sat with him, after hours, hour after hour, as he tried to find a reason to continue his life.

My Guilt looked up at the two figures and slumped further towards the floor.

I moved to cradle him. 'I'm sorry,' I whispered. 'I'm sorry I did this to you.'

Still My Guilt looked at the two figures at the bar. 'This is your reality. This is what you do.'

'I can't change what happened in the past,' I told him, 'merely live with it. But the best thing I can do is to live well.'

My Guilt said nothing, so I continued. 'As one person I cannot change the world... but I can change the world for one person.' I nodded towards Tian at the bar.

My Guilt turned sunken eyes towards me at last. 'You need to let me go.'

'I don't know how.'

'Be kind.' The breath rattled in his throat. 'Be kind to me and to yourself'.

Helplessly I shrugged. 'How?'

'Release me...' he hissed. 'Forgive me.'

That came easily. 'I forgive you.'

'And... forgive *yourself*.'

That came harder, but I said the words anyway to save him further pain. 'I forgive myself.'

He smiled then... a serene smile... a smile of peace... and he crumbled away to dust in my arms.

I opened my eyes and I was back in Alessi's sanctuary with the sweet scent of burning herbs.

Alessi bent over me. 'All well?'

'All well,' I confirmed as I sat up and stretched. I felt the years falling away from me.

'You are... recalled to life?'

'I am.' I smiled, shaking away the last of the tension, and turned to my friend. 'He... My Guilt, that is, he wanted release and forgiveness.'

Alessi smiled his quiet smile. 'They always do.'

Since then much has changed in Fallsend... and much has stayed the same. Perhaps it's just me who is different? My wounds, both physical and spiritual, are healed. I sleep well at night. Surkka has raised my wages, but I still keep my attic room over *The Crown*, although now it's more comfortably furnished... but not opulently so. Alessi travels widely but maintains his sanctuary in Upper Clay Street. When he is in town we spend much time together. We are close, but not chesna, not even lovers, but close all the same... All else may follow in time.

With my guidance, Surkka has opened another tavern in a poorer district than *The Crown*. *The Traveller's Rest* may not serve such exquisite fare as *The Topaz Crown*, but the destitute know that a hot meal will be served for the needy each day in the back room. The long, snaking garden is also home to many of the stray animals of the town, and the patrons enjoy tossing them scraps. Each day I grow in strength and happiness, and one day perhaps I shall visit Tian in Kalamah.

Fallsend will never be beautiful or cultural or *the* place to be but it can be... *better*. Barge loads of stone have been ordered to pave the canal district, and there is a proposal to plant cherry trees in the town square. At this latitude the fruit, of course, will be bitter, and this seems only right for Fallsend, but in spring the blossoms will be pretty enough.

Author's Note:

[1] The title 'Recalled to Life' comes from Charles Dickens' *Tale of Two Cities*.

[2] This story had its origin as a piece of collaborative fan fiction from the days before Immanion Press and when fans used to regularly meet online in 'The Stone Inn'. Two such humorous collaborations, From *Har to Maternity* and *A Day at the Races*, made it into the Forever fiction archive but the more serious *Tales from Fallsend* foundered and was never completed. I always wondered how Toban's story would pan out and in *Para Spectral* I've been able to explore that.

A Handful of Sea Coins

Nerine Dorman

My first memory is that of the dull pounding of the surf on granite boulders, the grumble and growl of the restless tides forever dashing themselves to foam and flecks. As a harling, I was constantly near that liminal space, where the grey-green of the Girdle of Tiamat dragged its claws through the half-moon, pebbled strand that was the closest thing to a beach our islet had. Here I found the treasures amid the wrack and washed-up snakes of kelp, be they smooth sea glass and shells, or sometimes even artefacts from ancient times, for which I didn't have the words. The gulls and gannets would wheel about, their cries turned ragged by the salt-laden wind that never ceased in its howling as it whipped the tendrils of hair that invariably escaped my braids into my mouth and eyes.

I didn't have words for many things when I was young, but the shapes, textures, and smells remain embedded within my heart. The way the prickly anemone puckered its bright flowers at the intrusion of questing fingers. Little fishes that darted, slivers of silver that slipped past my feet as I picked my way from pool to pool. Cushioned starfishes spongy to the touch, and the little white, spiralled disks of the sea snails, discarded.

Sea coins, Feyrith called them when he accepted them from my tiny hands. He'd offer a rare smile then and save the treasures in an old glass jar he kept on the windowsill. One day, I said to him, we'd have enough currency to buy our own boat.

One day, he said, and his gaze would be drawn towards the window. He'd pause, not breathe for a few heartbeats, and then he'd shake himself.

Then he'd find tasks for me. The tide was coming in, I'd better fetch what fresh wrack I could find for our dinner. Or I must run to the pier to discover whether anyhar's sails appeared on the horizon. Or perhaps see if there were penguin eggs for the taking. Don't let the seals chase me again. Mind that I keep an eye on the tide. Don't turn my back to the ocean.

But return before it's dark. Always *be back before sundown.*

As soon as the sun bled into the ocean, and its stain turned from blush to orange and then cobalt, and the chill climbed up the walls and lodged in our bones, Feyrith would ascend the ladder to the top of the lighthouse, where the crystal was. I was too young to help him, he said, and had to remain below while he concluded his rites and woke the star that would guide seaborne hara to safety.

There are reefs here, like jagged teeth, he told me. This has always been the Cape of Storms, and always will be.

Old words in ancient tongues, *Cabo das Tormentas.* Yet also *Kaap van Goeie Hoop. Good Hope.* I played with the opposing idea of storm and hope, hope and storm. Slender hope was all ancient mariners could hold onto, I supposed, when their delicate barques were at the mercy of Tiamat's rages.

Yet there was no hope in Feyrith's gaze; only dull resignation.

He was the light keeper, a solitary candle who kept watch in the night.

During the early years of my harlinghood there was one shipwreck. The morning had been bright enough but by noon, the northwester blew up dirty clouds that crowded the sky from horizon to horizon. The swell was big, and the spray spattered even the glass of the cottage as we huddled inside. The oil burner's flame did little to warm our home, and the candles guttered in the insistent draughts that crept their chill fingers through miniscule cracks and crannies.

Even cocooned in our blankets, I shivered. My guardian paced from window to door, door to hearth then back again, his bare feet shushing on the cracked concrete floor. The dim light painted his features in long, gaunt planes, his hawk nose sharp, mouth downturned. We did not speak. We didn't need to. I could tell by the set of his shoulders, the way his hands clenched at his sides, that this was no ordinary storm. Each gust made the ancient tin roof groan and judder, and tiny runnels of dirt trickled down the walls. I feared the wind would knock down our walls, pluck us out and toss us into the turbulent sky.

By late afternoon, he went upstairs to ignite the crystal, before sundown.

'It's dark out already. I am deeply concerned,' was all he said as he began to ascend the rungs.

From where I hunched, I could hear him intone the words of his rites to call down the light of distant stars. The small hairs on my arms prickled with the incipient power, and I prayed then, though I knew no dehara by name, that our light would be enough.

Yet it was a night unlike any I'd experienced before. The rain came hammering down, a thousand fists beating upon the roof, against the window, the wind shrieking and ululating until I too was crying in terror.

Feyrith was not a har to offer comfort, and ordinarily he took a dim view on any unseemly displays of emotion, but this night he pulled me close so that I could hear the slow, wet drum of his heart, and his arms created a barrier between me and the world. I slipped into troubled sleep, but was awoken when he gave a sudden, sharp cry and sat up.

'What is it?' I straightened next to him on the pile of cushions that we shared.

The candles were all out but for one, and the light from the crystal above bathed the room in intermittent flashes – two short bursts, followed by one long, a pause, then the pattern repeated itself. The wind still lashed us with heavy, salt-laden rain, but there was a different quality to the night, one that I sensed more than I understood. *Pain. Fear.*

Waves dashing themselves against the bow, timbers squealing as stone fangs rend the hull.

'There's been a wreck!' Feyrith lurched to his feet and staggered to the door where his oilskins hung on a peg. 'Stay here! Don't come out.'

Light keeper's magic. I shivered in apprehension.

There I huddled, wrapped in our bedding, the skin around my eyes taut as I peered towards the window at the various graduations of dark on dark, at the haggard moon that occasionally leered at me through torn clouds. What could I do? I was but a small harling, barely counting three summers. The wind screeched around the corners of the cottage and the rain thrashed down in swathe after swathe. The oil burner went out for want of fuel and my breath misted before my face as the last candle eventually drowned in its wax.

And still Feyrith didn't return, and I must've sunk into fitful dreams, of grasping tentacles and dark, watery depths, for when the door eventually banged open, the interior of our home was bathed in dove grey dawn, and my guardian was not alone.

35

Feyrith was soaked through to the skin and carried a bundle wrapped in his oilskins. Another har, whose long, dark hair was tangled with wrack and whose limbs hung limp.

'Get the oil burner going,' was all he said, and his expression was such that I daren't gainsay him.

I'd disappointed him; I knew that look well. But I hadn't wanted to disobey him either. That's if I wanted to pick at his last command to me before he'd vanished into the storm. Yet even then I understood that I was lying to myself. I'd been too scared, too carried away by the thrill of the tempest to trouble myself with notions of self-preservation. The oil canisters were in the store round the back. He hadn't wanted me to go out. Yet I'd let the burner run out of fuel. There'd be no hot water for half an hour at least, and by the looks of things, he'd need more than just a cup of tea round about now.

Splinters came off on my hands as I shoved open the door and stepped into the gloomy store. I hated this room with its long, grasping shadows and the persistent smell of damp underpinned by the inescapable fishy tang of guano. I was just big enough to handle one of the canisters that the officials brought from the mainland every fortnight or so. Nevertheless, the container was unwieldy for a har my size, and I had to be careful lest it roll back on me on the incline and rattle us both into the gully where the surf sometimes exploded outward at high tide. I held no illusions about my chances dashed to little bits on the sharp, barnacle-encrusted rocks below. Though the crabs might complain there'd not be enough of a feast off my skinny bones.

By the time I returned, Feyrith had the har wrapped in all our blankets, divested of all his dripping garments. Pale-faced, the stranger shivered as Feyrith chafed his hands.

'Quick! You know what to do,' he commanded as I went through the drill of removing the tap from the empty canister and attaching it to the full one.

His scrutiny made my movements clumsy, but I successfully decanted oil into the burner and had it lit. Then I fetched water from the barrel outside, made sure there were no bugs or worse floating in it, and filled the kettle a quarter of the way. Rather get some hot water immediately then set more to boil later.

All the while I stole glances at the stranger. He was of medium build, with skin like sea foam – so different from Feyrith's olive complexion and my own. Sometimes Feyrith said I was part fur seal, for my hair held the colour of their pelts and my eyes were liquid dark. When viewed under a particular light, my brown skin was mottled, like the cusk-eel's, but with a deeper hue, like that of the kelp when still glistening wet.

This strange har was not like the others who sometimes visited to trade supplies and stories, hara who had the sea in their veins and whose dusky-gold skins told of a life immersed in salt and sun. He was soft, unblemished but for his near drowning, and I mistrusted him immediately.

As much as I feigned disinterest, he openly regarded me, which made me hope the heat flaming in my cheeks wouldn't immediately be apparent. He was an intruder, disrupting our little world, and the more Feyrith mixed herbal concoctions while asking him questions about the ship that had run aground, her lost crew and possible salvage, the more I huffed and fretted, awaiting whatever orders Feyrith had for me.

Yet if the stranger had questions, he kept them to himself for those first few days of his recovery, for he had been badly bruised during his ordeal, and despite his harish constitution, suffered a fever. He slept for the most part, and Feyrith had me busy beach-combing for anything useful that washed up. During that time, I dragged up such bits of flotsam – wood of any size was worth more than gold on our little rock. Bits of rigging and canvas tatters too, for these could always be repaired and repurposed. I wasn't certain what I would do with the oddments of clothing: one boot, a torn shirt and what appeared to be a felt hat. The one day I did spy what I thought to be a corpse, but it was too far out near Pilot's Pillar, and I noted the dorsal fins of sharks, accompanied by the tell-tale ripples of big fish worrying at the object, so I erred on the side of prudence, and refrained from swimming out. Besides, the tides were still unsettled, and a rip current swirled treacherously. While I certainly took chances on calm days, I knew when to remain ashore. I was only a harling, after all.

'A name, youngling,' the interloper asked, 'has your guardian never thought to give you one?'

Feyrith had gone down to the pier, to check up on whatever it was that he'd been mumbling about.

I glared at the har. That he'd sought to ask me if I had a name now suggested he'd possibly discussed my lack of it with Feyrith and had not gained an answer he liked. Or perhaps no answer at all, which was more likely. That he felt he was secure enough in his position to ask me rankled.

'I don't need a name,' I said.

His sudden bark of laughter made me start, and my flinching only caused him further mirth.

'Oh, you are such a sullen one.'

I cocked my head at him, my breath held. 'You presume much.'

A coughing fit wracked him at that point, and when it did not immediately subside, I went to fetch more of the tincture Feyrith had set aside for this very purpose. I might be sullen and ill-tempered, but I wasn't unnecessarily cruel.

'Thank you,' he wheezed as he accepted the tin mug with the concoction. Then he wiped his mouth on the back of his wrist and regarded me. 'My name is Edera.'

'I know,' I told him. 'Feyrith said so.' By admitting that I knew, meant I had to refer to this intruder by a name. He became a har to me.

'But we have not properly been introduced.'

'We don't often get visitors who stay,' I said, frowning.

Now that I considered what he said, Edera had a point. Always I'd been in the shadows, the scurrying little harling to fetch and carry, and remain silent by the hearth until needed. Nohar had remained longer than it took for the tide to turn or the winds to become favourable, which was a few hours, at most. And nohar, up until now, had ever asked after me.

'Has it never bothered you, that you have no name?'

I allowed myself a small, one-shoulder shrug. 'It has never been important. I know who I am. Names are limiting.'

'Yet your father has a name.'

Another shrug. 'He is welcome to it. And he is *not* my father.'

Edera raised an elegant brow at my admission. 'But surely your hostling had a name for you?'

'I have no hostling,' I replied.

'Everyhar has a hostling,' Edera said.

'Not I.'

'Oh, so you mean to say that you just magically appeared out of thin air, fully formed?' Edera gave a soft snort then grimaced at the mug he still clutched. 'Sweet dehara's arse, what does he put in this stuff?'

Feyrith cast his shadow over the doorway at that point, and when he caught my eye, he offered a meaningful glance at the bucket by the door. I still had mussels to pick for that night's dinner.

Yet whatever spell the ocean usually cast over me while I worked was gone. Unerringly I sought the biggest molluscs, giving a strong twist and pull to drag them from their anchors in the tidal pools.

The storm might've blown over, but winds of another kind stirred within me.

I shouldn't care about my origin, I told myself. Perhaps it had been living in the present, awash with the tides and the phases of the moon for my entire short life at this point, that meant it simply hadn't occurred to me to ask. I'd never admit to Edera, a perfect stranger, that I'd always taken this namelessness for granted and that I'd been here, on the island, and that this was where I'd remain for the rest of my life.

Yet the penguin chicks lost their drab brown down and became sleek, mottled creatures that eventually slipped through the grey-green waves.

On good days, I could see the shore through the haze of spray. The blue ridge of the mountains knuckled the horizon, where at night a light flared that was the partner to the one we called home. I fancied the towers winked at each other, silent sentinels sharing their tasks in solidarity. Perhaps there was another harling who stood on the shore at times, and stared across the restless waves, wondering at this very outcropping of rocks. Deep within me, Edera's questions stirred a riptide that undermined my understanding of my world, and slowly dragged my heart out to deeper waters.

The har remained with us for a fortnight. Feyrith sent a message to the keeper at the Gannet Point light, and he confirmed that the next supply vessel could put out a week early to retrieve Edera. It didn't help that during this time, Edera and Feyrith took great enjoyment in each other's company, and I was not blind to the fact that they often sought excuses to send me on errands so that they could indulge in aruna. There was a hunger to both of them, perhaps because they understood that their being together was limited. My guardian even smiled and told stories of the past when he'd not been a keeper and had rode with caravans through the thirst lands of the continent. I had not seen this side to him, and it rankled that he'd spill these stories to this interloper when with me he was usually so reserved.

'You never told me what happened to your chesnari,' Edera said on that last night.

Feyrith grew still, his knuckles momentarily white as he gripped the clay goblet that contained his brandy. Then he looked at me. 'Go see if the storeroom door is locked. The northwester is picking up.' His eyes were sea-tumbled pebbles.

For a moment I hesitated; I was warm in my little nest of blankets by the burner and had been content to listen to the adults speak while I was all but forgotten.

Edera raised a brow and glanced at me, but then feigned interest in picking wax from the table with his fingernail. There would be no support from him in this matter. The unfairness of the exclusion rankled but I knew better than to argue. Feyrith might cuff the side of my head and make my ears ring. I did not want to suffer the indignity of having Edera witness the spectacle.

My blanket pulled around my shoulders, I rose and kept my eyes downcast. As if welcoming me to its icy embrace, the wind outside shrieked, and the eaves creaked. The door was stiff on its hinges and the moment I was outside, in the dark, I could hear the two hara talking quietly. Yet with the breakers dashing themselves senseless on the rocks and the wind rattling the old tin of the roof so that it hummed its own, low song, I couldn't discern what Feyrith was saying.

I glimpsed them through the window as I walked round to the store, and I saw how Edera pressed his forehead to Feyrith's, a hand placed gently on my guardian's cheek.

The storeroom door was bolted firm. Of course it was. I'd been the one to lock it earlier that day. Instead, I stood there behind the house and lifted my face to the sky that was fast filling with thick, scudding cloud. Stars pierced patches then were quickly covered over as fast as more rips appeared in the firmament. Yet the wind would abate in the early hours. It wasn't one of the big storms. How I knew, I wasn't sure. By the dead hour, the rain would come down with fat, hard drops that would beat a tattoo on the roof, and by mid-morning it would be a fine day with patches of mist drifting on the ocean.

Some whim had me clamber up the pile of boulders behind the light. I'd done so on so many occasions that I knew my way up with my eyes closed – not that I'd do so, ever. Whatever Feyrith said to Edera, I knew when I wasn't wanted, and the jealousy burned its bright flame in my belly. Also, I had no way to fully explain the impulse that had me seek this high place. I had a view here of the horizon all round, the white stone column of the light shafting just shy of sixty metres into the sky. Fifty-nine metres and seventy-five centimetres, to be exact. Constructed ten years prior from fine sandstone brought from the quarries in the South Coast when the old, human-built light collapsed. That the original human light keeper's cottage still stood was a miracle in and of itself. The concrete around the stones was crumbling faster than it could be repaired.

And this was my world – a stony outcropping I could circumnavigate in just under half an hour if I didn't stop by every other tidal pool to search for sea glass and pretty shells. Despite the storms that often raged here, I still felt safe, encapsulated, that somehow we were cocooned by our little hollow of boulders where our home crouched. That no matter how high the swell, how angry the ocean, we would always endure. The world beyond our boundaries existed only in wrack that washed up.

Yet that night, I could feel myself on the cusp of something greater than I was, so that all the small hairs on my neck and arms prickled. It was cold, and my blanket did little to protect me from the wind's icy bite, but somehow the discomfort only awakened a cold fire deep within me as I turned in one spot to take in my surroundings.

Above me, the light continued its vigil, the bursts of illumination the steady pulse that provided the counterpoint to my heartbeat.

My skin prickled as my gaze was drawn unaccountably east, to the open ocean. The moon's sickle grin was but a thin sliver riding low, and that is when I saw the ship. A cutter, her sails tatters, and the remaining jib flapping loose as she dipped and wallowed upon the swell. A pronounced list to her port side made me fear that she'd capsize as she came ever closer to Pilot's Pillar. The only har on her deck stood to attention, one hand at the wheel and seemingly unconcerned about the disaster about to befall his vessel. Yet there was some sort of indefinable *wrongness* about the way the ship moved that I couldn't fully articulate.

Save that he intended to run the ship aground.

I sprang from my perch, my breath short as I shrieked Feyrith's name and ran back to the cottage.

My guardian was at the door before I could touch the handle, a shadow against the golden glow of the interior.

'What is it?'

'A cutter!' I pointed vaguely behind me. 'About to hit the rocks.'

Feyrith blanched. 'Which rocks?'

'The pillar.'

He ran, and I followed on his heels, aware that Edera came after. So soon for another wreck. This time I would not cower in the cottage.

Yet when we arrived at the half-moon beach that offered the best, unobstructed vantage point towards Pilot's Pillar, there were only the breakers foaming on granite and the sucking waves swamping our legs.

Feyrith peered out to sea, Edera standing to his left while I paced the length of the high tide line.

'It was there, I swear it!' I cried, my chest heaving.

'Was she listing to her port side?' Feyrith asked after what felt like an interminable silence. His voice was hollow.

I halted, stared at him, and nodded.

A soft snort escaped him, and he shook his head. 'Torn sails. Seemed to be moving contrary to the actual wind direction?'

Now that he mentioned it, I realised what had bothered me. A northwester was blowing. The schooner had been moving *against* the wind, as if pushed by an invisible hand. Against the wind with tattered sails.

'That's not possible!' I cried.

Edera glanced from me to Feyrith then back again. 'There's no ship now.'

'Of course there's no bloody ship!' Feyrith snapped. 'Come, let's go.' He turned and marched back to the cottage without further explanation.

Feyrith was sullen for what remained of that night, and he poured enough brandy to make both he and Edera sodden. The interloper made up for Feyrith's silence by recounting a mangled story of heartache and disappointment that rambled so much I could barely keep track of his slurring and sighs. Yet whenever I closed my eyes, I saw that ship, and my memories painted it in finer fantasies each time. Had it gleamed with some sort of ethereal aura? Had the har at the wheel turned empty eyes in my direction, raised a hand in greeting? A ghost ship, I was certain, and a quiet thrill of fear lacerated my heart and all the small hairs on my nape prickled once more.

When sleep eventually overcame me, my dreams were watery, of seals slipping between the kelp fronds into fathomless, emerald-barred depths. Silvery shoals flashed and darted, and I sank, weightless, as my body dissolved, and my awareness spread out along the currents that caressed the bones of old wrecks.

I was the first to awaken, spilled out onto the strands of awareness by night's ebb.

Edera snored softly at the table, his head cradled on his forearm. Feyrith bustled about the cottage, his movements decisive as he filled the kettle – it was the clink of the metal lid snapping in place that had woken me – and he opened and shut cupboards while he placed items he retrieved on the bed.

'Good, you're awake,' he said without turning.

I made a small sound of acknowledgement in the back of my throat.

He paused, holding up an old shirt of his. 'It will be more like a tunic on you for a half-year or so, yet, but it will have to do.' This he bundled up and stuffed into an old canvas bag.

I realised then, what he meant, and I found my words. 'You're sending me away with Edera.'

'You're a few years away from your feybraiha, yet it will do you no good to be here when you should be with others who can teach you more.' Feyrith's voice shook, whether from deep emotion or fear, I couldn't tell.

A sharp pain gleamed within my heart, of knowledge of the sundering, the snipping of the cord. 'You don't want me. Why?'

He turned then, his eyes wild and wide. 'It's not *safe* for you here.'

'I don't understand!'

'You won't understand. Not yet, anyway. I... I cannot care for you as I should.'

My vision blurred with tears that sprang up from nowhere, and I blinked rapidly until they cleared, but my throat was thick, and I could barely talk. 'I don't want to go.'

'What you want doesn't matter. You will learn to understand that we cannot always get what we want. You will not remain a harling forever. This life…' He gestured about the dwelling. 'This is not a gentle life. I have been remiss in so much. Edera will take you with him when he returns to Table Bay where he serves in a big house. The master has sons your age. He says they will welcome another to be their companion. They have already answered him.'

I narrowed my eyes at him. 'You had no intention of sending me away until I saw that ship.' How I knew this, I could not tell.

Feyrith betrayed himself with a miniscule flinch. Anyhar else would not have known what to look for, but I'd learnt to see it.

'Why?'

'Go down to the pier and see if you can spot the sail. And don't get any funny ideas about hiding until they're gone. You think you know every inch of this cursed rock, think again. You'll only wish you'd skinned yourself on barnacles by the time I'm done with you.'

When I didn't immediately move, he raised his hand and stepped forward.

I was out the door before he could take a second step. He'd not had cause to beat me often, but there had been a handful of occasions when he'd lost his temper with me.

There was no ship, just yet, but I remained on the pier, dangling my legs over the edge and watching the rise and fall of the swell against the pilings. My mortification at having Edera witness my chastising had my cheeks aflame, and it took a while for the chill of morning to assert its calm. What had gotten into my guardian that he was casting me off so abruptly? What was it about that cutter?

As always, the gulls wheeled and cried. Black-browed terns dropped like arrowheads into the now becalmed water, scything off with their silvery catch. Oystercatchers piped along the rocks, their bright red beaks like flames as they hunted for small crustaceans. All this was mine, the ebb and flow, the salty tang on the air. I could not conceive of trading this for the unknown world beyond the pier.

And yet the ship must come, as it always did. For now, the ocean had turned back to dull cobalt, the sky paler than a silver gull's wing. The northwester was mostly blown out, but made paws on the swell, telling me of another storm front coming. My throat was thick, my eyes swollen. Why did Feyrith want me gone? Surely he'd need me, especially now?

Closer to noon, I glimpsed *Golden Goose*'s sail – Meren Stormreier's yacht. Her jib and mainsail billowed, fat with wind as she set her course for the pier, and it wasn't long before she was within hailing distance. Usually I'd run up to the cottage to warn Feyrith, but I surmised (correctly perhaps) that Feyrith wanted this time alone with Edera before we departed. Consequently, I waited, was there to catch the mooring line when Meren's deckhand cast it my way. It was only Meren and one other this time, and I assisted with the unloading of the casks of oil and other sundry supplies.

If Meren suspected anything, the har said nothing, merely noting how much I'd grown since he'd last seen me and commenting on the precursor to the bigger storm to come – a not-so-subtle hint for us not to tarry. The har who accompanied him gave me the side-eye as we began to move the cargo up to the cottage. He'd not bother me none with Meren present, but I swore I caught him making a warding sign against evil.

The usual pleasantries occurred once we reached the cottage. Meren and Feyrith greeted each other with their usual banter, while my bag stood packed by the door, waiting to be slung over a shoulder. Edera sat by the table and watched, missing nothing while I stood awkwardly, half outside already. Feyrith would not glance in my direction, but lined Meren's palm with silver I'd not known him to possess: passage, for Edera and me.

Then, with much throat clearing and gesturing to the patchwork sky, Meren hurried us back down the track to the pier. Feyrith's hand made a claw on my shoulder as he all but pushed me ahead of him, as if he were terrified that I'd bolt at the last moment. Before I could protest at all, Edera had already taken my hand and Meren had cast my bag onto the yacht's deck.

A wordless scream tried to worm its way up my throat but Edera's grasp on me was firm, and he shook me once, hard enough to rattle my teeth. A near imperceptible shake of his head. *No.*

The deck lurched beneath our feet as Meren gave the order to cast off, and the deckhand shoved us from the pier. Canvas snapped full, and it was as if invisible hands already understood to guide us from the shore.

Feyrith did not stand and watch us depart. My last sight of him was of his retreating figure already hastening up to the cottage.

A har could compose an entire saga about what life is like when ripped from all that is familiar, cast out like seed upon barren ground with the hopes that it will somehow germinate and flourish, to bear fruit. This is not that story. Suffice to say that Edera took me with him as he returned to Table Bay. He had not lied when he said that he was in service of a wealthy har, and there were harlings close to my age who became my companions, though at first I was but a wildling who did not take kindly to his taming.

It was not an unpleasant life in that big house high up on the northeastern slopes, even if I could only view the ocean from the big windows in the dining room. Table Bay curved lazily, a crescent of white strand and dunes cupping the restless grey-green waves with their frothing heads of foam, yet it was only during winter, when the northwester gusted, that I could scent the salt-sweet sea.

I learnt my letters, wore shoes and could speak appropriately to hara of many stations. I accompanied Edera as his apprentice when he went down to market. The master's sons were kind, unlike the stories one reads about foundlings adjusting to live in a new family.

I became a patient young har, earnest. Sincere. A har of few words. Some said I wasn't all quite there. They looked upon me with pity, but Edera wasn't fooled, though he often despaired, and had the occasion to offer harsh words about my erstwhile guardian's negligence.

How could I explain to him that I'd been perfectly happy chasing the tides and studying the patterns of the breakers as they dashed themselves upon the boulders? Yet I understood, without argument, that he had a point. That Feyrith had been right to push me away so I could try my wings the same way the mottled gull fledgling eventually ventures forth from the nest.

Everything was different after my feybraiha, which had been rather civilised, unremarkable. He was a friend of Edera's, another fish-belly pale har with soft hands and eyes like tanzanite. His name, unimportant.

They named me. Of course they named me. I had to be described, placed within boundaries. Maaris, it was, two syllables that felt like yarn spooling out, loose. In my mind, my identifiers were the ocean, the sky, a scattering of stars half-obscured by a scrap of cloud. I was the moon, gibbous and pock-faced, rising red. I was a handful of sea coins pattering into a glass jar on a dusty windowsill.

I remained in Edera's service for another six months until one afternoon my feet strayed to the breakwater where the remains of the ancient human dolosse still pushed back the ocean. Barnacles crusted at the waterline and I picked my way along the interlocking concrete blocks with bare feet. My shoes I discarded on the pier, no doubt to be snatched up by an opportunist not long after my back was turned. What possessed me, I couldn't truly tell, except that it was that hushed expectance of a tempest about to make landfall that had lured me to the docks.

The masts of the windjammers rattled and clinked in the restless air where gulls cried and wheeled and squabbled over scraps. Decaying kelp was pungent, iodine-laced, and I sucked it in, taken back months, years to that little outcropping and its light. Who was to stop me now? I was a free har, was I not? To give Edera credit, he had tried, but I could feel the ebb in my blood, calling, whispering for me to return to the ocean.

Shastia Moon was but the first of many vessels upon which I served, and it felt somehow right that I answered that indefinable call. Secretly, I hoped that we'd sail past Gannet Point, that I might see the twin lights winking in the night, and draw comfort in the knowledge that Feyrith was steadfast at his post. Yet our routes had us travelling everywhere but along the South Coast. Majestic windjammers, their holds filled with a wealth of grain, bolts of cloth, fine wines, rare timbers, spices worth more than their weight in gold. We rounded the Cape of Storms many times, the Horn, we mocked the dehara of tempest and courted the spirits of fortune.

And I heard many tales at sea, of merfolk who lured foolish hara to their deaths, of serpents that snagged the unwary and feasted upon their bones within the depths. Each coast had its legends of spectres and ruin, and more than one story of some phantom cutter with ragged sails wracked upon a storm.

I'd sit still then, spine straight, my measure of rum clasped in suddenly tight fingers as I listened to the storyteller speak of some har upon whom a terrible doom was laid, to sail the seas forevermore. Cursed never to set foot on land. One should never cross the dehara, it was said.

I never spoke of that one night, so many years before, when I'd spied that ghostly herald that had seen my guardian take fright and send me away. Perhaps now I understood that I still bore him resentment and would never find rest until I'd looked him in the eye once more. Yet I lacked the wherewithal to do anything about it except fashion elaborate imaginary meetings while I stitched sails or repaired lines. Always our windjammer would be bound to another destination, and I'd be carried with, somehow pleased that the decision to do anything about my fixation had been taken out of my hands.

Yet all stories have ends, and mine is no different. The dehara in charge of our fates spun their wheels and conferred among themselves that I was a har cast adrift, too comfortable aboard *Nerissa's Splendour*, and too certain of the sun-bleached, scoured jarrah beneath his feet.

The storm came up without warning, the sky bleeding at sunset and filled with patches of fleece before it darkened to thick, boiling turmoil. We were due to round the Cape of Storms within the day. Instead we found ourselves embattled upon high seas off the South Coast where hundreds if not thousands of vessels had foundered during the centuries along this graveyard of ships. *Nerissa* pitched and yawed, sliding sideways up mountainous swell, only to plunge into the yawning chasm that followed. Rain was driven horizontally, mixed with lashings of saltwater as we battled to furl the sails. Our captain stood at the helm, chanting, pleading with the dehara to intervene, but whatever magic he usually possessed, his powers had deserted him this night.

The wave that washed me overboard dragged me into the fury, so that I knew neither up nor down as ice-cold, angry water robbed me of sight and breath. Some dim part of me wailed and gnashed its teeth at this abrupt end to a life hardly lived, even though I understood deep within my bones, with the ocean that ebbed and flowed with every heartbeat through my veins, that an end to the material form was as natural as the moon rising or whales breaching in a quiet bay. Even as darkness clouded my consciousness, I was able to find some sort of peace, that part of me would still endure, not lost...merely changed.

I did not expect to awaken with another har's arms around me, positioning me in a bed.

'Come now, Tiahaar, breathe deep.'

Every breath was fire, and I coughed until I could barely draw air into me. I tasted salt, and as my eyes adjusted to the candlelit gloom, I gave a choked cry.

The room hadn't changed much with the passage of years,

except that it seemed smaller and grubbier than my memories allowed. I'd been lain upon the same old pine bed. Somehar had, at some point, taken a bit of whitewash to the walls, but had evidently run out halfway through the job. The windows were tightly shuttered – the shutters were new – but the same antique candleholder stood upon the rickety table where I'd eaten so many breakfasts. That damned jar of sea coins still gathered dust on the windowsill.

Except the har who was rubbing me down with a piece of old blanket was not Feyrith. Dark of skin, and clearly a descendant of many tribes, he was small and wiry, his hair tight peppercorns against his narrow skull. When he smiled, his teeth flashed with gold. 'You are safe, Tiahaar. You are safe. Not drowning.'

'How?' I croaked.

'The storm. You are lucky I went out when the wards tripped. Tide washed you in. Thought you were a corpse, but the gulls wouldn't touch you. Like they were watchin' over you. Wouldn't let me close at first, until they seemed to be sure that I didn't mean you harm.'

Little by little, the events leading up to my near-drowning returned, the press and wash of the immense ocean, the marrow-deep cold, the pressure. My throat was raw, my lips chapped. Every breath burned, and that chill lingered, for I began to shiver.

'Name's Itshe,' he said and fetched me a cup that had been warming by the oil stove.

He eyed me as he helped me take the first sip of a herbal concoction that was liberally laced with brandy.

'Maaris,' I said.

'Just Maaris?'

I sipped more of the mixture that stung its way down my throat. 'Just Maaris to most.'

Itshe cocked his head, as if waiting for me to say more, but I feigned interest in the tea he'd given me. He was the octopus snaking out tentacles, undecided as to whether he'd take the bait. A har grew lonely out here. To him I must be the most tantalising of sea wrack, and I was not ready to spill my secrets, even though part of me was thrilling to do exactly that.

'How long have you been here?' I asked.

'Long enough.' He wheezed laughter then rose as he went to fetch a long-stemmed pipe. 'You don't mind?'

I shook my head then watched while he cleaned and packed the pipe with fresh weed.

'You'll laugh,' he said to me as he lit his pipe and puffed his cheeks to get the ember glowing. The sweet tobacco filled the room with the wash of cherry and vanilla.

'Try me.'

He regarded me evenly. 'It should be I who's asking you to spill the story.'

'My story can wait.'

'There's not much to tell. I came here a score of years ago, if not more. I've stopped counting. Came out here to think. Haven't stopped thinking.'

'Nohar just comes out here.'

'Seems like you'd know something about that.' He offered me a meaningful look.

'Mayhap.' A strange kind of brazenness had its grip on me, accompanied by an equally peculiar ache. Where was Feyrith? I wanted to spin out this moment, without a big "reveal", yet rush headlong into the inevitable.

'It's not the first time you've been here is it?' Itshe noted.

I caught myself just before I shook my head, but his eyes gleamed at the interrupted gesture.

'No use pretending. I saw the way you was looking at things. That jar there, that's your doing, innit?' He was too observant by half.

The pain in my heart dislodged, and I had to draw in a ragged gulp of air. 'Many years ago, there was a har here. The light keeper. The one before you. What happened to him?'

'Your chesnari?' His expression turned to pity in a heartbeat.

I shook my head, vigorously, like a gull shaking water from its feathers. 'No. My guardian.'

He drew hard from his pipe and smoke boiled from Itshe's nostrils like he was some dragon as he regarded me. Something about the gleam in his eyes suggested that he did not believe me at all. 'They say when a har is alone too long, he can go crazy.'

'Then why are you still here?'

'I am not crazy, am I?'

'I don't know. You tell me.'

Itshe laughed. 'Well, you wish to know of your... guardian. It is a strange, strange tale, yet I suspect it's even stranger tides that have washed you up here, so perhaps this is the dehara's way of telling that this is a story that needs finishing.'

He sighed, wrapped his blanket around his bony shoulders then made quite the production of pouring us liquor from a clay jar. Whatever it was smelled of aniseed and tasted of smoke and burned all the way down my throat and made restless serpents that coiled in my belly.

'A har will sometimes seek isolation. Whether it is to think or to make space for the greater silence that yawns about us. Feyrith was, as we could describe him, a haunted har, and it is my belief that he came out here so that he could be closer to his regrets instead of letting the wind loose them from his fingers like the downy feathers the gulls use to line their sorry excuses of nests. His chesnari had sold his soul to the spirits of the ocean. Some say Yala was more spirit than har, and like the foam you couldn't trap him on the sand for long before he simply disappeared. But he was flesh and blood, like all of us, and he had needs. Yet it wouldn't be long before he'd answer that call only he could hear, and he'd be gone. Sometimes three months, sometimes years. That's why Feyrith took this post, you should know. He wanted to be closer to the sea; he wanted to be the one to guide Yala to port though he himself could never bring himself to abandon land.'

'So Yala was Feyrith's chesnari?' I asked.

Itshe coughed dry laughter. 'If you could call it that. It wasn't what I'd call a happy affair. Nohar else would do for Feyrith, and he'd go weeks, months without so much as sharing breath with another har. Some said that'd drive anyhar mad in and of itself. I was running the supplies back then, back before the Big Storm, that is.'

'There have been many big storms,' I pointed out.

'Oh, this one was the storm to end all storms. Your pearl wasn't even a whisper in your hostling's heart back then. It was the storm that sunk *Kogoda's Triumph*, among others, and caused an entire fleet from Megalithica to run aground when their captain misread the signs. It was the only night that this light failed.' Itshe glanced up meaningfully at the light that was doing its duty even now. 'Many lost their lives.'

'The light has never failed. Feyrith said so.'

'Feyrith lied, but those at the Gannet Point light knew. We *saw*.' He wet his lips then drank more liquor.

'The storm came up earlier than we expected. I knew I'd be

chancing it, but we expected the seas to be high for more than a week, and we needed to bring the keeper's supplies. I was a young har, foolish then. I didn't respect Tiamat's Girdle as I should, so I volunteered to make the run. You see, I had my reasons, and Feyrith ranked quite highly in that list.'

'But if his heart was spoken for...' I said.

'So what if his heart was spoken for? You can't blame a har for trying, can you? I didn't mean to tarry but I did, and then through misfortune or not, depending on how you look at it, the tempest set in good and hard, driving the rain, lashing the waves up into a fury. All we could do was make the yacht fast and take down her mast. Already a tricky matter with the wind shrieking like some mad thing. I could pretty much imagine my superiors moaning about my folly, but secretly, I tell you, I was excited. I'd never been out by Pilot's Pillar during a storm. Lightning arced across the sky in sheets and burnt everything white-violet behind my lids. The thunder was so loud, I could feel it right here.' He thumped his chest with the flat of his hand for emphasis. 'You know that sort of storm that only happens every century, or so they say. The night was drunk with it, and there I was, on a little rock with the angry ocean dashing itself to foam flecks. It was the kind of night where you wondered whether the next swell would be larger than the others, and wash everything clean away.

'I don't know how long Yala had been away from Feyrith, but some of the madness in the storm had turned Feyrith a little...as his name suggests...*fey*. I guess that bottle of spiced wine I'd brought with me from the mainland must've helped too, because as the storm swept up, so did this particular passion in him. He was talking, more animated than I'd ever seen him, telling me how he expected Yala to arrive that week. How he'd dreamed that he would come.'

I shrugged. 'Dreams can be prophetic.' Not that I knew personally, and my stomach began to crawl, as I began to get an idea of where this story was headed.

Itshe regarded me evenly. 'Dreams... Pah. I can see you're making connections, and yes, I did seduce him.' A shudder wracked him, and his gaze grew hollow. 'And it was not what I'd expected, and nor was it something I wished to ever repeat. We all knew there was something not quite right with Feyrith, that he was possessed by his love for Yala, and I was not prepared for the exquisite agony of his regret. It was like I had been thrust upon a piece of driftwood caught out in the very storm that lashed us. In fact, the more I clutched at that little piece of flotsam, the greater the crests, the deeper the troughs. I was helpless, bashed hither and thither with each swell. I regretted my earlier boast to my friends that I'd conquer Feyrith's loneliness, for I had not expected how his isolation had gutted him. He was a hungry har, and took more than he gave, so that by the time I came to stillness, I was wrung out, weakened to the point of falling into a deep sleep from which I wasn't certain I'd ever awaken.'

Itshe pulled his blanket tighter. 'I still blame myself for what happened.'

I leaned closer, my breath short. I had never expected to hear of my erstwhile guardian lapsed into such wild abandon, and I feared that if I interrupted Itshe now, he'd say no more on the matter.

As if he understood my need, he caught my gaze and seemed to be fighting some sort of internal battle.

'You have a right to know, I suppose.'

I inclined my head slightly.

'I was the reason why the Pilot's Pillar light wasn't lit that night. Intoxicated, Feyrith had abandoned his post. The Gannet Point light wasn't enough. The vessel that hit the shoals near the Stillbay cliffs was Yala's. All hands gone down. In fact, no bodies were found at all. The cutter *Sonia's Arrow* carried precious cargo. Nohar is certain what exactly, though there are stories that for weeks after, harlings found gemstones on the beach during low tide, such gems whose like were never seen since.

'He didn't know at first. He seemed distant, somewhat agitated when I said goodbye to him that morning. It was only once I'd docked at the point that I was called up to the head keeper's office and pretty much keel hauled for having stayed away. He wanted to know why the light had failed, and that is when the news reached us.'

'Feyrith must've...' The slow horror crept over me.

'Aye, he blamed himself, all right. The *Arrow* had been due to dock at the Pillar. He'd even mentioned her name to me and said how much he'd been looking forward to seeing Yala – this was before I'd seduced him, mind you. We'd been quite in our cups.'

I didn't know whether to despise or pity Itshe. This was not a pretty tale, and all I could recall was the way that my guardian used to stare out to sea every time the northwester blew, how precise he'd been about the rites related to the light so that the crystal never failed.

'There's more, of course.' Itshe gave a little laugh. 'You'd like to hear your part of the story, I'm certain.'

I straightened. 'What?'

'There's an epilogue. You wouldn't be here otherwise. Unfinished business. I can smell it on you. I might be a simple har, but I'm not a fool.'

'What of it?' I narrowed my eyes at him and sipped more of the liquor.

'Your guardian refused to be relieved of his post. Truth be told, nohar would willingly live out here for longer than a few weeks at most, in any case. So he remained in his splendid isolation. Penance and a daily reminder of how he'd failed. Suffice to say that I was removed from the supply run in case I might decide to repeat my idiotic escapade.' He crowed dry laughter. 'I learnt, though. Guilt is a nasty thing if left to fester. I have my own devils. But that's when the stories started. We all know of ghost vessels. After all, there's that old Dutchman that's been sighted many times around the Cape of Storms, and now we have our own spectral ship here.' He leaned closer, so that his oily, somewhat fishy scent nearly overwhelmed my senses. 'It is said that the *Arrow* still sails, when the northwester comes up, and that anyhar who lays eyes on her is doomed.'

My laughter burst from me. 'What rot! Here I am, hale and hearty.'

'So you've seen her.' His expression grew crafty. 'Thought so.'

'I did not say that.' For some reason my heart beat faster, my mouth suddenly dry.

Itshe regarded me evenly, as if he was in possession of some secret joke he had no desire to share. He hid his smirk in a yawn as he stretched.

'It was a particular hell for Feyrith. Everyhar else who washed up at Gannet Point and Stillbay who claimed to have seen the *Arrow*. Except him. Some ill always befell them. Perhaps a vessel would spring a leak. An entire catch would escape. Cargo would spoil. A har would sicken, perhaps come close to dying after claiming to have seen the ghost ship. It might all be coincidence, but you know how folk love their stories. It was like that story of the phantom hitchhiker on the Eastway, begging rides from the hara running the tramway.'

'Hara love their stories, you're right,' I said. 'And stories are all they are. You know how we can sometimes think we saw something, but it might only be a trick of the light.'

She was a cutter, her sails tatters and the remaining jib flapping loose as she dipped and wallowed upon the swell.

I couldn't help but shiver at the memory, and Itshe laughed at me, then topped up our goblets with more liquor.

'You're a terrible liar, Tiahaar, but let me continue. It was after a storm-tossed night that your pearl washed up on the sorry excuse for a beach here on this cursed rock. At least that is what Feyrith claims. You're the spitting image of Yala, apparently. Those who met him said he had a queer complexion, even for some hara, as though he were more suited to the deep than life ashore. You have the shadows trapped under your skin.' He ran a finger along the smooth skin of my forearm, and I shuddered at his touch. It was not a pleasant sensation.

'He never said anything about my pearl washing up.'

'You've never asked, never wondered?' He cocked his head, his eyes bird bright.

'It never mattered.'

'Truthfully?'

I maintained eye contact, though every part of me wanted to rather examine my nails or pick at the frayed edges of the blanket I clutched around my shoulders.

Honestly, I had been putting off this very question for many years. Somehow, I'd known Edera hadn't possessed the answers I'd sought, and yet I had been too afraid to come sooner. Afraid of what I'd discover. That perhaps my guardian had been my hostling after all, even though I understood implicitly that this was not possible.

'Nohar thought that pearl was viable, yet the head keeper at the Gannet Point light sent for the Nahir-Nuri from Stillbay to come look. He was puzzled by your pearl's arrival as much as Feyrith was.' He raised his brow. 'No, I am not your father. The pearl washed up five days after the *Arrow* ran aground.'

'What, you're saying I'm some ghost's offspring?'

He lifted his shoulders, shrugged. 'There are many mysteries under the sun, Tiahaar. You are but one of many. Feyrith kept you for as long as he could.'

'Where is he now?'

Another shrug. Itshe wet his lips. 'Not long after you left with that storm wrack of a har, Feyrith simply vanished. Some fisherhara say they glimpsed a cutter, listing badly to her port side. They tried to hail her, but the northwester was gusting up, and she vanished behind a swell. They reported the incident to the point light, but when Feyrith's light failed at dusk, we sent an emergency crew to investigate. Just as well we did. This rock was deserted, and I've been here since.'

'Maybe he walked into the sea.' I knew my words were callous, but I'd grown weary of this roundabout telling that wasn't giving me the answers I wasn't even sure I wanted to hear.

'Mayhap he did.'

I raised a brow at the har. Itshe agreed with me?

'The place was swept clean. The bed made. Linen, such as it was, folded and placed in the kist. That jar there, with the sea snail shells, that was on the table.'

My heart beat a lot harder than I wanted it to, and I swallowed back my expectations. 'Was there a note?'

He shook his head.

But I didn't need a note, did I? I knew very well what he meant. I'd asked him, often, if I had enough sea coins to buy a boat. And then what sort of boat. A windjammer. Cutter. Schooner. Catamaran. Yacht. I'd gone through the list of names and each time he'd shake his head, his smile tight.

As an adult, I understood the meaning of useless currency. A harling's dreams.

Feyrith must've known I'd return.

This was his way of telling me that I must go, pursue my dreams. He'd wanted more for me; that I must grow without the burden of his guilt.

I regarded Itshe without malice, and he, in turn studied me, his dark eyes reflecting the wavering pinpricks of the candlelight.

'I am not your father,' he said.

'I know.'

He sighed deeply. 'They will send a yacht in the morning. Best make yourself comfortable. You are lucky to be alive.'

'I was never in any real danger.'

Itshe offered me a soft snort then rose. Another fierce squall hit the cottage, but somehar had fixed the roofing, for there was nary a shudder, and no fingers of cold pushed through under the door.

Itshe was like the rock; he'd endure. There was a determination to the set of his shoulders as he went about securing his dwelling for the night. The last thing he did was check up on his light, which left me alone for a spell. Enough for me to gather my thoughts and know what I must do come sunrise.

Sometime during the night, the wind had blown itself out and only soft rain sifted down, the kind that was more gull spit than downpour. The sea was restless, but the swell had subsided, and I made my way down to the small cove that served as a beach. It was ebb tide, and the wavelets rattled the pebbles with each wash. The sun was up already, though obscured by thick clouds that pressed their bellies low against the horizon, but the light had that particular hazed-out quality that spoke of a fine day later. The kind of blue that would be like a promise, a song.

I held my breath as I waded into the shallows until the water lapped at my thighs.

My fingers disturbed the fine patina of dust on the jar of sea coins. When I was a harling, my entire hand, past my wrist, could fit into the jar. Now I had to tip the contents into my palm so that I could examine the white, whorled disks. One side was spiralled; the other had bumpy, calciferous growths.

Feyrith had explained to me that these were the doors to their shells, and there'd been times when I'd disturbed the snails in their tidal pools, to find them with their little 'lids' pulled tight.

Yet there was that part of me that had secretly believed in the worth of these objects, despite the fact that they littered the beach in great profusion, and my guardian had humoured me.

I closed my fingers around a handful. There was so much unanswered. I was but an endnote for some greater tragedy that had been drawn out to sea. Mine was not their story, though it had begun with their end. Somehar else would rage against the secrets, shake their fists at the dehara for their cruelty. Perhaps this handful of shells was all I had of my past, and perhaps it was up to me how I would deal with it.

A great sorrow descended on me, for all that was disrupted, for the greater mystery in whose shadow I stood, that would never be solved.

Then a kelp gull nearby let out its gulping, gobbling cry, and I pulled back my arm and tossed that first sprinkling of sea coins as far as I could into the outgoing tide. Each fell with a small plop and sank immediately. Three more handfuls followed, until I held only the jar. Empty. The temptation to throw the receptacle was great, but glass was precious, and Itshe might still have a use for it.

I stood for a while until the cold hollowed out my bones and my ears began to ache.

I had no answers.

I wasn't even sure what questions I should ask, save that the harbourmaster at Stillbay might be able to offer news of the next windjammer that would put in for supplies. Whatever Feyrith had intended, I was of the sea, and there was no turning my back on the waves, and I had the feeling that I wouldn't be seeing any ghost ships soon. Some things were only found when a har wasn't out searching for them.

The Museum

Amanda Kear

'Leave the bottle.'

Drey tossed a handful of spinners on the bar and drained his glass in one swallow, feeling the liquor burn an angry path down his throat. The sensation matched his mood. It was barely lunchtime, yet he had a mind to get falling down drunk.

He seethed at the polite message which had been passed onto him by a househar from the Big House: that Falcon's Fire was rising in status and aspired to be a place of learning and culture, so certain hara and certain trades would no longer be welcome within its demesnes.

Certain hara such as the scavengers who made a living from forays beyond the Great Wall of Lund. Hara who in manner and appearance were habitually as feral as the Lund gangs; who salacious rumours said had unsavoury habits as depraved as any gang member and likely spent all their time plotting murder or worse.

No matter that the Phylarch's consort wore a diamond and emerald necklace which *Drey* had brought back from Lund, nor that the Heir's obsession with porcelain statuettes was a major reason so many scavengers came calling at the town. Rough, dangerous hara were out. Enlightened, civilised hara were in. Drey had received an ultimatum: morph into some forelock-tugging peasant whose purpose in life was to do tasks the Phylarch's get considered beneath them, or clear out of town.

Drey was instead going for option three: get very, very drunk, and then tell everyhar exactly what he thought of them, the Big House and their poxy "place of learning and culture". Afterwards, they'd more than likely forcibly eject him from Falcon's Fire lands. Assuming they still had a few rough, dangerous hara on their staff to do the ejecting.

Enlightened, civilised hara were apparently already in town. Gossip from the Big House swirled around the inn. Those in the know reported a trio of scholars from the Great Library at Kyme were currently being sponsored by the Phylarch. The chatter said their tribe was Tuaththua, not Sulh, and they were here to discover lore about animals – or perhaps come to repair the ravages done to nature by humanity? The rumours and tittle-tattle were rather vague on details.

Drey paid them no heed. The doings of scholars and high-ranking hara were not part of his world.

He had achieved a state of pleasant drunkenness when the stranger tapped him on the shoulder. Drey was staring at the label on his mostly empty, second bottle, contemplating the sheer volume of alcohol a har had to drink to feel satisfyingly legless. It had been a much, much quicker process when he was human.

'Excuse me, are you Tiahaar Drey?' The voice had the burr of a Tuaththuan accent.

Drey turned to see an elegant, dark-skinned har who wore the sigil of the Great Library on a burnished copper pendant.

'Ah, come to enlighten and civilise me in person, eh? The Great Library does house calls now, does it?' Drey muttered. He waved a hand at their surroundings. 'Well, pub calls, anyway…'

The stranger looked confused. He took a breath and tried again: 'Tiahaar Drey, my mentor Tiahaar Eburneus har Tuaththua wishes to hire your services.'

The har made a gracious gesture towards one of the larger tables in the inn, where the pothar was fussing over two bookish looking hara as they took their seats. The expression of both speaker and pothar indicated they severely doubted the wisdom of anyhar hiring Drey's services.

'So the learned and cultured still need the services of the rough and dangerous, eh? Has anyone told the Phylarch?' Drey grinned and pulled himself to his feet. Telling the great and the good of Falcon's Fire what he thought of them *after* he'd secured a new source of income sounded like a fine plan. Option three is dead – long live Option four!

He strode across to the table, fancying the path he took was more or less a straight line.

'I'm Drey the Scavenger. What do you want found?'

'No, that's *not* how it works. *You* don't go into Lund – *I* make the journey on your behalf.'

The conversation with the scholars was not going well. It had started out reasonably enough: once they were all seated, introductions made and a jug of water had been pointedly placed in the centre of the table, Eburneus quizzed him about how many times he had been into Lund, and how well he knew the central part of the ruined city. He peppered the conversation with human names for districts and landmarks, and Drey responded in kind, assuming this was the scholarly version of checking his credentials.

Of course, he had the advantage over Eburneus that he'd actually lived there, human and har, and could easily recall the human names for districts no human had walked for decades. All three scholars had the air of second generation about them, though Drey would guess the flaxen-haired Eburneus was far older than elegant, mahogany-skinned Nakara or mousy, nervous Verga.

However, Drey couldn't seem to convince them he was a scavenger, not a guide. Couldn't convince them, in fact, there was *no such thing* as a guide into Lund. Only the deranged, the suicidal or the very, very stealthy ever ventured past the walls and into the territory of the murderous, feral gangs which inhabited the ruins. He currently counted himself as one of the stealthy. If he agreed to escort three heads-in-the-clouds scholars into Lund, then he'd definitely qualify as both deranged *and* suicidal.

'You pay me part of the fee, I go in and locate whatever it is you need, then you pay the rest when I deliver. *That's* how it works. Nohar sane will take travellers into Lund. At least nohar sane who wants to get them out alive again. Though if the intention is to murder them and then blame the ferals, then I suppose somehar might...' Drey put on his best do-not-mess-with-me scowl, hoping they took the hint.

Please Aghama, make whatever they wanted be something small like a book, and not something ludicrous like a life-size, marble statue!

The three scholars swapped enigmatic glances. Probably communicating by mind touch.

'Perhaps if we explain what we need. There is a place in Lund – a human museum...' Eburneus began.

Drey sighed. Oh great, treasure seekers. 'Filled with great riches, no doubt. The wisdom of the ages, bedecked with gold and steeped in rare spices!' He laced his words with enough sarcasm to penetrate even a scholar's haze.

Eburneus stared at him, blinking in confusion. A small frown formed. 'No, no! Animals! A museum of animals!'

It was Drey's turn to stare.

Eburneus mistook that for ignorance and launched into explanation: 'A very large museum, dedicated to the natural world. It housed the bones, skins, and pickled remains of creatures from all over the Earth, as well as plants, fossils and minerals. We have its position marked on an old human map, and would like—'

Drey cut him off with a gesture. 'Yes, yes, I know the place.'

Eburneus beamed.

'Is it still standing?' the one called Verga asked anxiously. 'Have you been inside?'

A bark of laughter. 'Of course I haven't been inside! Nohar goes inside.'

'Why?' queried Scholar Eburneus with mild puzzlement.

Drey favoured him with his most withering glare. 'Because of all the dammed ghosts.'

Shadow was playing with the fish today. He ran up and down stairs and along corridors as shoals of them darted and swirled around him. In places reached by the sun, light glinted off silver scales of species which adored the shallows. In dark, windowless rooms lined with shelves and drawers, deep-sea denizens lit his way with flashes of bioluminescence.

He ran laughing into the middle of a school of fish, delighting in the way they parted before him and swirled round to coalesce behind. They sang tiny songs of predator and prey, of life and death in the oceans. A shark and its accompanying remoras cruised past, joining the recreation of ocean life.

Eventually he was so drained from running, laughter and sharing his energy with the fish that he had to stagger to a halt. Shadow padded at a more sedate pace to the cathedral-like great hall and climbed the steps to sprawl by the statue of a bearded human. The fish continued their play, treating the crumbling plaster of Paris dinosaur skeleton as if it was a shipwreck; darting in and out of the rib cage, sheltering under its spine.

This morning the salmon had decided the staircases were waterfalls, and were leaping up them, singing of their desire to spawn. Elvers joined them, trilling with the need to forge upstream. Soon the fishes of the world had divided the great hall into freshwater and saltwater domains: carp, trout and pike languidly idling near the ceiling while their marine counterparts claimed the "depths".

Other phyla were waking up and joining the ethereal dance. Krill, squid and jellyfish formed their own shoals. Seabirds dived into the depths, turtles swam upwards in search of air, corals grew on balconies and walls. Whale song echoed and reverberated from a neighbouring hall. Here and there the illusion of ocean and river was slightly awry: a trio of colourful parrots perched on a display case; a hedgehog snuffled and snorted its way up the stairs; and there was an excited swarm of bees chasing their queen amid the schools of fish and squid.

Shadow didn't mind.

He lay down on the stone floor and dreamily watched it all. His animals. His friends.

His sanctuary.

'Animal spirits? Oh, but that's marvellous!' Eburneus smiled like the doting parent of a newly-hatched harling. 'I was hoping to awaken some spirits, but if they are already active…? Marvellous, marvellous.'

'No, it's not bloody marvellous,' snapped Drey. 'It's dangerous. Nohar sane goes near that place.'

Only the terminally stupid. Or sometimes the absolutely desperate, taking a massive risk in the hope of shaking a pack of ferals off their trail. Drey shuddered.

'What harm can the spirits of animals do? If we are properly respectful…'

'Perhaps you'd care to ask the har who had all his blood drained by a thousand ghostly mosquitoes? Or the one who had his eyes pecked out by spectral crows? Or maybe talk to the har who was grabbed by an enormous thing with tentacles? Oh no, wait a minute – you can't. Because! They're! All! Dead!'

Drey realised he had stood up and was shouting, and the eyes of everyhar in the inn were upon them. He took a deep breath and crashed back into his seat.

Sometimes risks paid off. Sometimes they didn't, and you had to live with their consequences for the rest of your life. He grabbed his bottle and took a huge swallow, then another. His voice dropped to a mutter. 'It's a bad place. Not even the Lund gangs go there.'

'Ah, so it might be untouched? Intact?' If anything, Eburneus' enthusiasm had gone up a notch or two.

'Weren't you listening? The place is a death-trap!'

'It is a risk worth taking.'

'You'd risk death to speak to some animal ghosts?' Drey gestured aggressively with his bottle. 'There are animals and ghosts aplenty in the woods round here. Go speak to those ones! You won't have to risk pelki to find them, and they won't tear you to pieces when you do.'

A shake of the head. 'No, no – it has to be the museum. These are very particular spirits. Ancient spirits. Extinct animals, wiped out by the humans. We will return them to corporeal existence.'

'Bring them back to life,' one of his companions translated.

'In *Lund?*' Drey asked incredulously. 'They'll be extinct again in five seconds flat. The gangs will eat them.'

From Eburneus' expression, that particular possibility had not occurred to him. A flicker of doubt crossed the scholar's face, then was dismissed with another enthusiastic smile.

'I shall meditate on it, but I believe we can imbue the ritual with a degree of protection necessary to ensure their survival. The important thing is we won't know until we *try*.'

Nakara and Verga echoed his sentiment.

'You are all as mad as a sack full of stoats,' Drey said. Option four was a bust. Back to Option three.

The museum had been a part of Shadow's life as far back as he could remember. He recalled coming here as a child, as a regular treat arranged by a barely remembered grandmother. Then later, there were educational visits: a raucous group of school children, accompanied by world-weary teachers, hoping their charges might be inspired to learn something.

Shadow longed to learn.

He would have been happy to fill his whole life with learning. However, his mother and his peers lived by other rules. Black boys from rough estates were not supposed to be entranced by cases of seashells or arrays of insects. They were not supposed to want to learn animal names or memorise their habits. And as they grew older they were most certainly not supposed to want to eschew their duty to father the next human generation by being attracted to their own sex…

The museum became a haven. Whenever he could scrape together the Tube fare, he'd make a pilgrimage across the city.

Sometimes he fancied the bones and skins talked to him. Sometimes he felt as if he was being watched. Sometimes he thought he was going mad.

One day a youth followed him from the Tube station to the museum and shadowed his progress round the halls. A youth who was fascinatingly feral. A youth with eyes that reflected light like a cat's. Shadow found Wraeththu, found a pack to run with… and for a time became little more than one of the animals he so admired.

His pack was small, their needs and wants few. For a time, there was a golden age, when they played and partied in the dying city, moving from place to place when the food ran out or as the mood took them.

On a crisp winter morning Shadow emerged from his pack's lair and watched the city burn. He didn't know who had started it – human or hara – but it marked the end of human occupation of Lund. Humanity threw their resources into finishing their Great Wall, then abandoned their capital to the hara packs and gangs.

That day, his pack dashed through smoke-filled streets, crossing the river to escape the worst of the flames. Shadow was at the front of the pack, scouting for trouble ahead even as they fled. No point escaping the fire, just to run into the frying pan. Without realising it, his path veered towards the museum; icon of childhood safety.

It had not escaped unscathed. Pigeons fluttered in and out of broken windows. Walls bore gang tags in lurid colours. Bullet holes pock-marked the main doors.

At the top of the steps were a thousand mice.

His pack-mates were afraid of the myriad spirits. They had only seen spectres in ones and twos, never in a flock or herd or swarm. The hara stopped, milling about in confusion, filled with nervous chatter… eyes on the mice, not on the route they'd just travelled.

In that moment the other gang struck.

The air was filled with whoops and war cries and the screams of the dying. Shadow snarled and threw himself into the fray. Blades slashed, sending arcs of crimson into the haze of smoke. They were down to five hara… then three… then two – Shadow and his pack leader, fighting back to back.

A pistol spat death, and Shadow's companion went from vibrant life to a crumpled, broken thing, jerking spasmodically at the foot of the steps.

Run, run!

Shadow could not have said if the thought was his own or a mind-touch sent by the dying har.

He feinted with his knife, then hurtled up the steps; a waterfall of mice cascading down the stairs to meet him.

The bullet's impact plunged him into the midst of them. Sprawled bleeding in a sea of twitching whiskers and tiny feet. He began to crawl toward the main doors, in vain hope of shelter, of safety.

Help me! Protect me!

His sending went out to his dead pack-mates, to the building, to the mice – to anyhar who would listen.

A lion roared, and the pride answered. A wolf howled, and the pack replied. A baboon barked a challenge and the troop shrieked and jabbered in fury at intruders on their territory.

A thousand mice turned gleaming eyes on the gang members.

Mice are small, and hara are big. But a thousand is a very large number – and you cannot kill a ghost with blades and bullets.

A shock of cold water brought Drey abruptly to consciousness. He jerked and spluttered, then regretted the motion as his hangover kicked in. He slumped back to the floor.

'Is he awake?'

'Yes, Tiahaar.' The pothar moved aside, to give Drey a view of the Phylarch's Heir and two sour-faced househara.

Oh, Aghama's balls! He seemed to have skipped straight from the drinking phase to the being ejected from the town phase, without any recall of the venting his spleen phase. That was monstrously unfair. Drey glowered at the empties lying beside him.

The Heir settled fastidiously on a chair, flanked by his minions. 'Good afternoon, Scavenger Drey,' he said superciliously.

Drey made a grunt which might have passed for a greeting and hauled himself upright. Water dripped from his hair.

'Scholar Eburneus informs me you have turned down his offer of employment.' The Heir studied his perfect nails, then looked up. 'This is unacceptable. Falcon's Fire endorses his mission and has promised him a guide.'

It took Drey's brain a moment to catch up with what had just been said. 'Endorses? Seriously?'

'Yes. Very seriously. The benefits will be untold.' The Heir gave what he obviously thought was a winning smile. 'As our foremost scavenger…'

Drey gave a bark of laughter. 'Only scavenger left, you mean. Been a bit too efficient at running the rest out of town, have we?'

The servants frowned at this insolence. The Heir made an airy gesture, dismissing Drey's assertion as of no import. 'You *will* guide Scholar Eburneus' party. The Phylarch insists. You'll be well paid, and in return we will grant you permission to stay in Falcon's Fire. Or...' The Heir leaned forward to emphasise his words. 'Or we can provide written references to any future employers in other phyles.'

The unspoken threat hung in the air. *Or we can blacken your reputation with every phylarch in the south-east...*

Drey clenched his fists and bit down hard on the impulse to punch the Heir repeatedly in the face. The two servants shifted stance, alert to the possibility of violence, and radiating their own ability to do harm.

'It's suicide,' he said eventually. 'The scholars won't last five minutes.'

'Domana and Bellon will accompany you as protection.' The Heir indicated his two servants.

Oh great. Now he had to get *five* idiots safely in and out of Lund.

Shadow dragged himself into the belly of the museum, leaving a bloody trail in his wake.

A host of creatures greeted him. Scavengers – jackal, hyena, raven – padded and swirled around him, as they had attended the dying in life. Predators followed the blood scent, whispering of the hope for an easy kill. Prey animals chirped alarm calls or brayed in distress at one of their number fallen to the hunters.

Eventually Shadow could crawl no further, whimpering in pain and exhaustion. He lay panting on the tiled floor, eerily calm. Watching the creatures around him. As fascinated by their ghosts as he had been by their bones, shells and skins.

If he died here, perhaps he too would become a ghost, haunting the museum's halls?

Shadow found he didn't mind that notion at all.

The Walls of Lund loomed before them. The barricade was a haphazard relic of the human age: the last great construction project before the city was given over entirely to Wraeththu. Functionality and desperation had taken precedence over architectural niceties such as aesthetics, so the construction materials varied from rusting shipping containers to poured concrete to the tangled wreckage of vehicles. Razor wire snaked and curled over everything like some metallic cousin of brambles. In a few places the Wall had been designed to keep intruders out. In many, it was most definitely constructed to keep hara in.

Time had softened the grim reality of the barrier. Toadflax and moss patterned its walls. Birds nested upon its ramparts. Gang tags declared portions of it not as an obstacle, but as property.

For the Great Wall of Lund was a porous structure. It might appear impenetrable and imposing, but each gang, each clique, each scavenger, had ways in and out. Some were well known, well maintained and zealously defended by their current proprietors. Others were secret, precarious passageways though the blockade, known to a scant few whose lives depended on the denizens of Lund never discovering their carefully concealed access and egress points.

Drey's preferred entry was one of these. A crawl-way through a series of vehicles entombed in concrete. Squeezing and slithering through the gaps and air pockets where the wet concrete had neither filled the cars nor crushed them under its weight. Dark, claustrophobic – and ideal for staying concealed from roving gang members.

He cast a weary look at the Tuaththuans. At least he'd been able to convince them to exchange robes for neutral-coloured, hard-wearing clothing. He'd gone through their gear twice, each time making them dump a whole host of impractical and bulky objects which would slow them down.

'Ready?' he asked.

A ripple of assent. Drey carefully pushed aside the screening curtain of ivy and slithered into the darkness.

There was a kind of ecology to the gangs of Lund. Predator-prey relationships. Each crew had to be large enough and fierce enough to hold its own in the constant internecine warfare. Yet growing beyond a certain size brought diminishing returns. The early bounty of unwary urban wildlife and stockpiles of canned goods were long since devoured. If the gangs wanted to eat, they had to cultivate the gardens and green spaces of the ruined city.

However, in a culture of might makes right, the allotments and vegetable plots of one gang made a tempting target for another.

Farming was hard work and had none of the glamour and immediate gratification of violence. Gangs claimed land and tended a few crops until one faction or another grew big enough to eschew agriculture and opt to live entirely by pillage. A large faction by its very nature would be too voracious. To avert starvation, the targeted farmers would revert to raiding of their own. In short order the whole system would collapse since – without abundant crops to steal – the large faction would become unsustainable and splinter into fragments.

Had Lund been an entirely closed system, the gangs would eventually have warred to extinction. But the Great Wall was a permeable barrier. Hara ventured out on raids, and brought back food, resources – and knowledge. Knowledge such as the ability to make pearls.

The ecology of Lund changed. The resource which was fought over was no longer food, but flesh.

The enclosed microcosm within the walls ensured the gangs never became sufficiently stable and stratified to develop into tribes. Outside the walls, Wraeththu evolved and moved on. Within them nature remained red in tooth and claw.

Domana was the first to die.

Drey took point, eyes constantly sweeping the route for traps, ambushes or the myriad physical hazards of a derelict, crumbling city. Bellon was on one flank, Domana at the rear. Over the next few hours, Drey led them forward in fits and starts, pausing often to check for signs of pursuit, pushing energy into small magaris which he hoped would muffle sound or hide their – horrifyingly obvious – trail.

Precious few second-generation hara had had to fight for survival, and it showed. If there was a branch that could be snapped, broken paving slab to clunk or corroded can to kick, the scholars found it. On top of which, Eburneus – annoyingly – wanted to *know* things. He bombarded Drey with a constant series of questions. *Why are all the trees on this street dead? What do those painted symbols mean? Is the river still navigable?* Eventually Drey – and some pointed remarks from the two Heir-appointed bodyguards – convinced the scholar that silence was of the essence. Which only meant the questions now came as mind-touch, rather than as stage whispers. It was distracting as hell.

Lund was not the sort of place for anyhar to get distracted.

A flicker of motion – and Domana was down with an arrow in his throat. Verga's shocked screams almost drowned out the yips and howls of the gang's war cries.

'Run!' Drey locked eyes with Bellon. Each grabbed a scholar and hurled them into motion. An arrow shattered against brickwork in a near miss.

Where? Bellon sent, having the sense not to waste breath.

Border of this gang's territory. Look for fox skulls painted on walls. That was their only safety now – hope that one gang would not venture into the turf of another. They zig-zagged between the overgrown hulks of abandoned vehicles, ducking under listing lampposts, leapt over the roots of street trees grown to forest giants.

Dark shapes loped along rooftops, paralleling their flight. More arrows flew. Drey swiftly jerked Eburneus between himself and the archers, using the scholar as a shield.

Target the ones who look like warriors: capture the ones who look like prey – the eternal tactics of the ferals of Lund.

Bellon paused to fire a pistol at their attackers. Mistake. Drey glanced back to see a crossbow bolt puncture the har's calf.

'Run! I'll—' Whatever Bellon had been about to say was lost in the sickening *shunk* of a second bolt burying itself in his skull.

Drey grabbed Eburneus by the arm and fled. He never looked back.

Fox skull symbol. Another. Then a cluster of three on a wall and, fifty metres further on, an actual vulpine skull nailed to a tree trunk.

The sounds of pursuit faded. Rain began to fall; steady, insistent. Drey stumbled to a halt. His eyes sought out an open doorway and he headed for the shelter and bolt hole it offered. Eburneus and Nakara staggered unsteadily along in his wake.

There was no sign of Verga.

'So, we're calling quits on this, yes?' Drey said, as soon as he got his heaving lungs under control enough to speak. 'Best plan is to rest up an hour or two, then sneak back by another route.'

'No,' said Eburneus.

He glanced up at the scholar, expecting some half-arsed plan about rescuing Verga.

'We go on.'

'Go on?'

'Yes. We're too close to give up now. This is too important.' Eburneus pulled out his Aghama-damned human map and leafed through it. 'We're here, yes? We could be at the museum in less than an hour!'

Nakara appeared to be in shock, staring dully at the faded pages. 'But... Verga... the others...'

Eburneus gripped Nakara's hand. 'We're close, Nakara. Too close to turn back. We have to let their sacrifice mean something. We have to continue.'

Drey had been wrong. Eburneus wasn't an airy-fairy scholar – he was a fanatic.

The museum became Shadow's domain. He explored corridors, laboratories and storerooms barred to him as a youth. Opened drawers and was welcomed by armies of beetles... multitudes of rodents... throngs of wildflowers. Each carefully preserved skin or meticulously labelled jar a little shrine to the dead. The creatures were lonely. Their physical remains had been cherished by their human caretakers and visitors, seeking insight into their lives. With each painstakingly written label or detailed scientific examination, the humans unwittingly transferred tiny amounts of energy to the bodies of the deceased creatures. The creatures had felt appreciated. Loved.

With the ascent of hara, the spectral as well as the physical had become visible to those who walked the museum's halls. The creatures had briefly rejoiced.

It had been short-lived. The hara of Lund had no interest in the patterns and rhythms of nature, beyond what they must know to survive. The intricacy of a snail's tongue, or the life cycle of a barnacle, or the texture of a pollen grain meant nothing to them. Hara were violence and rage. Hara were the smashing of glass and the threat of fire.

The creatures drove them from their halls.

Until Shadow. He became their audience of one, and daily they danced the stories of their lives for him.

Drey insisted they stay the night in their bolt hole. He may have totally failed to convince Eburneus of the wisdom of turning back, but at least he could be adamant on the need to rest until Nakara's limbs had ceased shaking, and the har's glassy stare reverted to something reminiscent of normality. He also gave the scholars a tongue-lashing on the folly of wanting to creep around an unfamiliar, potentially unstable ruin as night approached.

Facing the ghosts would be bad enough in daylight. Drey was sure he'd end up a gibbering wreck if they tried it at night.

He was sorely tempted to leave the scholars and save his own skin. If it had just been Eburneus remaining, he probably would. But he felt he owed Nakara a chance at survival.

'Absolutely sure you want to do this?' In the grey light of a rainy morning, he tried one last time to make Eburneus see sense.

A firm nod. 'Absolutely. The world needs this.'

Nakara's gaze was fixed on the other scholar, like a drowning har watching the shore. Drey sighed and led them out into the rain.

By the time they were halfway to their destination, Drey suspected they were being watched, despite his concealment magaris. By the time they'd picked their way to the final street – with a portion of the museum distantly visible up ahead – he was sure of it. The eerie bark-yowl of foxes echoed across the deserted streets, and Drey was pretty sure not all the calls issued from vulpine throats. He couldn't quite shake the feeling that the watchers had figured out their destination and were tagging along for the sheer entertainment value of seeing three lunatics take on a whole building full of ghosts.

His suspicion was confirmed when they emerged onto the wide street by the museum frontage. While Eburneus – all caution forgotten – exclaimed in delight, Drey spotted a couple of hara crouched on a balcony further up the street, observing. Fox tails dangled from their unkempt braids.

Crap. They were all going to die. Or worse.

Drey kept one eye on the watchers as he followed the two scholars across the cracked tarmac. In their enthusiasm, he wasn't sure the Tuaththuans had even noticed the Fox hara, let alone recalled all his warnings about the spectres. A flock of pigeons circled the roof and Drey shivered, wondering if they were physical or ghosts.

'Hey, slow down! Ghosts, remember?'

'Yes, yes, we must be respectful. I will… My. Oh my!' Eburneus had stopped stock still, staring into the greenery beyond the museum railings.

A tiger paced through the trees, turning amber eyes to them. It bared its teeth and snarled.

Shadow was on the roof. Pigeons cooed and fluttered around him – some living, some spectral. Frogs from several continents were enjoying the rain, vying to utter the most seductive mating call.

He was distracted from his friends' antics by the activity of hara in the streets below. Shadow was confident in his friends' abilities to keep intruders out, yet he was simultaneously drawn to and wary of his own kind. As gang borders shifted to and fro, various different factions had held the turf around the museum. Some ignored it. Some chased victims or rivals towards its walls, letting the ghosts do their killing for them.

The Fox Hara held sway here now. They sent their younglings – barely past feybraiha – racing through the grounds, daring the creatures' ire as a rite of passage. Shadow politely asked his friends not to slay these youths, but the sight of fleeing prey sometimes proved too tempting for the carnivores.

Today the Fox Hara were flitting round the streets and buildings, which surrounded the museum. Their calls told of intruders, yet no attack was being massed. What size of force would make them hold back? Shadow was concerned. He requested the pigeons screen him from view and loped along the rooftop to a vantage point.

It was not a force – it was three hara. One had the air of a gang member or scavenger. The others, for all their similar attire, carried themselves in a different way. Excited. Stately. Scribbling notes.

Intrigued, Shadow headed down to observe more closely.

Eburneus was trying to communicate with the spirits. It was evident enough that the scholar had their attention – a whole ark full of creatures chirped and roared and bellowed just within the gates. However, every time Eburneus or Nakara ventured a step from street onto museum land, teeth snapped and talons slashed. Both Tuaththuans now bore cuts, bruises and ripped clothing, and were looking increasingly bedraggled and dispirited as the rain continued.

Drey wore his best 'I told you so' expression.

He was hunkered down with his back to the railings. He could cope with the concept of being close to dozens of ghosts if he didn't have to look at them too often. And *somehar* had to keep an eye on the feral hara. That wasn't likely to be Eburneus or Nakara.

Something snuffled at the back of his neck. Drey uttered a cry of alarm and leapt to his feet, spinning round. A cry of alarm – yes, that's what it was. Not a terrified shriek. Definitely not a terrified shriek.

A phantasmal elephant had poked the tip of its trunk through the railings, sniffing at where he had been. It rumbled and withdrew the appendage, turning away to lumber back into the greenery. Other creatures moved to let it pass by. Including a...

'Did you see that?' Drey squinted into the flickering shadows. There was a positive blizzard of ghostly animals in the grounds of the museum. Smaller groups of them would solidify for a moment or two, then meld back into the morass. He thought he'd seen... What? A human ghost amongst the animal ones? A harish figure?

'See what?' Nakara asked.

'I thought there was somehar in there with the ghosts.'

A brown, hairy creature charged at the railings and reared up on its hind legs, displaying front paws with a set of wicked looking claws.

'Grizzly bear,' said Nakara.

'Maybe,' Drey said doubtfully. What he'd seen had been tall and slender, not built like a brick shithouse. Maybe the hara killed by the ghosts still haunted the place? Lucky them.

Shadow cloaked himself in birds and insects, using their flight and motion to conceal his approach. The strangers had tried to enter and been driven back. Now two of them were attempting to communicate, but they seemed not to understand the replies. Or possibly they were simply asking the wrong questions?

His friends were happily engaging with the strangers by demonstrating their prowess at defending the museum. Territorial beasts were scent-marking and calling to proclaim their ownership. Other species were making threat displays and mock attacks to drive off rivals. The whole area was a frenzy of overlapping shapes, as creature after creature realised their audience had increased from one to four.

Shadow wasn't sure how he felt about this. If other hara wanted to learn his friends' lives, would they still dance them for him?

He might never find out – the Fox Hara had got bored. The pair on the balcony dropped to the ground. One uttered a vixen's yowl. From the streets around, harish shapes loped towards the museum gates.

One of the strangers raised a pistol. Another clutched a notebook protectively to his chest.

Shadow made his decision.

The Fox Hara advanced with the easy bravado of those who know their prey cannot possibly fell enough of them to survive.

'Shit!' Drey aimed his pistol at the closest and backed closer to the scholars.

Eburneus was belatedly realising the danger. 'What do we do? What do we *do?*'

The cacophony of animal cries fell abruptly silent.

Drey darted a glance over his shoulder. The maelstrom of ghosts was settling into stillness. The eyes of a hundred kinds of creature were fixed upon them. Whiskers twitched and tongues flickered, wings rustled and antennae trembled. Watching. Waiting.

Memories of that earlier time surfaced: a territorial grab gone wrong, a running battle, a handful of young warriors and a desperate gamble to flank their enemy and strike back... The end of Drey's life as a pack member. The start of his life alone. He found, to his surprise, he would rather be torn to pieces by spectres than grasp the thin chance of life which capture by the Fox Hara might offer. He took a deep breath, twisted past Eburneus and stepped into the museum grounds.

He braced in anticipation of teeth and mandibles rending his flesh. Incomprehensibly, the ghosts stood motionless and let him pass. The two scholars scurried after him. Could he survive this? Drey picked his way cautiously forward, fighting down the urge to run screaming in the opposite direction. Any direction. Just *away*.

Nakara and Eburneus picked up the pace, passing him and forging a way steadily towards the steps below the huge wooden and glass doors of the main entrance.

Drey hesitated, glancing back to the street, where a cluster of Fox Hara gestured at the spectres and shouted at each other. It would be ironic for him to survive the ghosts, only to be shot in the back by ferals. He shifted to a sideways, crab-like gait, trying to keep the Fox Hara in view as he followed the scholars. Trying not to think about the fur and scales and chitin he brushed against.

Eburneus was ascending the steps. Nakara paused, looking back and gesturing urgently for Drey to join them. With yips and howls, a handful of the Fox Hara charged towards the trio.

The ghosts surged to meet the ferals, and the feeding frenzy began.

Three hara were inside his sanctuary. Shadow crouched in a swirl of butterflies and watched the strangers. The one with a gun was jittery and on the verge of panic. That har had his back to a pillar just within the central hall, trying to keep a watch on all the creatures simultaneously – an impossible task. The other two were wandering up and down the hall, exclaiming in delight at everything and pausing to write feverishly in notebooks.

The creatures were dancing stories of arrival and change. Migratory species were re-enacting their travels, white winter coats were moulting into summer pelage or plumage, grubs and larvae were metamorphosing to adult form.

Now hara were here, perhaps Shadow would metamorphose too? Turn into something new? He wondered what it might be.

They were surrounded by a thousand animal spirits, yet Eburneus was complaining they were the wrong ones. The scholar had them poking about in galleries and back rooms, rubbing the caked dust from display cases and wrenching open storage area doors long seized-up solid from disuse. He had issued a shopping list of animal names and instructions to find the bones of each. *Megaloceros giganteus, Ursus spelaeus, Bos primigenius, Coelodonta antiquitatis, Stephanorhinus kirchbergensis, Mammuthus primigenius.*

Eburneus had, however, neglected to mention just how *large* these damn animals were. Drey had found a mounted skeleton of a *Megaloceros giganteus* and could only assume its name was some human language for "bloody enormous deer". It was taller than a shire horse, and its antlers were huge.

The rest of the set were: bloody enormous bear, bloody enormous ox, bloody enormous rhinoceros, bloody enormous rhinoceros with a differently shaped horn and bloody enormous elephant. Drey was splitting his time between freaking out that he was *surrounded by ghosts* and wondering what possible benefit rhinoceroses and bears – bloody enormous or otherwise – offered to Alba Sulh? Were the Tuaththuans going to open a zoo?

He was also increasingly of the opinion they were not alone here. There were all the ghosts, obviously. But animal ghosts did not leave bare harish footprints in the dust, nor place a container under a broken skylight to catch the drips. And on one balcony there was a "nest" of dried moss and autumn leaves, which was just the right size for a har to bed down in.

'Somehar is living here?' Eburneus seemed rather put out that the mystery inhabitant had not introduced himself.

'Yes. And since we don't know if that somehar is just terribly shy, or is a cannibalistic psychopath, I suggest we stay on our guard.'

'Cannibalistic psychopath?' scoffed Eburneus.

'Welcome to Lund,' retorted Drey. 'It's like Fulminir, but without the facilities.'

Paranoia kept Drey awake for hours, keeping watch over the scholars as they slept. However, eventually exhaustion claimed him. He came groggily awake and started to stir, and then froze as he realised the things surrounding him, pressed up against him – *on him* – were slumbering ghosts. A bunch of furry rodent things, frogs, coiled snakes and... Aghama's balls, were those hulking great brutes *bears?*

They're showing you how they hibernate.

Drey was too busy extracting himself from the pile to pay much heed to the explanation. It was only when he had put a distance of several metres and a nice solid wall between himself and the bears that he realised the voice had been in his head, not his ears, and it hadn't been the mind-touch of Nakara nor Eburneus.

A har was standing in one of the archways off the main hall, watching him. Naked, skin a deeper shade than Nakara's, hair twisted into dreadlocks. Old scars marred the scalp on one side of his head. Insubstantial butterflies perched on the stranger's shoulders whilst snakes and giant millipedes coiled round his limbs like semi-transparent jewellery. He was scrawny, ethereal... and beautiful.

'Tiahaar!' The call was part greeting, part warning to the scholars that they had company. 'Who are you?' Drey asked.

Shadow.

Was that a name or a job description? It didn't seem polite to ask.

Shadow was aware how he'd almost forgotten how to talk – how to interact with hara. He sat cross-legged on the floor near the strangers, his attention flickering back and forth between them and his animal friends. The creatures were playing at courtship this morning. Birds of paradise shook their feathers, crocodiles bellowed from imaginary pools of water, cuttlefish proclaimed their virility with bold stripes. It made Shadow think of aruna, and how long it had been since he had touched another har's body.

The blond har was explaining what Grissecon was. It was something to do with aruna and would somehow return dead animals to the world. Shadow wasn't sure he fully understood, but some of his friends were now dancing stories of long dormant spores returning to life, or dried-out eggs hatching when the rains came. He didn't think it was quite the same thing.

Shadow was sure of one thing, though: most of the animals the blond stranger wanted to resurrect had died so long ago their spirits had long since left the world. The reverence and enthusiasm which humans had displayed for their bones had not been enough to draw more than a few back.

He leapt up and bounded off to find one.

'I don't think he's entirely right in the head,' Eburneus remarked. 'Whatever gave him those scars has caused brain damage.'

Drey agreed, though he found himself holding the skittish, fey Shadow in higher regard than the pompous Eburneus. The Tuaththuan had still not expressed an iota of regret for the deaths of Domana and Bellon, nor the fate of Verga. Plus, Shadow called the ghosts his "friends". Drey wanted to be on good terms with anyhar who kept the ghosts docile.

'The Fox Hara have made themselves scarce, you know. We could leave any time we chose.' He said it more for Nakara's benefit than his own.

'Not until after the ritual,' said Eburneus firmly. 'We'll be ready in a day. Two days at most.'

Drey sighed. 'Don't your bloody enormous animals need, like, tundra and ice ages and stuff?'

'The aurochs and narrow-nosed rhino are forest animals. Alba Phorlakhan and Tuaththua have suitable habitat for the rest. The Freyhellans agreed to provide additional land if I was successful.'

Drey resisted the urge to roll his eyes. They were a long way from Alba Phorlakhan and Freyhella.

The scholars were in the midst of preparing their ritual area in the Mammal Hall, at the feet of the giant deer. Purifying the site and discussing the best placement of candles to light the cavernous hall. To Drey's eye, Nakara was fussing and fretting over these arrangements as displacement activity, so he didn't have to think about the horrors of their journey.

'Crystals. We didn't bring enough crystals!' Nakara wailed.

'Nonsense. Those we have are quite adequate for our needs,' Eburneus pronounced.

The panic over crystals and other trappings of the ritual was just a symptom of Nakara's distress. Drey intervened before Eburneus could make the situation worse. 'Hey, Nakara – there are signs to a Minerals Gallery and an Earth's Treasury Gallery. Bet those are full of crystals. Let's go find where Shadow went and ask if we can borrow some.'

His cynical scavenger side also told him it wouldn't hurt to see what could be safely looted.

'Yes – oh, yes. They'll already be attuned to this environment…'

He let Nakara burble on, as they headed off in search of Shadow. The har's chatter served to distract Drey from scuttling and scurrying things, and the insubstantial webs being woven by spectral spiders.

They found Shadow crossing the central hall, beckoning a large ghost to follow.

Mammuthus primigenius! he sent.

Drey stopped and stared. It wasn't a bloody enormous elephant – it was a bloody enormous, *hairy* elephant.

Eburneus hadn't quite put it in those words, but scruffy scavengers were not high on the Tuaththuans' list of purified objects to be included in their Grissecon. It was made clear that Drey should keep his distance – if he absolutely had to watch, then preferably he should do this from an upper level balcony or through a suitably distant doorway. The Tuaththuans had also tried to impart this information to Shadow. Drey was not sure how much of the message had sunk in.

Well, if he wasn't wanted, Drey could make better use of his time than watching scholars ritually wash each other. There were still all sorts of unexplored side corridors and back rooms which would be worth inventorying. Then later, maybe he could strike some sort of a deal with Shadow to pacify the ghosts on future scavenging trips? What would the fey har want? Clothes? Decent quality food, perhaps? What the hell did Shadow eat here anyway?

Drey slipped away to explore.

All over the museum, animal ghosts were mating; responding to the mounting energies of Grissecon.

Shadow watched, intrigued by this new kind of aruna, and the majhahn Eburneus was directing; pulling some of his animal friends back into the flesh they'd once had. A whole species poised on the verge of rebirth.

Today they were concentrating on Mammoth. She was pleased to be returning to the world. But the strangers were doing it wrong. Didn't they understand that Mammoth and Mammoth's kind was not a single thing? She was part of a pattern. The other animals the strangers had mentioned were pieces of the pattern, but not the whole. The pattern was huge and intricate.

Shadow would help them do it properly. He ran to seek out what he needed.

The ghosts were thankfully too wrapped up in their own affairs to bother Drey. He'd found a "staff only" door, which was ajar, and picked his way cautiously down an unlit corridor that led deep into the heart of the building. Fireflies and phosphorescent fish emitted an eerie light, just barely enough to see by. Dark rectangles hinted at access to laboratories and workshops. Drey flicked on his flashlight.

There was old, old blood smeared on the floor; an erratic trail that led to one of the dark doorways. At its terminus, a skeleton. Not the pristine and beautiful mounted skeletons of the display cases. This was a discarded huddle of bones, still clothed in mouldering rags and scraps of dried flesh.

The beam from his flashlight flickered over the corpse. Dried, brittle hair in dreadlocks. Left side of the skull cracked and broken.

A quiet sound behind him. Drey whirled to see Shadow standing within a shoal of glowing fish. 'Aghama's balls! You're a fucking ghost!'

Am I? Shadow peered at the bones.

'How can you not know you're dead?' Drey backed off, skin suddenly slick with sweat. Abruptly conscious he was retreating deeper into dark spaces, haunted by Aghama knew what.

Was he dead? Yes, he probably was. Shadow didn't see what difference it made. His animal friends still loved him.

Apparently Drey did not feel the same way. The har was afraid of him, the way he was afraid of all the ghosts. Shadow cocked his head to one side, considering this.

You don't like ghosts?

'Damn right I don't like ghosts!'

I will help Eburneus and make the ghosts go away. Become flesh. Live again.

'Great. Why don't you piss off and do that.' Drey had backed into a corner, nervously eyeing the shoal of fish which drifted around the pair of them. 'Get rid of a few.'

Not a few, Shadow told him. *All of them.*

'No more ghosts?' Drey's expression morphed into a guarded hope.

Shadow explained what they needed to do.

'Seriously? Eburneus was right – you're not right in the head!'

Drey couldn't believe he had agreed to this. His burning need to make the animal ghosts go away had fought his common sense. Apparently common sense had lost. Or maybe he had taken a fatal wound from the Fox Hara and this was all really the dying hallucination of an oxygen-starved brain?

Shadow-the-ghost ran caressing fingertips down his chest.

Grissecon with a ghost. While the corpse of said ghost lay only a metre away.

Well, at least he'd forever be guaranteed winner of any 'What's the weirdest aruna you ever had?' banter down the pub. Drey steeled his resolve and allowed Shadow to share breath with him.

His view of the universe expanded to infinity.

Shadow compared and contrasted. Laid his energies next to Drey's – living and dead, flesh and plasma – to attune himself to the difference. His very new comprehension of his own nature and Drey's instinctive dread of his Otherness smoothed the process. The opposites spiralled around each other, achieving balance. Yin and yang. Soume and ouana. Shadow began to weave a bridge between the There-Then of the *life-that-was* and the Here-Now of the *life-that-is*.

The ghosts ebbed and flowed around him, tasting what he

offered, and accepting or rejecting as their nature dictated. The numbers of those who accepted grew. At first a few hundred, then thousands, then numbers in the millions.

He tapped into the majhahn crafted by Eburneus and Nakara, feeling their surprise and alarm at the intrusion. Mammoth trumpeted a welcome and began to pace out a stately dance of the pattern of life and her place within it. Millions of happy ghosts chirped, yipped and croaked their wish for his ritual to happen, adding their own tiny energies to the mix.

In the face of so many eager animal spirits, Shadow felt Eburneus assent and lower his defences. Shadow drew on the scholars' knowledge, in turn feeding them his energy. The two majhahns became one.

One by one, a million ghosts were reborn.

Drey sat on a wall above the steps of the main entrance watching the mass exodus. Things crawled, galloped and flew – some vanishing immediately into the surrounding ruins, others patiently waiting for others of their kind to emerge and join them. Seeds and spores blew about in the breeze, drifting off across the rooftops of Lund.

The remaining Fox Hara had fled. They probably thought the animals were still unkillable ghosts. Drey speculated how long it would take the gangs to figure out otherwise. Or how long it would take the animals to get hungry and start eating each other? Or eating hara?

Flocks and herds were beginning to form and mill about, awaiting some incomprehensible signal to depart. Nakara and Eburneus had a herd of their own – a small group of mammoths, rhinos, bloody enormous deer and the rest, which gathered around them, apparently with the intent to follow the scholars to the habitat they'd been promised. Drey wondered how Eburneus felt about the scimitar-toothed cats and cave lions, which had subtly added themselves to the edges of his group?

He pondered another problem: how they were going to get all these beasts past the Great Wall? He shouted to Eburneus: 'Hey, scholar! You might want to tell them to follow the river and *swim* out of Lund. Sodding great wall in the way, otherwise.'

Eburneus frowned. Drey suppressed a snort of laughter at the realisation the Tuaththuan had not thought to plan how to get his bloody enormous animals out of Lund.

'Don't worry. I'll show you the way. Just got a few things to do first.'

Drey carried Shadow's bones from the dark corridor to the light and air of the main hall. He carefully laid out the skeleton at the feet of the plaster dinosaur and used his knife to scratch Shadow's name into the information display. *Shadow, first harish guardian of this museum.*

He'd expected Shadow too to become flesh. He'd felt it start to happen as they had been intertwined; the ethereal solidity of ghost flesh starting to take on reassuring warmth. But Shadow had halted the process, reverting to his incorporeal existence.

I am needed here. My friends need me.

Now Drey glanced up to where Shadow-the-ghost watched from a balcony. Anxious spirits flitted around him – fish, tropical insects, Arctic plants… even a bloody dodo. All the organisms that could not make their own way from the museum grounds to somewhere they could survive and thrive.

'I'll make the scholars promise!' Drey yelled. 'I'll make them promise to find a way to get your friends home!'

Shadow threw something. Drey made the catch, a hard, heavy object smacking into his outstretched palms. A hunk of fire opal, bigger than his clenched fist. Worth a bloody fortune.

Drey grinned. 'Yeah, that ought to pay for a lot of scholarly thinking and magical research. Few pints too, eh?'

But Shadow swirled round and darted off without replying, a flurry of ghosts racing after him. Whale song echoed round the hall.

'Definitely not right in the head,' muttered Drey. Which probably went for him as well, given that he'd taken aruna with a ghost…

He shoved the opal in a pocket and sauntered out into a world filled with new life.

The Kinder Lie

Fiona Lane

'But does he love me? Tell me truthfully, Tiahaar!'

Tanzen looked carefully at the young har sitting opposite him, hearing the pleading note in his voice and seeing the candlelight reflected in his unnaturally bright eyes. He knew what the har wanted him to say, and he was not about to disappoint him.

He looked down at the har's hand, palm up, cradled by his own, and traced the indented lines on it with the finger of his other hand. The skin was soft and pale. Not a har accustomed to physical labour.

'You are destined to connect with your soulmate,' he informed the har gravely, running his finger over the lines. 'I see two... no, three harlings. All beautiful and clever and kind. Wealth will be coming to you soon. If you have for some time desired a certain... object... you may feel free to purchase it without concern.'

The har gave a contented little sigh. 'You are most insightful, Tiahaar,' he informed Tanzen breathlessly. 'You have The Gift, of that there is no doubt.'

Tanzen bowed his head slightly in modest acknowledgement of his own talent, released the har's hand and looked at him expectantly. The har took the hint and produced a silk purse from his pocket, from which, after a degree of rummaging, he produced three coins. Tanzen looked at the coins, now deposited on the table, but pointedly did not touch them, and after a brief pause the har added another one, at which point they were professionally vanished into a small chest Tanzen kept under the table for this purpose.

Having completed the transaction, Tanzen rose fluidly from his seat to escort the har from the tent. He pushed aside the heavy velvet curtain fixed across the doorway, letting the bright daylight flood into the dim interior.

'... and please, Tiahaar, do inform your good friends and close relatives that I am available for consultation until the end of the week.'

'I shall most certainly do so, you may count upon it!' the har replied, gracing Tanzen with what he imagined was meant to be a seductive smile, before continuing on his way.

Tanzen watched as the har wandered away down the dusty track between the collection of tents that had sprung up in the last two days. Once his customer disappeared into the crowd of milling bodies, Tanzen retreated into the gloom of own tent. He pulled the curtain closed and smiled to himself. With any luck, the har's acquaintances would also seek him out, eager to learn what the future held for them. What that would mean for Tanzen's own future was more coins in his money box. If he told them what they wanted to hear.

Tanzen had long ago realised that hara paid far better for good news than for bad. That was why he had not revealed to his most recent customer that the current object of his affections was scarcely aware of his existence, that his future offspring would be hosted by an inconstant har who would leave him for a wealthier and more beautiful partner, and that his financial prospects were about to be increased only by the amount of money he thought he had lost but which he would he would rediscover between the cushions as he was cleaning his house next week.

Some called Tanzen a charlatan, and it was true that the whole palm-stroking routine was merely theatre. It was what the customers expected; tracing the lines that ran from fingers to wrist, staring down thoughtfully as if in a trance, then lifting his gaze to look directly into the eyes of the har opposite him, holding it just long enough for a shiver to run down the har's back...

Why should he tell them the truth? The truth was of benefit to nohar. It would certainly not have helped the har who had come to him seeking reassurance over a minor health matter. Tanzen had reassured him that his worries on that score were unfounded, and that he would have good health for the rest of his life. And then he had stood in cowardly fashion behind the curtain, eyes closed, listening as the runaway horse careered into the unfortunate har only a few paces from the tent, killing him instantly.

What good would it have done that har to know the future? It would only have blighted the last few minutes of his existence. Bad enough that Tanzen should know. Even as he had stroked the har's palm and seen the horse break free from its handler, rear and bolt, the vision forked and there were two scenarios: Tanzen reassuring the har. The har leaving. The horse. Tanzen telling the har the truth. The har screaming at him. The har leaving. The horse.

The vision forked again: Tanzen grabbing hold of the har, forcibly restraining him. The har punching Tanzen to the ground. The har leaving. The horse.

There was always the horse. There was always *a* horse, or something. The future never lied to him.

Tanzen could not remember when he had first realised that not every har could see the ghosts of the future. When he was young he had assumed it to be the natural scheme of things, that the world was full of shadowy effigies of the living, but as he grew older, he began to understand that most hara were not so blessed – if that were the right expression – as to be able to see the future selves of others and what would befall them.

Often he met hara who claimed to be able to do so, yet upon closer inspection proved to be the charlatans that many accused Tanzen of being. Rather less frequently he would meet a har who, with some effort involving props and rituals – and possibly an episode of Grissecon for good measure – could peer mistily into future times and extract from there some enigmatic information.

Never yet had he come across a har who encountered on a daily basis the apparently living, breathing avatars of those around him in their future incarnations, but for Tanzen it was as natural to him as breathing. When he took the hand of another har in his, that har's future self would walk away from his present one and begin the sequence of events that would multiply, time upon time, to lead to an inevitable conclusion.

It was a mixed blessing, and one that had led him to his current position in life, as a peripatetic fortune teller, travelling the length and breadth of the land in the company of various other hara of unusual talents and skills; moving from town to town, here and there, setting up camp for a few days but never staying long. Long enough, though, for word of his ability to get around. If there was good news in a har's future, Tanzen would be happy enough to let him know. If there was bad news... he simply lied. Hara remembered his successful predictions far longer than his failures, and he made enough money to keep body and soul together by this method.

One day – when the treasure chest he kept under the table was full – he dreamed of retiring. Of settling down into a permanent home, of no longer endlessly pitching his tent in some muddy field, only to break camp again a few days later, of no longer having to see the future lives of other hara in all their blighted imperfection.

But at the moment the treasure chest was light and rattled emptily when he shook it; it would be many years yet before his dream became a reality. In the meantime, there were more hara to lie to.

Tanzen was interrupted from his reveries by the sudden bright spear of light inside the tent as the velvet curtain was pulled aside to reveal a new har standing there, silhouetted darkly against the daylight.

Blinking, Tanzen rose to his feet to greet the newcomer. His eyes, not yet adjusted to the light, could not make out the har's face – the features were shadowed and indistinct – but as he approached the stranger to welcome him inside, Tanzen caught a brief scent of some expensive perfume mingling with the smoky incense that permeated every inch of his tent.

'Welcome, Tiahaar, welcome to my humble tent. Please come in and take a seat. I am Tanzen har Sukun, Seer of the Past, the Present and the Future, and if you dare to ask, I will read the lines of your life that are written on your palm and tell you where they will lead.'

Tanzen recited his customary introduction speech in what he hoped was a mysterious and intriguing tone and guided the har to the chair on the nearest side of the table. He himself took the chair opposite and sat upright and still, examining the har, looking for any clues as to what might have brought him here.

The har smiled at him nervously.

'You are most kind, Tiahaar.'

'Give me your hand,' Tanzen instructed.

The har hesitated a moment, then stretched his hand out across the table towards Tanzen, who noticed that the fingernails were long and lacquered, sparkling with some gleaming specks.

'My name is Ledah,' the har informed him solemnly, and Tanzen nodded, as if he were taking careful note of this, which he was not; he knew he would have forgotten it by the next day.

Tanzen continued to gaze at the har's outstretched hand on the table in front of him, but still did not touch it.

'Is there perhaps something *in particular* that you wish to learn about your future, Tiahaar?' he asked, slowly looking up from the hand to meet the har's gaze. He found himself staring into dark eyes fringed with heavy lashes. Thick dark hair coiled down past the har's shoulders and gleamed like oiled silk in the low light. The har raised his other hand and pushed away a lock of the hair from his face, but his eyes never left Tanzen's

'I want to know… There is… a har who says he loves me. I love him, Tiahaar, I know this to be true. Is it our destiny to be together?'

Tanzen nodded gravely, maintaining his outwardly attentive demeanour. It was an inquiry he had heard a thousand times before. Affairs of the heart often led hara to seek his services. *What was it about love*, he thought, *that left hara so unsure of themselves?*

Some tribes did not subscribe to the belief that hara could fall in love, all evidence to the contrary. The outcome of pursuing this philosophy to its logical conclusion often proved troublesome.

Experience had convinced Tanzen that love did indeed exist, and convinced him even more strongly that it should be avoided with great diligence whenever possible. Few hara, however, seemed to agree with him on that score. While vexing, this did at least provide a good income for one of his travelling companions whose speciality was concocting potions, charms and fetishes allegedly designed to provoke feelings of affection in hara who currently harboured none. And, of course, it benefitted Tanzen himself in his profession of dispensing predictions as to the longevity of these feelings.

'The lines on your palm do not lie,' Tanzen told the har, reaching forward to take his hand in his own. He pulled back the fingers and studied the lines that ran from the side across, and down past the thumb to the wrist.

They were, of course, only indentations in the skin. Mere mechanical folds without which a har would not be able to bend his hand. There was nothing in these lines that gave any clue to an individual's future life.

Which was not to say that there were no other lines which did.

Gently, Tanzen touched Ledah's palm, and as he did so it seemed to him that lines sprang forth from there; spreading lines, fine as spider's silk, criss-crossing in the air around him and across the table between him and the other har. He knew that Ledah did not see them. No other har did. It was Tanzen's gift alone to see these lines, watch them extend beyond the present and into the future and bring along them the ghosts of things that had not yet happened.

Even as the lines in the air grew brighter, the inside of the tent grew darker, the light somehow vanishing into the heavy fabrics, being absorbed within them. The scented smoke from the incense burners seemed to thicken and intensify, almost overpowering Tanzen with its intoxicating perfume as he drew it into his lungs. His head swam and an unexpected dizziness fell over him.

The lines embraced and coalesced, weaving a pattern of visions that played out before Tanzen's eyes – places, people, events. The light from a future world travelling backwards, through space and time, through the har Ledah and his outstretched hand, through Tanzen's fingers resting on his palm. How this could be possible, he did not know. He had never asked for this gift, never wanted it, but the ghosts demanded that he witness their fate, and so he did, watching in growing apprehension, and then fear, as the future made its shape clearer.

Abruptly, he pulled his arm away, releasing Ledah's hand, which dropped onto the table top. Ledah looked across at him with concern.

'Tiahaar…?'

'You must go!' Tanzen's voice sounded rough and too loud in his own ears. He swallowed hard and rubbed the hand that had been touching Ledah's on his clothing, as if to wipe away some contamination.

'I don't understand…'

'He doesn't love you. This har of yours. He will never love you.' Tanzen fought to keep his voice steady, trying to seem his normal self as he delivered the verdict to the bewildered Ledah.

'He has betrayed your trust. He has lied to you. You cannot be with this har. You must leave him. Never speak to him again. Never go near him again. It is for the best. Believe me.'

Tanzen watched as the expression on Ledah's face changed from confusion to disbelief and then to anguish. Tears were beginning to form in the other har's eyes as he stood up. His mouth worked as if he were going to say something, but no words came out, and without another word Ledah turned and ran out of the tent, shoving past the velvet curtain and leaving Tanzen alone at the table.

Tanzen hated himself in that moment, but there had been no choice. With slow, deliberate movements he stood up and followed the departed Ledah out of the tent. Outside, the sun was shining brightly, voicing its approval of the gaily-coloured clothing worn by the crowds. A breeze was blowing, and pennants fluttered busily from the tops of the tents, and in the distance the sounds of laughing and shouting could be heard. Tanzen fastened the rope across the front of his tent, indicating that he was closed for business, then turned and walked away in the opposite direction.

Tanzen sat crouched uncomfortably on the wooden seat at the front of the trap and flicked the reins over his horse's back, encouraging him to pick up the pace a little, but the beast continued his steady gait, ignoring Tanzen as he always did when his harish master suggested that he might want to proceed a little faster when pulling the fully-laden trap. Tanzen could not find it in himself to blame the horse, particularly on a day like today when the rain had turned the hard ground underfoot (and hoof) to soft mud, making the going that much harder.

Still, Tanzen attempted another flick, equally ill-received, because he wanted nothing more than to put as much distance between himself and the town as possible. He pulled the hood of his cloak up further, trying to protect himself from the steady drizzle, but the rain merely dripped off the edges and into his face and down his front.

No matter how far from the town he got and no matter how he hid under the folds of his cloak, he could still not leave behind him the face of the har, Ledah, whose fortune he had foretold the day before.

It had been a lie, of course. The one thing that Tanzen was good at. And it was as well that he had so many years' practice, that he could be so convincing and that Ledah had believed him without question. It wasn't a kind lie, Tanzen could admit that much, but the truth would have been of benefit to nohar. Except, perhaps, Ledah himself.

Tanzen closed his eyes, but he could not clear the visions from his head. He had seen that the har whom Ledah loved did indeed love him back, with an intensity that Tanzen had found at once both incomprehensible and wondrous.

He had seen them – Ledah and his har – in the throes of aruna, felt their passion, both physical and emotional, felt every thrust as their loins connected, tasted their sweat, felt their rapture as their union became something more profound, felt the child that was brought into being, the bloodline founded, one generation to the next, saw the walls fall, the cities burn, the bodies – Sweet Aghama, the bodies – so many dead, so many innocent hara dead and dying – and there, there in the cradle of conception between Ledah and his lover was where it began, and there was where it could be ended, because Tanzen had also seen another vision, another future, where that bloodline was never founded, where a broken-hearted har ran from a darkened tent, pennants flying in the breeze, sunlight pouring down from the sky, towards the river where even now they were pulling his body from the water, stiff and cold and lifeless, the grim future precipitated by his descendants no longer a possibility.

It was the kinder lie, Tanzen told himself as he rode on. If there was a purpose to his unwanted gift, perhaps it was to guide the ghosts of the future to a better, kinder place, even if that kindness did not extend to Ledah. Or himself.

Who else would come to him, trailing their future ghosts behind them, he wondered? And what lies would he tell them? Hara were not meant to know what the future held. All things were connected and knowing what was to come would irrevocably change the present.

Sometimes, late at night, out of the corner of his eye, Tanzen saw something or someone he thought he recognised. Some future incarnation of himself, perhaps. Older, wearier. Possessed of a knowledge that would change everything or nothing. One day he might have the courage to turn and look at that particular ghost and ask it the questions he did not want to know the answers to.

But not today.

He flicked the reins over the horse's back one more time, and together they travelled on towards the next town.

The Hardest Hue to Hold

E.S. Wynn

'Rain coming,' Phil says.

I don't know how he knows, but after ten years, I've come to trust his sense for storms. 'How long until it hits?'

'Six hours or so,' he says. 'It'll hit during the night, drag on until dawn and blow itself out before noon tomorrow.'

'We need it.' I stand, stretch. 'Been a long, dry summer.'

'Buckets and tarps,' Phil reminds me. Nodding, I turn to face him, regard the empty lawn chair next to mine, the one I know he's sitting in, even if I can't see him. I can feel his eyes on me, hear the rusty springs creak as he shifts. Of all the spirits to wander into my waystation, he's stayed the longest. 'And candles.'

I nod. A storm blowing in means a chance to collect water, and the tarps on the tin roof will have to be checked and patched if they have any holes. More than that, though, it means new spirits moving through, the ghosts of animals and humans, of stones, trees and distant shores. Spirits of all kinds, except one.

Hara. Never once have I seen the ghost of a dead har cross through the doors or walls of my waystation.

'I'll start getting things ready for our guests.' I leave Phil sitting on the porch, watching the sun drop steadily toward the horizon.

Preparing for the eve keeps me busy until dusk. Ratty tarps that have seen a hundred summer storms are raised and stretched tight between sturdy nails, wrap the cinderblock walls and broken windows of my ranch house until the whole thing is swathed like a wound in a cocoon of blue bandages. Dozens of plastic buckets scavenged from the little town that sprawls far below my hilltop house go out into the yard, their open mouths facing skyward to catch the rain I know is coming.

The whole time I work, I catch the subtle chill, the quick, jittery movement of another resident spirit shadowing me. *Mae.* She's always restless before each storm, as if she's worried, as if she knows something dark is coming.

'What do you see, Mae?' I finally ask her, feeling her just off my shoulder, watching me arrange buckets on the dead, flattened burr-grass in the front yard.

'The land is stirring,' she says to me. 'It is restless.'

'Because of the storm,' I offer, but I feel her shift beside me, hear the handles of the assembled buckets rattling as she moves between them.

'No.' She stops in the middle of the front yard, gives off a sensation I take as the wringing of hands. 'It *knows*,' she says.

I wait for Mae to explain, watch the open air where she stands, but she doesn't elaborate. She only stares, or does something that feels like staring, and then, like so many others who have come to stay with me, she begins to fade.

'Happy Trails,' Phil offers, watching Mae slip away like dust in a breeze.

Without saying anything, I turn back to my buckets, gather the last from inside and set them up with the others. I try not to think about Mae, try not to think about where she might be going, what waits for her on the other side. Most of the spirits that drift through my waystation are like moths in summer. A flash of sensation, of personality and presence, and then they're gone. The ones that stay, that linger and take the time to converse with me are few and each of them special. Some of them, like Mae, I grow attached to, miss when they leave.

And they do always leave. Every one of them.

Every one of them except Phil, though I know that even he won't stay forever.

'Where is she going?' I ask idly.

'To be with her grandchildren,' Phil whispers back. 'They'll take in a scraggly cat in a few years, care for it and come to love it as a member of the family. That cat is being born right now.'

I say nothing, only nod. What little of the dead that bleeds through into the world of the living is both cryptic and revelatory. Their sense of time, the agreements they make with one another beneath the notice of mortal minds – their world is so different in so many ways, and yet even there, nothing is permanent. Even there, change is a constant companion.

'Gonna be wind tonight,' Phil offers. 'Tent stakes and twine, if you want to keep any rain.'

'Rocks work too.' I nod, thinking of the cache of smooth river stones I keep in the garage.

Piling a few of the heavier rocks into the bottom of each bucket takes time, but the added weight should be enough to keep them from tipping over in the wind. Tent stakes and tight lengths of twine tied to bucket handles is just insurance, and with shadows already settling beneath the scraggly boughs of the oaks and madrones at the edge of the hilltop, time is running short. Better to pile the rocks and be done with it, move inside and make the place ready for the visitors that the winds and rain will bring.

Phil says nothing as I hurry, only watches in that silent way that spirits often do. I think about asking him if the rocks alone really will be enough, but I'm afraid of what his answer might be. I don't want to be wrong. Besides, Phil would warn me if he saw a vision of me parched and regretful in the future, a vision of me wishing I'd staked the buckets down.

Wouldn't he?

I put the worries out of my head, finish with the buckets, then secure and bolt the front door. A stout length of creosote-soaked board goes up on hand-hammered brackets, secures the only exit in and out of the ranch house but for the garage door. Floor locks I built myself keep that manually-moved square of aluminium and steel tightly shut against the elements, and then I close and lock the door between the house and the garage, cover it with a heavy woollen blanket hung with a pair of stout nails as old as the house.

I sense Phil as I light the first candle, set it up on the little altar I've made of the rusty electric range in the kitchen. True to form, he bypasses the locked door, walks through it as if he were but a whisper from another world, a memory playing itself out in person. The little metal flip-lighter I use to light the first candle takes a couple of clicks to work, but once the wick takes, I use the flame to light all of the others I've gathered for nights like tonight.

Other residents of the ranch house come out as I place candles on stands and holders in every room. Sweets is one of them. A cat, I think, or something like it. The spirit is blurry, timid, comes across as a tiny ball of hot static at first, only calms to cool and soft once I start to whisper to it. Reassuring thoughts and comforting, welcoming words encourage Sweets to slink up to my side, the spirit following me as I move, staying so close to my feet that I'd surely step on it if it were a flesh and blood animal.

Another resident I recognise is Stepper. Like Sweets, he seems to only become active at night, and especially when a storm is approaching. He never talks, in fact the name is something I've given him, something that seems to fit with the one thing he does do, the one way he makes his presence known. Footsteps, and always in odd places. When the ceiling creaks like an old floor, or when the tile walls in the bathroom groan and clack like someone is striding across them in heels, I know it is Stepper. What he is, what he was, I may never know, but I've come to find the sound of his slow, steady stride to be a comfort during the long nights when sleep eludes me.

Stepper and Sweets keep me company as I light the last of the candles. The ranch house is small, only two tiny bedrooms and a narrow bathroom clustered around a hallway that opens into the combined parlour and kitchen, so it doesn't take long. Gusts of wind are already whipping across the tarping like hands looking for a way in, but I know that we're safe in our cocoon. This isn't the first late summer storm that Sweets, Stepper, Phil and I have weathered together. The tarps holding our home together will hold. They always hold.

The last candle I light is a candle for me. A little green and white twist with a tiny wick to hold the smallest flicker of flame. I carry it as I make my way back to the kitchen, open one of the cupboards and pull out a dusty box that feels like it might be older than I am. Cake rolls, a dozen of them, and all so well packaged and so laced with preservatives that they haven't even a spot of mould. They're a little dried out, a little chewy, but the chocolate flavour of them is surreal, almost hypnotic compared to anything I could gather from the woods and cook myself.

Food from another world, a dead world. The perfect offering for spirits only briefly passing through this one.

Working carefully, I unwrap the little treats and place them on the altar, line them up and leave them. There is spirit in everything, and the essence of the old world contained in the cakes will be welcome sustenance for most of the visitors stirred up by the storm. Whatever is left, the elements of essence they leave and the material remains of the cakes will be mine to take and make my own in the morning, but until then, they are sacred. Licking the faintest flakes of chocolate off my fingers is the only indulgence I allow myself in the meantime.

The wind picks up quick, brings with it the first pattering waves of rain. The tin roof of the ranch house rings with each gusting brush of falling drops. Big drops, and no doubt icy, running down to gutters patched with steel epoxy, angled toward empty buckets. The last of the light from outside dies golden, leaves only the deep and distant blue in its wake. Summer thunder cracks and crashes, rumbles from far off, quickens as it comes closer.

And when the first spirit arrives, I become aware of it almost at the same moment that Sweets, Stepper and Phil do.

It isn't large, doesn't make a grand entrance, but practice has made me sensitive to little ripples in the spirit world, have sharpened my senses. The first spirit to come to us is simple, a little nodule of soul from a great and fallen oak, now wandering, looking for an acorn to settle into. Like so many others that have come before, the oakling comes seeking shelter from the dark and the whipping winds of the storm but stops and lingers at the edge of a wall, half in shadow, half in the light.

'Hello,' I greet the little oak spirit. 'You are welcome here.'

With a gesture, I direct the spirit's attention to the cakes on the range altar. It seems to understand the offering, seems to be weighing it when another spirit slides into the ranch house, attracts our eyes like a sudden flashing beacon. I recognise its kind immediately. Loud, frantic, erratic – the spirit of a human, and one who died suddenly, violently. One who is still angry, still hurt, still lost and unable to understand so many things.

Like a caring parent, Phil steps up to the new spirit and takes her by the hand. The move comes with so much more that I can't see, can't comprehend. A wash of images and concepts from Phil that soothe the other human in waves. A direct connection. Once she's relaxed enough to be receptive, Phil leads her away, carries her to a shadow where she can rest and reflect while the storm rages outside.

One by one, we guide each of the spirits that comes, welcome them and work with them until the ranch house is thick with them. Spirits of trees group together in the parlour, form up in like knots, most of them walnut, oak, manzanita and madrone. Spirits of flowering plants dreaming until distant spring play, trade stories with the spirits of familiar pollinators while the lone ghost of a Toyon tree sits watching. In other rooms, themes of feeling begin to develop, intensify as spirits drawn to certain shared energies and shared experiences gather together in the candlelight. Like stewards, Phil, Sweets and Stepper each settle into a room, set and maintain the tone of the spirits therein. Left alone to mind the kitchen and the parlour, I find myself missing Mae, and not for the first time since she faded on to her next incarnation.

As night deepens and draws long, I find myself sitting off to the side with the lone Toyon ghost, watching the other plant spirits dance and play. It's lonely, having no one to talk to, having only the soft, innocent impulse thoughts of the Toyon to bounce around in some simulacrum of conversation. Rarely do I catch a glimpse of Sweets or Stepper or Phil, and they're always caught up, busy with their crowd of like minds. When I concentrate, I can see past all of the activity, all of the spirits packed into the ranch house, and it is in those moments that I feel truly alone. Not only am I the only har, I'm also the only spirit on the hilltop clad in flesh. Even the few mice who normally skulk in the rafters or chew at the firewood in the garage have taken shelter elsewhere for the night, driven away by the preponderance of ghosts, phantoms and memories come to life. I am alone, just as every night that the spirits gather, I am alone. Even in the days, even when I hear the steady drawl of Phil advising me, or feel Sweets come up warm and soft against my hand, or hear Stepper crossing a stretch of ceiling, I know that I am alone.

Alone.

'Thank you for the cakes.'

I blink as the voice brings me back from my self-pity reverie. Glancing down, I notice that the Toyon spirit is gone, that many of the plant spirits have tucked away into little slumbering glowspots for the night. Candles that were once long and bright now gutter in stumps, short and nearing their own death. Pulling in a long, deep breath, I turn toward the kitchen, catch a bit of movement there, focus myself inward, try to resolve a form, a shape. Something rich, glittering and subdued moves by the range, dips into the dusty cakes there. Something like a shade of gold, shimmering and yet mellow, something like a bit of sheer silk shifting in a gentle wind.

'You're welcome,' I say, smile at the gold-glittering spirit. 'My home is your home. If you are peaceful, you may stay as long as you please.'

'I appreciate your hospitality,' the spirit says, and as it drifts closer to me, edges and lines begin to take shape. Legs and arms, the body of a person, a human…

'You're the first of our kind I've seen in a long time,' he says to me.

It takes me a moment to recover from the realisation. *A har. The spirit of a har.* I lick my lips. There are a hundred questions all trying to rip their way out of me at once. *Where are you from? How did you die? Are there others…*

There's a flicker, a brush of ice against my lips as fingers reach out, urge my mind to slow, to settle into silence. 'It's been a long time for you as well, hasn't it?' he asks.

I swallow, nod. 'I've waited. I've wondered, hoped.' I battle to get words out, to form sentences that make sense. 'In all the years I've lived here, I've never seen another har, never seen the spirit of a har. I was starting to wonder if we can even die, or if maybe we transition to some other place when we go, or…'

'I wish I had answers for you,' the har-spirit cuts me off.

In the pause, I feel all of my hope, all the fire and passion in me settling, draining out again. So many questions, and all of them laid aside, silenced with a single sentence. *How can you not know?* I find myself wondering, but before I can ask, the har-spirit speaks again.

'But then, I suppose you wouldn't have the answers to any of my questions either.'

'Questions about what?' I ask.

'The world. Politics. Which tribes are in control, who leads them, how the lands between here and the eastern coast of Megalithica have changed since the beginning.'

I consider his words for a moment, mull them around in my mind, finally shake my head. He's right. With all of the years I've spent in this ranch house, atop this hill, never so much as glimpsing anyhar else, never really caring about the flow of armies and nations, there's not a lot about physical things, about life that I can offer. 'I'm sorry,' is all I can manage.

'It's a bit of a disappointment.' The har-spirit fades a little, becomes less golden, less glittery.

'It doesn't have to be.' I wet my lips, expectant.

Nearby, the har-spirit seems to resist my quick optimism, only slowly turns his attention on me again. 'What do you mean?'

'What is your name?' I push ahead, unwilling to let the opportunity die.

'Name?' He asks, then drifts thoughtful, finally answers, 'I don't know. I can't remember it.'

'My name is Jyrathen.' I point to my chest, smile at the spirit.

'Jyrathen,' he repeats, sounds it out, as if feeling it, as if separating the sounds in an attempt to better understand it. After a moment, he perks up again. 'What name do you think would fit me?

What would you call me, if I didn't have a name?'

I think about it for a moment, look him over, up and down, then smile as it comes to me. 'I'd probably name you as I see you. I'd probably call you Gold.'

'Gold.' He shifts, brightens a little. '*Gold.* I like it.'

'Tell me of yourself, Gold.' I sit, gesture at a place on the floor beside me. 'Tell me what you've seen, where you've been. Tell me what you know, and what you remember.'

'There isn't much,' he says.

I offer him a soft smile. 'I'd still be honoured to hear whatever stories you have in you.'

Gold nods, and like an old friend, he settles in beside me, starts to unwind the fragmented memories of his life. Most of it comes hazy and out of order, but a picture of who he was before he died slowly starts to come into focus for both of us. It's interesting to me, all of it. With words, sensations, the occasional colour or strong image, he paints a picture within my mind of the har he was, of the life he lived on the pitted and abandoned highways far to the east, lending a hand where he could, killing when he had to. He tells me of the objects he carried as if he still carried them, tells me of every crack, every line on the gun, the wrench and the lighter that kept him alive in the desert wastes as if his survival still depended so keenly upon them. He tells me of a brief stay in a settlement called Saltrock, of the hara there, of the frantic, passionate aruna he shared with a har who wore his orange hair in long, straight tresses. Images of that night, of Gold's last night in Saltrock, break upon my mind like waves, awaken feelings in me that I'd forgotten I could have, and I find myself distracted as he meanders on through his memories. *Passion, aruna.* The stuff of life, of the living. The things I'd forgotten after so long living amongst the dead.

Hours pass, and as Gold spins through the last of his stories, he starts to ask me questions, starts to ask me about the life I've lived in this place that is so far away from everything. In all of his wanderings since his death, he's chosen to ignore so much of the spirit and soul stirring in everything around him. Drawn ever westward, he's run and run without looking back, without asking questions, without observing the entities that no doubt took notice of him, perhaps even attempted to communicate with him. For a spirit, Gold knows very little of the world of the dead, but the more I talk about it, about the nuances and intricacies of it, the more he seems to take an interest, asking questions the way a child might, taking in everything that I offer, digesting it. Flitting from memory to memory, I tell him about my life living in the hilltop ranch house, about the storms, about the spirits I've seen, the souls I've spoken with, lived with, even come to care deeply for. His hue seems to darken, become richer as I talk, and I wonder at what he's thinking, what kind of conclusions he's coming to. When he finally asks me about the fading, about the way spirits sometimes wash away to nothing, as Mae and so many others before her have, the subtle light at the edge of the coming dawn is already starting to peek in through the blue of the tarped windows. Most of the spirits of trees, flowers, rocks and nature have gone on to other shades of reality, faded or dispersed in flashes so tiny they're almost missed. Tired, and feeling a little hazy with the lack of sleep, I hug myself against the cold, consider my words before I answer.

'There are many things about the soul that I do not know or understand,' I tell Gold. 'Spirits don't have to be dead in order to wander, in order to visit others, dance, play or dream their way into other worlds. Most of the spirits that come here during storms are dead, but even they seem to exist in some transitory state, dreaming between lives, between minds, waiting to be reborn somewhere else, somewhen else.'

'There does seem to be a fluidity to it,' Gold says absently. 'I can feel it, just at the edges of my senses. It's like a crowd of voices, a veil of voices, and all of them talking at once. I feel as if I could pass into that, become one of those voices, and make an agreement that would pull me through into another life, into another living being.'

'Do you want that?' I ask him.

'I...' He hesitates, considering. 'I'm not sure.'

'Are you afraid?'

Gold is silent for a long moment. His light hangs steady, mostly still, but the shimmer he carries doesn't darken, doesn't fade. In the pause, I reach for him, feel the slight prickle of cold as his hand settles into mine.

There's a sensation like a drawing of breath, deep and resigned, and then the har-spirit speaks to me again, says, 'I am. I hate admitting it, but I am afraid.'

'What are you afraid of?' I turn to look directly at him, give him a soft, reassuring smile.

'Losing myself,' he says. 'Forgetting who I am, who I was.'

'But you've already started to,' I tell him. 'You've forgotten quite a bit about who you were in your last life.'

'That's why I'm afraid.' His hues soften, lose some of their vibrance. 'I've lost so much. I don't want to lose anything else. I don't want to forget.'

'You haven't.' I smile. 'In truth, you haven't forgotten anything.'

For a moment, he only seems to stare at me, waits as if ready to absorb even the smallest explanation. Waiting, looking away, I pull my knees up to my chest, clear my throat.

'Everything you were, every memory you carried when you lived that life you're trying so desperately to cling to, exists somewhere, in some form.' I look at him again, give him a moment to soak in what I'm saying. 'Your memories aren't lost. You aren't lost. You've changed, and you'll continue to change. The journey never ends.'

'The journey never ends,' Gold repeats the words, and on some level, I feel as if they've hit him exactly where they needed to.

Silence sprawls out around us, and then the harsh yellow rays of the newborn sun cut into the parlour, shine through tiny holes in the tarp to light up lines of shimmering dust. There's a heaviness as dawn begins to give way to day, an emptiness, a restoration of the material as the influence of the immaterial begins to wane and fade. Beside me, I feel Gold stand, turn toward the sun.

'You're afraid too,' he says to me.

I blink as I look up at him, considering his words.

'You know that if you leave, you'll change. You know that if you change, you won't be the same har.'

'What are you saying?' I ask him.

'This house, this place.' He gestures at the walls, the cold stumps of candles, the little pockets of phantom glow where a few spirits still linger in sleepy clusters. 'Why do you stay?'

It takes me a moment to push aside the rush of feelings his words trigger in me. I swallow, stand, come up with something to say, but it doesn't feel honest, doesn't feel genuine.

I force myself to say it anyway.

'I like it here.' I make a gesture to try to hide the emotions I'm feeling. Gold sees right through it, I know, and so I refuse to look at him, avoid eye contact as if that might make me more opaque to him. 'I have everything I need here.'

'Do you?' he asks.

My eyes dart back to him, back to the shimmering shape full of light and memories, and in his stare, I can feel pinpricks of what it means to live, wet emanations of what it means to run, to sweat, to hunt, to kill, to take aruna. It's soft, but the needs in me have been so long ignored, so long denied that the sensations hit me like a sledgehammer – and then he touches me, *he touches me*, and I lose everything. I lose the world, and all control with it.

What I gain is a dusty highway, a pale sun burning across black and pitted asphalt. What I gain is a memory shared, a moment spent within Gold as he was, as the ratty-haired and tanned highway har wrapped in patched leather and torn denim. With living clarity, I see what he sees, feel what he feels, live what he lives, and I drink in the richness of the experience like a greedy harling, flit from detail to detail, gorging myself on the sumptuousness of a life lived so viscerally. Hearing the stories in the feeble candlelight of the deep night was enough to tantalise me, but living them – it renders me powerless, utterly. All I can do is feed, lose myself in what he gives me.

Nothing is lost, yet everything changes, he tells me as we hunt as one, as we catch a jackrabbit in the crosshairs of his rifle and send its spirit scampering away to other things, other lives. The flesh is sweet as we tear into it, suck the fat and warm, spilling juices from the lip-like edges of soft fur. Like a guide, he shows me the crunch and sweet, sticky release of eating beetles, shows me the way fat grubs collected from under rocks roll across the tongue, soft and warm, with just the barest crunch when we bite down, savouring the fleeting taste of their buttery meat.

And then he shows me aruna, or rather reminds me of how much my body misses it, hungers for it. He shows me the sweet sweat that flies, flung from hair as backs arc, as mouths meet with a low and passionate howl. He shows me the tense knotting of hands and arms and thighs, the heat, the way it spreads, builds and draws all of the attention inward, in toward creation, toward such a fiery and profound need that it captures all and holds every ounce of breath and soul until everything flies apart in crashing, crushing release. He shows me the collapse, the return, the sweet wash of cool air that comes as souls settle back into bodies, as one melted, melding being becomes two again, two spent spirits wrapped together, sated and silent in the wake of the storm.

And when Gold finally lets me go, I am panting, sweating. My heart is racing, pounding in my chest, and if Gold were a living har, a creature of flesh and blood, I swear I'd pounce upon him and bite him, deeply and passionately. The needs swirling within me are so strong, so blinding and overpowering that it's all I can do just to clench my hands, and even then my nails bite into my palms so hard that they draw blood. I feel as if I've just been incepted, as if I've just awakened to what it means to be har, and the feeling clings to me, prickles my skin, burns at my nerves, inescapable.

'Why do you stay?' Gold asks me again, and this time I cannot answer him. I have no answer, and nothing seems important enough to tie me down, to keep me fixed in this place, this ranch, house, waystation at the fringe between worlds. *Stepper, Sweets, Phil* – but when I call out to them with my mind, none of them come, none of them even answer. It's haunting, the silence, the sudden, vacuous silence.

Gold says something to me, but I don't hear it. I'm so overwhelmed, I rush into the hallway, throw open all of the doors, shouting and staring, searching for movement, for any shift of glow or shadow, but there is nothing, *nothing*. The rooms are all empty, the candles dead and cold. There's no sign of Sweets, of Stepper, of Phil, and when I turn back toward the kitchen, I see that even the little cake rolls on the range are gone. Nothing remains. Nothing but cold wax.

Nothing but me, nothing but Gold.

'Where will you go?' he asks, picking up on my thoughts, the fragments of needs swirling through my mind. I don't answer him immediately, only shake my head, cross to the range to make certain I'm not missing something. The cake rolls – even the crumbs are gone.

The back door is still latched. Working quickly, I toss aside the woollen blanket and tear my way into the garage. Fingers snap loose the locks on the big car-port door, and then I'm shouldering it open, swinging it up into its tracks on the ceiling. Light streams in, and I blink past it, turn my eyes to the yard, to the buckets...

And every one of them is sideways, knocked over by the winds of the storm, empty of water.

'What is left to stay for?' I ask no one but myself.

Shaking my head, I turn back to the garage, let my eyes wander across the cinderblock walls of the ranch house. On the porch, Gold shimmers at me, watches me like a silent sentinel.

And it is in that moment that I realise he's already beginning to fade.

'Gold!' I cross to the porch, stand before him, wish he had hands to take and squeeze. Sensing my need, my thoughts, he raises his arms, settles his cold, ephemeral fingers in my open palms. 'You're leaving too, aren't you?'

There's no answer, no verbal answer, but I get the barest hint of a sensation. *Understanding. Relief.* I swallow back tears, hold my own feelings inside.

'I think I'll go East,' I tell him, answering his earlier question. 'I think I'll try to find that highway, try to find Saltrock or places like it. I'll find out what the hara of this world are doing, what tribes are in power, how things have grown and changed. I'll learn of life and living, and I'll whisper to the winds what I discover, whisper my thoughts to you when I lay down beneath the stars every night. I promise.'

Gratitude. That's the sensation I get just before he slips away, just before he becomes little more than a breath, ascending slowly skyward. Gratitude, and it is enough.

Even as I pack my few meagre belongings into a rucksack and start toward the mountains and the desert far to the East, it is enough.

The Ghost of Who I Was

Zane Marc Gentis

I hear their howls of fury as I run between the dead streets. They flit at the corner of my vision, deeper shadows against the hungry dark. A quick glance back – I know I shouldn't, as soon as I do it – and something catches at my ankle, tripping me up.

I kick wildly, imagining cold fingers clutching my foot, pinning me in place. The thrashing frees me, and as I scramble up I see it's no hand; just a tangle of rusted cables I'd run into.

My relief vanishes as the howls get louder. They echo off the tall concrete edifices, bouncing and coming at me from all sides. Heart hammering in my chest, I realise I can't keep running all night. I need to get my energy back, buy some time to think.

Each breath of the frigid air tears at my throat, but I need to keep going until – there! A dash around the corner and a quick dive into a deep, dark river that thunders between the ruins. The water is frigid and saps my strength but is dark enough to conceal me from watching eyes, and the roar of its passage would have hidden any splash I made.

Can ghosts smell? It doesn't matter – I'm hidden, but if I don't move and find somewhere to surface I'm going to become a ghost of the waters myself.

Everything's murky, and the cold lances into my joints, making them ache. Fingers brush against dirt, twigs and rotting leaves – I'm at the bottom of the river. I swim like the frog, arms pushing through the water and legs kicking it aside, flowing with the current. Perhaps I can hold my breath long enough to leave this cursed place and get to the ocean.

Perhaps is only half a yes, and I know I can't do it. I need another breath, my lungs burning from the earlier exertion and their current starvation.

Just a little further and I can take a breath. Just a little further...

If I don't surface now, I'll drown. I kick hard, pulling myself towards the surface. My head breaks through and I inhale deep lungfuls of air, desperate for breath but trying to keep as silent as possible. The howls grow softer, and angrier. I've given them the slip for now.

I paddle along the surface, trying to stay in the shadows at the water's edge. This brief respite is what I need to slow my heart, calm my body. I may need to duck under the water again soon, and I need to be ready for it.

I don't want to think about what'll happen if they get me. What's happened to Kageso...

Kageso's hands massage the stiff muscles of my back, strong fingers kneading the scented oils into my skin. The fresh, sweet sting of orange and the warm spice of sandalwood linger in my nose.

'That's a new blend you've got there,' I say, feeling the tension leave beneath Kageso's ministrations.

'I got some new oils today,' he says. 'Do you like it?'

'Of course. Something about it makes me think of the village, of home.'

'I'm glad,' he says, hands smoothing away the creases of worry. He's massaging my shoulders, kneading the tension out of my neck. I've been doing woodwork all day, my back stiff from bending over the bench and arms aching from the effort. 'The smells actually make me think of you,' he continues. 'The scent is strong but gentle, like your hands, and there's something about the scent of the workshop and long grasses of the fields outside your window in it.'

I turn and stare at him, despite his tuts of protest that I'm interrupting the massage. Kageso really is beautiful; his skin is the colour of the forest soil, giving away how rich with life he is. His eyes are just as dark, but they always gleam with whatever private joke Kageso's laughing inwardly at. His true pride is his hair; I know how long he spends brushing and oiling it, braiding the small bells, coloured leather strips and bird feathers into his locks.

'Do you think we'll still be together after the *Kaliwa* ceremony?' I ask quietly.

'Of course,' he says. All disapproval is gone. His hands delicately touch my cheek, bringing me back from my worries. My eyes meet his again.

'We'll both pass the initiation, and then we'll come back home together, and one day we'll even be chesna,' he said. 'We're meant to be, you and I. So long as we're together, we can do anything.'

But we're not together anymore. I'm alone in the freezing waters, swimming between the dark ruins of a tainted city, hunted by ghosts. I have no idea what's happening to anyhar else who was with me earlier. I've heard their screams as they were taken one by one.

How do any harlings survive this? How can there still be tribes if no harlings survive?

All the tribe's harlings going through feybraiha stand together on the village outskirts. Aurum, one of the tribe's elders and most in commune with the spirits, is waiting for us. He's clothed in the furs, feathers and mother-of-pearl jewellery that all hara of our tribe wear, the symbols of our connection to the world around us and our communion with the beasts of the land, air and sea. Aurum's familiar, a mottled python, is wrapped around his shoulders and testing the air with its dark, forked tongue, regarding us all with cold eyes.

We stand in silence till everyone's gathered. Kageso is beside me. He wiggles his fingers to catch my attention and sticks out his tongue before resuming a straight face. I smile back while I'm sure Aurum can't see.

When everyone's ready Aurum approaches each of us in turn, waiting as we strip. He hands each naked harling a blanket woven with the tribal colours of blue, white and black, before dipping his fingers into a bowl of blue pigment and painting stripes down their cheeks. There are fifteen of us in all, and he proceeds in utter silence. We understand the rules, including the ban against speaking. We haven't eaten any meat for three days, and now on the first day of our trials we'll be forbidden to speak until we arrive at the site of the Kaliwa ritual.

We're barefoot, falling into single file as Aurum leads us off. The farms and groves around our village make way for the wilder woods. We take leaf-strewn paths between towering yellow-woods and ferns as high as a fully grown har. Moss and orange stairs of fungus grow up the tree trunks. Bird calls stop as we near, and in the ferns you can hear the crush of animals backing away from us deeper into the woods.

I hear and smell the ocean before I see it, salt mingling with the cool scent of loam, rot and greenery. We're led through a gap in the trees and the sea comes into view, stretching to all directions of the horizon. It's a rolling, endless blanket of blue, waiting at the bottom of shrub-covered cliffs. What catches my attention is something I've never seen before: squatting below the cliffs to the left, on the edge of the forest, with black rubble tumbling out onto a white-sanded beach, is a shadowy ruin that feels cold even at this distance.

I remember the fires that struck in the drought a year ago. My skin, scorched from the sun and flames, had hurt for a week, and we had to be wary of wasting what spare water we had. Not all the tribes and villages had managed to escape unscathed. I'd walked through the burnt-out husks of buildings, picking among the ashes and still-smouldering coals and smoking ruins. Some of those villages had been resettled and reclaimed. Others had been abandoned and were being taken by the forest.

These buildings had been burnt, but they weren't reclaimed by hara or nature. They were dead.

I'm probably the only living thing in these ruins. Not even sharks ventured into the mouth of this river; there was no prey here for them.

The buildings had been sinister and strange then, when I first set my eyes on them, but they were even worse now, without the day to reveal the truth of their dilapidation. They gained a sinister vitality at night. That was when they and the ghosts that dwelt here came alive.

I wrap my blanket tightly around my shoulders. The ruins suck the warmth from the air. From the corners of my eye I see shadows, but whenever I look at them they hide themselves from view. At first, I think that they're another tribe, but somehow I know this is a lie I'm telling myself.

We walk along the beach, sand rough and warm between our toes. Even here, on the shore, it's lifeless. Dark rocks at the water's edge, pitted by erosion, are bare of the smaller creatures – the hard-shells, salt-snails, shore flowers and salt-crabs. No kelp has washed ashore, and none could be seen cresting the foam on the water.

We pass the first pieces of rubble. From a few paces away, they chill the air. A strange miasma is emanating from them, distorting the air like heat-mirages. No one else around me seems to notice. I get Kageso's attention and point at the stones. He shrugs and looks at me as though to ask what I'm trying to say. Can't anyhar but me *see* that there's something wrong with this place?

Other harlings wrapped in blankets are coming across the beach from the other side, and more are winding their way down between the trees and shrubs on the hills. All together there are over thirty of us approaching the ruins.

Aurum has us wait on the ruined city's outskirts. The other blanket-wrapped harlings join in silence, each group led by their own elder. I don't know or recognise any of the harlings, but I know their tribes by the appearance of their elders and the stories I've heard. The *Althunzi* elder is easy to spot by his ritual scarring and the animal bones he's put through his piercings. He's wearing a flute around his neck that's been intricately carved from a large animal bone. The stories say each tribe member has to carve the flute himself and must use it to commune with the spirits of the land. The *Ivuka* elder is tattooed with curving designs to remind other hara of his connection to rain, and his tribe's communion with the lightning birds that bring the water and an end to the dry season. He wears lots of copper jewellery in jagged designs that jingle as he walks.

Aurum is the one who speaks. 'Today begins your passage from harlings to hara. You have shed the clothes and toys of your childhood. Now you are on the journey, but you are not hara yet. You may drink water, but you are not permitted to eat food today. You are forbidden to speak until the sun has hidden his face. Once darkness has fallen, you will be tested three times before the sun rises. The price of adulthood is knowledge – the knowledge of who you are, and your place in the world.'

'Go now,' the unknown elder from the *Ivuka* tribe says. 'We will collect you at dawn, when each of you has become har in spirit and flesh. Beware: the trials are not easy.'

The hunger begins as an easily ignored irritation, but as the day progresses it settles as a dull ache in my middle. Kageso and I wander together, even though we can't speak to each other. We shake hands in greeting with some harlings, and hug others that we feel safer with.

The shade among the ruins is welcome in the scorching heat of mid-day. Despite that, a chill comes off the stones and pierces through the protective layers of my blanket. I stick close to Kageso, not wanting to be alone. The miasma coming off the ruins is even stronger here, distorting the air around me. I feel nauseous every time I stare too long at the larger buildings. As much as possible I try to stay near the river in the centre of the ruins, or near the outskirts; anywhere, so long as there's something to look at that doesn't knot my insides and make me want to hurl them out.

No one else feels the way I do. They don't seem to get cold either. I can't understand why I'm the only one so badly affected by the ruins.

I pick up flat stones and throw them into the lazy river, trying to see how many times they'll skip across the water's surface. As I watch the last one hop, counting each of the first ripples, I see a harling standing on the water's surface. My breath freezes and sticks in my throat. It's Kageso, standing on the water and reaching out to me.

'*Help me,*' he says. I can't stop myself: I run into the water, dropping my blanket without a second thought, my splashes disturbing the silence. The river is deep, and the water has gotten halfway up to my waist within three steps. My legs begin stinging from the painful cold, and I might have drowned myself had a hand not grabbed my wrist and yanked me hard, stopping me from throwing myself into the icy water.

I turn, trying to shake off the harling who's grabbed me, but a second tender hand to my cheek stops me from thrashing loose. I look into Kageso's eyes and see the worry in them. A quick glance back to the river, and whatever I'd seen there is gone. Kageso's here, beside me: warm and solid, not like the cold vision earlier.

I am har. I know these ruins are dangerous, and since I'm the only one who sees what I see, I should know better than anyhar else. My cheeks burn with shame at having been deceived so soon, before the tasks have even begun. Kageso tries to ask what's wrong with his touch and his glance, but I push him away and run off by myself. When I'm sure I'm alone with my shame, I bury my head in the blanket strung across my knees to block out the ruins and pretend I'm anywhere else but here.

If I paid more attention, I would have realised that what bothered me most about the ruins wasn't how strange they are, but how normal.

These buildings are like the dwellings in our village. Square masonry supports old ceiling beams made of charred wood. Floors of cut stone. Regular steps leading between collapsed floors within the stone buildings. I wonder if this is an old city belonging to one of our tribes. And if it is, then why was it abandoned? Where did its inhabitants go?

I run my hands lightly over the rough, cold stone. It feels like I'm being watched, but the eyes are before me, within the walls. Even if I can't see them, they can see me. My shame forgotten, I leave the house and try to find Kageso.

His eyes ask many questions, but a wan smile is enough to put him at ease. I'd save my secrets and concerns for tonight, when we could speak.

I've managed to float quietly through the city ruins, to where the deep river meets the sea and the tumbled masonry gets swallowed by the beach sand. I haven't seen a single harling, or any of my pursuers. Am I the last one left alive?

The sky's getting lighter behind the hills to the east. Just a few more hours and I'll be safe. My river journey is at an end. When my feet touch down on mud, I carefully begin to wade out of the water, letting the soft lapping of waves mask any noise I make. The mud sucks at my feet, trying to swallow them and pull me back. I stumble, fighting against the earth and water. The wind picks up then, blowing against me. It stole my blanket earlier, and now it's trying to stop me leaving as well.

I push against the elements, forcing my way past. I have to get out. I have to be free.

'Don't leave me!'

The wind dies, silencing itself so that I can hear those words. They're a whisper laden with pain and fear. 'Kageso,' I say, turning.

Kageso follows me like a shadow for the rest of the day. It all passes in a haze of waiting and hunger. As the sun begins to set, a sense of anticipation falls upon us. The energy changes, buzzing with excitement. All this time in silence around each other has left us itching to speak, hungry to find out what the trials are, yet none among us dare disobey the elders' commands.

We gather on the beach to watch the last of the sun's rays burn the horizon a deep coral and set the waves ablaze with shimmers of gold. As its edges disappear and the sky darkens, a harling in the ruins lets out a cheer, startling the rest of us. It's the first sound in a day of silence, and we all laugh in relief when we realise what's happened. The tension's broken, and the laughter bubbles out of us.

'Finally!' Kageso says, hugging me and slapping my back in joy. 'What happened earlier? It looked like you were trying to drown yourself. I tried to figure out what was going on, but you looked like you wanted to be alone for a while.'

'I...' I shake my head. 'Can't you feel it? There's something wrong with this place.'

'Well, sure. It's a bit spooky. Do you think anyhar died here during the fires? Is that why we're here?'

'It's more than that, Kageso! Everything here feels *cold*. When I look at the rubble I feel sick. Something's not right here. This place isn't safe.'

He touches my cheek again, calming me with his smile. 'If it wasn't safe, they wouldn't let harlings spend the night here.'

I nod. Kageso's right. He has to be. It doesn't make sense otherwise. My relief is short-lived, however. My skin begins to tingle, and all the hairs on my arms and legs stand on end. I turn from Kageso to look into the ruins. As the light of the sun disappears further and further over the horizon, a faint glow emanates from the ruins. Motes of warm light, like dust-mote sized embers, float out of the stone. They swirl in the air like dandelion seeds.

'Kageso,' I whisper, 'please tell me that you can see *this*, at least.'

He swallows and nods, mesmerised.

The other harlings are coming from the beach as well, drawn by the hypnotic dance of the lights. They try tentatively to tap the light motes with their fingers, but the motes drift away, almost playful. The harlings laugh. Those who are fast run their hands through the glow, the lights glowing brighter. The second time the lights are touched they pop into glowing smoke and the chime of tiny bells.

All the harlings come sprinting then, running their hands through whatever light they can. The motes drift deeper into the ruined city, and the harlings run after.

Kageso is laughing as well. He grabs my wrist and tries to pull me along after the others, but I jerk my arm back. The bell chimes haven't stopped. Each successive chime is getting louder and echoing longer, but it's as if I'm the only one who can hear them.

'You can't hear that, can you?' I ask Kageso, resigned to his answer. The bells have become so loud I can barely hear myself speak. Their chimes echo off the ruined buildings and bounce back, reverberating inside my mind. I grab the sides of my head, blocking my ears with my palms.

Kageso looks at me, puzzled. That's when I realise that the light motes have surrounded us. They all pop at once, and my world is engulfed in rivers of fire and the deafening ring of iron.

The light leaves my vision and I'm back in the city. Bells are tolling in alarm and hara scream in panic and pain. No, not hara. Something different. Hara are whole, are one, these creatures are of two flesh, separate. Each one is like half a har, like looking at half a soul that spent its life looking for another piece to make it whole. Their harlings are like them as well: incomplete.

It's night, but the sky's light as day, and sweat runs down my flesh in rivulets. Flames leap up, taller than the buildings, burning everything in their path. Parks and tree-lined streets burn to ash. Glowing embers fall from the scarred walls of the sturdiest structures.

I run with the crowd. Their sweat is sour with their fear. I sense their emotions in the air. It's like a series of blows to my heart, each one a stab of emotional pain that still bleeds as I run. They're all around me. Scared animal faces. Bodies violent, shoving and rushing and breaking. Smoke and sweat and death in the air, which singes my throat as I breathe it. Ground sticky beneath my bare feet.

A hand shoves me aside, pushing me to the ground. I push myself up, but hard-soled shoes crush my hand. I scream as more shoes knock me down. Feet trample me, knocking the wind from me. Bones shatter. Flesh is crushed to pulp as skin tears. Then the flames catch my broken form. All I know is pain. All I want is an end.

Kageso. I can't. Not yet. What's happened to him? Is he here too? Where *is* here?

Those thoughts come unbidden, but as they do the pain recedes; it isn't the only voice in my head anymore, panic no longer the lone emotion.

Kageso had been right here. Where is he, or rather where am I? I flex my broken fingers. The bones snap back into place, the flesh knits itself back together. As I push myself to my feet, everything else reassembles itself, like many fallen logs piling themselves up. I'm surrounded by the flames. Everywhere I'd felt my skin rip, the flames rush over me, cauterising my spiritual wounds.

The flames die away; my vision clears. I'm standing in the ruins again. Kageso has collapsed to the ground in front of me, thrashing, the lights enveloping him. I rush to his side and shoo them away, pulling him through the small, glowing explosions. I no longer hear the bells, but for all I know they haven't stopped for him.

I drag his body, half-slung half over my shoulder, to the sea. We fall into the lapping waves. The shock of the frigid, salty water snaps Kageso awake with a gasp, his tremors stopping.

'Kageso!' I say, hugging him. His heart hammers against my breast and his hands cling tightly to me, nails hurting as he grabs and doesn't let go. We'd lost our blankets somewhere back in the ruins, but I don't care. He's all right.

'What...what happened?' he asks, his voice shaking.

'The trials,' I say. 'They've begun.'

'It's not you,' I say, shaking my head and backing away from the wan figure before me. 'I couldn't save you. I know now that this is a trick.'

'You wish it were a trick,' he whispers, coming closer.

'No,' I say. 'It was you earlier, walking to me across the water. Kageso was with me the whole time. You're not him. You're this place, trying to get into my head again.'

'So, what do we do now?' Kageso asks.

'Daylight,' I say. 'There's a reason the trials take place at night.'

'That's when the ghosts come out!'

'I don't know if they're ghosts. These feel more like memories.'

'Is there a difference?' he says, shrugging.

'Kageso, we have to leave. This is just the first trial, and there are supposed to be three. It's not safe. We have to go and come back when it's light.'

'No,' he says, still hugging me firmly. 'This is how we become hara. We can't leave. If we do, we've failed.'

'We can't become hara if we're dead!' I say, pushing him away and hugging myself. His hands encircle me, and even though I try to shrug him off at first, I soon stop, grateful for his touch.

'We're not the first harlings to come here,' he says. 'And we won't be the last. There is a way to beat this. They wouldn't send us all here to die.'

'Not everyhar comes back, Kageso,' I say. 'Sometimes, there've even been strangers in the tribe, after the trial. Is that what happens if one tribe loses too many harlings? They divide the survivors up between the tribes?'

'We'll beat this,' he says again. 'Trust me. If we stick together, we can beat anything, remember? But we're not going to pass these trials by running. We have to face them. You knew from the start that there was something wrong here, and you were right. You've never experienced aruna, but you're more in tune with the magic of this place than anyhar. If anyhar can beat this place, it's you. So, please come with me. You saved me once already, and I might need you to do it again.'

Kageso's crazy. He can't want to go back in there, not after what happened. I turn to him and see that I'm right: he doesn't want to go back. But he's still going to, because that's who he is. His eyes are frightened, but his jaw is set.

'All right,' I say, 'let's go.'

The ruins that had been aglow only moments ago are now dark. The motes and flames have vanished. Kageso and I pick our way through the rubble, searching for any other harlings, but all is silent.

'Where are they?' I ask him. 'We should have found one of them by now.'

'Unless they're hiding,' he whispers back. 'Maybe they all managed to beat the memories, like we did. The first thing you'd do is try to find somehar else to protect you, or a place to hide so that nothing dangerous can find you.'

He's right. I point to a large complex of ruins; the walls have crumbled away in places and the roof has burnt away completely. It's a warren of hiding places, and any harling seeking to get off these exposed streets would be drawn to it. 'There. That's one of the best places we've seen so far.'

'Let's go,' he says, darting ahead of me. Kageso progresses silently, his moves cat-like. I feel clumsy following him, my every step creating a skittering of loose stones and dirt, noise that I'm not sure is real or imagined.

The ruined building is even more dilapidated inside. Fallen pillars and other debris create small caves and passages between the remnants of intact rooms. Parts of the floor have crumbled away into cellars that lead into tunnels of dirt. Stairs lead to a mostly collapsed upper level that we can gaze into through holes in the ceiling above us.

Kageso motions for me to stop, but there's no need. I hear it too: the sound of a harling whimpering. It's coming from within the warren of fallen masonry. We duck below a pillar and crawl through a passage strewn with rubble. The whimpering seems near, but each time we round fallen stones it's just an echo, pulling us deeper. I watch Kageso disappear into the dark and reappear later in moonlight falling through gaps in the masonry. My skin is tingling again, as it did before. No bells ring, so something different is happening, but what?

The passage opens up into a large chamber beneath a clear sky. There are three harlings squatting together, their backs to us, their faces hidden by their long hair. I stop, cold. Kageso notices how I freeze. The harlings' whimpers are of relief and punctuated by wet slurps and suckling noises.

Shadows slip through their hair and encircle their necks. As I watch, all three heads whip around. Their faces are dark, writhing shadows covering them like living masks. Their eyes are sickly-glowing yellow orbs. Blood drips from their mouths, and before them is the rent and twisted body of another harling.

The clear room becomes darker, and as I look around I see shadowy tendrils twist like smoke through the cracks in the walls and between the fallen rubble. Clouds of shadow tendrils block out the stars as they circle above us, like a noose drawing tighter.

'Kageso!'

He turns to me sharply, puzzled. He can't feel what's happening, can't understand. He can't see the shadows, he doesn't know how much danger we're in.

The three harlings aren't confused. They dart at us without hesitation, running and whooping like wild dogs. I turn and run, darting through openings between the shadow tendrils before they can close on me. I hear Kageso howl in pain behind me, but I can't stop and look back. There's no time. My blood is cold in my veins, but my cheeks burn with shame, and I cry as he continues to scream. I need to save him, but I'm overwhelmed. I can't do it. All I can think about is running, getting away.

I run through the passages. Shadows slither through holes and cracks towards me, others darting through the air. My way is barred, and I have to turn, have to run. I hear the sound of hurrying feet and whoops behind me.

They're gaining on me.

'I heard your screams,' I say. 'They were coming for me. I couldn't save you. No one could have.'

His face contorts, the flesh falling away from his jaw and his teeth chipping into sharp splinters. His eyes glow with feverish light and the shadows exit his nose and ears, enfolding the upper half of his face.

'You left me!' he shouts, pointing an accusatory finger at me.

'This isn't real,' I say, my legs weak. 'You're not real! *You're not real!*'

He runs at me, jaw opening wider, flesh pealing back from his fingers and turning them into bone claws. There's nothing around me to use in defence; I have only my bare hands. Kageso leaps and crashes into me with the force of a charging rhino. I hold his wrists as we roll on the ground, keeping his claws away from me. His snapping jaw lunges for my throat, and I must keep moving to dodge it.

He manages to flip on top of me and wrenches his hands free, but I use my greater strength to kick him off before he can strike me. A stray claw cuts my leg, pain lancing through it. He manages to dart away, ready to spring again but watching me carefully for an opening.

'Kageso would understand,' I say, getting up and limping backwards, keeping him in my sight all the while. 'Even if you were him once, you're not anymore.'

He runs as at me, and I know there's no way to get away from him. I trip over a large stone and fall to the ground, just as he jumps on me, teeth tearing into my side. I can't think through the pain. I grab him by his hair and pull him off, flinging him to one side, but he dashes back and bites me again.

The stone I tripped over! My scrambling hands find it, and I bring it down with as much force as I can onto the back of his head. His bite slackens, but I don't stop. Pain and fear are drugging me into desperation, and I beat his skull in over and over with the now bloody rock, crying tears of pain and relief and horror the whole while.

Trembling fingers drop the rock, too tired to hold on anymore. His slumped, bleeding body is on top of mine, but I'm shaking from tiredness and sorrow and can't move.

Kageso...

We were meant to be together. We were meant to be chesna. He's always there to protect me, to comfort me, and now what am I to do without him?

Until now, I never realised that what I've feared the most is losing him. I've never thought to be afraid because it's never seemed possible. Now he's gone.

I can't do anything except cry. My skin tingles at the magic in the air, and I see the encroaching shadows. Their touch is like dry water, whispering along my flesh. I feel it change, becoming cold as they wrap around me.

Soon my crying stops. The pain and loss of Kageso's passing are taken away, and replaced with a dull, numb ache. The world becomes lit as though it's day, the ghostly magic shaping my eyes. I can feel the kiss of the dark across my face, the shadowy miasma hiding me, making me just another ravenous creature like the others.

I feel strange. Powerful. The har I was weeping over earlier doesn't matter now. He feels like a stranger, unimportant. I flex my fingers. Shadows swirl around them like smoke. They swim over the wounds in my side and leg, filling the rents in my flesh with darkness and making me whole.

The tingling I felt earlier on my skin is now inside me, flowing from my core, up the back of my neck and tickling my scalp and forehead. It feels like the magic within me often does, but cold. I push myself up, my body rippling with strength. I can run, and jump, push myself further than I have before. I'm fit to burst with energy; it feels like I could set a tree alight simply by touching it, a cold flame burning within me.

The flame is hungry. It whispers to me in many voices, and I know them. They're whispers from the half-hara who lived here before and died in the fires. They're whispers from other harlings before me, who've come here for the trials. These are whispers of fear and rage, offering all the power within me now if I just sate my hunger, the hunger I've felt as a dull ache all day and that now begins to burn like acid within me.

I grab the sides of my head, but I can't block the voices out because they're within me. *Feed. Hunt. Rage. Kill.*

They would take my fear, take my rage, all of it, and magnify it a hundred-fold. Nothing could ever hurt me again like I've just been hurt. Nothing would ever be out of my grasp. I'm Wraeththu, born to power; this is my world, and they'd give it all to me.

The hunger surges within me, but more intoxicating is the power. I laugh, and it comes out as a dog-like whooping, the laugh of a jackal or hyena. It's *good* to be powerful, a warm embrace that makes everything feel all right. The hunger isn't frightening, it's empowering. I can feed it and have every right to. It's *right* to use my powers, for I've inherited the earth.

No! I rail against it. It's wrong. It doesn't *feel* wrong, but these aren't my thoughts or my feelings. It feels good, but the good feeling is dangerous. It takes away my ability to sense the danger. It gives me what I want. And it can't be trusted.

Despite my attempts I can't feel anxiety about not feeling bad. I wrestle with the hunger and the power, but my feelings won't come to my aid. I have to will this energy away, even though I want it to stay.

I deny the voices. Every ounce of will forces them to silence, tries to drown them out. My mind-words feel empty, ringing hollow in my ears, and the voices can sense it. They argue me down, trying to convince me to give in, but still I deny them.

The voices stop trying to convince me. The flame burns colder and flares up within me. The denied hunger needs to be fed, and if it can't get the sustenance from anywhere else, it'll consume me.

I'm burnt alive from the inside, swallowed by the shadows and their power, my frame no longer able to contain it all. In those last moments, every nerve in my body is singing with pleasure, crying out in ecstatic release as every sensation is burnt away from me.

Sunlight warm on my face. I blink my eyes open, and find I'm lying outside the ruins, on the beach, waves crashing near me. I'm not alone. All around me, other harlings awake as well. No, not harlings: *hara*. My eyes are different now, and I can see that my companions are subtly changed. They have glowing markings across their bodies. The markings are different on each one, though: some have dots, others solid lines, in some cases the patterns are curved and in others all straight lines.

As they wake, they look about at each other, and then down at themselves, realising they're wearing these marks. The har nearest to me stirs just then, and I feel a rush of relief and sorrow. 'Kageso!'

His eyes open at my words, and he stares at me. Written in those eyes is a wealth of pain and loss and sorrow to rival my own. His eyes say he's sorry, and they're filled with horror at the realisation that he tried to kill me, but there's a guarded reproach about the pain. In our final moments, I'd killed him. First, I ran when we were in danger, rather than turning back for him, and when he attacked me I killed him.

What can we say to each other? How do you rebuild any association after that?

I check my body. All the wounds of the night before have vanished. Nohar that I knew from our village is missing. Were all the deaths of the night just dreams, like the visions of our own deaths among the half-hara in the distant past?

'Look!' someone shouts, pointing down the beach. The three elders are approaching, each carrying a bundle of blankets slung over their back. They too have the glowing marks that we all now bear. And I see that, like the rest of us, their markings are different. They approach the young hara in turn and give them blankets in the colours of their tribe. Aurum comes to Kageso and gives him a rough blanket of antelope skin and woven wool. He walks past me, not even meeting my eyes.

The *Althuzi* elder arrives before me and hands me a blanket of heavy grey cotton with bones hanging from woven strings like beads. Wordlessly he moves on, handing out only two more before slinging the rest back over his shoulder. He gazes at each of us and beckons us over. We stand together, looking at each other. Our markings are similar to his, setting us apart from all the others.

'You have been marked as *Althuzi*,' the elder says. 'You have the will and determination to deal with the spirits that inhabit this world. Your old names are best forgotten, just like your former selves. You will be given new names to suit your new lives. You'll be able to visit your families in due time and reclaim any things you may still desire by the end of your training.

'There's no sense in tarrying. Are there any goodbyes you wish to make?'

I shake my head. It seems the others feel the same way.

'Good,' the elder says. 'Follow me.'

He sets a brisk pace. As we walk down the beach, I look back at Kageso one last time. I can't tell whether I'm relieved or sad that his back is turned to me. Could I have borne the look on his face one more time?

I turn my back on him, and the person I'd been, walking towards my future.

Winds of Vengeance

Martina Bellovičová

The view of the Phylarch's estate, as observed from the Eagle's nest, is one of the brightest Freyhellan jewels. It is seated in a lush pine grove amidst two massive mountain peaks, which create a small valley, cut in half by a lively stream. It runs around the east side of the outbuilding, passes the main house and rushes to reach the end of the plateau, where it dives into the depths of a chasm. At night, when nothing but the roar of the waterfall and the occasional hooting of night birds disturbs the peace of the rugged landscape, fires are lit in all the buildings and the entire estate flickers against the starlit sky, glows and shines from its privileged spot, not unlike a mansion of the dehara.

It is a place of great magic, or so our seers believe, because while laying the foundations, the workers uncovered what seemed to be the remains of an ancient temple. Sagga, the Second of Five, claims to have experienced a vision upon entering the newly-built estate for the first time. For a moment, he found himself standing in a large wooden temple, surrounded by men, women and children clad in simple white robes, who moved from one statue to another to receive their blessings.

The air was heavy with smoke and the metallic smell of blood, which pooled on the footworn ground in the centre of the temple. The crimson surface would stir in irregular intervals, upset by new droplets of liquid falling from above. Looking up, Sagga beheld a young male, suspended from the timberwork in a spread-eagle position, his deflated lungs expertly pulled out of the broken mess of his ribcage and folded on his back like a pair of wings.

We are, essentially, much closer to those seafaring Norsemen of the olden times who worshipped in that temple, reaching out in the dark towards a universe filled with divinity, than to their modern successors, whose attempts to rid the grand and rugged landscapes of their mysteries caused much harm. Of course, we no longer bring sentient offerings to our dehara, nor do we raid neighbouring lands for resources, but we do share the same spirit. A sense of freedom and perpetual passion for adventure, forged by the ocean, that continuously lashes itself into fury against the great cliffs of Freyhellan shores.

Those blue seas have been my second home ever since I turned twelve years of age. After 386 days on shore, tonight's gathering in the Phylarch's hall is of prime importance to me. If I fail to prove I am on the top of my abilities, I may not be assigned a ship and instead spend the summer in somehar else's crew, or worse – I could be stranded here for the entirety of a year. Another year I cannot afford to lose. Tonight, I will attempt to enter Aegira's Nayati and demand his covert support. Before the trail goes cold, I must sail.

Fires burned bright tonight under the midnight sun, as hara from wide and far assembled in council. Some sailed to Freygard and undertook the rest of the journey on foot, climbing up the rocky path beside the majestic waterfall. Others crossed the mountains and yet more rode their steeds through forests and plains from east and west. Several camps rose on the clearing surrounding the estate, each bustling with life.

Crossing the bridge over the river, I could already make out voices interwoven with the sound of laughter as well as a distinctive mixture of smells: mead, heavy ale, grassy smoke, fresh pastry and roast meat. As I approached, one familiar face after another appeared in the crowd, but I could also see many whom I did not recognise. Most were smiling, undoubtedly already a little drunk, even though the afternoon was only just about to spill into the evening.

It might have been due solely to the overall atmosphere of joy, but almost everyhar I happened to pass by offered me a handshake, a friendly greeting or a clap on the shoulder, and drinks were shared more easily than usual. When Mikkel, the best navigator in Freyhella and my former shipmate, passed me a horn filled to the brim with golden mead, I finally took the chance to stop and take in the entire gathering with a sweeping glance.

'I don't recall hara being this excited about the annual council since I was a harling...'

Mikkel raised a bushy eyebrow in what appeared to be a

conspiratorial manner. 'Curiosity is a mighty witch.'

'What's so important? I might have missed a thing or two during the last year or so...' Apparently, I really had, because my question instantly made him chuckle.

'Haven't you heard? Týr is going to present his soon-to-be chesnari at the gathering. A pretty young thing he brought home from Aislann, they say.'

'Is that right?' I brought the horn to my lips and took a deliberately slow gulp, pondering how this could influence Týr's mood and the decisions he was going to make. Surely the prospective bonding meant happiness and, by default, generosity...?

Having persuaded myself that this was definitely a good thing, I flashed my best smile and raised the horn. 'Well, then! To the Phylarch and his chesnari, may they have a long and happy life!'

The toast was the first, but by no means the last one I made that evening. The hall, tremendous in its size and splendour, seated a hundred and fifty hara comfortably and almost two hundred if they squeezed. Everything was festively decorated, a massive chandelier crafted out of a whale's ribcage illuminated the entire space, and Týr's househara kept the tables perpetually full. The usual Northern drink is ale, but this time, delicious mead was being poured just as often, and we feasted heartily upon huge portions of boar's flesh, then gorged ourselves to the full on cranberry pie.

A tall, handsome, stately har, Týr was seated on an elevated platform in the middle of the largest table, clad in regal robes with a full bearskin thrown over his shoulders. It was impossible not to notice the lively young har on Týr's right, clad in pure white robes with long flaxen hair, crowned with heron plumes. He was just about the right mixture of charm and boldness, laughing without inhibitions, yet keeping his voice down and his eyes on Týr, whenever the Phylarch spoke.

Once the main course was finished, and the assembled hara, sated and content, could fully concentrate, the Phylarch rose and silenced the hall with three loud knocks of his goblet against the table.

'Everyhar having a good time?'

The answer to his question came immediately, in the form of loud cheers — as though as he had said something spectacularly clever.

'Then let the annual gathering commence! Before we start

debating and continue feasting, I can already tell you that the upcoming season will bring forth many changes and provide ample opportunities for adventure. But first, I have an announcement to make.' The Phylarch's eyes shifted almost unnoticeably to his right and his companion obediently rose, reaching for Týr's hand.

'This is Galdra, an exceptional har, whom I have decided to make an important part of my, and thereby your, future. Starting from now, you will show him the same respect you show me. His word will be second only to mine. And of course, you'll be invited to our formal bonding in due time!'

The two of them enjoyed a standing ovation for a moment; Galdra remained silent through it all, though his lively eyes disclosed he had much to say. He was reading us, I was sure, perhaps more closely than the five seers, who dwelled in the shadows near the main fireplace. And finally, as soon as the buzz subsided, the main subject of my interest was brought up.

'I expect all of you are eager to hear where we are going to sail to.' Týr's steady gaze swept the entire hall slowly, as though he was building a fleet in his mind. Each year, as soon as the spring blessed the land with its colours and the last remainders of ice crust melted into the sea, the Phylarch would announce the destinations of voyages planned for the season, which lasted until early fall. After that, the northern routes were considered off limits, since ships were in danger of getting trapped in ice when temperatures dropped, as well as being exposed to volatile elements that made movement on the deck an impossibility.

'I decided to split the fleet into three divisions,' he announced. 'One of them will remain here in order to provide for Freygard and protect the capital in case of need, the other will embark on a journey to the southwestern lands, and the last one will sail back to the Land of Ice. As you surely know, we have a situation there that needs to be resolved – and I cannot stress enough that I would prefer to have it done peacefully.'

A hum of agreement resounded through the crowd, yet... Did I hear a sarcastic snort at the word "peacefully"? Apparently, Týr heard it too, because he looked my way, searching for a culprit. I remained completely calm as I met his gaze, giving a slight nod so as to show we were in agreement. The sea ice surrounding the large island made it accessible solely during the three warmest months of the year and I was not going to risk having to wait another full cycle to get there, courtesy of being sarcastic.

'Furthermore, a single ship will be sent to Alba Sulh on a diplomatic mission,' he continued, omitting all the details. They would only be disclosed to ship captains at a later date. 'Galdra and myself will retire to my study shortly, where we will be speaking to prospective captains one by one. If you have what it takes and are willing to command a ship, come to see me.'

The rest of the topics discussed that evening were of little interest to me. Sure, the rebuilding of the port, agricultural progress, reforms in the law, caste education, or trading with Alba Sulh were all good things, but I had my mind set on the land, where I had lost half of my soul. There was a score I needed to settle, and until that happened, I could not rest.

Not wanting to appear overzealous, I waited half an hour before visiting the Phylarch, allowing three others to have their chance. We were not rivals per se, as the fleet required a number of skilled sailors with experience in command. What endangered my position was not another har, but my own demons. Still, a year had passed since I had been temporarily demoted, and Týr was not a leader known for giving inadequate punishments.

He welcomed me with a smile and a goblet of dark ale, which I gladly accepted. Anything to drown the butterflies in my stomach. With an all-embracing gesture, I was invited to take a seat wherever I pleased, which consolidated the informality of the audience.

'I am glad to see you here, Njörd,' Týr reassured me. 'Your absence has been noticed – as was to be expected of one, whose name channels the god of the sea. Still, I have to ask.... How are you?'

'I am well. I have been helping Ville with building ships in the recent months, trying to contribute in a meaningful way... But I am ready to answer my true calling once again.'

'No, Njörd. I mean it: how *are* you?'

It was impossible to escape his piercing eyes or the sharp edge to his voice. I folded my hands in my lap, returning his look with what I hoped seemed like complete sincerity.

'I am... coping.' With a bitter smile, I took a sip of the ale, pondering how to elaborate. 'You know how it goes. It gets worse before it gets better, but now... I believe I've done all the thinking a har possibly can, and I am, mostly, at peace.'

'I hear you've been doing more than just thinking.' His tone made it obvious that he meant *who* I had been doing rather than what. Technically, that was none of his business, though.

'Whatever helps.' I shrugged, dismissing the concern. 'It wasn't really helping all that much, anyway. I toned it down. Now I believe I am on the right track. The best for me would be to return to the Land of Ice in order to gain closure.'

For a moment, there was silence between us, so profound that I could almost hear the sound of his thoughts as he considered my words.

'I know you are one of my best,' he said finally, 'and when you say you are ready to take over responsibility again, I have no reason to mistrust you. But the matter with the Land of Ice... it needs to be handled as smoothly as possible. The prosperous settlement we wanted to help create there is still very much my priority and it is my intention to send hara, who will be able to assess the current situation without bias and, if possible, resolve it peacefully. By this, I do not mean justice won't be served. However, a violent conflict of a larger scale should be our very last resort. I have to admit that your personal involvement doesn't exactly make you the most qualified person for the task.'

Nothing he said caught me by surprise; this was what I had prepared for. I let no emotion show as I shook my head and spoke up in the politest tone I could manage. 'In fact, I believe myself to be uniquely qualified, exactly because I am more involved than anyhar else. It was Ylwa's dream to help those people, see them content in their new lives. There is nothing I want more than to make certain the colony thrives and is self-sufficient. Otherwise, he died for nothing.'

My answer was well-rehearsed, and I had planned more equally fitting comebacks in case the discussion continued. However, it seemed that my first attempt was persuasive enough, because Týr's eyes cleared and he flashed a smile my way.

'I am glad to hear it. I will assign you a ship. You may reunite with your old crew or recruit whomever you see fit.'

The white nights of Freyhellan summers are unforgiving in a peculiar way. Whatever activity you choose to engage in, you have to count on the fact that there is no chance it will remain hidden under the cloak of darkness. Tents may offer a partial sanctuary, but after the official end of the council, most of them were instantly occupied by pairs or small groups, seeking bliss in heavy ale, mulled wine, particular kinds of mushrooms and in each other's bodies – not necessarily in this order.

I, too, felt a distinct longing for comfort after leaving the hall, but the idea of possible witnesses did not sit very well with me. These unfortunate circumstances drove me to the very outskirts of the camps in search of lonely wanderers, lovers of solitude and those who simply wished for a bit of silence. Preferably, I hoped to find a complete stranger. Had I been a bit less drunk, I might have hated myself for this desperation, but that night, I was far beyond the point of caring.

My steps aimed for the edge of the forest, where a hideout could easily be found. The Sun already shone high in the sky, but thankfully the day was turning out to be overcast. Thick fog suited the melancholic mood that overtook me after one too many drinks; above me, long grey strips of cloud drifted across the sky. A few fires were still smouldering; I chose one at random and followed the thin lace of its smoke.

The bony, disfigured body I found there, hunched under an old blanket, almost scared me at first; it had nothing in common with the lithe harish form I had hoped to see. I made a half circle around the fire, approaching cautiously, until I got close enough to make out his features. The face of this being... I had never seen such ugliness in my life. His skin sagged and wrinkled to an extent that could only be likened to an aged apple and its colour wasn't far off either. The eyes, dark and glazed-over, were almost entirely covered by overhanging lids, and the way his lips puckered indicated he had few or no teeth.

Observing this abomination, I felt great wrath rise from the pit of my stomach, growing like a landslide in early spring. Oh, to remove him from the face of Earth! It mattered little that this particular human had not caused me any injustice; no member of their species can be trusted. To find him there, in the vicinity of the Phylarch's estate, was nothing short of a sacrilege. My shock was so profound that I must have stared at him longer than I had thought, because I only came around when a cold hand gently squeezed my forearm.

'You have never seen old Mads?' asked a honey-sweet voice to my left. 'He lives in a solitary hut up in the mountains. I'm not quite sure what he's doing here – perhaps he longed for a taste of our way of life. In any case, the human is not dangerous, only exceptionally repulsive.'

My new companion was a petite har with impossibly blue eyes and long off-white hair arranged into an intricate pattern of tiny braids. He had a beautiful smile that somehow managed to capture both mischievousness and melancholy.

'I did not think him dangerous,' I was quick to assure the har, not mentioning that had he not encountered me, I might have been a danger for the old man. 'It is just that his appearance was so unexpected. I didn't even know there were any humans still alive in Freyhella.'

Just the one, I believe. You should quit stalking him. No matter how long you look, he will not become any younger. You'll only upset him... He must be quite sad already, living in a world where he is only a guest.' Despite the late hour, the har's bold make-up was not smudged in the slightest. The hand on my arm showed no signs of ever having done manual work, which was unusual in our lands.

'We are all but guests here,' I reminded him, not buying into the sympathetic melancholy. But he was, of course, right. I turned away reluctantly from the human and followed the har deeper into the trees, where he had built a tiny sanctuary for himself from branches and furs. The mixed smell of incense and aruna leaked out, tickling my nose. He crawled through the narrow opening and lay down on the furs, beckoning for me to enter.

Why would I not? It was, after all, what I had been looking for. Most of the wrath had dissipated by then and the rest could as well be released in a way more pleasant than others. Unceremoniously, I flopped down onto the pile of furs, looking up at him in expectation. The corners of his lips jerked upwards in a suppressed smile.

'Relax, Njörd.'

Before I could marvel at the fact that he obviously knew who I was, while I had not the slightest clue about his identity, we were sharing breath and in a few passionate seconds, he had me almost completely undressed. I refused to allow him to keep believing he was in charge here, and so I caught the hand that was just about to slide into my pants by the wrist.

'And who might you be...?' I hissed.

The har was not taken off guard at all. He calmly lowered his head and placed a gentle kiss on the back of my hand, urging me to loosen my grip. The golden rain of his braids spilled over his shoulders and into my lap, tickling my bare stomach.

'I am the dehar of consolation, sent out to kiss away the tears of mourners and pour balm into hearts wrung by grief.'

That hit a little too close to home. I felt somewhat humiliated because of what he might have heard of me, if this was what he believed I would like to hear. Perhaps my anger had not entirely dissipated after all, because I couldn't stop myself from stating what I had been suspecting for quite some time. 'You are a kanene.'

He remained surprisingly non-offended and the roll of his heavy-lidded eyes hinted at mild amusement. 'Does that have to exclude the former?'

That made me laugh and, as if by miracle, the heavy atmosphere in the shelter was lifted. 'It doesn't.'

He would do. In fact, he was ideal, because knowing he was going to see this through for the coin made everything so much easier. There would be no blame placed, no morning regrets, no hysterics, no explanations asked.

Sensing my willingness, he leaned in for a kiss, before expertly unfastening his robes. In the tiny space we had at our disposal, it seemed almost impossible to make undressing a sensual show, but he handled it most creatively. As he descended upon me, it became clear that this dehar of consolation belonged to those who tend to assume rather than ask, and in my case, he was in for a surprise.

'You want me to...'

I could see the confusion in his eyes as the realisation dawned upon him. In a way, it was understandable; most of those who were willing to pay for aruna only wished to claim their prize. 'If that is no problem.'

A mischievous sparkle lit up in his eyes. 'No problem at all.'

He took me with the vigour of a har, who burned with a bright fire, but did not often get to be ouana. Deep down, it pleased me to know that this act would bring each of us something we craved, even though physical satisfaction was of little importance to me. It only served as a vessel that enabled me to descend deep into myself, open all my secret chambers and navigate them to the one place I desired to reach. I could hear him gasp in shock as it happened, but I no longer saw his face, nor did I hear the faintest echo of his voice.

It is a both an immense blessing and a heavy burden to carry a gate inside one's core, through which the spirit can walk to the edge of our world and beyond, through the unseen and the uncreated to that long gone. The paths are only imagined here, but I never stray. In the centre of this timeless space, a large tree took root and grew to such marvellous height that even my mind's eye cannot see its top. Its evergreen branches provide a pleasant kind of shade, creating a misleading sense of safety. I rush towards it, only vaguely recalling the physical stimulation of the body I've left behind.

This is where we meet. Sensing his presence, I smile into the darkness, which slowly dissolves, touching my hair, eyelids, cheeks and lips with its fingers of smoke. There is an incessant buzz in my ears, a kind of pressure not unlike the one you feel when, after diving into great depths, you attempt to reach the surface too quickly. Knowing that it will subside, I ignore this inconvenience and reach out for the form that is only just taking shape.

'Ylwa.'

When we come together, it is both painfully less and infinitely more than an embrace. It feels as if somehar is hugging me from within, filling each empty space with raw emotion, whose depths no mind could fathom.

I miss you, I miss you, I miss you.

'So do I, Ylwa. Ag, you have no idea.'

For the longest moment, we simply hold on to each other with all we have, relishing the fact that here, in a place outside of space and time, our bond is as strong as ever and we can just... be. Yet we know we cannot let the agelessness of the here and now fool us, because down on the Earth, the seconds are ticking away. Sooner rather than later, I will be pulled back and forced to wait for an excruciating couple of days until we can briefly meet again.

Talk to me, Njörd. Tell me everything.

'Alright, let me tell you all the news. There was a gathering, and I got my ship back today. Everyhar and their hostling were there, because Týr is going to get bonded. His chesnari looks both cute and smart, I bet you would like him. Tomorrow, I will head home and get ready, then in a couple of days it's back to the sea for me.'

I am glad. It is about time, isn't it? You've been wasting your potential lately.

'You've been saying that a lot lately...'

I just want the best for you. My life might have ended, but yours goes on. I want to hear that you're living it.

All this time, and he still doesn't get it. I may be alive, but I only breathe for two things: these surreal moments and revenge.

'As long as I have this, I will be alright.'

His facial features are somewhat foggy on this plane, as though he's hidden behind a thin veil, but I still notice the melancholy that overtakes them.

Sometimes I'm not certain if our moments together are not harmful for you, but by all the dehara, I don't wish to give them up.

'Then don't! I need you, you know...'

But he is already slipping away into the darkness. Panic overtakes me and wrenches my very soul, until I realise he has not really moved on; it is me who is being pulled away from him – violently. I try to grip something I can hold on to, but the tree branches are too high, and my fingertips can only just about touch the lowest leaves, too fragile to grasp. Struggling like a fish out of water, I am snatched up and whirled away by a powerful force.

On the earthly plane, my body found itself on the verge of release and I was violently returned to it, so that I could experience the high. Yet my cry was more of frustration than of fulfilment. Instead of relishing the afterglow, I inspected the kanene's flushed face. Had he noticed anything? Most hara do, but they cannot quite put their finger on it; some fear they made me with pearl, others suspect I might have used them for some kind of magic.

This one was a professional. He mentioned nothing of the extraordinary connection as he pulled his clothing back on; all he did was outstretch his hand and give me a piercing, marginally intimidating look, which could only mean he had just decided I would pay a non-standard fare.

Home – a strange name for a patch of rocky land, a few fields and a lively stream surrounded by trees. There is a moderately large house made of red wood with stables and a barn, perpetually empty. Attached to it is a weak attempt at a flower garden, the remnants of last year's outplanting, either rotten or frozen, scattered on the ground in intricate patterns of decay. A northern-type sauna stands in the front yard, out of use for over a year.

None of that means much to me anymore. In a few days, I will embark on a journey. The strange vacuum of time until then is mine to fill as I please, so that day I packed a blanket and hiked upstream, hoping to find the one place that I actually might miss while I'm gone – a little clearing around the river bend, one particular pebbled beach on the waterfront. Just like I used to with Ylwa, I took off my shoes and waded through the stream, where it was shallow enough.

Ice-cold water, drowned in the sand. I savoured the needles of pain attacking my ankles, for pain is a privilege of the living. It distracts one's attention from the emptiness inside. Even the Sun was hurting, bathing its broken rays in the freezing stream and colouring it blood red.

I returned to the shore and looked around, comparing the groups of trees and the waterline with the images etched in my memory – yes, that was the place, our first fishing spot! We used to sit on the flattened stones over there, and... right there was where I accidentally dropped the can with bait into the grass. *You think the fish will come flying and start pecking on these?* he'd asked, laughing.

The day was for goodbyes. Not the hugs and cheers upon embarking on a sail that awaited us soon in Freygard, but for the silent, personal ones. Most were spending as much time as possible with their families, but all I had was there: that tranquillity, those memories. An insufficient bandage to cover the cleft of clefts, the yawning gulf of despair. Still, I would never exchange it for anyhar else's company.

Once upon a time, a wise har told me that if you wanted to know whether you could spend the rest of your life with another, you had to take them fishing. Those long hours of exquisite boredom, waiting for a catch, are perfect for learning everything you need to know about the other. With Ylwa, the time passed like a breath. I still carry them with me, those silver nightfalls, when even whispering sounded out of place, and so we remained silent, as the weight of the world evaporated in the growing darkness; those golden dawns after a sleepless night, when ice-cold dew could only be fought by a warm embrace.

I never took anyhar fishing after him.

Staying there overnight would not bring me closure, neither would it help me recapture the moments etched into my memory. Regardless, it was what I needed.

On the way back from my hike, I was surprised to find a tall figure clad in dark robes seated on my porch. Unusually dark hair, adorned with pearls and raven feathers disclosed the har's identity from afar: Skaddi, the Second of Five and Tyr's left hand. His right hand, I assumed, was still overseeing the guests, who had chosen to stay a couple of days longer, making certain no harm would come to the household. That meant the Phylarch had sent to me his second-best; this rang of great importance. What was Skaddi doing here?

I was in no rush to join him. Obviously, he was well-trained in the art of exercising patience, for he wasn't showing any signs of impatience as he watched me approach. As soon as I stepped onto the wooden porch, he rose so elegantly that I hadn't even noticed him doing so.

He nodded in my general direction. 'Good day, Tiahaar Njörd. I apologise for failing to announce my arrival in advance.'

Stiff as a stick and with more formalality than the Phylarch could ever hope to achieve.

'No problem at all. Sorry you had to wait. Would you like to join me for a cup of hot cider?'

'That would be agreeable.'

From the way he moved, I could tell he was even more rigid in his stance than usual. That made me wonder how long he had been sitting there. For all I knew, he could have arrived last evening and been forced to spend the entire night on my porch. I will not lie; the mental image was amusing.

Skaddi followed me to the kitchen silently, politely refraining from commenting on the mess my place was, but his eyes darted left and right and every now and then, his eyebrows would sharply jerk up.

'Yeah, I could use a househar,' I admitted reluctantly, although I couldn't have cared less about what he thought of my way of life. We used to have somehar to do the chores, but after Ylwa's death, I largely preferred solitude rather than clean floors. To make up for the inhospitable surroundings, I decided to share with him my favourite kind of cider, lingonberry.

'Alright, Skaddi. Spill it. What brings you here?' I asked directly as I knelt down to start the fire. I couldn't help it, his rigid formality had always made me act more casually than was appropriate with a har of his standing, perhaps to achieve some balance.

'I come bearing an urgent message from the Phylarch.'

That actually made me stop and stare – a fruitless attempt, of course, because his expression was, as usually, perfectly unreadable.

'Since when does Týr use you as a messenger? Don't you have your hands full, what with divining the future and all that?'

'There has been a change of plan.' Skaddi didn't take the bait and remained emotionally detached as he delivered his blow. 'The Land of Ice is off limits for you this summer. You and your crew are needed elsewhere.'

'...come again?' My eyebrows knitted together as I tried to process the information, betraying my refusal to accept it.

'You are to report to the docks the day after tomorrow at one hour past noon, prepared for a journey to Alba Sulh.'

I busied myself with pouring the cider, pondering the news. Alba Sulh... I recalled Týr had mentioned that a single ship would be dedicated to this diplomatic mission, the purpose of which hadn't been revealed. However, the discussion I'd had with him left me feeling that my wish was going to be granted. Why would he reconsider?

'The Phylarch doesn't trust me?' I tried to ask as calmly as possible while handing Skaddi his goblet.

'Oh, I am afraid this is entirely my fault. The Seers from Alba Sulh require my assistance in an intriguing ritual, which is to be performed six days from now. I asked for the most reliable ship, as my task is of utmost importance, and yours came to mind...'

My grip on the goblet tightened, and I could feel that I had burnt my hand a little, but that was of no consequence. Not when this untouchable creature had effortlessly destroyed everything that still mattered to me. If I only could, I would have knocked him off his chair then and there and used it to break his conniving skull, but that would have gotten me nowhere. Trying to hurt Skaddi for the stab in my back would only belittle me in Týr's eyes. Since it was crystal clear to me that he wouldn't be reasoned with either, there was only one thing left for me to do.

'Fine, you may deliver the message that I'll be there. I will be expecting you, as well as any cargo the Phylarch wishes us to transport, thirty minutes prior to our departure at the latest.'

That finally squeezed a hint of surprise out of him; he had probably expected me to cause more trouble. In the next second, though, Skaddi's features settled back to complete indifference, which I now knew to be feigned. The only thing left was an unsettling kind of gleam in his eyes. As he tilted his head in order to get a better look at me, I was almost intimidated. It felt as if he was trying to see inside my head and strip me of all my secrets, and his piercing gaze was further enhanced by the birdlike quality of both his thin body and feathered attire.

'I shall see to it.'

When he finally looked away, there was a light smirk on his lips, hinting he might have been successful at finding out things about me nohar else knew. And perhaps... Perhaps he had known all along. In either case, I had already been unsettled enough for one day.

'Good,' I said icily, crossing my arms on my chest. 'And now, get out of my house.'

Skaddi's right eyebrow flew up, making him look rather comical. 'Excuse me?!'

'I mean it, Skaddi. Get out and don't ever try to fuck with me again.'

For a moment, I thought he was going to implode, but after a second of unbearable silence, he shrugged and huffily turned on his heel, slamming the door behind him. The momentary justification was totally worth it, but I still found myself in a disastrous situation. The abrupt change of conditions had made it crystal clear that the only possible way for me to sail to the Land of Ice was a mutiny. And I had exactly a day and half to organise one.

I gathered them in Ville's loghouse; a skeleton crew of twenty-nine hara I trusted most, handpicked from those I had sailed with in the previous years. The shipwright had constructed his home in a secluded place. Far away from the rush of Freygard, it was surrounded by dense forests, overlooking the sea. The only other settlement nearby was a lumber mill that kept Ville supplied with all the wood he needed for his projects, and at the time I had chosen for our meeting, it was already closed for the day.

The ship is a world apart from anything else. After spending so much time with a group of hara in a very restricted space, going through the same hardships and sharing all kinds of experiences and adventures, you get to know them in a most profound way. The crew becomes a proud, tight-knit community, and bonds between shipmates often last a lifetime, regardless of societal or generational divides. Such ties cannot be found elsewhere or recreated artificially. Once exposed to the elements, you can't afford to keep around anyhar you can't absolutely rely on. This time, though, I had to handpick the special few, whose bonds to the ship run even deeper, overshadowing whatever relationship they might have with their homes or their families. Those, about whom I could surmise that they shared my opinions. Adventurous souls, who placed honour first and doubts second.

And even still, it was a betting game.

Aegir, my third in command on our last journey, was the first to arrive. 'Njörd! What amazing news!' he called, halfway through the door. He hurried to shake my hand. Innocent in their cluelessness, his eyes shone with excitement. 'I can't even tell you just how happy I was to hear that we all get to sail together again.'

'Trust me, so was I.' I returned the sentiment, but my insides were squirming.

The loghouse slowly began to fill with friends, some of whom I had been out of touch with during the past year, and their cheerful attitude created an atmosphere that made it extremely difficult to ask them to make such a hard choice. They were glad we would soon be back together, and I let them enjoy the reunion for a while, because once I revealed my intentions, there would be no going back.

When the door had closed behind the twenty-ninth har, I finally began to speak. 'It is good to see you all.' My eyes locked on those closest to me. 'Tomorrow will be a fateful day and I couldn't ask for a better crew to share it with.' I quieted the murmurs of agreement, pleasant as they may have been, and proceeded to what needed to be said.

'However, there's something we must discuss before we set sail. And the nature of the matter at hand demands complete secrecy. Therefore, I must ask all of you to swear that whatever you hear tonight won't leave these walls.'

As I spoke, the expressions on my shipmates' faces slowly changed from joyful through confused to a broader mix of emotions.

'Drat, I should have known this wasn't a reunion celebration,' Mikkel chuckled, eyeing the pitcher of mead he had brought with him.

Ville gave him the look that usually made his dog crawl under the bed. 'Njörd is being serious,' he said, keeping his voice down as though somehar could hear us even there, in the seclusion of his home. 'As far as I'm concerned, you've never been here. That's my story and I'll stick to it if anyone comes to ask.'

Silence spread its wings over the entire group; Ville wasn't a har of empty words – or even words in general. He was completely content to spend days polishing his woodworks into perfection without saying anything at all, and when he did speak, there was always a meaning in it.

'Alright,' came an uncertain voice. 'Of course we'll keep silence.'

One after another, they all swore that no matter their opinion on what they were going to here, nohar would speak a word about it to outsiders.

That was the easier part.

'As you may or may not know, we've been assigned the special task of transporting the seer Skaddi to Alba Sulh, where he's expected to attend some kind of ritual. Meanwhile, others will continue preparations for the return to the Land of Ice and they'll depart in a week, by which time we won't yet have returned. This mission will effectively prevent us from having any influence on the situation over there, and I won't stand by that.'

The picture I painted was rewarded with a handful of heartfelt invectives as well as sounds of disbelief.

'We can't let that happen... right?' Fjaer demanded, rightful anger making his voice shaky. 'If anyhar should have a say about the colony, it's you!'

He was damn right. According to our law, the family of the victim decided on the murderer's punishment, and Ylwa had nohar else but me on this world.

'I *am* going to seek justice on his behalf, no matter what,' I confirmed, taking a deep breath and releasing it slowly. 'But I cannot do it alone. Which is why I have a proposal for you. Let them think we are sailing to Alba Sulh – the route is identical for the first two days. Then we change direction and start heading North. At that rate, we will arrive in the colony first, and it will be us who captures the murderer.'

The silence that followed was full of muffled whispers and half-concealed signs, which made me feel as if I was standing on a pillory, uncomfortably exposed. It was unclear whether or not agreement would be reached, when finally Mikkel spoke up.

'I do believe that Marluk should be punished according to our law. And I think your concerns are valid. This change of plans... The only logical reason can be that either Týr or Skaddi want to take that away from you. I can't stand for that. Count me in.'

'But why?' Dagný wondered aloud, absentmindedly playing with the lucky rune pendant on his neck. 'Makes no sense to me.'

The shadow that was Ville detached itself from the wall and, again, make a shocking observation: 'Týr thinks Njörd lost it a while ago. He doesn't expect him to be lawful once he gets to the Land of Ice, if you know what I mean.'

I certainly knew what he meant, even if not the others did. Despite the impression I hoped to have made the night before, the Phylarch labelled me a lunatic.

'He coddles the colony like a bunch of harlings,' Fjaer, our youngest, burst out. 'Not so long ago, it was full of filthy humans, half starved to death. They need to be taught, not spoilt. And all this lack of trust in somehar, because they mourn in their own way, that's just low.'

His honest words bought back memories. Around this time last year, we had arrived in a desolate land occupied by a few barely-surviving, half-wild humans, yet what we left behind was a small colony in its beginnings, populated with new hara. Ylwa was more than willing to teach the inhabitants of Nuuk everything they needed to thrive. Instead of receiving gratefulness, the only other Freyhellan present had to escape the island alone on a small fishing boat. It was only thanks to the mercy of nature that he lived to tell us the story.

'I realise I ask a lot of you. Too much, perhaps.' I lowered my eyes, afraid that they would reflect the sudden weakness that threatened to overcome me. 'And if you agree to support me, there will be consequences. This may very well be a one-way journey. But I still hope some of you will join me, because you knew and loved Ylwa, which means that, hopefully, you want him avenged as much as I do.'

It was unrealistic to expect the entire crew would throw away their lives in Freyhella, but I didn't need all of them. Twenty, or twenty-two would be just enough to man the ship. Which, on second thoughts, was still a considerably high number.

Of all the things that could have broken the silence, it was the sound of liquid being poured that did it. On the other side of the table, Mikkel took a long swig from his cup and passed the bottle of mead to the har on his left. 'I hear there are truly amazing lands down South.' He wiped his mouth with the back of his hand and leaned into his chair in a relaxed manner. 'Places where nohar has ever seen snow, and you don't have to wait until bedtime to see a beautiful, naked body, because they hardly cover themselves.'

As though the stone of decision had been removed from their shoulders, others seemed to open themselves to the idea after his absurd remark. Some began making tentative plans, concealing their concern with jokes, others took the liberty to put their rightful anger on display, cursing Skaddi and promising Marluk a painful end. Only two of them left the loghouse, and even that was with reluctance; they had families in Freyhella and couldn't abandon them.

This was understandable. What I found harder to believe was that the majority chose to stay. They were all with me, twenty-seven of them, and the gravity of the moment overwhelmed me to the point that I had to blink a few times to clear my vision. If only Ylwa could see this, I thought. He would be so proud...

Ironically, the world was painted in gorgeous colours on the day of our departure. Deep green forests, glistening jewels of lakes, grand mountain tops, colourful thatch-roofed houses and, of course, majestic fjords with clear blue skies above – all the beauty of nature seemed intent on mocking me. Upon my arrival at the port, I couldn't help but notice the swell of overwhelming optimism that usually comes with the first voyage of the season. I used to feel this drive myself, but this time I was only nervous.

The voyage that lay ahead of me was not going to be easy. Moreover, it would have a negative impact, not only on my own future, but also on the fate of the entire crew. As I watched them greet each other with back-slapping, pull up the sails, share a bottle of mead and toss supplies on board, I began to have second thoughts. I could still decide to back down and obediently sail to Alba Sulh, giving up the chance of confronting Ylwa's murderers personally, thereby sparing the others a life spent in exile.

It was but a momentary lapse in conviction, or so I attempted to persuade myself as I chased the thought away. I had my priorities straight, thus I would play the only card I had up my sleeve and wait to see whose hand was stronger: mine, or fate's. According to the position of the Sun, it was almost noon when I put two fingers in my mouth and gave them my loudest whistle. Every head in my field of vision turned.

In previous years, I had usually given a little speech before the first sail of the summer, which served to embolden the crew, tighten the collective and help them set clear goals. This time, they all knew they could not expect anything of that kind from me, as the cards had already been laid out on the table. In approximately an hour, we were to pass the point of no return, and I needed to make sure they were still in.

'You know I trust you all with my life,' I claimed, looking across the upper deck in an encompassing glance. My crew: capable and courageous, tempered by many hardships, independent yet loyal, always prepared to have each other's back. 'And I hope that once the blood debt has been paid, there will be only adventures of the best kind waiting for us on our way south. But I do have to ask you one last time: is this really what you want? I don't have a choice, but you... You may still return home.'

There was no debate, no insecurity in their body language, no apparent doubts. 'Captain,' Aegir stepped forward, 'I believe I speak for all of us when I say that going home would also mean going back on our word, and we would never do that.'

And so we embarked on our journey, the sea welcoming us with its best demeanour. Its surface wrinkled only in small, timid waves, whose quivering and changing hues were a joy to behold. By day, the Sun graced us with warm rays of gold. At night, the Moon shone brightly in the sky, accompanied by plentiful constellations that helped us navigate the ship. The most prominent one, shining the brightest, was the Spinning Wheel, also called Orion's Girdle by hara from the South. Favoured by gentle breezes, we were being wafted towards Alba Sulh without great effort on our part.

Among the crew, the enthusiasm characteristic of the beginnings of each sail prevailed. If any of my shipmates had doubts about what we aimed to do, they were keeping them to themselves. During the first two days, one could almost forget the pact we had made and the consequences it could have. Skaddi made himself scarce, which everyhar felt grateful for. He kept mainly to the lower deck, praying, as he had haughtily announced, to the spirits of the sea and wind. Prior to his arrival, we had decided not to disclose our intentions to him until he himself noticed that our supposed destination was nowhere in sight. So far, there was no way in which he could have suspected anything untoward, but I was keenly aware that this circumstance would change very soon.

Still, it was amazing just to be in the moment, to breathe the salty air and feel the wind playing in my hair. Just like the good old days. While my heart belonged to Ylwa in its entirety, a part of my soul was tied to the sea, in which I was able to find deep consolation. It was only in the evenings, when the singing and drinking was all done with, that I felt a touch of loneliness. Along with it came the desire to share the positive experience of our journey with the one I sorely missed.

On the second evening, Fjaer and myself were the last hara still awake, because we had found a common topic. Among the deep, peaceful breaths and somewhat annoying snoring sounds, we talked silently in mind touch about humans in general and the inhabitants of the colony in particular. Fjaer's first sail had been the cursed journey, during which our fleet had discovered the hostile shores of the Land of Ice, and it had left a deep impression on him. He remembered the state in which we had found several small settlements on the massive island – each a frightening vision of sickness, famine, death, ugliness, decay and primitiveness.

I believe we had all been shaken by the discovery, most likely because it showed us what the entire post-apocalyptic world might have looked like, if Wraeththu had not been created. Or perhaps because it showed us where we came from? Of course, many of us had once been human, but after their transformation such hara had forgotten all about their past life. I do not remember a single occasion when humanity had been mentioned in association with anyhar I knew. It seemed no more than a discarded snakeskin.

In any case, for those born har, that discovery represented the first contact with a large number of humans. For those who had been incepted, it brought back unpleasant memories and sparked off a realisation: *this could have been me*. Most of the inhabitants of the measly settlements, slumped on the waterfront, had been sickly or malformed, some outright dying. All of them had been dirty, dressed in rags and furs that hardly shielded them from the biting cold, with inadequately-treated wounds. None had eaten regularly in what must have been years. And that was just the beginning. They had seemed violent and primitive, more like a pack of wild animals than our ancestors, treating each other with brutal cruelty, stealing anything they could get their hands on and speaking in an inarticulate way.

Yet there were some younger ones among them, fewer than forty when collected from all the settlements we'd found. Týr had thought we ought to help them, undoubtedly enthusiastic about turning the freshly discovered island into a prosperous colony of Freyhella, thereby expanding his dominion. It seemed to be an easy victory, since the only blood spilled belonged to the decaying old men and frail women. Once the prospective hara were incepted, we would aid them with the first steps of their new lives and provide for them until the colony became self-sustaining. One day, it would hopefully become our formidable northernmost outpost.

Ylwa, the most generous creature ever born, had not been interested in the economic side of the endeavour. He had made the colony his project, hoping to make their transition from human to har as smooth as it could be. As a renowned Hienama, he'd chosen to stay behind and perform all the inceptions, while we were supplying the colony with food, seeds to grow crops and herds of live sheep. Along with him, the farmer and fisherman Ottar had remained, helping the newly-incepted learn how to take care of themselves, repair their houses, learn what it meant to be har and fight against the relentless winter. In spite of this, Ylwa ended up dead within a year, and only thanks to Ottar's escape did we learn who was responsible.

Marluk – a name ringing with the insidiousness of the far North. He haunted my dreams as a faceless monster, since I had no recollection of the har from the brief time I had spent in the Land of Ice. Yet I was certain that I would recognise his sinister aura the moment I saw him. In my visions, that moment was often his last.

'Týr should be more resolute with them,' Fjaer claimed passionately. 'He should establish a permanent guard and teach them to respect laws. Marluk should be made an example, else they may never learn.'

'We have to work with what we've got,' I said, resigned to my fate and heavily under the influence of mead. Once I'd had my revenge, I didn't care what would happen to me, but I was going to have it, one way or another.

'I hate that he would withdraw your right from you.'

The echo of actual care in his voice surprised me. Tall, slight of build, with deep-blue eyes, so often characteristic of those who go out to the sea in ships, Fjaer was a more than pleasant sight for anyhar's eyes. And more importantly, intoxicated with passion and mead, which he, too, had drunk in liberal quantities, he was willing. I allowed him to take my face into his slender hands and kiss me. Through breath, I communicated to him what I longed for, and he was more than happy to oblige. Taking aruna with somehar I actually liked was different than doing so with a stranger, in that I felt guilty for using them as fuel for my vessel. That time, I hoped Fjaer was drunk enough that in the morning he wouldn't remember how little I had been there as he quenched his fire in me.

The rush of being close to Ylwa again can only be compared to Nature's resurrection after the long death of winter. As I peel away the layers of reality and enter the nowhere, the shine of his long golden hair, which he always wore flowing loose over his shoulders, restrained only by a golden circlet, leads my way. The ethereal wind is blowing the sun rays away and in the semi-darkness, he is an otherworldly vision of beauty. Even the evergreen tree seems to be decorated with gold today.

You are here.

He reaches for me, and I fall into his arms without hesitation, taking in the wonderful smell of his hair. It is odd, this complexity of experience, all the sensations that are inexplicably present, when they clearly shouldn't be, but I accept whatever I am given without analysis.

I can sense your happiness.

'And I can sense your smile.'

For the longest while, we simply sit there, touching yet never touching, together yet far apart. Then, I begin to talk. I tell him about our journey, without mentioning that we had gone against the Phylarch's orders. I explain, though, that the entire crew supports me in any decision I make and tell him how much it pleases me to belong among them. He feels better when he can believe I might achieve happiness again one day. I tell him we have Skaddi on board, too, which turns into a short session of badmouthing the unpopular seer.

You seem to be doing better, he decides eventually. Soon, you might not need me anymore.

'That day shall never come,' I assure him.

Sometimes, we play this little game. He asks me, when will I finally find somehar else. I ask him if he is thinking of rebirth. It is a formality really; neither of us can leave the other behind. Although... I would never admit it to him, but I am marginally concerned that one day in the very, very distant future, I will no longer be certain about my answer. One day, perhaps dozens of years later, I might realise I am nothing but a lonely lunatic, a fading har with nothing to show for himself but a ghost. Yet at the same time, I fear I might never be able to give him up and see his light disappear, knowing that it could have kept burning within me.

On the third day of our sail, I could see Skaddi growing restless as the morning spilled into afternoon. It was something we had to expect, because the journey to Alba Sulh rarely took three days, and we had been blessed with marvellous weather the whole time, which meant that we should have been nearing our destination. Minding their own business, everyhar was feigning ignorance as the seer paced across the deck in large circles, stopping to cast an expectant glance at the horizon every now and then. It took him no less than two hours to swallow his pride and approach me with an impatient spring to his step.

'Excuse me, Tiahaar, but shouldn't we be able to see the shores of Alba Sulh by now?'

I had never been a particularly good liar, therefore it surprised me, how easy I found it to answer his justified query.

'Yes, you're right. We have drifted a little southwards during the night and I had to correct our course, which slowed us down. But it's nothing to worry about. We will get there in time for... whatever it is you plan to do there.'

His eyebrows knotted together as he inspected my face. Unable to read me, he eventually nodded and relaxed a little. 'Very well. Please, inform me when we are close.' With that, he retreated below deck.

Mikkel, who had been a witness to our short exchange, joined me at the handrail, where he stared out into the wide open blue. He scratched his head, looking distinctively displeased. 'That won't help for long.'

'I know.'

Skaddi may have been lots of things, but an idiot he was not. It would dawn on him before sundown at the latest. Then things could get rough very quickly and some of my shipmates might end up regretting that they'd agreed to the change of plans.

'Don't worry, I'll back you up,' said Mikkel, as if he had been reading my mind.

Just as I'd predicted, the sun was nearing the still empty horizon when the seer returned in all his feathered glory. He reminded me of a bloodthirsty vulture as he looked down on me from his somewhat greater height, shooting daggers from his eyes. This time, he cut right into the heart of the matter. 'I demand an explanation.'

I was torn between playing dumb and giving a hearty laugh, but

I managed to suppress both urges and gave him the answer he deserved. 'Oh, we are not sailing to Alba Sulh after all. I'm afraid this is entirely my fault...'

Recognising his own words being used against him, Skaddi made one intimidating step closer. An angry red crept into his cheeks, making him look like a somewhat overcooked bird. 'You will turn the ship around right now,' he said very quietly. 'Then, you will apologise to me, so I might consider not mentioning this incident to the Phylarch, but you will owe me a favour.'

I stared at him, dumbfounded. 'You can't seriously think this is what will happen.'

Seeing he was getting nowhere with me, Skaddi turned to Mikkel, who seemed to be next in the chain of command. 'If you help me end this mutiny, the ship will be yours and I will speak to the Phylarch on your behalf.'

Mikkel actually snorted at the offer. 'No, I will not help you. And it's only a mutiny if the captain's not involved.'

Bewildered, Skaddi looked at the present sailors with defiance, searching for those who appeared most tense. 'The offer goes to anyhar, who...'

'Nohar on board will listen to you,' Catgar, at whom Skaddi was currently looking, cut him off. 'We prevail together, and we go down together, but you are not one of us. You may as well give it up now.'

The atmosphere was so tense that one could cut it with a sword, but the unity Catgar spoke of could be felt in the air, familiar and binding.

'There will be consequences,' the seer warned me, as though as I was miraculously unaware of this.

'And I will face them if we ever return to Freyhella. Until then, the ship is under my command. You may stay below or make yourself useful up here, I don't care, but the fact is that you'll have to miss your ritual, because this ship is sailing north.'

Somewhat deflated, Skaddi gave me one last scorching look, before turning on his heel. 'You don't know who you're toying with. The ship may be under your command, but the spirits are not, and neither is the universe.'

As he retreated down the ladder, seething with anger, a chuckle could be heard here or there. Personally, I didn't have a good feeling about this – his words did have an ominous quality, so I saved the laughs for later. At least, the cards were on the table and we could focus on a single task: reaching the Land of Ice as quickly as possible.

Several days passed and Skaddi's sinister prediction had been forgotten. We were making good speed, and even though five days on the open sea still lay between us and the distant shore, the north could already be sensed in the air. It acquired a different quality, which could be best described as the crispiness of winter, for she never gave up her reign in these parts. The seer kept mostly below deck and we hardly ever saw a hair of him. The wind was not so favourable now, however, so we took to rowing during the day and relaxed in the evening, telling stories and playing the games Fjaer had brought on board.

Mikkel and I grew even closer than we had been before, and a great deal of our time was spent planning our strategy once we arrived in the Land of Ice. I felt good in his company, even though (or because) everything was telling me he was eager to get to know me in all the ways he hadn't been able to while I was in a chesna bond. Perhaps that was why making a move on him three nights later felt so easy.

Looking back, I should never have done that. I should not have endangered that newly-strengthened companionship the way I did, but at that time, it was stronger than me. I hadn't seen Ylwa since my one-of-a-kind encounter with Fjaer, and the gap within my chest tormented me with the direst kind of pain, making me desperate for the only balm I had access to: a connection of two bodies that would open the door for me and trigger my descent into the waiting room.

After hundreds of similar encounters, this was the first one I actually felt guilty about, because Mikkel was offering me more than just consolation, a random roon or a night of drunken fun. As we kissed, there were real, honest feelings in his breath, laced with a vague promise of a future we could never have. Perhaps promise is too strong a word, because none had been asked – or made. It was more of an offering, which I was about to deny, despite acting as though as I was accepting it. I hated myself for that, but at the same time I found myself unable to do what was right. Who knew when I would get my next chance at the encounter I so desired...

The tree is evergreen, its leaves never withering, but today they are covered with soft rime. Ylwa is waiting underneath its branches, sitting in a meditative repose – a personification of the hard and frozen earth, who reluctantly yields to my warm embrace. Something is wrong here, terribly, irrevocably wrong. Confused and terrified, I hold him as I always do, but instead of waves of comfort, deadly chill runs up and down my back.

'*What is it, Ylwa? What happened, please, talk to me...*' *I plead, my eyes filling with tears I am unable to release on this plane... or anywhere really. I have not wept since losing him, which might be part of the problem.*

You are going to do something horrible, *he says in the saddest voice I have ever heard in my mind.* And it is my fault.

'*What are you talking about?*' *I croak, even though deep inside I realise he must have discovered the purpose of my journey. What I cannot fathom is the how.*

You know how important the colony was to me, yet you are willing to spill blood on its ground, and you have persuaded yourself you are doing it for me. Do you not see the irony?

This, right here, is my worst nightmare coming to life. A part of me has known all along that Ylwa wouldn't have approved of a severe punishment, that he would have been forgiving and generous, even though these exact same qualities had cost him his life. But I didn't expect him to feel so strongly about it, especially not after his death.

'*It is my right,*' *I object meekly. That, and it would feel so good. Has it really taken me so long to realise that I wanted Marluk dead for my own sake, not his? But then, why should that make a difference? Regardless of the motivation, he still deserves to suffer.*

It is my fault, *he repeats.* In my unwillingness to give you up, I have made myself more important than a soul who has crossed over ever should be, overshadowing everything else in your life. I should have given you more space, a chance to build something new. Something material.

'*Don't be a fool. All I ever wanted was you. Why don't we just drop this? What do you say?*'

It upsets me that we are wasting the precious moments we have been granted on a petty argument. In our old life back in Freyhella, I would have either kissed him and indicated that spiked emotions are best smoothened in the sheets, or announced I needed a break, after which a long walk would have followed. Under the current circumstances, the immense pressure of time complicates things, because if a conflict is not resolved immediately, it will become irrelevant by the next encounter. This exchange of opinions is wearing me down.

Don't jeopardise your life in Freyhella, it is not too late, *he insists, completely ignoring my attempts at reconciliation.* Turn that ship around! *'Haven't you just complained about having too much influence on my life?' I retort sarcastically. 'Why don't you just go and take a rebirth instead...'* If our encounters keep having a negative effect on you, I may have to consider it.

I give the mental alternative of an exasperated sigh. 'Come on, Ylwa, you know I didn't mean it. We should...'

I didn't have time to finish the thought; a towering wave of physical sensations swept over me and violently pulled me into the physical plane. Distraught, I pressed the back of my hand firmly against my mouth, biting down in order to muffle the noise that threatened to come out of my throat, lingering somewhere on the fence between an annoyed groan and a moan of pleasure. Rather than basking in the afterglow of aruna, I immediately began to blame myself. Even though this was the longest encounter we'd had in quite some time, release still came too soon. Leaving on such a bad note was making me feel somewhat hysterical. This time, I knew I couldn't wait several days until I returned to him. As desperate as that would make me look, I had to find somehar the next evening, perhaps even morning...

It was only when I felt two firm hands sharply squeezing my shoulders, shaking me into full consciousness more harshly than I would have liked, that I realised I had a more pressing problem to settle right there and then. Mikkel's face slowly swam into my view and the expression upon it was far from the gentleness he had been treating me with in the past few days. I tried to slip out of his grasp, but apparently I wasn't all there yet, because he had me pinned down without a sweat.

'What the Hell was that?!' he hissed at me, quiet enough not to wake up the rest of the crew, but no less threatening for it. 'What did you do?'

'Let go of me...' I huffed, not really in the mood to explain.

'Njörd...'

'We took aruna, I spaced out and now you're hurting me, that's what happened. Let go.'

His breathing grew heavier and more irregular, which I attributed to suppressed anger. Pale eyes bore into me in the darkness, earnest, pointed daggers made of the bluest ice.

'Oh yeah, you spaced out alright. Your eyes rolled back into your skull and you were totally gone most of the time. I'm not so pleased to have served as a tool for your private grissecon, and I think that at the very least, I deserve an explanation. What did you do?'

I ground my teeth as the words sunk in, making me realise he was, of course, right. I had used him and explaining why was the least I could do.

'Alright.' I stopped struggling and Mikkel finally loosened his grip on me, so that both of us could sit up and make ourselves more comfortable. 'Once, as a harling, I was supposed to die. I fell out of my father's fishing boat and the water closed above my head. There was no light, just freezing cold dread and slimy things that wrapped their tendrils around my legs. I don't really remember being saved, or what happened while I was out. Now, I believe the experience opened a door within me. A portal, through which I can see to the other side...'

To begin this story was incredibly hard, and I spoke slowly, careful where to tread, as if clawing my way through a particularly dense copse of trees. I had never talked about this to anyhar before and, if not for the circumstances, I never would have. Yet as I went on, a certain urgency made me hasten the pace. It was as if everything I had been holding inside wanted to spill out at the same time, now that the dam was broken. I told Mikkel everything: how I had discovered this ability by chance during a grissecon years ago, how I'd decided to use it after Ylwa's death, how I kept switching partners every night, so as not to be suspected of the very same thing he accused me of – that I was just using them. I admitted I had got into a vicious cycle and couldn't step out of it, even though there were all kinds of rumours circulating about me, how the real world had begun to lose its importance...

After such a confession, I expected to feel purged, yet the relief I had hoped for didn't come. Perhaps Mikkel's understanding could have brought it to pass, but I was not to be granted that. As I looked up at him expectantly, he lowered his eyes and shook his head in what might have been disbelief or disgust.

'Do you realise how unhealthy this is?' And even though he said "unhealthy", I clearly heard "sick".

'As a matter of fact, I do,' I admitted half-heartedly.

The sad fact? I had always known the truth, I'd just never cared enough to do anything about my destructive behaviour. I was fully aware of just how disrespectful it was of me, using others to feed my addiction without even telling them. And I also knew that one day, the "real" world could become completely irrelevant to me, while these stolen moments would become my reality. It was happening already, but I still couldn't find it in myself to care.

'I understand Týr's concerns now,' came Mikkel's gloomy voice from the darkness. 'If I had known this, I wouldn't have given you a ship either.'

'What I just told you is a private matter,' I replied dejectedly. 'It has nothing to do with how I perform...'

'Like it or not, this is an addiction,' he interrupted me resolutely. 'And addicts are dangerous. If you were a part of the regular crew, sure, but for Ag's sake, you are the captain and your priorities are... out of this world.'

He was wrong there, or so I hoped. My... indisposition didn't interfere with my responsibilities and he wouldn't ever have needed to doubt that if I hadn't made my problem his business.

'This was a mistake.' I pulled myself back to my feet, about to retreat to my hammock in the lower deck. 'I am sorry. For everything.'

He was silent for a while, but I lingered, waiting for closure. Just when I thought no reply would come, Mikkel looked up at me, the weight of the world reflecting in his eyes. 'Me too,' he said in a low voice. 'Do me a favour and... Quit this madness, while you still can.'

I didn't see how that could be achieved.

The following morning brought with it an unfavourable wind blowing from the north, which kept growing in intensity as the day progressed. It seemed that I had angered not only Mikkel, but also nature itself... or the Vanas, sea and wind deities to whom a large number of Freyhellans attribute great powers. Like the addict I apparently was, I couldn't stop thinking of Ylwa. A large portion of my day was spent pondering who I could approach for aruna and trying to invent new ways of reaching the other plane, but in the end I rejected all my ideas as implausible.

As the cold blasts wouldn't cease battering at the ship, we had to take down some of our sails and slave behind the oars all day. Yet despite our unending efforts, we were barely moving forwards. Ruthless waves toyed with the ship, throwing us off-balance every few minutes and jeopardising our course. I organised the crew into two shifts, which took turns rowing, but by the evening, everyhar was utterly exhausted nonetheless. At one point, Fjaer even asked Skaddi, who was hiding as far away from work as possible, for help. Naturally, the seer excused himself with sea-sickness and further ignored us.

Late at night, the wind finally stilled, allowing us to share a light dinner and try to rest. Some climbed into the hammocks, but most simply flung themselves down wearily on the floor to sleep. As it was apparent I would not be able to reconcile with Ylwa that day, I too fell into a restless slumber, but was soon disturbed by a peculiar noise. More than the thunder we were all familiar with, it sounded as if the sky was being ripped apart by a vindictive spirit. Even the wooden deck under our feet trembled.

'Everyhar on deck!' I yelled, setting an example by rushing to the ladder as quickly as possible myself.

Outside, it seemed as if all the dehara were having a vicious fight; it was unlike anything I had ever seen. Tremendous forces were at play, and the ship, disadvantaged by being almost unloaded, was in great danger. Towering waves rolled against the vessel, while high winds pulled at the remaining sails and dumped huge quantities of water aboard. It would be tricky to keep the ship moving into the waves, while not placing too much strain on the sails and masts and making certain it had enough momentum.

'Secure yourselves with ropes,' I reminded the arriving crew, because a har overboard was a har lost forever. 'Alfarr, Lethra, Fjaer, Dagný, up on the masts. Take down all the lower sails! The rest of you, with me.'

At that point, we were running from the wind and with it being this strong, the stern of the ship was in danger of being broken. Our main effort had to be turning the ship at an angle to the wind, while striving to face it directly into the oncoming waves. As the majority of the crew was doing this, a few hara went to help the group I had originally assigned to the masts, attempting to protect them. Without the remaining two sails, we would be left with no forward momentum, completely at the mercy of the sea.

It was a constant battle during the next few hours. Even though we did manage to gain control of the vessel, everyhar knew it could be lost at any moment. Soaked to the bone, we struggled not to slide on the slippery deck beneath our feet. The height of the waves added yet another layer of danger – sometimes, they were taller than the ship, effectively cutting us off from the wind. I kept gazing up to the sky, but there was no sign that the storm was about to abate. If anything, it seemed to be gaining even more strength.

And then, at one point, somehar squeezed my shoulder in order to attract my attention, because the wailing of the storm made it nearly impossible for us to hear each other's voices. 'Look! Over there!' he mouthed, pointing to the west.

My eyes needed a while to penetrate the darkness and focus on what he wanted me to see, but once I did, I was sure we were lost. A ghostlike shape towered in the distance, taller than even the largest waves. Huge and monstrous, it was neither ethereal nor made of water. Covered in seaweed, it seemed to be sitting in a boat of mist, rowing across the waves in our direction. The holes where its eyes should be were hollow, yet it seemed to notice me looking, for it reached towards me with a hand of smoke and emitted a terrible scream.

In spite of its destructive power, especially in the long months of winter, Freyhellans do not typically dread the storm. The principal theme of our entire history has been the perpetual struggle against the tameless forces of nature. Not unlike our ancient human ancestors, we brave the dangers incurred by hunting and fishing under these inclement skies and face the suffering entailed by long cold winters when the Sun never shines. But this storm was different. There was nothing natural about it and, after the sighting, even the least superstitious of us had to admit that.

'It is a Draugen,' Fjaer cried out, causing the entire crew to descend into a state of panic.

Draugen, ghosts of those who died at sea, were often blamed for the sinking of ships, although nohar I knew of had actually seen one. Something in me refused to believe that we were the first, despite the fact that the thing was slowly drifting closer.

'We shouldn't have disregarded Týr's orders,' Mikkel muttered gravely, wiping the water out of his eyes, so that he could have a better look at the spectre. The entity responded by lifting its large oar and sending a fresh shower in our direction. 'The dehara put a curse on our journey.'

In that moment that something dawned on me... a suspicion that had been taking form in the back of my mind for quite some time. Fully devoted to saving the ship, I hadn't given it the attention it deserved, but when Mikkel spoke of a curse, it suddenly became clear to me.

'The dehara... hardly. But somehar might have. Come with me!' With that, I began to move towards the lower deck.

Mikkel lingered behind, hesitant, but I needed him with me, not only to prove I was right, but also because there was strength in numbers.

'Mikkel! Come on!'

The urgency in my voice made him listen, although his expression spoke of confusion, if not lack of trust. Slipping, falling, stumbling and occasionally sliding across the entire length of the ship, we finally made it to the ladder. For the last few feet, we had to progress without the safety of the ropes, because they weren't long enough, and it was only by sheer luck that neither of us was blown overboard.

I rolled down the ladder rather than descending it, pushed forward by a particularly strong blast of wind, and immediately found out that the lower deck was filling with water. There wasn't much of it yet – once I got to my feet, it reached more or less to my ankles. I could not tell whether it had been dumped there from above, or whether the ship was leaking. Alas, I had a more urgent problem to deal with before I could start looking for a possible breach.

'We have to find Skaddi,' I whispered to Mikkel, gesturing in the direction I wanted him to take, while I inspected the corner in which the seer had spent most of the voyage. No luck. There was no light down there, and everything had gotten so wet that lighting a candle was out of the question. This meant we had to progress slowly and allow our eyes to become accustomed to the darkness. As I stumbled through the lower deck, arms outstretched so as not to bump into random objects, I registered that one area seemed somewhat less dark, as though a very dim glow was diluting the night.

Mikkel must have noticed it too, because we met halfway there. 'It's coming from the storage,' he hissed in a low voice.

Whatever Skaddi was doing there, I wanted to catch him unaware, and so we crept forward in silence, our efforts slightly hampered by the abrupt movements of the ship. Having reached the small room first, I kicked the door open, and my eyes fell on a peculiar sight. The storage was indeed filled with an opalescent, greenish glow, which was much more radiant here. In the centre of it, the seer was sitting in meditation repose, with his legs crossed and eyes shut tight, his lips reciting runes or incantations. It took a second glance to realise that he was not in fact surrounded by light, but rather the source of it, as if so much energy was coursing beneath his skin it needed to seep through.

Another massive wave picked up the ship and we were flung forward, into the glow. I gasped for breath, expecting it would affect us in a destructive way, but all Skaddi's efforts must have been directed outwards, because I only felt a slight electric prickling on my skin. Encouraged by that, I bent down and picked him up, shaking him into consciousness. Mikkel didn't hesitate to go a step further. He made use of the fact I was conveniently holding the seer in place and sent a strong fist into his face.

Skaddi's eyes snapped open and he broke out of his trance, but the storm didn't seem to cease in the slightest. What was worse, I could hear voices screaming from above, which could only mean one thing: the Draugen was gaining on us.

Furious, I grabbed Skaddi by the hair, forcing him to look at me, and yelled into his face. 'End this immediately, or I swear I will end *you*!'

His face twisted in an uncomfortable smirk as he attempted to shrug. 'I warned you. I could not help you anymore, even if I wanted to. The events will play out as intended.'

This time, it was me who struck him, strong enough to make us both stumble. His robe opened slightly in the process and I noticed a flash of something on his skin... something alarming that hadn't been there before. I swiftly grabbed his arms and pulled them up in order to give Mikkel access. 'Strip him!'

This time, Mikkel didn't question my order; he took a knife and started unceremoniously cutting away Skaddi's robe, until the seer's skin was almost completely revealed. At first sight, it appeared that Skaddi had painted magical runes upon the entire surface of his body – arms, legs and torso. Only when I looked closer did I notice that most of them were freshly tattooed, never to be removed. A cold, heavy stone of fear settled in my belly, as I came to understand why he claimed he was not going to be able to undo his curse.

'Fuck.' Mikkel realised it, too, and threw a side glance in my direction. 'Let's... I don't know, throw him overboard?'

I shook my head: no.

'The runes will still be there. Who knows what will happen, if the water takes them...'

And then my eyes fell on the knife in his hand. Suddenly, I was utterly calm, because it had just become blatantly obvious to me what had to be done.

'Tie him up,' I said matter-of-factly, strengthening my grip on Skaddi, who must have realised what I was about to do, because he started to struggle. 'I will skin him alive if I have to.'

There was plenty of extra rope in storage and after a short skirmish, we managed to incapacitate the seer and tie both his wrists and ankles. Even then, he wouldn't stop budging, and so I had to sit on him, while Mikkel was holding his arms up. A high-pitched scream from the deck reminded me that time was not a commodity we had enough of. Without further delay, I placed the tip of the knife on the uppermost rune on the left side of his chest and pressed down until I saw a droplet of blood. Then I made an incision all the way to his groin, interrupting each rune in the column.

'Being you, I'd stop jerking like that,' I warned Skaddi, who wasn't making it any easier for me. 'My hand could easily slip.'

Would he bleed out after I was finished with him? Maybe, maybe not. I was keeping the cuts superficial, but many were needed, as Skaddi had been very thorough with his incantations. Five more down his torso, two down the length of each limb. With every incision, the seer's moaning grew louder, while the wailing of the wind outside faded out exponentially, along with the greenish glow surrounding us. Just as I was about to destroy the last column of runes, the entire ship rose as though lifted by an invisible hand of gigantic proportions. Driven by fear for my crew, I sunk the knife into his leg and cut harder than before. The immediate drop that followed made all of us tumble across the floor, bumping into crates and barrels. And then there was darkness.

The peace that settled upon the sea seemed almost out of place after the raging hell we'd had to go through. I dragged myself up slowly, suddenly mindful of the blood staining my hands, knees and chest. Outside the door, the underdeck was filling with hara. Soon, one of them would open the door and see the crimson picture we had painted. Mikkel looked at me over the seer's convulsing body, running a hand through his hair, unaware, or perhaps uncaring, of the stain he was leaving. 'Good call, captain' he said.

The next impossible task I had to face was making a decision regarding the seer's fate. Now that the immediate danger had been warded off, it seemed unnecessary to kill him, even though he indisputably deserved it. The fact remained, however, that he was still one of Týr's favourites, and while what we had done so far qualified us as outcasts, this would have created a blood debt. Having no proof of the seer's vile intentions, the Phylarch would probably suspect that removing him from our way like an obstacle had been our plan all along.

'Somehar should see to his injuries,' I suggested. We did not have a crew slot reserved for a healer, but I knew that Björn and Dagný had some experience in the area.

'We are not throwing him into the sea?' Mikkel sounded quite surprised; he must have been convinced that we were only waiting until it was safe to get Skaddi off the ship.

'Týr can have him back, if he's so fond of him... I will not needlessly jeopardise your futures more than I already have.'

If anyhar had perished in the storm, I would have felt differently, that much was certain. But under current circumstances, I could afford to be generous rather than give in to the urge to gut the bastard. I might dream about it, though. Well, there was still the chance that he would succumb to his injuries.

'I have thought about what you said,' I told Mikkel the next evening.

'Oh yeah?'

We were alone on the stern of the deck, observing the gentle waves trailing behind our vessel. It was a well-deserved, peaceful moment after a day spent repairing everything the storm had damaged and putting the ship back on course. Once Skaddi's incantations lost their power, gone was the wind and the rain. Clear skies had provided us company ever since, and though the air was growing gradually colder, there was nothing unnatural about it.

'I think you're right,' I continued. 'I do have to focus on the here and now. Perhaps if I hadn't been preoccupied, I would have realised what Skaddi was up to sooner.'

'Well, you did save us. You handled that pretty well, if you ask me.'

'Going easy on me now?' I couldn't help but give Mikkel a little smile.

'I still believe you should let Ylwa go, though.'

'Right. But to do that... I cannot simply leave him waiting and never see him anymore. We both deserve a proper goodbye.'

Our eyes met; mine hopeful and pleading, Mikkel's widened with displeasure. I could immediately see that he understood what I was asking of him, even though I hadn't spoken the question. 'I don't think I can...'

'Mikkel, please!' I interrupted before his refusal was fully formed, aware that I wasn't being fair to him... but then again, when have I ever been fair when it came to Ylwa? 'Just this once. One last time, just to say good bye. If you grant me this, I will never go back again.'

'Just this once?'

'Yes. I promise.' I was quick to answer, even though, like every addict, I didn't even believe my own words. To quit visiting Ylwa entirely was simply more than I was ready to ask of myself. I wasn't completely lying, though. I intended to take a break from this form of astral travelling until our future was certain. I must keep my head clear for time being, so that I could deal with the situation in the colony without distraction. Moreover, it was unbecoming of a captain to throw himself on his crew like I'd done – yet another reason why I needed to restrict those encounters. And I was positive I could do that for the time being, if only I was allowed to make up with Ylwa after our falling out.

Mikkel studied my face for a moment, perhaps trying to decide if I was to be trusted. Then he took the kind of deep breath hara usually take before agreeing to something they would rather not do, and nodded. 'Alright. Have your goodbye.'

Our intimacy was somewhat forced this time; gone was the intensity of his original genuine interest. At least I didn't have to pretend with him. For the first time, my partner knew where my true interest lay, which was a great relief. The physical mechanisms worked just fine to get me where I needed to be anyway.

Something is horribly, irreparably wrong. Gone are the green fields and flowery meadows, in which we loved to roam. Everything is dreary in the extreme, enveloped in darkness. Even the evergreen tree is barren, devoid of leaves, the stream that bubbled nearby dry. Dismayed by a sinister anticipation, I begin to call him – not only with my voice, but with my soul, my entire being. The fibre of the ethereal realm resonates with the call, but all I receive in response is an echo of my own voice.

Where all was warmth and brightness, now there is only darkness. Unwilling to give up, I start to run, struggling through hundreds of shadows, pursuing shapeless forms with my arms outstretched, but he is nowhere to be found. This is it, then. Death may have kissed me, but his gift is useless to me now.

Defeat has the taste of swallowed tears and words unspoken. I lie down on the frozen ground, allowing the ethereal mist to lick my face. My thoughts wander, still searching for tendrils of hope. Anything to stop me from facing the reality: Ylwa is gone.

We managed to complete the rest of our voyage within a week, no longer plagued by nature's more sinister face. During those long days, I felt myself slowly harden as the despair caused by an acute sense of loss melted into lust for revenge. Perhaps, had I been allowed to mourn, I might have felt differently, but the weight of responsibility was too binding. Moreover, everyhar else had buried Ylwa a long time ago; they wouldn't understand that he was freshly gone for me. And so the thought that I would soon see Marluk face to face was the only force driving me forward, my sole purpose.

My cold heart was filled with both relief and suspense when the Land of Ice appeared on the horizon, submerged in a sea of fog. Summer was approaching the island, but it wasn't yet in full swing, which meant the temperature would climb a few degrees above zero during the day. The midnight sun's lingering light wouldn't allow it to drop too deep below freezing. At first sight, this might have seemed like a blessing, but the absence of true night also meant that no matter the time of our arrival, we wouldn't have the benefit of approaching unseen.

'What is your strategy?' Mikkel asked as we watched the colourful wooden sheds of Nuuk appear in the distance. The original settlers had built them right on the waterfront, at the mercy of the tide. They sat in clusters on the cliffs like perched hens, their overhanging parts supported by wooden pillars. The inhabitants of the Wraeththu settlement we had created stubbornly insisted on building in the same way. It was a mystery to me how these toy houses hadn't collapsed and drifted into the open sea. The fog that was spreading from outlying islands to the east rolled over the mountains and down the streets of Nuuk, carrying with it an air of spookiness.

'An outright attack would not only be uncalled for, but also difficult,' I pondered aloud. 'We would have to circle half the island and march through hostile land for hours, and they might still see us coming, because natural hiding spots are few and far between. Unless we decide to cross the mountains, which would be unnecessarily exhausting. I would prefer to approach them directly.'

Mikkel's brow furrowed. 'And negotiate?'

'I was thinking more of demanding they give up Marluk on the grounds of his crime. If they agree, we will carry out the punishment in accordance with our law, if they don't... then we'll wreak havoc on this funny little village.'

'I'd prefer to finish this without the spectacular bloodshed of the innocent,' said Mikkel in a voice colder than the wind that continually swept down from the north.

'If they back him up, they aren't innocent. He decided to bite the hand that feeds him. They'd better not make the same mistake.'

The truth was we knew little about Marluk's motive, neither did we know whether he'd had any help. In Ottar's words, he appeared to have been completely out of his mind. That might have very well been the case, for only a mad har would turn against those who had saved his pitiful excuse for a life. Perhaps that was why Týr acted with untypical benevolence, hesitant to enact punishment until he knew what had really happened and why

I hadn't come here for explanations, though. It was too late for those. The recent loss seemed to have awakened an urge for blood within me, stronger than ever before. Regardless of how calmly I managed to present myself to my crew, a primal anger that could only be sated by vengeance was stirring under my skin. I would have Marluk's head for this, followed by the heads of everyhar who assisted him.

As soon as the ship got closer to the shore, manoeuvring around the rocky patches, we dropped anchor in the bay and boarded our landing boat. It soon became apparent there was no need to announce our arrival. A welcoming committee of three had already formed on the shore, waiting motionless like sad statues against the backdrop of grimly towering mountains, where the everlasting snow glittered. Once we moored the boat, I thought I spotted some movement in a window of the closest dwelling. Yes, there were definitely more hara inside, and I couldn't tell whether they were observing us with mere curiosity, or with bows in their hands.

'Mikkel, Fjaer, with me. The rest of you, mind those houses,' I shouted as I jumped out of the boat. I landed thigh-high in the ice-cold water. While going alone would have been preferable, matching their numbers was highly important in a possibly hostile environment. As we waded through the tide, I could swear that the clanking of our weapons made the one in the middle step back... or was that just my wishful thinking?

We came to a halt a couple of feet away from the small group, biding our time. I made a point of measuring each har with inquisitive sight. They didn't impress me. While their bodies were tough, lean and muscular, which spoke of great endurance in extreme conditions, the expressions they wore were bleak, their features expressing weakness. Waiting was obviously making them nervous, which was why I remained purposefully silent, until one of them caved and started showering us with stiff official greetings.

'...and has the Phylarch also decided to grace us with his presence?' he finished his litany.

That was my cue.

'Why would he do that?' I enquired, lifting an eyebrow with what I trusted to be an air of superiority. 'He has more important matters to tend to than visiting colonies that have proven to be a disappointment. As do I, by the way. We will leave as soon as we have finished our business here.'

Finally, another member of the triad dared to speak up. 'May I enquire about its nature?'

So very, very careful. It would be my pleasure to destroy their last shreds of hope in my benevolence.

'Oh, quit acting as if it wasn't obvious.'

The three of them exchanged resigned looks; clearly they weren't dumb enough not to understand why I was there, but wouldn't quit pushing their luck. 'We have, in fact, hoped that you were sent with a delivery of supplies... Last winter was harsh and our harvest only covered a small percentage of our needs.'

Did they not understand that it was justice I came to deliver? Half shocked by such insolence, half pleased they had provided me with some leverage, I took the liberty to ignore their question and ask my own instead. 'During the time our hienamas spent here, did they explain to you the particularities of our law?'

'Yes, they did.'

'And what happens, then, when somehar kills another tribe member?'

At that point, their facade of denseness started to come off, revealing nervousness bordering on fear. The looks they gave each other were pathetic attempts at choosing the poor bastard who would have to recite the answer. 'The closest relatives of the victim decide the murderer's punishment,' the tall one on the right spluttered.

'Very good.' I praised him as if he were a dog, loading my voice with as much sarcasm as it could take. 'And as Ylwa's chesnari, I demand to be granted that right. Point me to Marluk without further meddling and afterwards, we may *perhaps* discuss supplies for the colony.'

The boldest of the three, (from what I could gather from their initial speech, he was the self-proclaimed governor of Nuuk), asked for a moment of privacy in order to discuss how they could be of assistance to me, which only highlighted their incompetence and fed my impatience. Mikkel noticed the way I was clenching my fists as well as the tension in my jaw and attempted to calm me down by placing a hand on my shoulder. I promptly shook it off and Fjaer, channelling my feelings, made a disgusted face and spat on the rocky beach.

Restless like a caged animal, I watched the governor make a few steps towards us. 'We will accommodate your request.' His voice sounded like raindrops on glass, both fragile and stiff, and he held his hands clasped in front of his body – a gesture that was peaceful, yet also subconsciously protective. 'However, we do have one condition.'

So, Ylwa might have taught them something after all. Instead of digging for roots, they knew how to use words like 'enquire', 'however' or 'accommodate'.

The fact that I was grinning seemed to make the governor fret; his pupils dilated. 'It is undisputable that Marluk killed a har. But the circumstances are complicated... We believe you should hear them first. And you should know him for the har he is now, as well. With all due respect, you have never been human, much less married to a female. You don't know what it was like for us, in the beginnings. We will gladly bring him to you, but we demand an actual hearing, because justice...'

And that was when I snapped. The shift was so smooth and sudden that in one moment, I had been chuckling at the way his nostrils quivered when he was tense, and in the next I came down upon him like a bird of prey, toppling him over into the slippery rocks before anyhar could stop me.

'You demand!' I screamed into his face, pinning him down with my own body, knife pressed to his throat. 'You have no right to demand any damn thing! I am the only one, who can make demands here, *the only one*, and I order you to bring Marluk to me. I want to know how it happened, see where it happened, and once that is over, I want his filthy head. Otherwise your heads will roll along with it, *do you understand?*!!'

From the corner of my eye, I noticed that a small skirmish was occurring somewhere above my head. The har's companions must have tried to help their mate, but Mikkel and Fjaer had my back and promptly got them into an impasse. Weapons had been drawn, but it didn't seem anyhar was in a rush to use them. I shifted my weight to get a better view, disregarding the governor's pleas, and my knee sank into his gut, eliciting a rewarding scream.

'I had a girlfriend,' said Mikkel, all of a sudden. 'Several, in fact.'

That effectively made half of my anger evaporate due to shock and, from what I could observe, it had a similar effect on everyhar else.

'I used to be quite the ladies' man a few decades ago. I had a younger sister, too. Riitta. We lived in the Electric City.'

So, there it was: the thing nohar ever talked about. The huge taboo, unexpectedly dragged into the light for... whose sake exactly? Mine, or that of the locals?

'You did...?'

I looked up at his ageless face with just the faintest trace of wrinkles in the corners of his eyes, from challenging the wind that swept across the ocean day after day. It seemed impossible to make the connection between this har I thought I knew and my experience of humans.

'She had this dream, once things went wild in the city – violence, poverty, robberies, illness and all that – that we could go up north, to Karelia and wait out the apocalypse somewhere in nature. Live on a reindeer farm, like the one she'd visited with her class when she was little. When our mother died of cancer, I thought why not give it a shot. It wasn't like we had much to stay for.'

By this point, everyhar had lowered their weapons and although they remained on guard, a large part of their attention belonged to Mikkel. Even I stopped cutting off the governor's supply of air, waiting for the dark ending of the story that was sure to come.

'I was taken and incepted before we got there,' Mikkel continued. 'We were separated by force, and I never found out if she made it; that's how things were done back then. Now it feels like it all happened to a different person, but I do remember that guy was really desperate. Yet he survived without going batshit crazy, and he never raised his hand against anyone who offered him any kind of help. If he had, by the way, I probably wouldn't be here. It wasn't a time of pleasantries, such as hearings or laws.'

His speech must have been for my sake, then. A way to shame them into doing what we demanded without stooping to physical violence; and it worked so marvellously that I caught myself wondering if he hadn't made it all up on spot for that very purpose. But even though there appeared to be things I hadn't known about Mikkel, I knew for sure he was not a liar.

'We will take you to the former Nayati now,' promised the one who had been silent until that point, putting away his dagger. 'And at sunset, we will have Marluk brought to you, to judge as you please.'

In the Land of Ice, it was – ironically – fire that had devoured the Nayati. The entire building including all the interior décor, had been built of white spruce wood, a perfect treat for the flames. Only the foundations remained untouched, outlining the rough shape of the place, where Ylwa used to commune with the dehara. They'd never built a new one, even though a year had passed since the incident, which alone told me a lot about the community.

Death by fire is often but not always quick. Sometimes it has little to do with flame's embrace of the combustible body. Not even flesh melting off one's bones and skin dripping away automatically grant merciful death. Seeking oxygen, a burning person sucks fire down their airways, searing them shut. It is a horrible way to go, and the only thing I could comfort myself with were the governor's words that I was only partly inclined to believe.

'The position in which we found his body indicated that he was not trying to escape the flames. We believe that Marluk attacked him during his regular evening mediation, either killing him on spot or rendering him unconscious.'

The vision of Marluk burning down what was supposed to be the safest sanctuary in Nuuk resonated with the way I had always pictured him: demonic, inherently evil. Now my vision took an even more detailed form, marking his skin with ashes and illuminating the misshapen features of his face with the dancing reflection of flame.

'And he tried to set Ottar's house on fire next.' I stated what I knew to be true.

'He did. But Ottar was not asleep, he had a visitor. They surprised Marluk, scaring him away. That was when they noticed the light coming from the Nayati and alarmed the town, but the structure collapsed before we managed to put out the flames.'

I kneeled down on the ground, tentatively touching a charred balk. There was a Hienama in Alba Sulh, I heard, who had a very special talent. By touching objects at a crime scene, he could invoke detailed visions – echoes of the violent act. Perhaps a masochistic part of me hoped that I could somehow make that happen for myself, but all I felt was wood, rough and firm at first, but quickly disintegrating under my fingers.

There was no consolation to be found there and no answers waiting for me. However, the place would still serve me well. Its central position, overlooking the entire settlement, the mountains and the sea, would provide a perfect setting for my retribution. A befitting end to my journey and Marluk's life.

The ruins of the Nayati took on a sinister appearance in the dying light of the day, and so did the faces of the small crowd that had assembled around what would become the sacrificial site. Only five hara remained on the ship, guarding Skaddi as well as all of our belongings. The rest of us slowly approached the group, features set in silent concentration. I counted approximately forty of them, which coincided with the expected total number of inhabitants. Nohar stayed at home; two even carried harlings who were too little to walk.

What might have seemed like a murder to them was ritual killing for me. I had spent the few hours I had at my disposal preparing for it, carving runes onto my axe and braiding my hair in an elaborate manner. I wore my finest cloak, wanting to clothe myself in confidence and status worthy of the occasion.

I'd been told Marluk had gone through several stages of insanity since his inception – something I could not understand. Unlike them, I had never been human, nor could I imagine what it felt like to have everything that made up my identity twisted and turned, no matter that the result was on a higher branch of the tree of evolution. Marluk had had time to adjust over the past year. He'd changed profoundly, settled down, and – just a few days ago – had birthed a pearl. None of that was of importance to me. It could not help Ylwa.

The locals kept their distance from us, and so I separated myself from our group and walked half way toward them, locating the welcoming committee from earlier. My body was experiencing a rush similar to the bloodlust that often took hold while hunting an animal, yet not completely identical. Time seemed to have slowed down, or else I was moving through it with unnatural speed, aware of everything around me a fraction of a second sooner than under normal conditions.

'It is time for justice to be done. Where is he?'

This new kind of haze that surrounded me did not call for rash acts of violence. Rather than that, it gave me the feeling that I had all the time in the world to draw blood.

And then something unexpected happened. One of the hara who had attended with a harling carefully handed their offspring over to another and, after giving it one last gaze, left the safety of the crowd and walked towards me.

Despite his dark hair and tanned skin, a sign of Inuit blood, he looked nothing like the demon I had imagined. There was not a glimpse of defiance in his almond-shaped eyes as he wordlessly knelt in front of me; a har resigned to his fate. Perhaps this entire display, along with the fact that he brought his offspring along, had been orchestrated in order to weaken my resolution, but I would not reconsider. I was going to enjoy this all the same.

Would you take a hostling from his newly-hatched pearl? I was willing to go that far for a love that lasted beyond the grave. I was willing to execute a har, who did not fight back, in cold blood. Perhaps I had even more in common with our Viking ancestors than I used to believe, because I knew for certain that this was how my story should have ended: in blood.

I could literally hear the thumping of blood in my ears, feel its pressure at the back of my head. Everything so far had been building up to this very moment. I closed my eyes for a second, giving the most internal kind of signal. Then I raised the ritual axe.

And then the harling began to cry. The wailing sound made me look at him, actually *look*, and the road I had chosen to walk took a different turn.

Bringing death, while sneering in its face at the same time. Restless, agitated. Hands covered in blood, dragging on the lifeless body that had lost its footing moments ago. Striding away from the scene in long, powerful steps, finally relieved. Cleaning the axe in utter exhilaration, finally having been given the chance to drive it through the murderer's gut. Eyes still calling for more blood, a rage-filled scream echoing through the air.

That was how I had pictured myself when I let the axe fall an inch away from Marluk's head.

'Bring the harling to me,' I said.

The har looked up at me, horror written in his eyes, and I enjoyed this cruel little victory as he began to plead.

'Please... Do with me what you like but let him live. He is just three days old. He's done nothing in this life that...'

'And what if I don't care?' I snapped at him, interrupting the pitiful begging. 'What if I let *you* live and take away the only thing you love, just like you did to me. Why should I take away *your* life, now that I see how little it matters to you?'

Without waiting for answer, I stormed to the first row of onlookers and unceremoniously ripped the screaming bundle out of somehar's arms. The sound died down and I immediately *recognised* him.

Three days.

He didn't know me anymore and perhaps he would never remember, but the memories were still palpable in his little mind, enough for all my senses to pick up on them. The evergreen tree. The fresh grass we would lie upon. The sharing of thoughts that even the pain of rebirth could not have completely wiped out. The promises and hopes destroyed by untimely death mixed with the joy of a new adventure, in which I had no role to play.

Was I to finish my job and take him with me? Burden a harling with a history he couldn't possibly recall, because even the subconscious shards of memories, our sacred moments, would eventually disappear? That was something I could not do. And he had known that, known that this was possibly the only step I would be reluctant to take.

Our distant ancestors would have considered this to be a grand joke of a trickster god, whereas I knew that the deities did not make us. *We* created them. No, this joke was Ylwa's doing. Well played, my darling.

This final lesson of his was supposed to teach me something important, but I was not willing to understand it yet. Perhaps in time, I would – and I suspected time was something I would have a lot of once Týr found out we had skipped Alba Sulh. But then again, I might not. The heritage of my ancestors resonated strongly in me, and no matter how much Ylwa prompted me to move past that, I would always believe in the cathartic power of taking blood for blood.

I handed the harling back to the har I didn't know or wish to, and turned back to my own tribe, since they were the only ones who deserved an explanation here.

'The dehara have spoken to me. Nohar will die here today.'

Did my crew understand fully why I had not taken Marluk's life? I didn't think they could. But they *were* painfully aware of the fact that I had experienced something from beyond the threshold of this world on the sacrificial site, saw it shake me to the core and had the decency to accept the message of a dehar as an answer – for now. Their inherent respect for the dehara and various forces of nature did not give them room for doubts.

As agreed before, we left Skaddi in Nuuk. I was positive that eventually Týr, or an emissary of his, would arrive to pick him up and enquire about everything that had occurred there. It was highly doubtful that he would be told the entire truth from anyhar present, but that didn't concern me. By that time, we would have been already days into our journey south, to the lands where hara dressed skimpily, unburdened by snow.

At least that was what Mikkel said. As we sat at the stern of the ship, watching Nuuk disappear in the distance, he opened a bottle of mead and helped me drink the day away.

'One day, will you tell me what really happened tonight?' he asked as I passed him the alcohol.

'One day I will. Will you tell me about your life as a human?'

'If you really want to listen.'

There were no more words that needed to be said, and so we sat in silence until the bottle was empty. Then I retreated to sleep alone, as for the first time since losing my chesnari, there was no ghost for me to chase.

The Strangest Ghost of Apaley

Christiane Gertz

Zeboah sighed, tilting his head slightly to avoid the sunlight coming in through the large window, as he did every morning, when he woke up in the large, white bedroom. Alone, as usual. Not that he cared much.

He didn't have time to feel lonely or get lost in thoughts – his work kept him busy. He got up, quickly brushed his long black hair, grabbed a shirt, then hastily put on some tea to brew. Usually, he didn't have to hurry in the mornings, (one of his clients had stitched the words 'The Dead Can Wait' into a cushion to remind him of that), but today was a special day.

For more than two years, Zeboah had been the most successful spirit subsessor Apaley had ever known. Apaley was an ancient city by the river Huxholl, many of its old buildings still intact, in which humans used to live. Its large university brought all sorts of young hara into the town, making the grey streets a bit more colourful.

It takes time for hara to realise they aren't immortal – they just have much longer lifespans than the humans before them did. And they don't die like humans, they fade. Some might stay around for a long time, to remain by their loved ones, until they become ghost-like, semi-transparent beings. Some might communicate with certain friends or members of their family, until they pass onto the next plane of existence. Slowly and consciously.

Others, however, are not that lucky. Hara might die by force, suddenly and unexpectedly.

There are stories that humans had the same problems: When they died unprepared, they could not reach the next plane, (whatever that might have been for humans), and became trapped as spirits in the physical world.

Zeboah had chosen to help hara who found themselves in such a gruelling circumstance, and their loved ones, who had to watch helplessly. He had found ways to communicate with lost souls; it turned out he was more skilled at this than his teacher at the time.

He developed his techniques, gaining a reputation to solve even the most difficult cases, and had found that he was at his best when working alone.

But today this would change. Zeboah sipped his tea and sighed again. His workload had become too much for one har to manage alone, and Thamar, the director of the university responsible for organising Zeboah's work, had informed him about a new case for which a mysterious client had requested a team.

The way to the university was short, and the day was sunny. Students were everywhere; the semester had just begun. Zeboah was sometimes kept awake by young hara celebrating in the streets and couldn't help but think that he had been so different as a student – always concentrating on his spiritual training. Before he could think about this further, somehar bumped hard against his shoulder and nearly knocked him over.

He saw a young har with spiky, blond hair, who yelled at him: 'Can't you look where you're going?'

'Hey, it was *you* who…' Zeboah began.

But the har grabbed him by his shirt and pulled him roughly, so their faces were almost touching. His dark blue eyes flashed angrily, and his tone was quiet, threating: 'Get out of my way *now*.'

'Let go of me! How dare you…!' Zeboah struggled in the stranger's grip.

The har suddenly pushed him away, and Zeboah fell to the ground. When he got to his feet again, he saw the stranger walking away with long purposeful strides, his long black coat flying behind him.

Zeboah was shocked by this rudeness. But he needed to prepare for what lay ahead: The university was about to present him with the only candidate they had found suitable to be his partner. It seemed the requirements for this job had limited the choice somewhat: Ulani, Pyralis or higher caste – most of the Pyralisits would surely prefer more enlightened work in one of the beautiful cities in the South.

On entering the university campus, Zeboah regained control of his breath and heartbeat, through one of the breathing exercises he'd learned during his training. His anger with the stranger waned, and he felt calm enough again to face his task. He pushed open the heavy door that led to the floor of the administration offices, welcoming the chill of the old building.

'Welcome, Doyenix Zeboah', Thamar, the director of the university, greeted him formally. 'We've finally found a candidate for you!'

'Finally?' Zeboah inquired, 'I asked you to look for one only three weeks ago!'

'Hmm, yes. I hope you don't mind me saying that you… well sometimes you gave the impression of being overworked, a bit tired… So we decided to look for an assistant for you some months ago. It was hard to find somehar, but we had to act, as your new case requires a team.'

'I see… well then, let's have a look at the har in question, shall we? Anything I need to know about him before we speak?'

'Well, his name is Altavi har Altarim and he's quite young, but has excellent references from the local spirit subsessor, from whom he received his last level of training. He has some knowledge that might be useful.'

Zeboah pulled some notes from his pocket he'd prepared for the occasion. 'Good, I'll see. Just let me talk to him now.' He wanted to know more, and not only about the experience of his new assistant. He might find out something about his personality, too. Zeboah didn't like surprises and wanted to be prepared for their work together.

Thamar opened the door for Zeboah, who entered the room with his eyes firmly on the papers…*Where was that first page?*… He almost stumbled over two long legs, which belonged to a har sitting, in a relaxed outstretched position, in one of the big armchairs provided for guests. Zeboah's eyes met a pair of strange, dark blue ones. He drew in his breath sharply. Sitting before him was the stranger who had pushed him over some minutes ago.

The blonde har appeared as surprised as Zeboah and uttered something like: 'Whoops'. Then he regained his composure, got to his feet and bowed. 'Doyenix! So…' He flashed a smile at Zeboah, 'I trust your spiritual level enables you to forgive our little mishap earlier!'.

Zeboah couldn't believe it. He had hoped for some quiet, unobtrusive har who would help him from the background, and not… *this*. 'Well if *your* training allows you to stay calm in every situation and not push strangers around …yes!', he shot back.

Altavi laughed loudly: 'Well, that's one for you!'.

Zeboah turned to the director: 'Can I speak to you for just a minute?'. They went into an adjoining room.

'Are you serious?', Zeboah said in a low voice, 'that *individual* out there is the best you can find after a search of three months?'

The director made a placatory gesture with both hands. 'Look, he's attained the required level, and he's even got experiences in closing portals.'

'He closed a portal?' Zeboah was baffled. To close a portal to another level of existence was not only a very rare event, it could only be accomplished by the best practitioners. Zeboah himself had only closed two portals in his time as a subsessor. It was a dangerous procedure. Some hara died trying to close gates between the worlds. The usual practice was to persuade the beings from another plane or world to return where they belonged.

Zeboah took some deep breaths and quickly reviewed his options. He could refuse to work with this har, but that would mean he'd upset Thamar and the client. Or, he could put aside his personal feelings and give Altavi a chance. After all, the har seemed talented enough to have completed his training successfully. Zeboah just hoped he wouldn't be too troublesome.

Zeboah and Thamar returned to the main office, where official paperwork was signed by Zeboah and Altavi, who had become somewhat quiet.

Thamar inspected the new team for a moment and appeared satisfied. 'Now, I'll provide brief information on your case, since I'd like you to start on it immediately. The client called me again this morning and was insistent he needed to speak to you today.'

'Who is this har?' Zeboah asked.

'He is an artist,' Thamar replied, 'and, because he's fairly well-known, would prefer this matter to be treated confidentially. I assured him that's our usual practice, but I mention it to remind you of it too.' He looked at Altavi. 'You both might know this client. His name... well his real name doesn't matter... He calls himself Yael.'

Altavi uttered a sound of surprise and looked at Thamar with wide eyes: 'You mean...*the* Yael? The singer? Silver-haired, violet eyed, world-famous Yael?'

Zeboah winced at these remarks. He'd had famous clients before; there was no reason to make such a fuss about it.

'I don't know anything about his current hair or eye colour,' Thamar said stiffly, 'but yes, that is the har. Please keep in mind

you'll be talking to a client with a problem, and not some...'
Thamar waved his hand as if to shoo away a fly. It was clear he
didn't think much of Yael as an artist, perhaps scornful of the har's
flamboyant lifestyle. 'He claims to have been *pestered* by a spiritual
entity for some time, and five days ago, things got worse. He didn't
want to give me any further details, but when he called again this
morning, he was clearly upset, scared even. Matali from Immanion
has asked me to give this case preferential treatment, so I said you'd
arrive at Yael's address around lunch time.'

The carriage journey that Zeboah and Altavi took to Yael's house
on the outskirts of Apaley took far too long for Zeboah's taste.
Altavi talked non-stop the entire time.

'Did you hear that he has ten hara living in his house just for
aruna?' Altavi said, in an excited tone. 'And that you can actually
apply for that job?'

'Well, might that be an alternative for you, job-wise?' Zeboah
replied, with a vicious smile.

Altavi was silent for a moment, then said, 'Doyenix Zeboah, as
I already said, I'm sorry for my behaviour in the street. I was
nervous and anxious to get to my job interview in time, so... I kind
of lost it, you know?'

Zeboah didn't know.

Altavi renewed his observations about Yael. 'And did you hear
that he actually wore a chain of living butterflies during his "I Never
Killed a Human" tour?'

Zeboah closed his eyes and tried to concentrate on calming his
mind. Would this har never stop chattering?

Eventually, to his relief, the carriage pulled up in front of an old
house.

Altavi was quiet while they waited in front of the old wooden
door. Zeboah half expected some beautiful or eccentric-looking
house-har to answer their knock, but the har who opened the door
was pale, average looking, with long, dull hair. He wore a plain grey
robe.

Zeboah bowed politely. 'Greetings, Tiahaar. We are Zeboah and
Altavi, subsessors from the university. We've been engaged by the
head of the household.'

'That'll be me, then,' said the har at the door. 'Welcome.' He
stepped back and gestured for them to come inside.

So, this was the famous Yael, without all the paint and decoration. Zeboah was amused by the transformation. But now he must be professional. No matter who or what his new client was, only the work ahead mattered.

Yael led them to an expensively-furnished salon. 'I'm grateful you could come so quickly,' he said. 'This... problem I have has been going on for some time now. Please, sit down.'

Yael, sitting across from Zeboah and Altavi, appeared nervous. His hands pulled constantly at his hair, tucking back stray strands behind his ears.

Zeboah smiled in an attempt to put this har at ease. 'I'll begin with standard questions,' he said. 'When did you first see something unusual and what was it?'

'I first saw him two months ago,' Yael replied. 'A ghost. A strange ghost. He never talks. He just stares at me and gestures, as if he was... mute.'

'If you don't mind me asking, why did you take so long to call us?' Zeboah asked.

Yael grimaced. 'Well, at first he was... a bit scary, but useful. I first saw him a day or so after I moved here, in one of the upper rooms. I found him standing by the window, looking out. At first, I thought it was a real har, but then realised he wasn't entirely... *solid*. I knew then it wasn't somehar who'd sneaked into the house... They do that, you know, some of the fans – try to meet me or become a member of the famous harem I seem to have somewhere.' Yael smiled in a tired manner. 'It's strange, but whenever I see him he looks different, but I know it's always the same har. Ghost. Whatever. He's hard to describe... I can never see his face clearly.'

'Did this entity react to you in any way?' Zeboah asked.

Altavi was writing notes and, much to Zeboah's relief, not saying anything. He'd been afraid that Altavi would do something embarrassing, such as giving Yael silly compliments or asking for an autograph.

'He just stared at me,' Yael said, 'as if he was astonished I was there. Then it *looked* as if he tried to say something, but I didn't hear a sound. I tried to indicate I couldn't hear him, and I think he understood me. He felt kind of sad to me, and then he just disappeared. I thought that was it.'

'And what did you mean by him being useful?' Zeboah asked.

Yael's grey eyes lit up. 'Simply this… Before that encounter, I had what I call a *blank time*, when I don't have any new ideas, and find it hard to work. I needed inspiration for a new song. Just one hour after I saw that… ghost… I wrote "Heralds of a Different Time". That's what I mean by "useful". I saw him three times in the following weeks.' Yael got up and began to walk around the room. 'Each time I wrote for hours afterwards. It was as if something in my brain or my heart had broken free! I remembered feelings I'd forgotten. I had ideas I'd never had before!'

Zeboah realised that the reservations he'd had concerning this new client had diminished. He didn't seem to be the egocentric maniac that he appeared to be in public.

'He became your muse,' Altavi said.

Yael nodded approvingly. 'Yes. That's why I didn't call a subsessor. We met at various places in the house; he seemed to be looking at me sadly. I spoke to him, tried to comfort him, and thought he might find his way to the next world on his own. I played songs to him. He appeared to like that at first. But when I played him the songs he'd inspired me to write, that changed. And what's more, he became envious of the time I spent with others.'

Altavi addressed Zeboah and asked, 'May I?'

Zeboah waved a hand at him, nodded, hoping Altavi wasn't about to fulfil his worst expectations.

'Before we talk about this entity's apparent "envy", as you put it, please could you describe him in more detail? Can you guess his age? Is he tall?'

Yael looked tired again. 'No, I can't guess his age.' He frowned. 'It's as if I see him in different stages of his life. The first time I saw him, he had long, dark-blond hair. He's not very tall, but slender, like all hara. He's a bit peculiar-looking, but I couldn't say why exactly… It's as if he keeps his face in shadow. The second time I saw him, his hair was short and blonde, and he had strange trousers on, with… you know what I was wearing on stage for the Water Festival?' He addressed this question solely to Altavi, instinctively choosing the younger har.

'You mean braces?' Altavi asked. 'It's an antique accessory to keep your trousers up, which was popular in certain decades of the human era. I noticed you'd appropriated this fashion for your costumes on tour.'

'You know a lot of human history?' Yael asked, perhaps a little archly.

'Yes,' Altavi answered simply. 'But your ghost is... he's not *human*, is he?'

Yael laughed. 'No, I'm sure he's a har, so I guess he simply picked up on these... braces somewhere before I made them fashionable again.'

Zeboah didn't follow the cult around Yael and other contemporary singers that much, but awareness of this celebrity's ever-changing and ever-more-outrageous appearance was unavoidable in a city like Apaley, with all its festivals and concerts, and the large population of young, student hara to enjoy them. They adopted the fashions worn by artistes at the festivals, and Zeboah saw the results in the streets and cafés. Lately, hara had begun to wear spectacles, a contraption of sight-correcting lenses humans had used when their eyesight was poor. Humans had suffered from all sorts of physical deficiencies but had generally developed means to overcome them. Now, certain of these items were used as fashion accessories by the young.

'I loved the walking stick you had last year, and the monocle! You looked... so cute!' Altavi, who so far had maintained an air of professional competence, now began to sound like the excited young har he'd been during the carriage ride.

Zeboah felt obliged to curtail this. 'Ahem... let's keep on track. The entity has an undefinable age and average stature. On the occasions you see him, he wears different clothes, and his hair styles are different. You can't see his face clearly. What else?'

Yael thought for a while. 'He once danced.'

Altavi glanced up from his notes. 'He...*danced?*'

'Yes, before he got nasty, when I played him one of my old songs. Before that, I wasn't sure if he could hear me. He seemed to listen, but... I just wasn't sure, because he couldn't answer. One night, I played him "Sun Light Song". He smiled and did some funny, slow dance. Then he stopped, looked at me, and just disappeared.' Yael sighed. 'Two weeks ago, things changed. I met him in the room where I keep my guitars, and spontaneously played one of the songs he'd inspired me to write. And he didn't like it. I couldn't see his face, it was in shadow as usual, but his whole appearance became dark grey, as if he was filled with smoke. I could sense his anger. Then I asked aloud: "What's wrong?", but he just disappeared and didn't show up again.

'Then it got worse. I had a har living here, Jabin. We weren't chesna, but together for some time. He never saw the ghost, and I didn't tell him about it, because I didn't want to scare him away. Then, one time, I saw the ghost in my bedroom, and he seemed to be waiting for me. But Jabin was directly behind me, so I made a sort of shooing gesture, so the ghost would go away. My friend came in but didn't see him. The ghost went up to him, stood directly in front of him, and stared at him for a minute or so. This was while Jabin was undressing, and it was very disturbing to watch that scene. The ghost disappeared, and I acted as if nothing happened, but I had a hunch that things wouldn't be easy from then on.'

Yael had begun to pace the room again. 'Strange things began to happen. I didn't see the ghost anymore, but my friend kept having accidents. Glasses broke in his hand or even against his mouth. He cut himself with most knives he tried to use for cooking. His possessions were forever disappearing. All the while I kept thinking: "Are these just coincidences? Or is it more?". Jabin started to joke that the house didn't like him, or I was bringing him bad luck. I could see he was getting more concerned about it all, as it went beyond something you could joke about. He saw a picture slide down a wall, a glass break into a thousand pieces *before* it hit the ground. He had to jump back quickly, or he'd have been hit.'

Altavi had stopped to take notes and stared at Yael open-mouthed, clearly taken in by his story.

Zeboah touched Altavi lightly but firmly on the arm to bring him back into professional mode. 'And you took no action whatsoever?' he asked gently.

Yael glanced away briefly, as if embarrassed. 'At that time, I called in a... semi-professional subsessor.' He looked back at Zeboah, as if expecting a negative reaction to this disclosure.

Zeboah knew that there was a whole scene of "ghost hunters", who used a variety of peculiar tools and methods. Generally, they didn't ask too much about the family history or mental health of their clients. In some cases, hara preferred their services, because they were cheaper to hire and less officious, often embellishing their work with spiritual practices. Zeboah didn't care about this – he saw these amateur rivals as fairly harmless – as long as he didn't have to clean up any mess these ghost hunters left behind them. 'And what did this semi-professional attempt to do?' Zeboah asked.

'Well, he tried some rituals, which didn't help, and later we ended up in a rather... unprofessional situation. Very unpleasant.'

This time, Zeboah did react. 'Unprofessional and unpleasant meaning...?' If there was a charlatan out there, he would have to take action.

'Umm... we smoked something as part of a ritual, ended up in bed, and when I asked him to leave after aruna, he was furious.'

Zeboah couldn't help but smile. So, no need to notify the authorities just yet! Simply an aruna encounter gone wrong.

Yael sat down again, his eyes somewhat narrowed. 'I realised I needed the help of professionals, and also... a team, so I'm not distracted... although, well, when I look at you...' He leaned closer to Zeboah, who winced away in distaste.

'You're seeking help concerning a potentially dangerous discarnate entity that's threatening you, and still find it appropriate to make a pass at me?' Zeboah snapped, and instantly wished he'd not said those words aloud. Normally, he remained composed, under any circumstances.

Yael laughed. 'You're right. I'm an awful har. I could say I was testing you, but you'll never be sure about that, right? I heard that you're a no-nonsense, serious har, and that's why I wanted you for this, plus this bright young har there, because a second pair of eyes might see more. And now it seems he might even have witnessed what happened five days ago.'

Altavi, whose expression had remained unreadable for the past couple of minutes, raised his brows. 'What do you mean, Tiahaar?'

'Did you go to see my show in *The Quarry* last week?'

Altavi nodded. 'Yes. You sang four new songs.'

'And you didn't notice anything unusual or... different about me?'

Altavi shrugged. 'Well, now that you mention it, you seemed... distracted. I'll be honest – I thought it was drug-related. Everyone knows there are some new highs on the market now, and they can have strong effects. I thought it was that.'

'You're too polite,' Yael said. 'The truth was, I had to stop the performance briefly twice, and eventually fell over, although fortunately it appeared I'd slipped.'

'There was nothing serious enough to be in the media,' Altavi said, reassuringly.

Yael snorted. 'Oh, come on! The show was a mess. And the truth is: I was completely sober. I always am on stage. But *he* was there. At the side of the stage. He simply stared at me. I think even some hara in the first row might have been able to see him, but how can I know? I couldn't exactly go up to them and ask: "Oh, by the way, did you see a strange creature with fiery eyes at the side of the stage. He would have appeared to be filling up with grey smoke when I sang?"' He shook his head, rubbed his face. 'I felt I was going to choke up there. And then I couldn't see anything. I guess at that point he'd figured out how to get physical control over me. I called the university the next day.'

Now Yael buried his face in his hands. 'And then, two days ago, he pushed my friend Jabin down the stairs. He broke a leg. It could've been even worse, you know. Once he was in the care facility, I had to tell him everything. I asked him to keep quiet about it. He will, but our relationship is over. He never wants to set foot in this house again, nor see me again either. He thinks I've invented the ghost, and it's some kind of negative energy within me that pushed him down the stairs.'

Zeboah said nothing but felt sympathy for Yael. If the entity was a fading har who'd latched onto Yael, or a bona fide ghost, it was unusual for such manifestations to be able to affect physical reality in the way Yael had described. 'Thank you for telling us your story,' Zeboah said. 'I appreciate how distressing it is for you. But you did the right thing in contacting us.' He glanced at Altavi, who now seemed somewhat bewildered. 'We'll act quickly, since the entity appears to be gaining strength and mobility. It's not chained to one location. We'll go back to our department and discuss the situation and possible strategies with our colleagues. We'll return tomorrow and attempt to contact the entity, in order to discover what this is all about.'

'Thank you. I appreciate it.'

'Now,' Zeboah said, 'do you have somewhere you can stay where you won't be alone?'

Yael nodded. 'Yes.'

'Good. Please go there and meet us back here tomorrow morning at 10. Is that convenient?'

'It is.'

Yael showed them to the door, but at the threshold, put a hand on Zeboah's arm. 'Please excuse me – I know this is trivial,' he said, 'but what do you use on your hair?'

Altavi uttered a smothered laugh, while Zeboah snapped, 'Excuse me?'

Yael shrugged. 'I mean, it looks beautiful – such shiny black. Mine's so dull, when it's not full of feathers, beads and so on. I guess I colour it too often…' He smiled hopefully.

To his own horror and Altavi's apparent amusement, Zeboah blushed. 'Er… I use coconut and argan oil, with a drop of lemon juice. I make it myself…. Would you like me to bring some for you tomorrow?'

'Yes, that'd be great, thank you.'

Once the door was closed on them, Altavi said, 'My favourite singer without make-up and a glass-shattering ghost. Nice first day at work. Oh – and advice on hair care.'

Zeboah sniffed in disapproval. 'Be quiet. We need to form a strategy for tomorrow.'

They walked back to the waiting carriage.

Altavi stretched inside the confined space and yawned. 'It's weird. I feel so tired, as if my energy's drained.'

'It is. I feel the same,' Zeboah said. 'I'm not sure if it's entirely down to the entity or Yael himself. Celebrities need attention like vampires need blood.'

'I'm not sure I'm up to planning strategies. I'm also starving. I don't know if I'm able to think!'

Zeboah realised he too felt out of sorts, and very tired. 'I'm going to go home and freshen up, then perhaps we could meet at my favourite Souvli restaurant. I still think you were too rude this morning and strongly disapprove of your behaviour, but I'm too hungry to care, so I'm inviting you to share my meal.'

Zeboah didn't take much time to rest at home but dressed in less formal garments: a dark green silk shirt to match his eyes. Remembering Yael's compliments, he freed his hair from the pencils he used to hold it up in a bun.

When he arrived at the restaurant, it was already full of hara, as this place served the best Souvli in town: traditional dumplings with salty or sweet fillings, all of them delicious. Zeboah spotted Altavi in a corner – he couldn't be missed with his almost white hair surrounding him like a spiky halo. He wore Kajal around his eyes and a strange old-looking shirt, plus red chequered trousers: a peculiar outfit but it looked good on him.

Altavi jumped up when he saw Zeboah. 'Oh, you…', he started, but broke off and appeared a little confused.

'Doyenix is the proper salutation,' Zeboah said and proceeded to sit down. He still hadn't forgotten their first encounter.

When the pothar arrived at their table to take their order, Zeboah picked something for Altavi and himself to eat. He noticed that Altavi was still staring at him. 'Do I have something on my face?' he asked, unnerved. 'Why are you looking at me like that?'

Altavi appeared uneasy. 'You look quite…different.' he said.

Zeboah didn't want the conversation getting too personal. 'I'm curious,' he said. 'How would *you* start with our new case?'

Altavi straightened his face, clearly aware of the rebuff. 'Well, one thing is clear, the entity in Yael's house isn't somehar he knows – no relative, chesnari or friend – so we can exclude the usual questioning. As the entity has already manifested on the physical plane, I'd suggest we begin with a level two incantation, then set up a trap, maybe with Casarea stones, to keep it where we want it. Obviously, we don't yet know if we can communicate with the entity properly, as Yael has told us it's mute, but maybe we could use a Hesbron board.'

Zeboah was impressed. 'I concur with your observations,' he said, and smiled. While Altavi might grate on a personal level, professionally he promised to be a help.

By the time the Souvli arrived, Zeboah and Altavi had already made notes on how to proceed, as well as a list of what equipment they'd require. Now they could turn their attention to the meal.

'Delicious!' commented Altavi, shovelling up a third helping of Souvli with his fork. He managed to eat and speak at the same time, a trait Zeboah generally disliked.

'Have you ever encountered a human ghost?' Altavi asked without looking up from his plate.

'No, never,' Zeboah replied. 'To me, it's clear they simply weren't strong enough to cling on to their existence in that manner.'

'But human lore is full of ghost stories!' Altavi exclaimed. 'Ghosts and ghost hunters were popular in films and fiction. Did you not know that?'

Zeboah noted that Altavi didn't look tired anymore. He considered for a moment that his new partner might be one of these crazy humanity fans, who rummaged for the last pieces of human daily life in antique shops or even dressed in their clothes. 'You've studied human forms of entertainment?' Zeboah enquired, being sure to inject a sliver of disapproval into his voice.

'Yes, I wrote papers on it during my studies.' Altavi licked his fingers. 'Their music was the best!' He gulped down his second glass of wine. 'I'm involved in a project devoted to conserving the recordings of human music. What they called digital media was mostly lost, but recordings on vinyl survived. We collect whatever we can, and also the devices that allow us to listen to the records. I've heard so many different kinds of music, a lot of it absolutely amazing. Have you never...?

'No,' Zeboah interrupted. 'The fact is, it doesn't interest me, Altavi. I'm sorry.' He smiled to soften his remark, even if his teeth were somewhat gritted. He was aware that humans had left behind some fine literature, art and music, but he still thought that most of them had been idiots and fools to lose the world the way they had. He believed hara should make their own art and not dwell on the past.

Altavi grinned. 'Ok, you're entitled to your opinion, but I think you're missing out.' His face fell. 'Sadly, the project is... under threat. I don't know if...'

Zeboah refused to continue that line of conversation. 'As for human spirits,' he interrupted, 'of course I've heard the tales about how some are supposed to haunt various properties in this town, but I've never come across one myself. I believe it's merely stories. If there were human ghosts at one time, they're gone for good now.'

Altavi shrugged. 'You might be right, but I keep an open mind.'

Contrary to his expectations, Zeboah enjoyed the evening. He and Altavi talked about their work, comparing experiences. Altavi's enthusiasm was irresistibly contagious. Altavi was bright, and good company, even if he could be irritating and impulsive. Zeboah put this down to the other har's relative youthfulness but decided he could put with that.

The following day, Zeboah and Altavi met at Zeboah's office. Here, they packed all the equipment they'd need for the work ahead – the Hesbron board, and appropriate crystals and incense.

'Did you remember the hair oil?' Altavi asked, grinning widely.

'Yes,' Zeboah answered shortly. 'Shall we go?'

On the way to Yael's house, they discussed details of how to invoke and control the uninvited entity.

When he answered the door to them, Yael looked pale and

anxious. After the initial greetings, Zeboah offered Yael his gift. 'Use it sparingly,' he said, feeling Altavi's amusement behind him.

'Thank you for remembering,' Yael said and put the jar down on a table in the hall. He gestured for his guests to go into the living-room.

Here, Zeboah and Altavi took seats, and after the offer of refreshment had been attended to, and Yael sat with them, got down to business.

'We'll begin as soon as possible,' Zeboah said to Yael. 'First, I'll tell you what will happen. This is so you'll know your part in it and will be clear on what the procedure entails. Once we get started, there might not be the time or opportunity for you to ask questions, so if you're not sure about anything, or need further explanation, let me know.'

'OK,' Yael said warily.

Zeboah nodded briefly. 'Thank you. Our task today is to invoke the entity and attempt to communicate with it. For that, we have a piece of equipment know as a Hesbron board, which will provide a means for the spirit to answer our questions and reveal why it's here. It's mainly a board with letters and an indicator that discarnate beings can move, to spell words. We will be cautious, since the entity is able to act on the physical plane and has exhibited violent behaviour. We'll construct an energy circle with crystals, which will keep the spirit locked in place, so it won't be able to attack us or simply fade away. Perhaps you could explain this part, Altavi.'

The other har nodded. 'Of course.' He lifted the pouch of crystals and let some of them spill out into his hand. He held one transparent stone out to Yael. 'Take it, he said.

Yael did so.

'That's the purest clear quartz,' Altavi said. 'These crystals amplify energy and facilitate communications between a spirit and an incarnate being.' He took another stone in his fingers and held it out. 'This is haematite, which is an iron oxide. These stones conduct energy and ground it. They'll provide a level of protection for us.'

Yael took the stone from him, examined it.

'We'll also use amethysts in the circle to help amplify our psychic abilities and rose quartz to bring a calming, compassionate influence. Altavi handed examples of these stones to Yael. 'Finally, we'll include agates for further energy amplification and to aid in rooting the entity in place.'

Yael handed the stones back to Altavi. 'Thank you,' he said.

Zeboah brought out the pouch of loose incense and offered it to Yael to smell. 'This is the incense we'll use. It's a blend designed to facilitate the summoning of spirits and the heightening of psychic senses. It includes copal resin, lavender, rose petals, cedar wood, wormwood and lemon grass.' Zeboah took the pouch back from Yael. 'We'll first purify the space with the smoke of sage and myrrh.' He leaned forward. 'You must understand, Tiahaar, the grounding of this spirit will only be effective for a short time, meaning our questions will be limited. Is everything clear so far?'

'Yes, Tiahaar,' Yael replied, flicking a glance towards Altavi, perhaps for reassurance.

'Good,' Zeboah said. 'Your role will be to sit in the crystal circle with us. As soon as the entity manifests, I'd like you to place the remaining crystals so as to close the circle. Can you do that?'

Yael nodded.

'After this, it's best you do nothing more than observe. However, if the entity should want to interact with you, I have a list of the questions you must ask. Now, do *you* have any questions?' He held out a sheet of information to his client.

Yael took the page and shook his head. 'Not really, but… are you sure you'll be able to see him? Jabin couldn't…'

'Yes,' Zeboah answered. 'Our training enables us to observe manifestations, even entities that intend to remain hidden. Also, we'll smoke an herbal mix that will deepen our perceptions and help reveal otherworldly visitors to our inner senses. Are you ready to begin, Tiahaar?'

'Yes…' Yael replied. 'In this room?'

'We'll at least start here,' Zeboah said. 'May we roll back the rugs?'

'Of course.'

Zeboah and Altavi undertook the preparations, clearing a space in the room. While Zeboah arranged the crystals on the floor, Altavi first purified the room with sage and myrrh, then lit the incense, which emitted a pleasing scent. Once everything was ready, Zeboah placed a bowl of dark fluid at his side; his Anani bowl, an indicator for spirits. Then he gestured for his companions to sit with him, in a triangle formation, within the circle of crystals. The crystals were closely-placed but for one area where there was a gap. At Yael's side were the crystals that would close that space eventually. In his lap, he held a guitar.

Altavi lit the smoking pipe with the herbal mix and passed it around their small circle. Once this was done, Zeboah and Altavi began a chant of invocation. Yael sat between, watching them keenly, holding an amethyst in his hand.

After some minutes, Zeboah ceased chanting. Altavi faltered to silence too.

'This is strange,' Zeboah said. 'Nothing's happening. I'm not picking anything up. What about you, Altavi?'

Altavi shook his head. 'No, nothing…'

Zeboah turned to Yael. 'Usually I make contact with spirits easily. This one is resisting. Might I ask how you managed to invoke it with that… semi-professional subsessor?'

'He had the same problem,' Yael said, 'so I whistled one of my new songs. That made the ghost come to us straight away.'

Zeboah nodded. 'I see. Well, perhaps you could do that again.'

Yael started to whistle a tune, and Zeboah watched a frown form on his junior partner's face. Before he could ask what was wrong, he felt the familiar chill in the room. Before them, a slim figure materialised in the centre of the circle. It wore an ancient-looking bright blue suit. The entity appeared almost solid, but his face was blurry. He emitted rays of orange and blue light.

'Close the circle!' Zeboah said calmly, and Yael put the missing crystals in place.

'Welcome,' Zeboah said softly to the spirit. 'I see you have chosen to visit our plane of existence.'

The ghost turned its head, so Zeboah guessed he could be heard. 'I know you cannot speak to us, but before you is a Hesbron board, which allows you to spell words. Do you understand?'

The entity seemed compliant but began to emit flickers of orange light again. Zeboah noticed that Yael and Altavi had begun to shiver. Altavi murmured to the others that he saw the curtains move, but reassured Yael they were all safe within the circle. Energy was building up around them. The entity was attempting to escape but was anchored by the crystals. Perhaps realising this, it turned slowly in Yael's direction, then leaned over towards the Hesbron board, its hands flickering quickly upon it.

Altavi leaned forward to read the words that had been spelled out. 'Play for me.'

For a moment, the spirit's features became clear, as if it had forgotten to hide its face. A pale, beautiful har, wearing heavy makeup. Then the image faded to blurred features once more. The entity pointed at Yael.

'You mean, one of my new songs?' Yael picked up the guitar and started to play the song he had whistled before.

Within moments, the entity became semi-transparent, its silhouette filling up with thick black smoke, which reached out into the room in waving tendrils. A deafening, high-pitched noise filled the room.

Yael jerked backwards, dropped the guitar, his hands pressed to his ears.

'Be calm,' Altavi said, raising his voice to be heard over the noise. He put a reassuring hand on Yael's arm. 'The ghost can't break out of our circle.'

The entity moved the planchette again.

'Mine!' mumbled Altavi, reading the word. 'The entity claims this is HIS song!'

'Is this why you're so angry?' Zeboah asked.

The entity turned to regard him, and the noise in the room diminished. The smoke dispersed. Now, the entity sat down – like any living har – in front of the Hesbron board, where its form slumped. Slowly, it spelled out another word.

'Confused,' Altavi read aloud.

'About your state?' Yael asked. 'You know what happened to you?'

This question was on the list Zeboah had given Yael.

The entity's hand moved on the board. 'Dead,' it wrote.

And then it was gone.

After a short silence, Yael was the first to talk. 'Do you really think it was his song and he… well, put it into my head?'

Zeboah had to smile. Yael didn't seem to be afraid of the entity anymore but was worried about the song and his rights to it.

'Actually,' Altavi said, 'when I heard you whistle the song, I thought I knew the tune. If I only remember where I heard it…'

'Did you see his face?' Yael asked. 'He looks really strange, but I couldn't find why in that second, something with his eyes… and he didn't have any eyebrows!'

Zeboah had remained silent since the entity had vanished but had been staring into the bowl of dark fluid he had beside him. 'I don't understand why there's no reaction in my Anani bowl…' He glanced at Yael. 'This water is from a very special well. It reacts to all kinds of entities and changes its colour. It's an indicator as to how old an entity is and can sometimes even reveal the location of where it lived before its body died. But this time, the water remained unchanged…'

'Almost as if the entity wasn't here at all,' Altavi murmured. 'As if we only imagined it.'

Zeboah nodded. 'We have an angry and confused spirit here, which behaves like no others I've ever seen, who looks like a har but could be something else. Why is he confused? He knows he's dead, so that can't be it.' Zeboah stood up and stepped out of the circle to pace the room. He just couldn't get his head around this.

'What if…?' Altavi began.

Zeboah and Yael both looked at him.

'What if he *is* human, after all?'.

Zeboah tried not to roll his eyes at this remark. He felt Altavi's words merely reflected his distasteful enthusiasm for anything human. *Stupid, youthful fad!* 'Altavi,' he said sternly. 'You know my thoughts on the idea of human ghosts…'

Altavi jumped up so suddenly that Zeboah winced backwards. As he headed for the door, Altavi turned and said: 'I know who he is! I'll prove it. Wait right here. I'll back in half an hour or so.'

'Altavi, wait!' Zeboah snapped, but his partner ignored this command and slammed the door behind him.

Yael raised his eyebrows at Zeboah.

'I apologise for my assistant,' Zeboah said, 'he's… young, enthusiastic…' *And should do as he's told,* Zeboah thought. 'He's only just started with…'

'Oh, don't apologise,' Yael interrupted. 'I can see Altavi is bright and eager, and I'm sure he just had some fabulous idea. I can see his way is different to yours, and this might seem like insubordination…'

'Well…' Zeboah was rather taken aback this client, whom he did not know, could make such assumptions on short acquaintance.

Yael smiled. 'He respects you greatly. He stares at you whenever he thinks you won't notice.'

Zeboah frowned. 'I'm here to do a job, Tiahaar. I can't discuss my colleague with you. It's against…'

'Oh, come *on*!' Yael said, laughing. 'Loosen up a bit. The world is serious enough as it is. He's got a little crush on you – that's not a crime. Why not simply enjoy the attention? He'll work harder just to please you.' He got to his feet. 'I think we could use some refreshment. Tea OK for you?'

'Yes… Thank you.'

When Yael returned with the tea, he'd clearly decided not to pursue personal remarks. He handed Zeboah a large cup and said, 'Have you considered Altavi might be right? After all, just because you've never seen the ghost of a human doesn't mean they don't exist.'

Zeboah grimaced, sipped his tea. 'The entity *looks* harish. It… *he* even reminds me of paintings of the Aghama in physical form. Also, this spirit emits a tremendous amount of energy. What kind of human could maintain that for any length of time, if at all?'

Yael gestured with both hands. 'I understand your view, but sometimes I think we underestimate humans. We've written them off as inferior beings, the idiots who nearly killed the world and who were certainly mainly responsible for their own extinction. But they *are* our ancestors, since the original hara all came from human stock.'

'That's an inconvenient fact most hara struggle with,' Zeboah said, smiling wanly.

'I know, but I believe humankind simply didn't learn fast enough how to adapt to their changing world, and how to survive.' Yael picked up his guitar. 'But they made beautiful instruments like this…'. He played some chords and looked up at Zeboah, smiling. 'They made beautiful art. Doesn't that suggest they weren't *all* evil or stupid?'

Zeboah leaned back in his seat and for some minutes listened to Yael play and sing. Perhaps this har was right, but that still didn't mean Zeboah could accept the spirit of a human had appeared to them that day.

The relaxed mood was interrupted by the return of Altavi. He was breathless from running and carried a large leather bag.

'Is this your proof?' Zeboah demanded.

'Do you remember our first encounter?' Altavi asked him.

'That's pretty hard to forget,' Zeboah said stiffly, 'but I fail to see its relevance…'

'I was rude to you, but I haven't explained why... the cause. Remember I told you yesterday about this project I'm working on, collecting recordings of human music? Our group buys them from all over the world, as well as the devices to play them.'

Altavi sat down and took a drink of Zeboah's cold tea. 'That morning, before I met you, I'd just heard the project is being cancelled, our funding withdrawn. I was furious! I wanted to make a huge archive of recordings, so hara from everywhere could access it and listen to all the different music. But now...'

'Altavi,' Zeboah interrupted. 'I'm sorry to hear your little enterprise is no more, but this is hardly...'

'Please,' Altavi said, 'just listen. I wanted to tell you this when we went for that meal, but you shut me up! Just hear me out? Please?'

Zeboah sniffed. 'Oh, very well. But I really hope this is relevant to our current work.'

'You'll see,' Altavi said. 'Anyway, the rooms where we store the records will have to be cleared. None of us involved in the project have room to keep them in our homes, and storage is expensive to rent. There's a chance the records will have to be destroyed.'

'That's terrible,' Yael interjected. 'All that music, lost forever.'

'I know,' Altavi said. 'It's a part of the only remaining cultural heritage we have, except for printed literature and paintings. So much lost because it was stored electronically. Records have survived because theirs is the only medium still playable.' He turned to Zeboah. 'Can you understand now why I was so frustrated yesterday morning? I couldn't believe some older hara have the power to decide about that, just because they don't care. They said human music is "inferior", but they've only listened to the wrong kind of music.'

'OK, I sympathise,' Zeboah said, 'but what has this to do with our work, Altavi?'

'I'll tell you. When Yael whistled that song, I knew it. I'd heard it before. I have a very good memory for music but couldn't quite place it until after the session. Then it came to me. This was a piece I'd found extraordinary, and I'd wanted to present it to my friends, before the project was stopped.' He pulled out a flat, square, cardboard package from his bag. 'The original cover is lost, of course. It was destroyed long ago, along with the information that was on it. But I wrote a description on its new casing, so I'm able to tell the records apart. Unfortunately, the device that can play it is locked away in the university of Altarim. They must be afraid I'll run away with a precious antique because they stopped my project. This means I can just show you...'

'Wait', said Yael. 'I have a record player... or two. Not electronic ones.'

'You have two *gramophones*?' Altavi asked, wide-eyed. 'You know how rare they are?'

'Well I got them from a friend, along with some of these... records. I just didn't like the music much, so I forgot about it completely. Let me see... Excuse me a moment.'

Left alone with Altavi for a short time, Zeboah had intended to scold him for running away, but now he was curious. When Yael came back into the room with a heavy case, Altavi jumped up to help him carry it to the table.

Altavi opened the lid, inspected the device, then pulled out a large black shiny disc from its packaging, holding it carefully at the sides. He put the disc down on the device, turned a crank he had put in the side, and carefully lifted a silver arm on the disc.

From the little round mesh at the side of the box, they heard a crackling. Then, music. Someone played the guitar, and a voice sang. The three hara listened in fascination.

'That's so different from the music I heard!' Yael said in wonder. 'This is beautiful!'

Altavi carefully lifted the silver arm and put it down in another place of the revolving black disc. The sound of a piano came out of the machine, and presently a voice.

Yael froze. 'That's... not possible', he said slowly. The unknown voice was singing the same tune Yael had sung just an hour ago, but with different words.

'This is him,' Altavi said. 'He's human. Or was. And the connection between you, Yael, is music. I think he came to you because he doesn't want his music to be forgotten. But maybe he's angry you've claimed it as yours.'

Yael slowly nodded, his eyes unfocussed. 'Yes... It all makes sense now. Who was it?'

Altavi lifted the disc from the gramophone and hand it carefully to Yael, who took it gently by the rim. 'His name is on the label in the middle.'

Yael peered at the ancient faded print. 'The inspiration to write the songs came from this man, his work. When I was writing them, they *felt* like my own, but also new and strange.'

'I believe the energy you received from this connection must have gone back to the entity but amplified,' Zeboah said. 'You could say it *fed* him.'

'But what kind of human can still be around, after all this time?' Yael asked. 'And why does he look like a har?'

Zeboah pursed his lips. 'From what I felt, he was an *unusual* human. Maybe he even had a bit of har in him. Some of our scientists believe there were intermediate stages between human and har. A development. Not just one step from them to us. Perhaps humans that didn't fit in, that were looked upon as strange. Combined with talent, that might have helped make a person famous.'

'They called famous people "stars", Altavi said. 'Like something high up in the sky, that you can't really understand.'

Yael smiled. 'That would also explain my ghost's jealousy. When you're famous, you get so much attention you can become addicted to it. And I was obviously the only har he was able to make contact with. He must've felt alone in this world.'

'And that's why he said he's confused,' Altavi said heatedly. 'Maybe he died before the human world fell apart completely, before we came. Now he sees the world has changed and can't understand what has happened and who or what we are!'

'That's all rather simplistic,' Zeboah said. 'Discarnate entities rarely have complete awareness of their surroundings, or even their condition, when they're trapped in the material realm.'

'I think it's clear this entity is different,' Altavi said defensively. 'I believe he has a stronger spirit and will than most humans had.'

Zeboah nodded slowly. 'Well, that's an assumption, Altavi, but perhaps a correct one. So this is what we'll do. It will take time and energy, so we have to prepare. We'll call to this entity again and let him know that we understand that he wrote these songs. We can even play some of him on that... device.' He pointed to the gramophone. 'We know his name now. So, you can assure him, Yael that in future you'll credit him for his music. If we establish he is able to communicate with us properly and understand what we tell him, we can relate a short summary of Wraeththu history. Maybe that will give him peace.'

For the next session, they would gather at night. Zeboah felt this would allow them to establish a better connection with the entity.

Altavi said to him, 'Humans believed that ghosts visit mostly at night. They called midnight "the hour of the ghosts", isn't that beautiful?'

Zeboah smiled. Since they last met Yael three days ago, the three of them had studied antique human books from the university and had combed through the archives. Zeboah had found that Altavi's enthusiasm concerning humans didn't get on his nerves as much now.

On the night they chose for the invocation, Yael had prepared his music room as instructed. He had taken care to remove anything with shining surfaces and had prepared a space on the floor with candles and cushions. Altavi moved clockwise through the room to ignite little bowls of incense and resin. Zeboah laid out the crystals. Finally, he looked around the room, hands on his hips.

Yael carried the gramophone into the room. 'I know you won't want to hear this,' he said, 'and, yes, we have to concentrate on what's ahead, but you look fantastic!'

Zeboah didn't remark on this observation but pulled the girdle of his robe a little tighter around him. He was wearing his hair loose, the long black waves falling on the silky robe. 'Can you wind up that thing, so we can play his music once he shows?', he asked, pointing at the device.

Yael nodded. He also had a guitar with him, claiming he felt that the ghost would be attracted by his singing again.

When they sat down, Zeboah noted that Altavi was quite pale. 'Are you alright?', he inquired.

'Well – I was just thinking, this might be historic!' Altavi answered. 'The first time a human will learn about how Wraeththu have changed the world, the society we've built. We were created in a time of upheaval and violence that led to the extinction of the human race. Now, we have a more or less peaceful world, completely different from theirs. I wonder how I would feel, if I were him... His kind are no more. He's alone.'

Zeboah sighed. 'Altavi, as you know full well, discarnate entities do not travel in packs, and by their very nature are *essentially* alone. It might be this being won't be able to understand what we try to tell him. Our aim is to reassure whatever essence is left of this man that he and his art aren't forgotten. Anyway, it's time to begin. The hour of the ghosts is upon us.'

Yael had put an old clock on the mantelpiece, which promptly began to chime.

As before, Zeboah and his companions sat within a crystal circle, but this time the composition was aimed more towards attracting a spirit and enabling it to manifest rather than to trap it.

Zeboah closed his eyes and began to speak. 'You who lived yesterday, I call from my mind to yours. Come back from the shadows and show yourself here.' He raised a hand, which was a signal. Yael picked up his guitar and began to play and sing softly. This time, he used the original words he had picked up from listening to the record.

The air in the room began to turn chill. Presently, the entity appeared in the centre of their circle. Zeboah could no longer think of this being as "it". He was surrounded by orange light, which matched the colour of his hair.

Altavi draw in his breath sharply beside him. Yael had stopped singing. They were able to see the entity's face clearly and for longer than a brief moment. He looked nothing like the humans they knew from historical documents and pictures. He possessed a strange, pale beauty, with high cheekbones and the strangest eyes Zeboah had ever seen – they were of different colours, one bright blue, the other darker.

'Welcome to our plane of existence,' Zeboah said, inclining his head. 'On this occasion, we do not seek to bind you here, but rather – we ask you to stay and speak with us. We mean you no harm. We know who you are, or rather, we just know this…' Zeboah made a gesture to Altavi, who activated the record player. Once again, music filled the room.

The entity's eyes grew wide. He could clearly hear it, and he understood: whoever or whatever these beings in front of him were – they knew about his music, his existence.

'We have brought the Hesbron board again,' Zeboah said. 'You may tell us and ask us anything you like. We have all the time you need.'

The entity inspected each of them, and then he smiled. Zeboah noticed that his teeth looked rather big, but this imperfection, like his mismatched eyes, mysteriously made him more beautiful. He sat down in front of the Hesbron board and began to move the indicator around the letters quickly.

'You live in my house,' Altavi read out aloud. He glanced at his companions. 'In life, this was his home... at least for some time.'

'Have you ever appeared to hara... people... here before?' Yael asked.

'No', was the answer. 'None saw.' The ghost pointed to Yael's guitar.

'The music brought you back!' Yael exclaimed.

'Yes...' Altavi read.

The entity began to form words again: 'How long am I dead?' and 'What are you?'

'We can't answer your first question accurately,' Zeboah replied. 'After the human era, we started a new calendar. A lot of human history is lost. During the Upheaval, when catastrophes battered the world, all information stored digitally was destroyed. Humanity became extinct. From my words, you will know we're not human. We're what came after: hara, as you were people; Wraeththu, as you were human. Our kind live in harmony with nature. We don't endanger the planet through ignorance and greed. The world is a better place.'

The entity hung motionless between them, perhaps processing the information he'd been given.

'Of course, many relics and artefacts of human cultured survived the turmoil,' Yael said, indicating the gramophone. 'And I found this in the archives I was exploring with my friends...'. He reached into the pocket of his robe and took out a small, faded picture on cardboard, which he held up to the spirit. It depicted a young human man. 'This is an ancestor of mine. He was human and got turned into... one of us. I don't know much about him, but it seems he carried this with him for a long time. His name was Jones and he claimed to be the grandson of a famous, eccentric artist. Could that be you?'

The entity stared at the picture for a while. Then he spelled out a word on the board: 'Kin.'

'I am Zeboah, and they are Yael and Altavi.' Zeboah indicated his companions. 'Yes, Yael is your kin, your descendent. He is har, a whole being, for in us the genders are not divided. We are neither male nor female, but both.'

The room echoed with a strange laugh, which clearly derived from the entity, even if it had not come from his etheric body. He spelled words upon the Hesbron board.

'Hunky Dory,' read Altavi.

'What does that mean?' Yael asked.

'It means,' said Altavi, 'something like approval... I think.'

'He's pleased,' Yael said.

'Well, we all thought he was a har to start with,' Altavi said. 'He was more than a typical human, wasn't he?'

The entity spelled more words: 'Play my music'. Then he shook his head. He pointed to his lips, as if desperate to speak. Acting on instinct, Zeboah reached out to him. Even though this spirit wasn't solid matter, maybe he could be fed enough energy to be heard.

Where Zeboah's fingertips touched the entity, the orange glow grew brighter. He closed his eyes to concentrate. 'Help me,' Zeboah murmured, and became aware that Yael and Altavi were with him, channelling their energy into the spirit. Zeboah felt that although this being had somehow manifested in this world, and had clung to his tenuous existence, he was now at peace, almost ready to let go.

When Zeboah opened his eyes again, he was almost blinded by the bright orange light of the energy surrounding them, softly humming like a sacred chant. He looked directly into those strange mismatched eyes. And then he heard the dark silky voice he knew from the record, speaking slowly: 'Remember *all* our music! Play it, sing it!' With that, the orange became darker, the humming lower, and the ghost was gone.

Three weeks later, Zeboah and Altavi were standing in the middle of a large crowd of hara in a beautiful park. Everyhar was in a festive mood, and there was excitement in the air. A fanfare sounded upon the stage, where a drummer had started to play. Now other musicians came on stage, accompanied by cheering from the audience.

Yael appeared last, a guitar in this hand. The cheering became almost hysterical. He wore a dark grey shirt and flared trousers, which was a relatively modest costume for him, but his hair was dyed bright violet. Hara were clapping and whistling, jumping around. Yael stepped to the front and cleared his throat. 'Thank you for coming, friends,' he said, his amplified voice ringing out around the park. 'This is a special concert.' He paused to hang the guitar around his neck. 'Whatever you want to give at the end, depending on whether you like the music or not...'

Some hara laughed and cheered.

'...all proceeds from this event will go to a special project, which a friend of mine helps manage. It's all about music. You know that humans made music too, right?'

He stared into the audience. The reaction was muted, perhaps confused, because nohar present had expected Yael to say anything like that. Then somehar whistled, and somehar else called from the back: 'Yeah, but yours is better!'.

Yael smiled. 'So, I take it you liked my last songs?' He grinned, waiting for the cheers to ebb away. 'Well, most of them were written by a human. How I came to play them and think they were my own is a long, strange story that I'll tell you one day. But there's one thing I want to make clear: whenever you think back to those who came before us, don't assume everything they did was bad. Their extreme emotions, their aggression, their love and their suffering didn't only result in chaos and war. Beauty came out of it too. Art came out of it. Read their books, seek out their pictures. There is much to discover. You might not like all of it, but some of it you will. This also applies to human music. Through the project my friend is involved in, some of this music will be saved, all that can be found. It is not for us to decide what is good and what is not, because that's simply a matter of taste. The important thing is that it was written, and came from the heart, and that is one organ that both humans and hara share.'

The audience had gone silent, did not even laugh at the joke.

Yael strummed a couple of bars on the guitar. 'Here is some music I love,' he said. 'It was written many, many years ago by a great artist who is still around somehow…'

As Yael announced the song and spoke the name of the artist, Altavi nudged Zeboah with his elbow.

'Look,' he said, excitedly, 'at the far side of the stage.'

Zeboah did so and saw a shimmering figure in the wings. Its light became brighter, like a star, so that other hara in the audience saw it too. Perhaps they thought it was some kind of special effect Yael had created. They pointed at it and yelled elatedly.

The figure turned to the audience and became more solid, revealing a beautiful face, which was clearly visible now.

Let the audience believe it's a har, Zeboah thought, smiling. A har who can emit a flickering orange light.

The spirit stayed to hear the song, never moving. Then, as the last strains of the song ebbed away, he vanished. Zeboah knew that this time he was truly gone.

The stage lights dimmed to darkness and for some moments the entire park was silent. Then the cheering began.

A faint wind shivered the nearby trees. Altavi shivered. He looked sad. Zeboah knew this young har had wanted more than the spirit had been able to give. Altavi had been hungry for knowledge, for more music, more songs. But the spirit's visit had been necessarily brief. He had another place to be.

Above, the sky was crystalline, weirdly ablaze. Zeboah put an arm about his assistant's shoulder. 'Look...' He pointed up to the sky. 'The stars look very different today.'

The Emptiness Next Door

Storm Constantine

The house itself was never the problem. Tucked into a mellow suburb of Ferelithia, *Inglefey's* design was quirky, with its carved lintels and eaves painted palest red – certainly not pink, but cream with a hint of blood. When Seladris moved into it, as it was a perk of the job he'd taken, he thought the design must have been deliberate, only discovering later it was an old house and had been built during the human era. Seladris was a maestera baker and had come to work for *Confitteri*, the celebrated establishment whose sumptuous confections were sold even in Immanion. In keeping with this, but only coincidentally, *Inglefey* resembled an elaborate yet tastefully-decorated cake.

Seladris arrived at his new home in the early afternoon of a summer's day. The season had not yet broken, and the aching vividness of spring still throbbed from the trees and flowers. The sky was a clear deep blue and the chimneys of the house stood tall and starkly white against it.

Inside, the house was peaceful; its air seemed to hum languidly. Light fell in mellow bars through the tall windows, which were curtained only with sweeping drapes of dove-grey muslin that hung quiet in the windless day. The floors were mostly bare, here and there mosaiced with rugs of deep auburn, purple and gold. The furniture was old, and while somewhat battered upon the legs or surfaces, possessed an ageless elegance without being fussy. Floral perfume, spiced with an herbal undernote filled the air – Seladris could see through the open doors to rooms left and right that bowls of fresh-cut roses, jasmine and honeysuckle had been left for him, garnished with sprigs of thyme.

Seladris felt at once welcomed, protected and comfortable. He put his travelling bag beside the table in the hall, where he found a note advising him the larder had been stocked for his use: this was complimentary, but thereafter he'd be responsible for providing his own supplies. He would be expected at *Confitteri* at 9 the following morning. The noted was signed by Veredis har Mith, the owner of the bakery, who Seladris already knew was something of a "character" and a celebrity of the town.

Seladris put down the note and stood for a moment with closed eyes, soaking up the sun that fell into the hall. He took several deep breaths of the aromatic air, then glanced at himself in the tall, narrow mirror above the table, unsure as always whether or not he liked the tall, narrow har who stared back at him haughtily. His pale hair hung loose over his chest, devoid of style, which might be abnormal in Ferelithia and require a change. The light in the hallway flattered him, as if the mirror sought to make him feel at home. *Here, you are somehar else...* It had been the right decision to take this job. At such an esteemed establishment, known for its unusual sweet delights, he could exercise his creativity with flavours and textures to the full. And in a place such as *Inglefey*, hurts of the past would fade, be rubbed out, replaced with kinder feelings.

On his first morning at work, Seladris went to receive his orders from Veredis, who occupied a spacious office beyond the display galleries. The entire premises smelled of vanilla, ginger, anise and cinnamon, of lemon, and butter and sage. He walked through the viewing galleries, where remarkable edible sculptures rested upon plinths, spilling marmoreal limbs or swatches of hair, or falls of vine tendrils and blossoms, all fashioned from sugar and paste.

Inevitably, he had to pass by various members of staff, which led him to realise his colleagues would take some winning over. They stared at him with suspicion and, in a couple of instances, open resentment. Perhaps they'd expected somehar else to be promoted, somehar they knew.

Veredis sat behind a large desk of the palest bleached oak but stood up when Seladris came into the room. His family must have derived from a multiplicity of human ethnic types. His skin was dark, his lips Olathian full, yet his eyes were orientally poised, and of a rich violet hue. His shock of artfully-messed hair was dyed (presumably) deepest indigo. He was of moderate height and extremely thin but possessed the gracefulness to carry this off and not appear merely malnourished. The components of his being complemented each other well, and the results were, Seladris thought, quite arresting.

Seladris took the seat Veredis indicated. After the initial

introductions and listening to a repetition of the extent of his duties, Seladris felt he should mention the attitude he'd detected from the staff. His impression was that Veredis would not object to this enquiry. *Would* there be a problem with colleagues?

Veredis sighed through his nose. 'Their insolence is because I had to fire Plerander, the previous maestera. He was popular among the staff, and I liked the har myself, but I discovered he'd abused my facilities, *and* stolen from my stocks, to fulfil private commissions.'

'Oh... I see.'

'The hara here are still rumbling about it, but they also know I had little choice. He stole from me and had to be punished. Precedents to the contrary cannot be set, for obvious reasons. His two closest friends were dismissed along with him.'

'And they... were *also* popular?' Seladris asked.

'Yes,' Veredis said darkly. 'Still, I must make it clear I'm particular about these things. You've seen *Inglefey*. Do you like it?'

'Yes... of course...'

'Then don't I provide sumptuous accommodation?' Veredis interrupted. 'And isn't the salary reasonable?'

There was a pause, during which Seladris realised he was expected to nod and say yes, which he did.

'I have very high standards,' Veredis said.

'Then I look forward to impressing you,' Seladris responded, smiling. He was in fact quite confident about the quality of his work.

Veredis called for his personal assistant to show Seladris around. This was a pale, small creature with watery blue streaks in his platinum hair, which was confined in a loose plait. His name was Kizzy. Seladris thought the young har resembled a harling's drawing of a sprite, but he was affable enough. While Kizzy flitted at his side, Seladris mulled over his interview with Veredis. He thought the har's displeasure was valid, but he could also tell his new boss was finicky, with a tendency to pettifogging, a har who might take offence easily and be slow to forgive – if at all. However, Seladris was adept at handling difficult types; they did not bother him. He prided himself on his calm, serene nature, which had taken years to perfect after a tempestuous youth, when he'd learned the hard way that a hot temper and flaring emotions were not the best tools with which to fashion an easy life.

While taking the tour of *Confitteri*'s buildings, Seladris took care to introduce himself to every har, making no mention of the previous maestera, ignoring any mulishness, and smiling pleasantly to all. He made sure to *waft* through the kitchens and store rooms, exuding an air of unflappability. He would give them no reason to carp or criticise. He undertook a stock-take to familiarise himself with the ingredients favoured here. He met the hara with whom he would work most closely and encouraged them to speak about their own techniques and accomplishments. He examined all the display confections and began thinking about how he might improve upon the designs. In another life, he mused, he might have been a sculptor rather than a baker.

He returned to Veredis's office for tea in the afternoon and reported his thoughts. Already, he had ideas for two confections but asked if he might first take on a commission – a cake already ordered – to demonstrate his prowess.

'Generally, I'd have you create from your own imagination first,' Veredis said, 'to see what you can do, but in this case, very well. Your eagerness and confidence intrigue me. Now, please go home early today. I expect you still have things to unpack and want to get a feel for your new home.'

In fact, Seladris had already arranged, cupboarded and drawered his meagre possessions within the house. He'd not brought many clothes with him, since he'd decided to restock his wardrobe completely. In any case, the blood would not wash out entirely from certain items.

On his way home, Seladris explored the town, orienting himself to its landmarks. He went to the harbour and walked along the beach but didn't enjoy it. Perhaps there would be other places more to his liking, where there were fewer or no hara obscuring the landscape and making noises.

Once back home, Seladris made himself a mug of black tea and wandered out into the front garden. While *Inglefey*, situated at the end of Shadey Lane, had only a small yard at the back and not much more than a patch of lawn at the front, there was space around it. The houses across the street, to the south, were larger, set back, and with longer front gardens, but there was no obvious sign of occupation. To the east, there was a crossroads, so the nearest house was some way off. To the west was a wide empty space, (much larger than that occupied by *Inglefey* and its modest plot of land), where perhaps another house had once stood, or else, long ago, the land had been planned for a property that had never been built. Now the area was like a miniature wilderness. There was a rough lawn that appeared to have been kept cropped by deer or rabbits. Flowers and shrubs, unkempt and wild, grew in profusion. There were tall and ancient trees, one of them a Cedar of Lebanon. To the north came down the old forest, its rumble of dark hills.

Seladris did not care for close relationships with neighbours and thus appreciated the relative privacy. He'd use the plot next door as an extension to his garden. He noticed that a pair of long washing lines had been erected further up the lawn. Perhaps Plerander had put them up, since there wasn't much room in *Inglefey*'s back yard for that. He couldn't see that anyhar living nearby would object; Shadey Lane appeared so quiet. The nearest house to the west was a good two hundred yards away, down the gently-sloping road, and from where he stood he could perceive no activity in or around it. Since the Devastation, Ferelithia had been claimed and renamed by hara. Its population was significantly smaller than that of the throng of humans who had once burgeoned here. One day, all these beautiful old houses might be reclaimed, but for now, it appeared many stood empty. Perhaps Ferelithians preferred to live near the centre, by the sea. At Shadey Lane, the northern countryside butted against the order of the town, and in some cases had clearly broken through it. The unused plot next to *Inglefey* sloped upwards to the north, where trees and shrubs grew thickly. He would explore there soon.

Seladris went inside and prepared himself a simple early dinner of cold chicken sandwiches and salad. He poured himself a glass of tart white wine. This house was such a luxury to him, and at first he couldn't decide where to eat, though he eventually chose the western sitting-room, where plump and faded old sofas stood around the unlit fireplace. The softly-ripened light of the sinking day poured into the room. Again, Seladris perceived an almost inaudible hum, which at one time might have been associated with an electrical appliance buzzing away to itself somewhere in the house. But there was no electricity in *Inglefey*. While the service had been restored near the town centre, it was not yet available out here. The lamps were oil, and there were candles. The stove in the kitchen was a huge, antique range that once Seladris lit it, would undoubtedly have to be kept compliant with fuel and cosseting, like a domesticated dragon; it provided heating and hot water for the entire house. As a baker, Seladris knew it was essential to establish an almost spiritual relationship with your stove, because they could be capricious. He intended to honour that code and keep his beast sweet, since he expected to work at home in the evenings. But not, of course, for the purpose of trading behind Veredis's back.

He sat on – or rather in, as it seemed partially to swallow him with cushions – the sofa opposite the fireplace, the surround of which was wood, intricately carved with patterns of vines and birds. Above the mantlepiece a painting hung on the wall. It was a peculiar picture, Seladris decided, being of a blue leopard, which seemed to have been caught in the act of jumping and twisting – or perhaps it had been flung or was falling from a height. Its face was turned to the viewer, snarling, its claws outstretched from the paws of its flailing limbs. There was no background landscape to provide clues as to the circumstances of the leopard, merely a wash of colours – blues and greens, with the occasional crimson streak – perhaps to represent foliage and flowers. The painting did not look that old – perhaps it had belonged to the sacked maestera, but why would he leave it behind? Unless, of course, he simply didn't like it. Seladris wasn't that keen on the picture. It made him feel curiously uneasy. The leopard was long and thin and strangely elastic. It bent in places it should not bend. It was a mottled, deep-turquoise blue, but its gaping mouth was scarlet, the long teeth yellowy-brown. He had a feeling it wasn't a leopard at all but a symbol of something else. At the weekend, he'd remove it, perhaps swap it with another painting in the house, as he'd noticed there were quite a few to choose from.

The rest of the week passed without any dramatic incidents. The staff at *Confitteri* became more amenable, once they discovered there was little about Seladris to dislike. He was fair-minded, easy-going and if criticism was required, he delivered it graciously. However, he was careful to keep his distance. He didn't want the hara to dislike him, but neither did he want them to like him too much.

There was a minor difficulty near the end of Aru'sday, when a few of his colleagues asked Seladris to join them for a meal the following night. On this occasion, he was able to insist he had too much to do at home – there'd been so little time during the week to get anything done. He promised he'd join them another time, and knew this event might have to be faced, since excuses can only go so far, and he was meticulous in preventing opportunities for hostility to creep in. Still, he knew how to be a dull companion, which discouraged hara from asking him out more than once or – at worst – twice.

Inglefey had already become a secure refuge, and there was little he didn't approve of. The sheets on the wide bed, however, smelled unpleasantly musty and marshy, perhaps taken from storage after Plerander had left, but he'd wash these at the weekend.

Wind came up from the sea on Pelf'sday. Seladris did his washing and then crammed it into a wicker pannier he'd found in the small laundry to the back of the kitchen. This he carried out to the empty plot beside the house. The air smelled of salt, and gulls hung in it, uttering complaints. Seladris had once heard a tale that the voices of those drowned at sea spoke through gulls. A few birds lumbered down onto the roof of *Inglefey* and watched him.

The sheets made crisp, cracking sounds as he pegged them to the line. He had to fight the wind for them, as the heavy wet fabric seemed to cling to him, as if in terror of being carried away to sea.

As he pinned the last in place, he saw he wasn't alone. Through the flapping linen, he could see another har, also hanging out washing; his shadow stretched long on the ground. Seladris was instantly annoyed. Clearly, this plot was used by others to dry their laundry, most likely by more than a few, since this other har hadn't commented on Seladris being there. He picked up the empty basket and for a few moments stared at the long, slender shape as it danced up and down behind the sheet, almost like a shadow puppet. Then, sighing, Seladris walked back to his house.

At the threshold, he turned once and was surprised to see that there was no washing other than his own hanging on the lines next door. There was no other har, not even a shadow.

Once in the kitchen, he concluded it must've been his own silhouette he'd seen, or the shadows of sheets mixed with the wings of gulls that were circling around. Some mundane explanation, anyway. He'd felt no rising of psychic senses, no unease, not even a prickle to his skin.

Upstairs, he found other sheets folded in a linen cupboard on the landing outside his bedroom but was reluctant to make his bed

with them. Like those he had just washed, they smelled distinctly…
off. Fortunately, he hadn't damped the fire beneath the washing tub
and could throw the whole lot in there. He went to smell the quilt
on the bed. It too would benefit from being hung on the washing
line to air in the fresh breeze. He didn't relish the thought of
washing it, since it was stuffed with feathers, which would clump
and mat and thus ruin its comfortable plumpness.

He struggled downstairs with the enveloping quilt and dragged
it over to the empty plot. There were no inexplicable shadows. He
hoisted the quilt over the spare line and pulled it into place.

Billowy summer clouds moved fast across the sky; sunlight
beamed and dimmed. Seladris squinted up at the rising land beyond
the washing lines. There were tall conifers and what appeared to be
spurs of natural rock rather than a constructed rockery, no doubt
because Shadey Lane had once been part of the hill forest.
Undulating patches of sunlight and darkness between the tall trunks
were somehow inviting, but Seladris did not respond to this call. He
went back inside to finish his laundry.

Once this task had been attended to, and he'd hung out to dry
as much as he could in the available space, Seladris returned to his
bedroom. He'd finish the drying tomorrow. Now, he'd turn the
mattress, since as he'd removed the sheets he'd noticed a kind of
faint yellow greasiness on its surface. He was worried this might be
sweat left by a previous occupant – and not necessarily one as
recent as a har. Wraeththu were magpies; they scavenged where
they could and used what they found. It was likely most of the
furniture in this house derived from before the Devastation. He felt
slightly queasy that he'd slept in this bed all week and it hadn't been
as clean as he preferred his sleeping place to be. The mattress, apart
from the slight staining, appeared to be relatively fresh, but when
he turned it, Seladris jumped back and uttered an involuntary cry.
There was a hideous mass of mildew on the underside, roughly in
the shape of a body sleeping on its side. One arm was raised above
the head, as if curled beneath a pillow.

'No!' Seladris said aloud. 'Absolutely not!'

He didn't want to dwell on the cause of the stain, mainly because
it was quite possible a human had once died in this bed, and their
corpse had perhaps lain there for some time. The turning had also
released a stench of mould and rot, which was clearly what had been
polluting the sheets. Plerander must have been a slob to sleep in

this foul mess, Seladris thought. He shuddered and dragged the mattress out of the room. It was beyond cleaning. He must dispose of it.

Clawing and heaving the cumbersome article, while swearing beneath his breath, he managed to throw the mattress down the stairs. This was no easy task. It was heavy and awkward. It slithered reluctantly like an immense dead body, then caught on the bannisters and needed kicking and punching, seeming on the whole resentful of being removed. But eventually it was on the lawn.

Hot and breathless, tingling with exertion and annoyance, Seladris went back inside.

There were beds in other upstairs rooms, which Seladris inspected carefully. While none were as wide as the one he'd slept in, he chose to replace it with furniture not sullied by mould or smells. He didn't need a large bed. He always slept alone. These other beds must have been used only for guests, as the mattresses looked new. He moved one into his room and hauled the discarded base into an empty chamber next to his own. He also appropriated a fresh quilt from one of the other rooms, after smelling them all meticulously.

After this, he went downstairs and opened a bottle of wine. He intended to drink for some hours.

That evening, Seladris went into the sitting room where the leopard painting hung. He was going to remove it, but then, standing before the hearth, he changed his mind. The picture was strange and somewhat unsettling, but simultaneously also compelling. He wondered what its message was, what its artist has been thinking as he'd daubed the pigment on the canvas. Seladris drew closer. The paint was applied thickly, as if with a knife, yet the detail of the leopard was precise.

That night, he dreamed, and the leopard spoke to him. He was in a darkened place, outside, surrounded by densely-packed pines. The throb of drums filled the night, and the smell of wood smoke. He walked through tall, ancient trees, coming at last to a hungry fire where hara were dancing. They cast flame shadows that leapt alongside them. These were proto-hara, Seladris thought. Memories of the birth.

The skin of one of the dancers was tattooed or painted in varying shades of blue. He wore the mask of a leopard and gloves adorned with long black claws. He noticed Seladris and shimmied towards him, playfully lashing out with his paws. This was not threatening, but more like flirting.

Then Seladris saw shadows beyond the reach of the flame-light; tall, motionless figures garbed in black with vague suggestions of pale faces. Were they watching or waiting? These Seladris feared greatly.

'Close the door,' said the leopard-har, his voice muffled through the mask.

Seladris woke abruptly, to the echo of a noise fading away through the quiet house. Had somehar knocked at the door? He had not heard the sound exactly but felt the vibrations of its passing. He glanced at the clock on the opposite wall, which told him the time was 4.30 a.m. Light was starting to bleed across the darkened sky beyond his window. The town held its breath. Even the gulls were silent.

Seladris lay blinking at the ceiling, breathing hard as if he'd been running. He put a hand over his chest, felt the panic of his heart. A dream. They could not find him here.

Once he'd calmed down, he was wide awake, so got out of bed, put on a dressing-robe and went downstairs. He checked all the doors, which were closed and locked. He ate his breakfast of fruit and milk, standing up in the kitchen, gazing out of the window at the hurrying clouds. Perhaps he should move the leopard painting, after all. It must be poking old memories somehow and for this reason was bad for him. He might ask Veredis about it, see if it could be removed from the house.

After breakfast, Seladris finished drying his washing. He hung what was left on the lines, and there was no shadow to haunt him. He walked up into the pines at the back of the plot, and took a leisurely walk through them, gathering fallen cones and gull feathers. Why had this area remained empty? It was superior to its neighbours, having so much more land. If it was his, he'd build on it, raise a new, entirely harish house, full of light and air. He fantasised for some minutes about one day purchasing the land from the local Municipallion, or simply appropriating it. A lot of harish townships supported rights of occupation. If you found a place and liked it, and nohar was living on it or using it for trade or communal services, you had only to register you were taking possession and it was yours. As long as you paid civic tithes to contribute to local facilities, you became an accepted member of the town's society. Seladris didn't know if Ferelithia had adopted this practice, seeing as it was such a thriving, popular centre. But then, if its properties were so much in demand, why was Shadey Lane virtually unoccupied? He must ask Veredis about this too.

In the early afternoon, Seladris went indoors and prepared a lunch of steamed smoked fish with aromatic lemon rice. He carried this meal into the sitting room and sat in his now usual place on the sofa. The leopard gazed over and through him, as if yearning for the outside. As he ate, he became aware of a strange smell, which grew gradually stronger. It was the reek of boiling greens, like the hideous stinking cabbage that was all he'd had to eat when... no, he mustn't think of that time. It was gone.

He put down his plate and went into the kitchen. The smell didn't appear to emanate from there, but it was everywhere – foul, rotten, thick and stomach-turning: to Seladris the very essence of insatiable hunger that could never be assuaged. Somehar else must be cooking nearby and the stench had drifted in. He went outside, sniffing the air, but the smell had gone. He couldn't imagine anyhar in Ferelithia dining on rotten vegetables, boiled or otherwise.

I will not be haunted by my own stupid imagination, he told himself firmly and returned to the sitting-room to resume his meal.

On Lunilsday, as soon as Seladris reached *Confitteri*, he went to Veredis's office.

'I suppose you've come here for praise,' Veredis remarked tartly, but through a smile. He was watering the plants around the room from a silver jug with a long, ornate spout.

'Excuse me?'

Veredis stood on tiptoe to reach a high shelf. 'Your work. I'm very pleased with what you did last week. So is our client.' He put down the watering jug.

'Oh, thank you. That isn't why I'm here.'

Veredis indicated Seladris should sit down and did so himself, clasping his hands on the desk. 'Is there something wrong?'

'Well, not wrong exactly. I simply wanted to ask you a few questions about the house.'

Veredis made an expansive gesture. 'Of course.'

'First, I've had to throw a mattress out and wondered if you could have it removed from the property. It was... full of mould and smelled bad.'

Veredis frowned. 'Oh, sorry about that. The har who conducted an inventory of the place after Plerander left didn't report it, which is odd. He's usually thorough. But yes, of course, I'll get somehar to see to it.'

'And...'

'Yes?'

'There's a painting in my sitting-room.' Seladris then realised he didn't want to continue because what he was about to say sounded ridiculous.

Veredis raised his eyebrows in enquiry.

'Oh, maybe I'll let that be.'

'No, what is it? You appear quite... distressed.'

'OK. Could that be removed too?'

Veredis grinned. 'Does it smell of mould?'

Seladris managed a smile. 'No, it's just not to my taste.'

'Then move it. There's a lumber room on the top floor, I believe.'

'I'd rather it was gone.' Seladris laughed nervously. 'This is going to sound stupid, but the picture's giving me nightmares. I hate the thing. And before you start thinking I'm deranged or paranoid, I'm not given to fancies of this type, which is why it's unnerved me.'

'I'll have to come and see this dreadful daub for myself,' Veredis said, still grinning. 'You've intrigued me!'

'You're welcome to come. I'll make you dinner as a thank you for my employment.'

'I'm happy to accept that offer,' Veredis said, 'assuming your culinary skills extend to full meals as well as baking.'

Seladris laughed affably, then paused a moment and said, 'Do you know anything about the empty plot next to *Inglefey*? It's such a beautiful area, you'd have thought it would have been used... in the old times. Was there ever a house there?'

Veredis stuck out his lower lip for a moment. 'I've no idea. I asked Kizzy to appropriate a dozen or so empty properties for the business a couple of years ago, and *Inglefey* was on his list. He chose the most whimsical places he could find, of course. That's his way. We claimed a couple of other houses on that street, further down from you.'

'I didn't know colleagues lived nearby.'

'They don't. I lease the properties out at present.'

'That's allowed? You can just... *collect* houses in this town?'

'Of course. If anything, long-term residents are encouraged to take over the buildings. Ferelithia has many visitors who often need accommodation for lengthy periods. Whoever claims the properties is required to renovate them and keep them in good order. My rents are fair and comply with local...' Veredis stopped speaking abruptly, his eyes narrow. 'Why am I telling you this?'

'I didn't mean to pry,' Seladris said, raising his hands in a placatory gesture. 'I just wondered what the system was, that's all.'

Veredis made a careless gesture with one hand. 'Forget it. May I come over this evening, or is that too short notice? I really do want to see this picture.'

'Yes, by all means come tonight. I only hope you think the leopard is as weird as it seems to me.'

'The leopard?' Veredis asked sharply.

'The painting is of a leopard.'

Veredis had a peculiar expression his face, and Seladris thought at once his employer was concealing something. 'You know of it?'

Veredis smoothed his features. 'No. For a moment I thought you meant there was a big cat in the house!'

You didn't think that at all, Seladris thought, but smiled politely.

With Veredis' permission, Seladris left work an hour early to prepare a meal. He had learned the art of making seafood risotto at one of his previous jobs, which the har who'd taught him had claimed required skills more like alchemy than cookery. To achieve the perfect texture and flavour required a kind of culinary magic. Seladris decided this dish was most likely to impress Veredis. He would lace it with saffron, bought from the sea-front market and *not* appropriated from Confitteri stock – tempting though it was to steal a few expensive strands.

An hour or so after he'd begun cooking, a pair of hara with a cart drawn by a skewbald pony arrived to remove the mattress from the front lawn. 'Looks like somehar died on it,' one of them said.

Seladris grimaced. 'I'm sure *something* did...'

'We'll take it to the burning yard,' said the har.

Veredis arrived at 7. A sleek carriage, drawn by a beautiful black horse, and driven by a beautiful black har, dropped him off and then departed. Once across the threshold, Veredis took a deep breath of the aromatic air. 'I was merely hungry, now I'm ravenous,' he declared.

'I can't leave the food for long,' Seladris said, 'but come into the sitting room. You can look at the picture while I finish off the meal.'

Following Seladris into the room, Veredis stood before the fireplace and folded his arms. 'It's unusual,' he said guardedly. 'But frightening? I can't see that.'

'Unfortunately, I can't share my dreams with you,' Seladris said lightly.

'Hmm, I wonder why it bothers you so much.' Veredis's voice held a thread of what Seladris feared might evolve into suspicion.

He answered without hesitation, keeping his voice low, even slightly amused in tone. 'I think the painting might have a history. Perhaps the har who painted it *invested* feeling or memory into the work, even if unconsciously. *That* could be what disturbs me, rather than the actual image.'

Veredis pulled a face. 'OK. Maybe. I'll take it home with me tonight, see if it affects *me* in any way.'

Seladris doubted that was possible, because he suspected Veredis had a psychic skin so thick it was immune to subtle influences, but at least the thing would be out of the house. He turned to leave the room, but Veredis put a hand on his right arm.

'Wait a moment. There's something I didn't tell you.'

'What do you mean?'

'This house, or rather this area, *is* associated with a leopard. There's a story from the early times.'

'I must see to the food,' Seladris said. 'Will you tell me about it while we eat?'

'Yes, of course.'

Seladris was surprised – not because Veredis knew something but because he'd decided to share that information. In his experience, hara with secrets tended to keep them.

Veredis praised the risotto and drank a large quantity of Seladris's stock of wine while eating it.

'So… the leopard,' Seladris prompted after Veredis had put down his fork.

'Mmm, it's an odd tale. During the latter stages of the

Devastation, what's now Ferelithia was the site of intense conflict – between different factions of humans, and later between human survivors and hara. There was a kind of Doomsday cult, a band of humans who wandered around uttering depressing prophecies and – if the tales are true – murdering anyone or anyhar they considered their god might find pleasing as sacrifices. Then they ran into the Blue Leopard.'

'A har, like in my dream?'

Veredis shook his head, took a sip of wine. 'The Leopard was rather more than a single har. It was an egregore, the projected personification of a tribe. When you speak of it, you're really speaking of a group of thirty hara or so who called themselves the Cerulopard – blue leopard…. But the leopard was not merely *them* – it was an expression of their energy – their souls. But anyway, whether tribe or spirit, the Blue Leopard was called upon by the local phyle leaders to help dislodge the remaining human resistance in the area. The situation came to a head at midsummer around thirty years ago. There was fighting – naturally – some of it allegedly magical in nature. And the humans did not survive it. As for the Blue Leopard…' Veredis shrugged. 'Nohar knows what happened to it. Its hara disappeared that night and were never seen again. This left a scar on the psyche of the local phyles. They had come together to defeat a common foe, but there had been a high cost. They lost what I assume they regarded as a potent weapon that was *theirs* and yet it was taken from them. I would imagine that the painting here is a symbol of the Leopard. But…' Veredis turned the stem of his wine glass in his hand.

'But what…?'

'The Blue Leopard is considered unlucky, that's all. A symbol of harish hubris. The Leopard thought itself superior to any human group but was somehow vanquished by the failing remains of a beaten community. The saying, "don't be blue" in Ferelithia doesn't mean "don't be sad". It means "don't be so bloody arrogant".'

'I see.' Seladris refilled Veredis's glass.

Veredis drank, wiped his mouth. 'Anyway, this is probably what you're picking up on. A pity you find the picture unbearable, though. It's clearly of historical interest and a relic of our collective past. I quite like it.'

'Did it belong to Plerander, do you think?'

'I doubt it. It was most likely here when we acquired the house.'

'And hara lived here *before* you acquired it?'

'I assume so, as it had been cleaned up, renovated... There was no record of a claim, but that system only came in here around fifteen years ago. Took a while for the phyle leaders to settle down, wash off the war paint, and become a Muncipallion.' He grinned. 'Anyway, I can't see a human painting *that*.'

'Perhaps Plerander – or whoever else lived here before – found the painting somewhere, bought it from a market maybe? Just because the painting hangs here doesn't necessarily mean it was created here.'

'Well, yes...' Veredis began, then shook his head. 'Who knows? This hill and the forest beyond was known as Leopard's Shade – a term not used so much nowadays – but I guess it proves the Leopard *is* connected with it.'

Seladris pondered what he'd heard, while Veredis moved on from this subject but continued to talk volubly, regaling his new employee with anecdotes about *Confitteri*. As Veredis was a skilled story-teller, Seladris enjoyed hearing the gossip and appreciated not having to make conversation himself. He was able to listen and think at the same time. He was sure, however, that whatever the blue leopard's history might be, and however interesting, he wanted its image out of his house.

As time wore on and midnight approached, Seladris became slightly concerned he too might be considered part of the evening's menu. Rather than endure a difficult conversation, which might affect his working relationship with Veredis, Seladris changed his body language to appear forbidding. Fortunately, Veredis made no arunic overtures, either finding Seladris unappealing, or else had sensibly resolved to keep business and carnal pleasure at a distinct distance from each other.

Around 12.15, the carriage returned to take Veredis home. Before he left the house, he went with Seladris into the sitting room, where they carefully removed the leopard painting from the wall. It was extremely heavy and cumbersome, and now it was off the wall seemed far larger than it appeared. Even for hara, carrying it to the vehicle waiting outside wasn't easy.

'Are you sure about this?' Veredis asked, as they inched their way to the front door. 'It seems... well, it's part of the house.'

'I'd prefer it,' Seladris said, 'if you don't mind. Should we ask your driver to help us?'

'Sweet dehara, no!' Veredis exclaimed. 'He'd be most insulted. Tika's very particular about his hands. He's a musician.'

Seladris smothered a smile. He wondered if Veredis and Tika were related or perhaps chesnari.

Once the painting was stowed – a complicated manoeuvre regarded inscrutably by the beautiful Tika – Veredis thanked Seladris for the meal, hugged him stiffly, then leapt into the carriage with a farewell wave of his hand.

Once Veredis's vehicle had rolled off into the night, Seladris thought he might as well finish what was left of the wine. He felt strangely reluctant to go into the sitting room, with its bare, cleaner patch of wall above the fireplace. Was it odd that Veredis hadn't asked about the dream he'd had? Seladris would have done so, in his employer's position. Veredis was, however, a little self-obsessed, so perhaps had no interest in knowing. If he *should* be affected by the painting, perhaps it was best he didn't know, anyway. They could compare notes on the experience afterwards.

Seladris sat at the kitchen table in candlelight, gazing at his reflection in the window. He could see little of outside.

Just as he was about to take a sip of his wine, a loud, cracking noise exploded through the house, and its walls and furniture shook violently. Crockery, pans and cutlery were thrown from the counter, dresser and table, and a series of crashes beyond the kitchen could be heard, as if every painting and mirror had smashed to the floor.

Seladris sprang to his feet, clinging onto the table top to keep upright. The shaking and groaning of the house seemed to last an eternity, but then ceased abruptly. In the following silence, Seladris heard what sounded like the occasional tinkle of falling shards of broken glass.

An earthquake?

Cautiously, as his feet were bare, he picked his way through broken plates and edged into the hall. The mirror above the little table remained on the wall, but the glass in it had shattered; its pieces now lay glittering across the floor. All was still, but Seladris felt *Inglefey* held its breath; its atmosphere shivered, as if with fright.

'A quake, that's all,' Seladris told the house.

He went outside.

The night air was tranquil, not what you'd expect after an earthquake, even in this quiet suburb. The town below lay peacefully, its myriad coloured lights hung like jewels around the neck of the sea. Seladris glanced up and down the road, but no neighbours were out, and most houses were in darkness. He had to admit to himself there had been no tremor.

That's when he saw them.

They came in a crowd down the hill, unnaturally tall, thin figures, dressed in what appeared to be black robes or cloaks, their heads hooded, framing indistinct white faces that glowed faintly in the dark. They seemed to rustle and bustle, stooping forward slightly, uttering no sound. There must have been around fifteen to twenty of them.

Seladris stared at this unbelievable sight for several seconds, which stretched into what seemed like long minutes. The bizarre group paid no attention to him, glided past him swiftly in the middle of the road, then veered off as one and made their way onto the empty plot beside *Inglefey*.

Seladris had focused so much upon these figures he'd failed to notice an even more peculiar phenomenon that had manifested behind him. Upon the empty plot, beyond the lawn where the washing lines stood, the windows of a house now blazed with radiance, as if a hundred lamps had been lit within each room. The light was yellow, bright as sunlight. If he should draw nearer he'd see into every room, even though... there *were* no rooms. All that existed, painted on the night, were the lights from windows. There was no house to support them. These windows were ghosts.

The group of weird figures hurried towards what appeared to be an open front door and was absorbed swiftly by the glow shining from it.

Then all the lights went out at once, as if some mysterious being had turned off a switch.

The night was still and empty as before. All was silent but for the sudden mournful moan of a ship's horn from a vessel coming to harbour.

For several minutes, Seladris stared at the spot where the lights had shone, trying to process and understand what he'd seen. Those figures... no. Surely not hara. They'd been human, hadn't they, or *in*human? Phantoms, yet so solid to the eye. Something had happened here, something significant or bad. It remained. These things always remain.

Seladris felt light-headed, with several different aches crawling over his scalp. He found his way almost blindly to the door of *Inglefey*. Inside, he ignored the wine and went straight to the bottle of quite expensive Ferelithian yenayva he'd bought for "special occasions". Inexplicable manifestations must surely come into that category. He drank it straight from the bottle, winced pleasurably at its potency and the bitter yet aromatic flavour. This would calm his nerves.

When he went to bed, quite drunk, he slept undisturbed until the morning, and could remember no dreams.

The moment Seladris arrived at work, he went to Veredis's office.

Without preamble, Seladris asked, 'Did you dream anything last night?'

Veredis – to his considerable satisfaction – appeared troubled. 'No. There were no dreams, but… something else happened.'

'What?'

Veredis gestured for Seladris to take a seat. 'Well, I left the painting in the carriage as I didn't want to ask Tika to help me with it…' He sighed. 'No, that's a lie. By the time I got home I simply didn't want it under my roof. Tika's my househar as well as my friend and has a room in the house. He took one look at the painting and said, "Are you mad, bringing that here?" Clearly, I was. So we left it in the yard and went to our separate beds. I like a bare room to sleep in, so there isn't much furniture there. A beautiful old floor, though. Anyway… As I was undressing, I saw what at first I thought was somehar lying on the floor in front of the dressing mirror. There was this… this long, dark *mass*. I was wary of approaching it.' He made a jerky, perhaps nervous gesture with one hand. 'We get little trouble round here with rogue hara, but you never know what might come in off the sea or down through the hill forests. Anyway, when I drew near the shape, I saw it was a length of fabric; flimsy dark stuff, like a veil. The way it lay on the floor made it appear uncannily like a body. I picked it up, let it hang from my hand, wondering how it had got there.' He shook his head. 'It felt almost… *sticky*, like cobwebs.'

'How vile,' Seladris encouraged.

'Yes. I was compelled to tear it in two,' Veredis continued, miming the action, 'but couldn't, so let it go, and it fell back down exactly into the long shape that looked like a body. It was so light, yet it fell… *heavily*. I knew this *thing* wasn't right… didn't *belong* in this world. I had to get rid of it, so bent to pick it up. But... here things get weirder... It drifted away from me, bunching up like some kind of... *insect*. I found myself – and this sounds ridiculous – *chasing* it round the room. Then it sort of billowed up and threw itself out of the open window. I was right behind it and leaned out to see where it went, but there was nothing outside. Not a wisp of it.'

'And you've had nothing... like that... happen before in your house?'

'No, never.' Veredis grimaced.' I didn't sleep well after that. Kept waking up and hearing things, but that might have been my imagination. I was spooked.'

Seladris pulled a sour face. 'Maybe. Let me tell you what happened to *me* after you left last night.' He related his own experience.

Afterwards, Veredis shook his head slowly. 'It's like you've poked a nest of... something,' he said. 'I don't mean to suggest it's *all* down to you but... I told Tika about it at breakfast and he said nothing's happened up at Shadey Lane for years.'

Seladris blinked, spoke more sharply than he generally allowed. 'What does that mean exactly?'

'Meaning hara had reported witnessing phenomena up there at one time, but the activity faded away. Until you came. Plerander never experienced anything and, believe me, we'd all have known about it if he had.'

'Could Tika offer any further insight into my situation?' Seladris asked, unable to keep a thin blade of ice from his voice.

Veredis appeared not to notice the tone. 'Well, first he advised we return the painting to its original place, and second we should consult one of the original harish settlers, who'll know far more of the history and can perhaps give us more specific advice. I agreed with his suggestions.'

Seladris was silent for a moment, then said, 'Well, thank you, I suppose... for taking this seriously.'

Veredis laughed. 'I could hardly fail to, since I took some of the haunting home with me last night.'

'There's more to it,' Seladris said abruptly. 'I've experienced... other phenomena in the house.'

'Will you tell me about it?'

'OK.' He related all that had occurred since he'd moved in,

Veredis expressing surprise and interest as he spoke. At the end of the story, Seladris said thoughtfully, 'It began simply when I washed the sheets. *Are* these phenomena all down to me? I don't know. I'm not scared easily, but it feels to me as if whatever force is responsible is getting stronger, heading towards some kind of peak. Then who knows what might happen? I want all this to end before we find out.'

'Understandably,' Veredis said. He paused. 'How busy are you today? Could you finish early again?'

'Yes.'

'Then let's begin our investigations as soon as possible. Tika knows somehar who could help us. Meladriel was one of the first settlers here. Eerie creature but knows his way around the weird. I'll come and find you when I'm ready to go. Around 3, maybe?'

'OK, thanks... and the painting?'

'Tika will help us replace it after we've seen Meladriel.'

Seladris nodded. 'Again, thanks. I'd better get on now. See you later.'

Leaving the office, Seladris could tell Veredis was enjoying this situation. Perhaps he should adopt the same attitude, but then Veredis didn't have the history that was attached to Seladris like a festering growth. Seladris scraped its surface afflictions away as much as he could but he knew the roots went deep, couldn't be scraped out, at least not easily. He knew he should face the fact that unpleasant situations and events throughout his life were most likely the suppressed ghosts of his youth and its horrors, bursting out into the present, causing calamity. He'd brought the sickness with him. He took it everywhere he went. One day, if he should feel he must leave Ferelithia, (as he'd had to leave so many places before), somehar might have the idea to start investigating *him*, and would discover his history, his *plague touch*. Perhaps Shadey Lane wasn't haunted at all, and everything came from him. In that case, it must be time to confront the mean and hungry ghosts and lay them to rest, before they damaged his life irreparably.

Meladriel lived in a sprawling low house right next to the sea. At high tide, water lapped over the end of his long, sloping garden where it merged with the shore. Pale little crabs sidled through the flowers. A jetty poked out of the sand beyond the garden, and here a small, green rowing-boat was moored, riding the incoming tide. Meladriel walked up the garden to meet them. He was 68 years old, not counting his human years before inception. He was a friend of Tika, who had driven Seladris and Veredis to the meeting and now made the introductions. Tika had visited Meladriel earlier to arrange this meeting. He had also explained Seladris's situation for the har to ponder.

Meladriel's skin was the colour of an acorn and his eyes were a golden orange. His hair was of many shades, but not dyed, simply streaked by the weathers of the seasons. He possessed a sinewy beauty and appeared youthful, if rather pensive in nature. In harish terms, of course, he was young. He stared at Seladris for long, uncomfortable seconds, then nodded curtly and said, 'Come inside,' gesturing at the green back door of the house, which was hung with knotted netting, glass balls and the bones of large fish. 'We'll talk.'

In a dark low-ceilinged kitchen, where the window was small and not situated to let in much light, Meladriel made a hot drink. It had a tart herbal flavour, yet was undeniably, essentially black tea. He offered his guests home-made biscuits tasting strongly of lemon yet smoothly-sweet, kissed with oil of rose and a hint of salt.

While they drank the tea and ate the biscuits, Meladriel spoke of the history of Leopard's Shade. He told the story as Seladris had already heard it, adding little to the narrative. But then he said, 'Now you may ask me your questions.'

Seladris spoke without pause. 'How exactly is the Blue Leopard connected with Shadey Lane and the empty plot there?'

'That plot has been uncanny since long before our time,' Meladriel answered. 'Many tried to build on it. Strong energy lives there, and some humans had the sense to know it, but no house would stand for long. Only a vision of a house, to be inhabited by an individual who could drink the essence of the land. Leupardra considered himself to be this, wanted to be.'

'Who was that?'

'The pard-witch of the Cerulopard, who danced to summon flame, life – and sometimes death. He tried to live there, and he found the hidden gates to the cellars, the only part of a house ever begun in that place. They had been fastened shut and buried for a reason.'

'I think I dreamed of him,' Seladris said.

'Yes, you did. Called him, didn't you? But too late for that.'

'I'm not aware of calling him, or *anything*. Can you explain to me what you mean?'

Meladriel glanced briefly at Seladris's companions, then fixed him with a stare. 'Do you want me to?'

Seladris felt he was trapped, balanced on a wire above a gulf. He could fall now, so easily, for he guessed that this strange, shamanic har *knew* him, and would say what he knew, connect it to the present and the past. And then Veredis would know, and Tika. Dare he ask them to leave him alone with the shaman now? But perhaps there was a price for knowing the truth and one of them was candour. Seladris couldn't decide if he wanted to pay that price.

The seconds expanded. Tika shifted uneasily on his seat. Veredis examined his fingernails far too intently.

Seladris was tempted to try and communicate in mind-touch with Meladriel but was aware this presumption would not be taken well. He knew this type. They revered clarity. They exposed secrets and expected the costs of fate to be met.

'I did not call upon anything knowingly,' Seladris said carefully. 'But there were incidents – periods – in my life, which perhaps resonate with the history of Shadey Lane. If you know of these things, I request you honour their privacy and respect my position.'

Meladriel nodded once, his expression stern.

'I'm not first generation,' Seladris continued, 'but I was born to a small phyle that consisted mainly of incepted hara. We lived in an area that was... unsafe, and we paid for the risk we took. My hara were killed but for the three harlings they had, of which I was one.'

'Seladris,' Veredis cut in, 'you don't have to tell us any of this...'

He held Meladriel's gaze. 'I believe I do,' he said, thinking *or he will tell you more*. 'I was the only harling to survive to adulthood. Those who took us were... brutal, cruel. They had no respect for life or for the gifts we've been given. I was tough, though. Eventually, I escaped, but I had to kill to manage it – become like *them*, I suppose. The legacy of that time has... lingered.'

'You are... what? Forty years old or so?' Meladriel asked.

'Thirty-seven.'

'A long time not to clean away the dirt of the past.'

'I don't consider myself dirty.'

'You are,' Meladriel said in an eerily mild voice. 'You carry the dirt with you. You stain others with it.'

'*Please*...' Seladris said, very softly, with the palest flicker of outrage in his breath.

Meladriel closed his eyes for a few seconds. 'Very well. I'll tell you this: you can use this opportunity to heal your hurts or you can simply run away, as you always do. Ghosts have smelled you out, put a hook in you, but it's more than it seems. If you want to end this, you must clean the dirt away.'

'OK. Will you tell me how?'

'Will you pay me?'

'Yes. If that is what it takes.'

Meladriel laughed. 'Oh, far more than that. Shed a skin. *That* will hurt.'

Seladris could tell that both Veredis and Tika were growing increasingly uncomfortable with this conversation, which had ventured into territory none of them had expected. No doubt they wished to leave the house but weren't sure how to escape without interrupting or giving offence. Leaving without words would be worse.

A brief stroke of mind-touch feathered Seladris's thoughts. Of course, it was permitted for Meladriel to take this liberty; he was higher in spiritual rank: *You have blood on you, fairly fresh.*

I did not spill it, Seladris replied.

Bad things happen wherever you go.

Yes. But isn't it also possible that's just the way of the world, coincidence?

Telling yourself that is one way to live with it. Can you wander the world forever?

I'm prepared to face it now, if you can help me understand what it is I'm facing.

You must find that out for yourself, but I can help a little.

Aloud, Seladris said, 'The Blue Leopard told me to close the door. Is this what I must do? Which door?'

'You must clear out what lies behind the door before you close and seal it forever,' Meladriel replied. 'Make what lies behind all it should be.'

'How... how do I even begin?' Seladris asked.

'The phenomena are unleashed now. You do not have to wait. You...'

Veredis interrupted. 'Must he do this alone or can others help?' His voice seemed like a blast of harsh, intrusive brightness in the taut atmosphere.

'That's up to the har,' Meladriel replied sharply, without moving his gaze from Seladris. 'As I was about to say... you should wait for the night and watch. The Pale Ones will lead you.'

'Those weird figures I saw?'

Meladriel nodded. 'It's better not to let them become aware of you. If they do, they'll be harder to shift than anything else out there. And that's not something I'd want to help you with.' He stood up. 'I'll give you salt,' he said. 'Sea salt. I've blessed it. You will know what to use it for.'

He took down from a rough shelf a small earthenware jar, stoppered with aged cork and bound with dried seaweed, which he handed to Seladris. 'That will be a week's wage, Tiahaar,' he said. 'Bring it to me when you're done.'

Seladris blinked wordlessly at the cost.

'*I'll* pay it,' Veredis said.

'No,' Meladriel said. '*He* will.'

Seladris nodded. 'As you say.'

Seladris sat in the carriage with the jar on his lap. For some minutes there was silence in the dim, enclosed atmosphere; the sounds of the horses' hooves outside seemed to come from another world.

Veredis stared at his companion, fidgeting like an excitable puppy, at last unable to stop himself saying, 'Please talk about it, Seladris.'

'No.' Seladris softened the refusal with a smile. 'You heard everything back there. I'd rather my past was kept private. It's not who I am now.'

'But maybe it would help...'

'Really... no.'

'I'll come over again tonight. We'll face this together.'

'No...' Seladris frowned. 'Or rather... *why?* Is this entertainment for you?'

Veredis exhaled impatiently through his nose. 'I guess I'm supposed to be insulted by that and say "pelk you!" or something. Throw you out onto the road. Won't work. I'm coming over. No argument. Show me a har who's a saint and I'll show you a har who's probably got something wrong with them. For Aru's sake, Seladris, let's get this done, get to the bottom of it. It's my property, remember, and I'd rather find out what's going on. I promise to keep in confidence anything I learn about you.'

Seladris raised his brows. 'Like all the hara you gossiped about at dinner last night?'

Veredis rolled his eyes. 'That was different. You think I can't tell the difference? I know I'd pay for it if I betrayed your confidence over this. I'm a superstitious har at heart and believe in consequences. Also, Meladriel terrifies me. I'd never want to invoke *his* disapproval.'

'All right, then,' Seladris said. He sighed. 'All right.'

Tika drove the carriage to *Inglefey*, and here they carried the painting of the leopard back into the sitting-room. Regardless of danger to his hands, Tika helped place the picture back on the wall. He was a har of few words, but Seladris found his presence soothing, reassuring. He was like a pure muscle of strong energy. 'Will you stay?' he asked.

Tika glanced briefly at Veredis, then said, 'This seems *your* business, Seladris.'

'If Tika stays, it'll be too easy,' Veredis said in an airy tone. 'Also, I wonder if the apparitions would even dare to appear.' He patted Tika's shoulder. 'Go home. I'll stay to offer support. If I need you, I'll send a shriek into the ethers, I promise.'

Tika was clearly not happy about leaving Veredis behind but made no further objection and left the house.

Seladris and Veredis stood before the picture in silence for some moments. In the afternoon light, it appeared innocent enough. The house was quiet, calm, filled with honeyed light and the scent of flowers.

Seladris said, 'I hope you're right to send Tika away. I'm not sure about this. Meladriel's instructions were vague to say the least.'

'Time to trust your instincts,' Veredis said, 'you know, those super-honed ones we're supposed to have.'

Seladris smiled grimly. 'I don't think either of us are super-hara, Veredis.'

Veredis linked arms with him. 'Ved,' he said. 'It's what my friends call me.'

Seladris brought food into the sitting-room that they could pick at and also a large stoppered jug of wine.

'We mustn't get drunk,' Veredis said, pouring them both a glass.

'Slight drunkenness might help,' Seladris replied.

They clinked glasses, sitting side by side on the sofa, staring at the leopard.

The sun lowered itself into the sea until it hung like a half-shut eye, leaking crimson tears of light.

'We take so much for granted,' Veredis murmured into a comfortable silence between them. The wine jug now was empty. 'Like you, I'm second generation, and I can't really imagine what it was like in the beginning, the violence of it all, the catharsis. No wonder there are ghosts left behind.'

Seladris paused before answering. 'I don't have to imagine it,' he said. 'I *know* it. But maybe it was inevitable, the bloodiest of births, struggling out of darkness.'

Veredis nodded. 'Perhaps.' He was sitting sideways on the sofa, leaning against the arm, his brown narrow feet up on the cushions, his wine glass cupped in both hands. Now he extended a foot and nudged Seladris's arm. 'You can trust me, you know. I'm not quite the idiot I choose to appear.'

Seladris laughed softly. 'I can see that, and quite early on in our friendship too! I imagine that's a privilege.' He squeezed Veredis's foot. 'We all have our armour, Ved.'

'So?'

'So, what?'

'What happened to make you come to Ferelithia?'

Seladris stared at Veredis for some moments. 'You're quite relentless, aren't you?'

'I'm thinking that maybe we should begin to invoke… whatever it is in this place. Connect with it.'

'OK. I came here because the hara I lived and worked with in Margenya all died. They died around me.'

'How?' Veredis's voice was almost a whisper.

'I was a chef in a large, expensive and popular inn. There was an explosion. My world went black and when I could see again, I was surrounded by the pieces of everyhar I knew.'

'An *explosion*? How did it happen?'

'Nohar knew. There was talk of an oven malfunctioning, of gas underground, an unexploded device from the old wars, a deliberate attack… Nothing was ever proven. Not even the psychic investigations turned much up. To everyhar in the immediate area, the world went black. None standing close to me survived and whatever caused it didn't leave a trace. But…' He glanced at Veredis. '*I* knew. Whatever follows me will never let me rest or be content.'

'Were you hurt at all?'

'Cuts, some quite deep, a few burns, a ringing brain... Disorientation.' Seladris shrugged. 'Took a month to recover, but considering where I'd been standing I should be dead.'

'Hmm,' Veredis murmured. 'Am I risking my life by even knowing you?'

Seladris grimaced, took a swig of wine. 'Probably.'

'So everyhar you befriend dies?'

Seladris shook his head. 'No, no... I don't mean it to sound like that. But bad things tend to happen around me. I've learned how to control it to a degree, by keeping my distance from hara. For years, things had been fine. But what happened in Margenya simply proved to me I'm ultimately powerless.'

Veredis wrinkled his nose. 'You know, it *could* just have been a coincidence.'

'Meladriel said otherwise – in mind touch.'

'Well, he's Tiahaar Doom, isn't he? Likes to make pronouncements of horror. I don't think we should simply believe you're a walking curse. Colluding in that belief merely helps make it real.'

Seladris stared at the har he now realised was becoming a friend. Was this dangerous? Would everything be taken from him again? Dare he believe that at last he could be clean, and live like a normal har? He held onto Veredis's foot, felt the prick of tears in his eyes.

Then the house shivered.

Veredis jumped to his feet, while Seladris put his glass down slowly on the low table before them.

A series of shuddering creaks sounded, like those made by expanding wood, yet coming from a distance, as if through a gate between the worlds.

Seladris stood up, took Veredis's arm and led him to the window. The sun had nearly vanished, but the stars and a half moon were bright. Seladris wrapped them both in one of the diaphanous curtains, not sure why he did so.

Out in the hall, they heard the front door open slowly with a screeching whine, and then bang against the wall with a crash. There was silence for a moment.

Then, a faint sound of shuffling, and a hum like bees, or almost like bees. It was as if a million voices whispered together, heard from a long way away.

Veredis and Seladris clung to each other, their backs pressed against the window. Seladris held his breath, afraid of making even the slightest noise.

Shadows spilled through the open doorway of the room, stretching long across the floor. Seladris knew these shadows must not touch them. Following these insubstantial inky blots, the figures came. In the confines of the house, they seemed to pour into the room for ever, but Seladris could tell there were no more than he'd seen in the road the previous night. They rustled and buzzed, mimicking the sounds heard in dark woodlands at dusk. They clicked, like tiny bones breaking. Close to, they were immensely tall, their faces almost devoid of features, the eyes mere black holes, the mouths black slits. They didn't appear to be aware of the living hara in the room, simply reached in front of themselves as if blind, feeling their way. Their hands were grotesquely long and spindly, like sea-bleached sticks. They moved towards the fireplace, filling the room, bringing with them a smell, not of death or rot, but dampened fires, old wood, shuttered rooms.

In front of the painting, they reached out eagerly, touched it with their spiky fingers. Then, they *pushed*. The painting sank into the wall, plaster folding over it as if wet. And the figures followed after.

For some moments, Veredis and Seladris did not move. Veredis had buried his face in Seladris's hair, the curve of his neck. He was panting, as if he'd been running. Then he whispered, 'Is it over?'

'Well, they've gone,' Seladris murmured.

'What happened? I couldn't look.'

'They went into the wall.'

Veredis shuddered. 'Are we meant to try and follow? Is that what Meladriel meant by them leading us?'

Seladris put a hand on the back of Veredis's head. 'No, I don't think it's that. Remember what else he said. The cellars of a house.' Gently, he pushed Veredis away from him. 'Last night, those things went into a light that was like a door. That's where we'll look.' He paused. 'You can wait here if you'd prefer.'

Veredis shook his head. 'No. I'll see this through. If I back out now, it'd break the spell.' He shook his head, grimaced. 'I mean the *luck*, the timing… everything happening in order.'

They went out to the plot next door. The night was undisturbed as it had been the day before, but a thin, chill wind came down from the hills, smelling of earth, eclipsing the aromas of the sea. Seladris had fetched a lantern from the kitchen. Its buttery beams spilled over the empty plot, revealing nothing but scattering shadows.

Seladris found a long stick and handed the lantern to Veredis. 'Light the ground for me,' he said, and began to beat at the longer grasses and weeds beyond the cropped lawn.

'The lights appeared about here,' he said. 'I'm sure of it.'

Veredis held the lantern high. 'There,' he said. 'A stone. Where you were clearing a moment ago.'

There was no cairn, no great slab, merely a single rock, maybe five inches high, standing up from the earth.

'Hara would have seen this when they searched for the Cerulopard,' Seladris said. 'Surely?'

Veredis shrugged. 'Dig around it. Let's see.'

Seladris put down the stick and clawed at the soil and roots at the base of the stone. He tugged at it. 'Goes deep,' he said.

Veredis squatted beside him and put down the lantern. Together they tore at the earth. After some moments, Seladris rested his hands on his knees. 'We need more than our fingers to clear this. Would you go to the kitchen, Ved, and bring gardening tools? There are some in the cupboard near the back door.' He smiled. 'I don't want to leave you out here on your own.'

Veredis rolled his eyes. 'Thoughtful of you.'

Left alone, Seladris crouched beside the stone. From what he could see there were no markings upon it, and yet it appeared to have been planted deliberately. When he touched it, he felt nothing, but perhaps a dozen old hexes masked its purpose, sealed its magic.

Veredis returned with a garden fork and a spade. He'd also had the foresight to bring another lantern.

They dug for two hours or so, until Seladris's spade hit stone or metal. The buried rock was revealed to be a carved pole, and they'd still not reached its root. But they had found *something*.

The hole they'd excavated was six feet deep, like a grave but far wider, and hadn't been that difficult to dig with the appropriate tools. Beneath their feet, still partially buried, was what appeared to be a pair of horizontal doors, like those of a storm cellar, but fashioned of iron not wood. The handles were bound with chains and a huge padlock, wound with strings of bones and leather, and plaits of disintegrating fabric. The stone pole pierced the metal above the handles, as if – impossibly – it had been shot into it. *Something* had certainly been bound in this spot.

'Must we open it?' Veredis asked.

It was a rhetorical question, voiced merely, Seladris thought, to indicate that Veredis really didn't want to see what lay behind the iron.

Seladris nodded. 'We have no choice. Now we need the lump hammer from the tool store.'

Veredis sighed and climbed out of the hole. 'On my way.'

Seladris laid a hand flat against the metal, found it inert. No energy pulsed into his fingers.

When Veredis returned with the hammer, Seladris took it and began swinging at the lock. Below or within the resounding clunk of the strikes, there was another sound, like the deep tolling of a bell. He wasn't sure if this sound was real or in his head, but couldn't ask Veredis about it, only apply himself to the task as if bewitched. Eventually, the lock splintered apart, as if made of glass. Shards flew off it, and Seladris protected his face, but nothing hit him or his companion. If anything, the remains of the lock looked as if they'd melted into a shapeless lump.

Before opening the doors, Seladris pulled Veredis into an embrace and for some moments they crouched together in silence. Then Seladris drew away and hauled at the heavy doors. With a crack like thunder, the stone pole snapped in two and the doors burst wide. Seladris was thrown onto his back.

Veredis raised the lantern, peered into the darkness beyond. 'There are steps,' he said, then glanced back at Seladris. 'No horrible smell, though. That has to be a good sign, surely?'

'There may be another door beyond,' Seladris said. He lifted the second lantern. 'Shall I lead?'

'By all means,' Veredis said. He bowed and gestured widely.

There was a stone staircase of about a dozen steps, which led to a large, low-ceilinged chamber. Dusty strands of cobwebs and earth hung down at the entrance. The glow of the lanterns didn't penetrate very far, but from what they could see, the cellar was empty. The light, however, did reveal images upon the wall. Paintings of leopards and hara that resembled cave pictures of prehistoric times. Seladris went closer to examine the images near the door and realised the cellar was in fact a natural cave; the walls were solid rock, plastered over sporadically, so that lumps and spurs poked out of it in places. The place smelled of dry, rotten brick, earth and, strangely, of musty flowers.

Veredis ventured ahead, diminishing into the darkness, haloed by the feeble radiance of the lantern, as if its light was weakened by the room. After a minute or so, he said in an odd voice, 'Seladris…'

Seladris went to him, raised his lantern.

'The Blue Leopard,' Veredis said forlornly.

The bodies were piled in a corner, reaching to the ceiling, spreading out across the floor. Little more than mummified skeletons, still draped with ragged clothes. Seladris saw the wink of jewels in the light. There was no smell of death here, only a rather sickening, lingering aroma of old blooms and – bizarrely – face powder left too long in a drawer.

'Did those vile things do this?' Veredis said.

'That would seem to be the explanation,' Seladris replied. 'Yet I can't see *spectral* entities being able to bind those doors and bury this chamber, place the stone lock. Living hands did this.'

He hunkered down at the edge of the pile of corpses. He didn't feel afraid, or even particularly nauseated. These husks were empty. Disposed of. Hidden. He stood up. 'Let's look at the walls.'

They held up the lanterns and examined the paintings. There were scenes of ritual, and what looked like some kind of initiation or bestowing of rank. The figures were depicted as both hara and leopards, and also were-leopards, shape-shifters.

'This place must have been theirs,' Seladris said. 'Their headquarters, lair… whatever you want to call it. I think the Cerulopard made these paintings.'

'I get that feeling too,' Veredis said. 'Who else would paint them like this?'

'Sweet Aru,' Seladris breathed. 'Ved, look. My dream.' He held the lantern high, illuminating a further section of wall.

There was Leupardra, the pard-witch, adorned in his leopard skin, with its dangling paws, the snarling mask over the top half of his face. He danced before a raging bonfire, his hands curled into claws. His tribe mates were merely blurred shadows around him, caught in poses of leaping and striking. And beyond them, the Pale Ones, tall, motionless, blank-faced and dire, against a backdrop of soaring bleak pines.

And to the side of this image the words daubed in flaking white paint: *Remember, I sent them out. This is your blood debt to the Blue Leopard. Remember.*

Seladris moved further along the wall, and there was Leupardra, depicted in skilled detail, lithe and beautiful. His left arm was held out stiffly, his index finger pointing. And the Pale Ones were clustered behind him, their spiky hands curled at their chests, their pose that of *listening*.

'He *sent* them,' Veredis said, in a tone of awe and also grudging respect. 'He summoned and sent them. By all dehara, what *were* they?'

'What lived here,' Seladris said. 'Ancient *things*. I'm sure Meladriel knows. He just wouldn't tell us. This is clearly how Leupardra dealt with the human problem in the area.' He swung the lantern over to what lay in the corner. 'And that, presumably, is the price he paid.'

'And what has this to do with you, I wonder?' Veredis said.

'Well, that's obvious, isn't it? *I* dealt with a problem once, and although I didn't call upon etheric entities to aid me, I did leave a pile of bodies.'

'Sel...'

'Dris, they call me Dris. The few.' He smiled weakly.

'Whatever you did in the past, it was as necessary, surely, as what Leupardra did.'

'Was either incident *necessary*?' Seladris said coldly. 'Ferelithia evolved into a tolerant culture that harboured human refugees. Perhaps that compassion should have begun sooner. Did the Blue Leopard and the hara who used them ever seek a way of peace, of decency? I know I didn't. All I wanted was bloody vengeance. I wanted to make the hara who'd tormented me and murdered my tribe suffer. What good did it do me, ultimately? I could simply have taken my freedom and slipped away to a new life, learned to live as a normal har. Vengeance is never free. It comes with chains and a cost.'

'Are you sorry for what you did?' Veredis asked quietly.

Seladris sighed through his nose, glanced at his companion. 'I wish I hadn't done it, because of its legacy. I feel no pity or compassion for those monsters I killed, but I realise now my actions were wrong. I had no right to take their lives. At the time I was in too much of a state to realise that.' He paused. 'Is that enough repentance?'

Veredis smiled at him. 'Well, that sounds enough like regret for me.' He paused. 'So, what do we do now... with this lot?' He gestured at the floor.

'We need Meladriel's salt,' Seladris said. 'Shall I go or…?'

Veredis was already heading towards the entrance.

Seladris stood motionless for a while, staring at what remained of the Blue Leopard. Such hubris. Had Leupardra's conjured servitors turned on them? How had this happened? The answer, of course, could not be painted on the walls. Who had sealed this tomb?

A compulsion came over him. Without thinking, he placed the lantern on the floor and began tearing at the bodies, scattering bones. 'Where are you?' he muttered. 'Where *are* you?'

He was looking for Leupardra, sure he'd know when he'd found the har, even if only a shard of bone remained. He only stopped clawing at the remains, when Veredis called his name and caught hold of his arms from behind.

'Dris, what are you doing? Stop!'

Seladris dropped back limply against him. 'We *have* to find him,' he said. 'We *must*.'

'Find who?'

'Leupardra, of course.'

Veredis turned Seladris to face him, shook him slightly. 'Don't be ridiculous. It's just a pile of bones, all mixed up. How could we ever tell?'

'I have to do this. I'll spread them all out. You don't have to help.'

'In this case, I won't. I think you're mad.'

'At least hold the light up.'

'OK. I brought the salt. It's by the door.'

'We don't need that yet.'

Veredis held up a lantern, while Seladris laid out the bones in a calmer manner. They did not speak for some time, until Seladris said, 'This can't be all of them. There isn't anywhere near thirty bodies here.'

'Hmm, maybe half that?' Veredis said. 'Perhaps the rest escaped.'

Seladris stood up. 'He's not here.'

'I'm not going to ask how you've come to that conclusion, but perhaps it's possible Leupardra and some of his tribe fled, and dared not come back.'

Seladris shook his head. 'I don't think that's what happened.' He stared at the floor for some time. 'I think *he* did this.'

'How can you possibly…?'

'I don't know. It's coming to me…'

Veredis sat down heavily on the floor. 'Sweet Aru, of course!'

'What?'

'This is a wild theory but… there are around fifteen of those weird pale things, aren't there?'

'Well I didn't count them precisely, but…' Seladris gasped. 'Yes! Perhaps he didn't simply summon those entities, but *made* them, provided them with… vessels?'

'And whatever he did…' Veredis gestured at the carpet of bones. 'This was the result. Perhaps these hara gave themselves willingly, who knows? But ultimately they were sacrifices.'

'Would Leupardra do that? Would *any* har?'

Veredis grimaced. 'I don't want to believe so, because I rather like the idea of the pard-witch, but it makes sense to me. I *feel* it's right.'

'He might not have understood the risks.'

'Well, it's comforting to think that.' Veredis stood up and walked to the entrance, returning with the jar of salt. 'Shall we say a few words?'

Seladris took the jar from him. 'Just that? I'm not sure what to do. It doesn't seem enough to scatter salt, utter a few ritual phrases and simply lock them away again, down here.'

'The alternative is notifying the Muncipallion, resulting in a *big* fuss. I don't think that'd be right either. I say we scatter the salt, bless the bones, then burn them.'

Seladris nodded. 'Yes… I have oil in the house.'

Veredis laughed. 'This is becoming a pattern. Just tell me where.'

While Veredis was away, Seladris walked between the bones carefully, on tiptoe. This felt to him like a ritual dance. Would the actions he and Veredis were about to take end the disturbances in Shadey Lane? Had they even discovered the truth? Perhaps Leupardra's remains were here after all. Perhaps the Blue Leopard had never been more than the hara who lay dead around him.

We have made a story, Seladris thought. *We've imagined an explanation. Perhaps it's up to us to make it real.*

When Veredis returned, they dribbled the oil over the bones and scattered the salt. Then they backed to the door and lit the oil.

Seladris said, 'We give you freedom, hara of the Blue Leopard. Be purified by this untainted salt. Take flight to the realms beyond on the smoke of these cleansing flames. We release you and bless you, in the name of the Aghama, he who is first of all, the star and our master.'

For a while they stood watching the growing flames, which once they took hold seemed to devour the bones with increasing hunger. Then Seladris led the way outside, where he and Veredis pulled the doors shut. They had no lock now, but perhaps one wasn't needed. Seladris had kept back a little salt and oil, which he now applied to the doors and rubbed into them. 'Let nothing disturb the peace of this land,' he said. 'May seen and unseen walk in harmony, each in their proper realm, and there be amity between us.'

He stood up, took a step back.

The earth shook.

Veredis grabbed Seladris by one arm and yanked him out the hole they'd dug. The land seemed to scream, and the soil itself writhed underfoot. Stumbling, they tried to run across the grass, but it was difficult to remain upright. Before they reached *Inglefey*, there was a mighty crash, and a hollow moan, and they were thrown to the ground. Desperately, they clung to one another, trying to shield their faces from flying earth and sticks and stones, their bodies curled up instinctively. A storm of earth raged around them, seeming to last an eternity. Until the world shifted and there was only calm and silence.

As one, they raised their heads, scrambled uncertainly to their feet.

Veredis sucked in his breath in shock, exhaled slowly, said, 'Well, I'll need to fill that in. Can't have such a mess next door to my property.'

The ground had collapsed, bringing half the slope of the empty plot down with it. All that remained in the bright moonlight was a huge ragged wound in the earth, as if a meteor had struck it.

'And there's no doubt the Cerulopard are truly buried now,' Seladris said.

He began to laugh, and Veredis did too. Relief, release, the hope their work was done.

Seladris went home with Veredis that night, as he needed distance from Shadey Lane for a while. They sat up till dawn with Tika who'd waited up – no doubt anxiously – drinking to level their nerves.

'Do you want a new house?' Veredis asked Seladris.

He shook his head. 'I… hope not. I want to live in *Inglefey*, because I love the house. I think it likes me too.'

'Well, if you need to move, just tell me.' Veredis raised his glass. 'Here's to a peaceful home.'

They clinked glasses, drank.

In the morning, Tika drove them once more to Meladriel's dwelling by the sea. Meladriel clearly wasn't surprised to see them. In the dark kitchen, Seladris returned the earthenware jar, now empty, to the shaman. Veredis had lent him the payment Meladriel had demanded, which would be deducted from his salary. This Seladris also handed over. Meladriel took it without comment and secreted it in the dresser drawer.

'We'd like to tell you what happened,' Seladris said. 'Get your opinion. Is that possible?'

Meladriel consented and bade them be seated at his table.

Seladris told the tale in as much detail as he could recall, with Veredis occasionally adding a remark. At the end of this narrative, Seladris said, 'Do you think our suppositions are correct, Meladriel? Did Leupardra summon etheric entities into some of his hara and use them as weapons against the humans in the town?'

Meladriel did not reply for some moments. He stared at Seladris. 'You are making one big assumption,' he said.

'Which is?'

'That the bodies you found are, in fact, members of the Blue Leopard.'

'Are they not?'

Meladriel gestured gracefully with both hands. 'I'm simply offering my opinion, as you asked. It's not for me to say who those bodies belonged to. I'm merely suggesting you can't be sure either.'

Seladris glanced at Veredis who shrugged, then returned his attention to Meladriel. 'You mean Leupardra sacrificed hara of *other* phyles?'

'Are you sure they're hara?'

'Well… some of them wore jewellery.'

Meladriel raised his brows.

Seladris sighed. 'No, I'm not sure. So, you think they were human?'

'I've no idea. They could equally have been the bodies of

Leupardra and his elite.'

'He wasn't there.'

'No? How could you be certain? You and Veredis are har, psychically aware, yet the information you picked up was muddled, a riddle, a trick, a blind. Clearly, it was meant to be. I do think it's likely the local phyle leaders ordered the bodies to be concealed and sealed within that mass grave, but as to why, and who died there...' He pulled a face. 'The history is dark. No record was left to us.'

Seladris sighed deeply. 'So, we'll never know. Any of the explanations could be true.'

'An open mind is a wise mind,' Meladriel said. 'At least you've attended to your troubles.'

'It's truly over, then? Finding the cellar, burning the bodies... we did all that we should?'

'That was certainly the appropriate thing to do, but *your* healing began when you sacrificed your secrets, your dirt. This severed the link to the unclean energy in the area, and now it has nothing to feed on.'

Seladris blinked, then laughed in a caustic manner. 'I'm sorry... I can't accept that. It's too glib.'

'As you like,' said Meladriel. 'It is merely my opinion.'

Later that day, when Seladris returned to *Inglefey*, he went alone. The house was as it usually was – warm, humming, quiet. He walked into the sitting-room and found the painting of the leopard in its normal place. He stared at it for some time. Who had painted it? Hara of the Blue Leopard? Leupardra himself? The style was primitive yet colourful, yet now it was clear the picture was nothing more than an empty decoration. The artist would remain unknown.

Seladris went to the window on the western side of the room and gazed out at the empty plot. Already, the crater shaped by the landslide appeared less raw. There was no cellar left, no buried secret beneath the land, and the plot was more level now, perhaps easier to build on. And yet...

He saw a shudder of movement in the remaining pines at the top of the plot. Was that a figure between the trees? At once, he ran out of the house, overwhelmed by a powerful yet weirdly unidentifiable sensation. It comprised recognition, pleasure, certainty. He scrambled up the slope of the empty plot, still able to see that motionless, tall shape above him, mottled by shifting sunlight, the shadows of leaves. Mottled like a leopard skin.

But when he reached the spot, there was only light and shadow between the ancient trunks.

'You're not unwelcome,' he murmured. 'We are the same.'

He held his breath for long moments. But the day was serene, unmarked by uncanny influences. The feeling within Seladris ebbed away like the fading cry of gulls.

The Municipallion later reported in the Ferelithian newssheets that the landslide in Shadey Lane had been caused by a fault in the cave system beneath the northern hills. Small tremors had been felt for a short while prior to the event. Hienamas who'd inspected the area had ascertained there would be no further disturbance. To them, the ground was quiet.

Alas, What is Done in Youth

Wendy Darling

An adaptation of 'The Old Nurse's Story' (Elizabeth Gaskell, 1852)

'It'll be fine,' I assured Ailis, squeezing his small hand as we trudged up the hilly carriageway in the near dark.

Our arrival in what was to be our new home in Alba Caledon had not played out as planned. Arriving in town late, we found nohar there to meet us, and yet there we were with our luggage and a carriage just departed. We'd found an inn with a pothar who'd agreed to hold our things overnight and then given us directions up to the manor house.

Carrying only a small valise of clothes — my own and the harling's — we were now trying to make good time to meet the household. If we could avoid freezing to death, that would also be ideal. It was so cold we could see the thick clouds of our misted breath even in the muddled light of the clouded night sky. My face burned with the wind and I blinked my eyes to clear my vision. I did not want to miss a turn.

Ailis, only three, had better winter clothes than I did, I'd seen to that, but still I worried after the little thing. He was to be my responsibility, and it wouldn't do for him to arrive at the steps of his new home frostbitten.

'Do you really think it'll be alright?' he asked me, after we'd rounded another turn in the road.

'Oh, yes,' I responded, smiling even though he likely couldn't see my face. 'He's high-hurakin and he'll surely be delighted with you. I imagine the house will be something splendid.'

We walked another fifteen minutes before we came to a straightaway lined with tall hedges and ending in darkness. Not seeing any other turns in the road, we approached.

Ailis and I were quite frozen by now and sensitive to the wind, which is why I was surprised when I felt it blowing in from the end of what I'd thought to be a row of hedges.

Taking the harling's hand, I hurried over to the tall, iron gates. They stood not wide open, but ajar, with a brief note in neat handwriting:

> *Struan — Manus waited in the village at length but evidently you are not punctual. If you are reading this note, please hurry to the entrance of Leven Manor and make your presence known. Hopefully before midnight. You and my sori will be accommodated. — Lorna har Leven*

Nonplussed, I turned to Ailis and then gave the open side of the great gate a shove.

Leven Manor was not much brighter than the road we'd travelled up. Beyond the gate grew great, gnarled trees, surrounded by humps of rhododendrons, whose stiff, curled leaves rattled in the wind. A gravel drive led us to a sleeping giant of a house, three stories I judged, with wings spreading into the darkness further than I could make out. From the sconces aflame beside the entrance I picked up the smoky tones of old sandstone, half-covered with ivy. I could make out the shape of windows, but no lights flared in any of the front rooms.

My quick inspection over, I trundled Ailis up the few steps to the great oak and iron door. Although the landing had an overhang, it offered no protection from the wind, and so I quickly took hold of the knocker – as large as my hand and heavier – and announced our arrival as loudly as I was able.

'You have to knock hard for anyone to hear you in such a great, big house,' I said to Ailis, who was hunching into his coat collar, intent on nothing but getting warmth back into his blood.

After a minute, I heard the clicks of a lock tumbling and soon the old door groaned inward, revealing a tired but affable-looking har holding a lantern.

'Good evening, Tiahaar, and harling dear,' Manus greeted us warmly, gesturing us to cross the threshold. He spoke with the accent of the Caledii, as had the pothar at the inn. I was further from home than I'd ever been.

'Tiahaar Lorna had me leave that grumpy little note, but I understand… these things happen.' He reached out for my valise and I handed it over, relieved after carrying it frozen-handed for an hour. 'What an awful night to be walking. Here, come in, come in.'

Within five minutes, he had us out of our coats, hats, and every bit of frozen outerwear. We were assured that everything would be dried, tended to and returned to us by the next evening, along with our bags left at the inn. 'There'll be tea and a late dinner, just as soon as you've seen Lorna and Innes.'

'Innes?' I inquired, having not heard that name.

'Lorna's personal assistant, served him since they were young hara... since a bit before I came here myself,' he explained.

It's difficult to judge a har's age by appearances, but I'd been told that Lorna was close to a hundred years old.

'Over time, Innes has become more like a friend than employee really,' Manus continued. 'They're together most of the time. And with some of Lorna's, pardon me... peculiarities... Innes can manage him best now.'

Turning over the possible meaning of "peculiarities" and holding Ailis' hand as I followed Manus towards Lorna's sitting room, I took in my surroundings.

The entrance hall was massive, at least three times the height of a har, with floor-to-ceiling wood panelling. A great golden chandelier hung from the coffered ceiling, though there seemed to be only half as many candles as would be needed to light up such a large room, and there were no other lights.

The great fireplace, though unlit, was a thing of wonder, so large I was certain I could fit a bed in it. Deer, quail and ducks were carved amongst a forest of stone surrounding the fireplace mouth. Andirons jutted out, reaching higher than my knees.

On the opposite side of the room, taking up most of the wall, loomed a pipe organ, neatly accommodated by the hall's high ceiling. I only learned later, after asking, what it actually was. That night I simply assumed it was a great magical device of some kind, which isn't far from the truth, now is it? The organ pipes appeared half-covered in dust, but below the dust gleamed fine metal worthy of the rest of the hall.

Manus led us to a door just past the organ. He didn't mention the doors to the left and right of the fireplace, and in all the time I lived in the house, I never saw what lay beyond those doors.

We found the venerable hara together in a dimly-lit salon at the back of the house. One side of the room was nearly all curtains, covering a wall of windows. Various thick rugs covered the floor.

Lorna was writing in a notebook when we entered, Innes close at his side, seemingly sharing secrets into his ear. The table beside them held a delicate glass orb lit by mage light; it was the first bit of magic I had seen since arriving in the village. A few candles made up the only other light in the room, so shadows hung over most of it.

'Tiahaar Lorna,' Manus announced, 'our awaited arrivals – your sori Ailis and his guardian Struan.'

Lorna of course did not look "old" per se – there were no wrinkles, grey hairs or thinning of the face as with human's – but nevertheless his appearance confirmed his age. His eyes showed a great passage of time, in their depth and in their stillness. He didn't have the ethereal quality I'd been told much, much older hara attain, but there was a subtle difference I couldn't put my finger on.

'We've been waiting all night.' When he spoke, it sounded like the wind. 'Haven't we, Innes?' He set down his notebook next to the light. 'Why are you so late?'

I bowed slightly, doing my best to be polite, despite the fact he hadn't even said hello.

'Our carriage arrived late – so late that Manus missed us, and we had to walk all the way up here.'

'Best not use that driver again,' he declared.

The rest of that meeting proceeded much the same way. Lorna was upset we'd kept the household up late and wanted it clear that I should learn to adapt to the manor's ways as quickly as possible.

He did, finally, acknowledge his young surakin, whom he'd never laid eyes on before. 'It's the least I can do,' he said, 'giving you a decent place to grow up, in a home with at least one family member.'

Ailis of course made clear his gratitude and promised to do his best to make the family proud.

They were a few other bits of business discussed before we parted for the night. Manus would be settling us in upstairs and beginning the next day, for the most part we could expect to spend our time with him and his chesnari or manage our days independently. It was, however, expected that we would visit Lorna (and Innes) at least once a day.

'I'd like to keep an eye on the harling,' Lorna explained, in that sighing voice of his. 'He's my responsibility as well as yours.'

After our farewells, Manus led us through a sitting room, up a great flight of stairs, and across a broad gallery filled with books, until we arrived at what I later came to think of as my home.

A change in atmosphere was immediate. I smelled dinner on the air and somehar had lit candles all around the cosy dining room we entered. Manus gestured for us to sit down while he went to bring the food.

'Finally, something warm in our bellies,' I said to Ailis. 'And soon we'll have warm beds, too.'

He leaned in towards me and, checking the door, whispered, 'Is that grouchy har really related to me?'

Leave it to a harling. Well, at least he'd known not to speak in front of the househara.

'Yes,' I hissed, patting his arm and backing away. 'You'll have plenty of opportunity to get to know one another better.'

Just then Manus returned through the doorway, and he wasn't alone. He introduced his chesnari Dorlit, who did the household's cooking and shared some cleaning chores with Manus. They'd been together decades but had no harlings of their own. Dorlit was delighted by Ailis' arrival and the harling was soon at ease with both these strangers, a very good sign. He was, after all, still mourning the recent and very sudden death of his parents.

'So, how did you come to be Ailis' guardian?' Manus wondered. 'Do you not have family of your own?'

The question caught me off guard, comfortable as I'd been made by the stew and dumplings and company.

'Actually, I do, though it's just my hostling and I. He lives in the far south of Alba Sulh. But he's the main reason I'm in the business of caring for harlings'

I paused, as usual feeling obligated to share this bit of history but bracing for the reactions. 'Are either of you familiar with the old Varrish breeding experiments?

Both of them quickly drew back their heads, a tad startled.

'No,' Manus murmured.

Dorlit bit his lip. 'A little, more like a rumour.'

'Well, my hostling's story is this. When Marigold was a harling in Megalithica, he was stolen from his parents by Varrs to take part in a breeding experiment. This was in the days when harlings were still a rarity. A large group of harlings, all similarly stolen, were taken to a special "home" and indoctrinated into thinking they were designed to create the next generations of harlings.' Dorlit's lips parted, either in recognition or in horror. 'And once they went through feybraiha, they were taught how to submit as soume and how to make conception easy.'

'They didn't...' Manus growled.

Dorlit's eyes checked Ailis, to see if he was upset by this talk, but the harling was untroubled. He knew all about this.

'Once harlings like my hostling were ready, groups of Varr soldiers would arrive and make them all with pearl,' I explained. I hated this part of the story. I had half-brothers I would never know. 'After they'd birthed the pearls, the harlings would be taken from them, mostly to become soldiers, and then these young hara would have to make more pearls.'

Dorlit's eyes had teared up. These hara were far more compassionate than those who'd raised my hostling.

'It's all right,' I said, wanting to move on. I decided to skip over the fact my hostling had birthed eight pearls. 'In the end the Gelaming won the war, and so it all came to a stop. The pearls stopped. There's a story about how Marigold got away, but it's not important. He made it away from Megalithica.'

'And somehow got to Alba Sulh, where he had you?' Manus surmised.

I nodded. 'Yes. Growing up in that awful place, Marigold had done a great deal of work raising harlings and so over here, he kept that up, working in various schools, harling programs, harling-care, and so on. At times he's even helped hara with dropping pearls.'

'How did that lead to you?' prompted Manus.

'Well, after being liberated, Marigold wanted a harling of his own for a long, long time, but put it off because, well, there were painful memories for him. Finally, after a number of decades had passed, he found he was ready. My father's no chesnari of his but a friend, who I hear from now and then.

'But as for how I got into this "business", it really is from Marigold and just doing what he does. I was raised with him always teaching, providing harling-care, even had a few foster brothers now and again. So I went into it myself and have worked with my hostling or on my own for years. And when the need came to help with Ailis, I was called.'

'And haven't left him since,' Dorlit finished for me.

'No, I haven't.'

Actually, I hadn't left Ailis since he was in the pearl and I was called to watch over his hosting and the birth. I was part of the household for just over three years, helping to raise him while his busy parents shouldered the responsibilities of their estate. But then came the accident. When a bridge above a deep gorge on the estate collapsed, Keir did not live long enough to see a doctor. Antine was grievously injured but made it to his bed, where with his last breath he entrusted me with the harling. After a few days' deliberation, an inquiry was sent to a grandhigh-hurakin with an estate in the north. Would he be interested in taking in an orphan, who would be provided with a guardian? He answered promptly and now, here we were.

'It's good you're here,' Manus said, tipping his teacup towards us in a friendly gesture. 'At our age, and with everything so settled, it'll be grand to have a wee bit of youth and laughter back in the house.'

I glanced over to Ailis to say something, but he'd fallen fast asleep in his chair.

Over the next two or three weeks we settled in quite nicely.

On some days the weather warmed up enough that Ailis and I could walk about the grounds, albeit still wearing our coats and hats. The flowers may have faded, but there were all manner of interesting places to explore – enchanting groves of huddled trees, lines of tall evergreens cut like great spikes, and a circular hedge cut with a single entrance that led to a stone table and two chairs. I remember one day we took tea outside. Admittedly it was chilly, but we did so want to take advantage.

The house, where we spent most of our time, seemed endlessly fascinating. It took us several days just to sort out all the rooms and even then, I couldn't always find my way back to them or from one room to another without a few false turns. And this was leaving out Lorna's set of rooms, which was private, plus the section of the house beyond the grand fireplace in the entrance hall. That area, Manus informed me, was strictly off limits. As to why, we were provided no explanation, but with an enormous house to explore and a head househar as gracious as Manus, neither Ailis nor I pressed him.

There was a grand library, multiple parlours, a morning room, a dining room, all sorts of bedrooms, water closets, bath chambers –

and all of it filled with antique furniture of fine woods, wrought iron, brass, mirror glass. It smelled musty, yes, but Manus and Dorlit did dust and keep up appearances. The windows stood free of cobwebs, the drapes were not moth-eaten. The one exception was the organ, which as I noted on the first day was covered with dust.

For company, we quickly found ourselves fitting right in with Manus and Dorlit, who were kind and gentle hara, more so as we got to know them. They remained tight-lipped on some matters, owing to their loyalty to the estate and the family, and their long residence, but anything to do with Ailis or when helping me by ordering something from town, giving me ideas on things to explore outside or in the house, they were generous and chatty.

The one dark spot in all this were our visits with the rather intimidating and at times forbidding Lorna. I didn't plan them as dark spots but tried to approach them with optimism. Surely, he'd be more sociable as he grew to know us? Who wouldn't be beguiled by Ailis? But every day we came in and every day it was the same. He'd look up, blink, open his mouth for a brief greeting then gesture for Ailis to come forward. After inspecting him, he'd motion for us both to sit. Then Lorna would speak with Innes in his low, breathy voice, sometimes remarking on us as if we weren't there, sometimes apparently resuming whatever conversation they'd been having since we arrived.

I'd heard this was what happened to hara sometimes when they grew ancient and close to death, but neither har was near that age. Had they lost their wits? Their manners? Or was this some deliberate slight? If so, why? It would have eaten me up more had Lorna not always dismissed us within a quarter hour. Also, when I spoke to Dorlit about it, he said not to mind it. Lorna had told him privately he enjoyed seeing his sori, but simply didn't think he was good with harlings, never had been, and would just as soon leave Ailis entirely to me, using his wealth to support him.

It was coming up on the end of the first month that Dorlit mentioned he was going to be dusting the portraits.

'Do you mean the paintings of all the family in the study with the dark panelling?' I asked. Ailis and I had encountered it, but the room was so dark, and the drapes so heavy, we hadn't been able to see much.

He nodded, packing an array of rags and cleaning solutions into a bucket. 'Aye. It's barely used, but Lorna does visit it at odd hours and likes it clean.'

As he turned to leave for downstairs, I had an idea. 'Wait, Dorlit. Would you mind if Ailis and I came along?'

The househar cocked his head. 'That harling hasn't any business cleaning, Struan.'

'Oh, not for that,' I quickly explained, 'but to see the portraits. It was so dark when we were in there, we couldn't make them out.'

'Ah,' he said. 'That I can understand.'

'And I'd like to know who some of the hara are. Ailis should know, too.'

Dorlit set his bucket down on the floor. 'You're probably right. Fetch the harling and we'll be off.'

The room was as I'd remembered it, the heavy curtains drawn but for a few inches, walls of heavy, dark wood broken up by the lighter coloured wood and metal of portrait frames.

'How can you clean in the dark?' I asked as I ushered Ailis in.

'Well, first off,' Dorlit huffed, 'open up one of these.' Groping behind the drapes, he found what turned out to be a massive cord like a snake and tied it around one side of the drape. Once the other side was up, the light was markedly improved.

'We could also do the others, but I prefer this lovely lamp,' he said, moving to a corner where two reading chairs stood with a beautiful lamp of coloured glass between them. 'It's from Human times and originally wired for electric power, but Lorna's father, Tiahaar Fingal, had it converted to run on something more practical.'

Motioning for quiet, he placed his hand on the rounded lampshade for full minute while staring down at the table with great intensity. At last the light began to glow, then shine. Dorlit was right; the light filled the second half of the room nicely.

Ailis meanwhile had rushed forward in excitement. 'My hostling lit lights like that all the time,' he recalled breathlessly. 'That wasn't the only thing he could do, of course, but that reminded me of it. Are you trained in other arts?'

Dorlit offered a deprecating smile. 'Not much, dear. Simple matters, like certain types of healing, setting myself right and centred, those sorts of things. But only those workings that everyhar I grew up with knew. I never studied with a hienama like some hara.'

'Isn't it wonderful, though?' I gestured to the lamp, with its metal base wrought like a tree trunk and shade like a pergola of flowers. I was even less skilled in the arts. 'You'll learn how to do it yourself one day, I expect, Ailis.'

Dorlit was now rolling out a cloth on a windowsill and setting down his cleaning things. 'I expect he'll be tutored by a hienama here at the house. Manus tells me Lorna and his brother Alpin both received the best of education in such matters, as well as reading, music and more.'

The houshar stated this quite matter-of-factly, but these facts crowded my head with questions. The first of which come out was: 'Lorna is highly skilled in magical arts, then?'

'Of course,' Dorlit answered. He was apparently going to start in the corner by the door and work his way over, so I walked across to hear him better. 'I shouldn't say "of course", I suppose. You wouldn't know it. He doesn't flaunt his skills at all and, truth be told, it's seldom he uses them at all anymore, or I don't see it leastways.'

That was one question answered. Now the more pressing. 'And he has a brother?'

A slight shudder ran through Dorlit's body, quickly squelched by the tightening of shoulders. 'Yes. Alpin. But he died long ago.'

Not a lot of things can kill a har. 'How long ago?' I asked.

'Before I came to this house,' he answered, wiping down a set of candlesticks. He moved on to a marble bust, but stopped after a few minutes, I think sensing I still stood behind him with questions.

He set down his rag and turned. 'Come, I'll show you something. Ailis, too.'

The harling, who'd in fact been right beside me listening in the whole time, followed me as Dorlit gestured toward to a large oil portrait hung beside the fireplace. I'd gotten so caught up in my questions I'd completely missed it.

Lorna.

Though portrayed decades earlier, he looked nearly unchanged, with a few exceptions. The artist showed him in splendid clothes, with a wrap of thick white fur over a robe of what looked to be green silk. His intense red hair was long, pooling over his shoulders and dipping over one eye. Now he dressed more austerely; not like a pauper or a har of the land, but in clothes meant mostly for warmth, not for show. And his hair was cut short, just above the collar.

But the biggest difference from the Lorna of the past, at least as shown by the artist, was the eyes. The younger har's eyes were prideful, challenging: *'I am the best, the most splendid, and I dare you to prove it otherwise.'* Lorna was still prideful, but his eyes were often unfocused, or they deliberately seemed to avoid things and hara he did not wish to see. And something else: from the very first I had noticed flashes of pain in those eyes.

Ailis and I had our fill of the portrait, the harling asking a few questions. I thought we'd be done then, but Dorlit walked over to a bookcase and beckoned to us.

He went to the end of the case and began to pull out a large rectangular object. Once I recognised what it was, I stepped forward to help him. It was a second portrait, turned backward to face the wall, and further hidden away.

'You can't say anything to Lorna – or Innes or Manus,' he told me, as he swung it around. 'This is just between us.'

Alpin.

He was, if anything, even more beautiful, more splendid. About his shoulders hung a wrap of blackest fur, closed with what looked to be a silver and ruby pin. His silk robe was of darker green than his brother's, with slender yellow stripes. Alpin's hair was the same shade as his brother's, only it fell in ringlets to his shoulders. And were the eyes the same? Yes, they were. Prideful and challenging. I'd never know what they would have looked like now.

After we gazed upon the painting for a while, looking between it and its twin on the wall, Dorlit slid it back, and then for about fifteen minutes showed us some of the other portraits around the room. The most interesting besides those two was that of the father, Fingal, whose face looked down from a medium-sized frame over the desk. He wore no fur, instead a woven wrap of warm wool, but his eyes had the same look as his sons'.

After that, we left Dorlit to his cleaning and went about our day. I can't remember what we did, but I know it did not include questioning Lorna about his brother.

Not long after this, I found myself going to Dorlit for the answer to another mystery.

Every night, following a routine of washing and reading and singing, I'd put Ailis to bed and sit in my room adjacent or sometimes in another of the househara's room and enjoy a few hours alone before going to bed myself. Or I'd chat with Dorlit and Manus, if they were done with their work for the day. Evenings were pleasant and quiet.

But about three weeks into my stay, on a stormy night when I was alone, as the other hara had gone to visit friends in town, I heard what sounded like a far-off moan or a wail. Startled, I sat still and tried to decipher whether it was Ailis or some other har. It didn't sound like Ailis. I went to the window and searched the darkness with my eyes and ears. But the sound was inside the house. And it sounded like music, not random moans of sorrow.

I turned around and wandered out toward the entrance to the househara's quarters. The music grew louder. Its origin was certainly inside the house, and somewhere downstairs. But it was an hour before midnight, and I was loath to leave the harling alone and, to be honest, loath to go about the house with naught but a candle. So instead I stood at the top of the stairs listening to the unearthly voice of… What?

The next morning, out of earshot of the harling, I asked Manus and Dorlit about it.

'The wind plays tricks,' Manus told me. 'That great oak by the maze garden can play like a horn when a storm is coming through.'

A horn, a flute, an eerie voice – he compared it to all those things. But all of them were outside things, and I was sure the sound had come from inside – and it was music.

Dorlit meanwhile had mostly nodded along with his chesnari's explanations. 'I wondered about it myself, when I first started on here, as curious as you are, but Manus is right, it's the wind.' Yet something in his eyes told me he wasn't sold on the idea either.

About a week after I'd seen the portraits and learned about Alpin, the long-dead brother, I tried my hand at getting the truth from him. Ailis had already been put to bed and Manus was down in the town having a rare night drinking with friends, so it was just Dorlit and I.

'Those sounds I've been hearing at night,' I began. 'They're not the wind. They're music, and they're from inside the house somewhere, though I don't dare follow them to discover where.'

One of Dorlit's hands gripped the chair arm, while he drew the knuckles of the other to his lips. 'I shouldn't tell you,' he allowed. 'You've not been here long.'

I took a sip of my tea and waited. He'd already shared one secret.

But after nearly a minute, Dorlit hadn't budged.

'What would it take for you to tell me?'

He dropped his hand into his lap and gazed briefly at the ceiling. 'Well, I've been wondering,' he said, now looking at me levelly. 'When your hostling was in that... place...'

Inwardly I groaned. He was asking for an exchange of information. 'Yes?'

'You didn't say, so I was wondering... Couldn't *stop* wondering. How many pearls did your hostling drop?'

How... *unpleasant*.

'Eight,' I answered, setting down my tea. 'Four one year, three the next, and then only one the last year, before the Gelaming came.'

Dorlit's eyes dropped to the table. 'I'm... sorry I asked.' He was blinking back tears. 'He didn't get to keep any of them?'

When I answered, I spoke quietly. 'Not a one. Marigold didn't even see them hatched. And even though the place was filled with harlings, he never knew which were his.'

He shook his head and shuddered. 'I can't conceive pearls,' he whispered back. 'There was an... incident... back before I came here, and somehow I just... can't.' Finally, he looked up, but his eyes went to the wall and not me. 'Luckily Manus had no trouble with that. He's never wanted to bear pearls, always said having me was more than enough for him, didn't need more. We're kept busy taking care of the house anyway.'

He turned back to me, a sudden shift of mood. 'But there's a harling here, and you for company as well.'

I hoped we were now done with the topic. 'And now will you tell me about the music?'

And so he took a breath, looked around as if to check for Manus, and asked me – naturally – to swear not to tell a soul. The music, he explained, was from the pipe organ in the entrance hall. And who was playing it? He'd been told, by Manus and, years ago, a few other househara who'd once worked in the house, that it was Tiahaar Fingal. He liked to play, no one knew why, on stormy nights.

Well. I had asked, hadn't I?

Not long after this, I went into the village to seek out a bit of companionship for myself. A night's worth of warmth and affection, as any har is wont to do. I found it with a har who I believe might have been hoping for manor secrets from me. He didn't get much from me that way, but did get my body, happily given, and we both drifted off to sleep content.

I dreamed I was at the harling-house, which Marigold had described in vivid detail, written about in in a memoir even. I'd dreamed of it before, and the dreams were never pleasant.

I was in one of the delivery rooms, by myself. I wasn't with pearl but knew I had just delivered one. Since there was no doctor there to stop me, I decided to get up and go back to my own room.

The hallway was cold, tiles chill on my bare feet. I wasn't sure whether it was night or day, but I knew there was a staircase somewhere In fact, I was about to turn to the stairwell door when I heard a low sound, a moan. It stopped me in my tracks as it wasn't something I'd ever heard there. But then I understood. It was the organ.

The music grew louder, and I realised it was coming from somewhere up ahead of me. So, stepping away from the door, I proceeded down towards the dining hall. Sure enough, when I reached that first set of doors, the organ music swelled from inside. I pushed through and although I saw no organ, every chair was filled with harlings, all staring at me accusingly, mouths open, singing those eerie notes.

At the manor, the organ music continued, wafting up every few days, as storms big and small rolled through. I said nothing to Manus nor Ailis, and I refrained from exchanging looks with Dorlit. I didn't even ask him the obvious follow-up questions. A dead har was playing the organ? I was both intrigued and fearful. I knew little of magic or what happened to hara once they passed from life.

One night, as I sat in the dining room listening to a concert filled with high notes, it occurred to me: Could it not be Lorna playing? He'd had training in music and must've learned to play the organ. How did Manus really know?

I got my answer when, one day, headed out the front door, I stopped at the dusty organ. It was a curious thing, with knobs and wooden pieces and rows of black and white keys, then metal pipes of all sizes. I hadn't the faintest idea how it worked. Poking at it, nothing happened but some clicking. Examining it thoroughly, I spotted a door with a hinge at the end and had the notion of opening it up for a clue to its workings. I pulled a knob and suddenly I knew it couldn't be Lorna playing.

Every rod below the keyboard was broken, looking like it had been bashed out with a blunt instrument, like an axe driven straight back perhaps. I don't know anything of mechanics, but I did know the keyboard was the start and if it wasn't connected with the rest of it, the instrument's throat was cut.

Tiahaar Fingal was perhaps the musician after all.

After that discovery, the music brought on a sense of unease in me more than curiosity, though I tried pushing it to the back of my mind.

As Shadetide pushed toward Natalia, Ailis and I were settling into the household nicely. A tutor had begun to come by once a week to give reading and writing lessons and after the tutor left, Ailis would read, which coincided nicely with the weather. It was far too cold for explorations or games about the grounds. Curling up on a couch with a book was a much better option.

Lorna continued to have Ailis for regular visits, even if they were brief. Some days he was attentive, asking questions about the books the harling was reading, while other days he was listless. On those days we did not stay long. But overall I was pleased by what I thought was some bonding between Ailis and his hura.

It was a freezing cold morning in January that I headed into town, determined to buy some yarn. Cold or no cold, I thought I ought to familiarise myself with some of the locals. And besides, I could begin to knit some mittens and blankets and suchlike, which I could do beside Ailis as he read.

I went alone, leaving the harling with Lorna and Innes, to whom I'd mentioned my intention the day before. I could've left him with Dorlit of course, but Lorna had expressed an interest in spending time with him. Another opportunity to get to know one another.

I did indeed make the acquaintance of a few hara in town and filled a bag with lovely yarn. I'd never seen wool so fine or dyed so beautifully. I walked up to the manor having to brace myself against the cold but feeling quite glad I'd gone and pressed ahead with my idea.

As soon as I was back at the house, and before I'd had the least chance to warm up, I headed to the salon at the back of the house to collect dear Ailis.

There I found both Lorna and Innes sleeping in their chairs, under thick, musty-looking furs. A tea set sat on the table. Of the harling there was no sign.

'Ailis?' I called softly.

I walked about the room, assuming he was curled up somewhere not immediately obvious. I circled the room. I bent over and looked under the tables. I drew back the drapes. No Ailis.

It was when I went back to the entrance door and called out a bit more loudly that the hara came awake.

'What are you doing there, Struan?'

'Looking for Ailis,' I said, turning. 'I thought you were… looking after him.' I spoke carefully, not wishing to sound accusatory.

Lorna did not betray a shred of embarrassment when he said. 'I was, but as you must've seen, I drifted off.' He leaned forward and took a sip of tea, which he quickly set down again. It was cold, I presumed. 'I assume the harling "drifted off" as well. He'll be in the house.'

He was not in the house.

I searched the ground floor and then enlisted Dorlit and Manus' help for the second and third. Innes searched Lorna's rooms. Ailis was simply not about.

'He's got to be sleeping somewhere,' Dorlit assured me. 'There are an endless lot of hidey holes a harling could find in here, and then, sleepy, disappear in. He'll wake up and come to me looking for a meal.'

When by dinner, he still had not appeared, everyhar was as worried as I was. I was not content to wait. 'Could he be in that other wing of the house?' I asked Dorlit.

Not a chance, he told me. It was locked up tight, and only Manus and Lorna had the keys. He'd never been in himself.

The weather was far too harsh for Ailis to have ventured outside, we all agreed. There was snow on the ground and great clouds formed when a har breathed out there.

Dorlit pressed a cup of tea into my hands and told me to rest in my room for a bit. We would find the harling, he assured me. Most likely Lorna would scry for him, now that we were in desperate straits.

In my room, I could not sit, but rather went to the window, taking my lamp with me. The moon was waxing, though not full, and there was no storm that night, so by and by moonlight shifted across the ground. And staring down at the snow I noticed the shapes of what looked like footprints in the snow out on the front drive.

I threw on my cloak and raced downstairs, down two long

flights of stairs, then out the front door. It had stopped snowing toward midday and I wasn't wearing proper boots, only house shoes, but I didn't care. I followed the set of small footprints, climbing up a hill and through a stand of apple trees. There, I nearly collided with a figure dressed all in wool, naught but his eyes showing for the scarf and hat he was wearing. He carried a bundle in his arms.

Ailis!

'Found him frozen under a tree not far from here,' the har told me as we rushed to the door I'd come from. 'Begging your pardon, I was shepherding the flock, moving for the evening, when I saw a dark lump there and…'

Thank Ag for that shepherd. I dashed upstairs and cried for my friends, begging for anything to warm the harling up.

'Ailis, why were you out?' I demanded with a touch of anger. I loved him dearly, but after hours of worry, I wanted to know why he'd done such a daft thing.

He was barely sensible but managed a few words. 'I was playing…' he murmured. 'There was a harling, saw him out the window. Waved to me…' His eyes drifted shut and he spoke no more.

We did manage to warm him up, but on the matter of why he'd done something so foolish and dangerous, we had no further inkling.

'Ask him later,' Dorlit advised. 'When he's rested and feeling better. In the morning.'

I was too impatient for that, however.

An hour later, I peeked into Ailis' bedroom and found him stirring.

'Hello,' I said, sitting down at the bedside. 'Warmed up?'

He nodded and looked about himself as if wondering how he had gotten there.

'I left you with Lorna and Innes this morning, dear, as I'm sure you remember. When did you leave?'

He pushed himself up in bed. 'I stayed for a while, long enough I had some of Dorlit's biscuits. But then the hara started talking, boring stuff, and they bored themselves I supposed, because they fell asleep.'

As I often did, I was grateful the harling kept his impertinent comments for my ears only. 'And then?'

'I decided it would be all right to explore for a bit,' he admitted with some guilt. 'Not far and not long.'

'How did you end up outside?'

Ailis closed his eyes for a moment. 'I was in the entry hall, poking at that "organ", then looking at all the carvings on the fireplace, and finally looking out the window at the snow on the drive. And that's when I saw a little harling, my age.'

That caught me off guard. 'A harling?'

He nodded gravely. 'Yes, not far off either, so close I could see his lovely red hair, sprinkled with snow. He as waving at me, motioning me to come out.'

'And so you did.'

'I haven't seen another harling in months, and he was waving and waving. I thought maybe it was somehar from the village.'

'Come all the way up here on a freezing cold day? To see you? Few hara even know you're here. How would a harling know you're here?'

Ailis shrugged. 'I don't know. I just know I wanted to go out and see, so I did.'

Without a coat or boots or hat or anything, I thought. 'Then what happened?'

'He smiled and looked so happy. His cheeks were rosy red. Then he took my hand and tugged, like he wanted to show me something.'

With a start I realised something about this story. 'And you're telling me you followed this harling out into the yard?'

'Yes, of course I did. How else would I have seen the crying har out in the field?'

I'd never been cross with Ailis, because I'd never had cause. But now I leaned forward and took him by the shoulders. 'Your parents didn't raise you to lie and neither did I.'

'I'm not lying, Struan!' he pleaded.

'You are,' I insisted. 'I found you because I spotted footprints in the snow. *One* set of footprints, leading from the drive. Not two. There was nohar else with you.'

'But there was! There *was!*'

'No, there wasn't. There couldn't have been.'

'There was a red-headed harling and I went with them out into the yard and we…'

'You didn't,' I said, letting go of his shoulders. 'You're being fanciful… to put it mildly.' I gently pushed him back, so he was lying down again and adjusted his blanket. 'You're tired and probably looking for something to excuse yourself. We'll talk about your naughty behaviour in the morning.'

I rose and was just turning to leave when I heard a sniffle. My dear harling was in tears. 'I'm not lying.'

It broke my heart, but I knew I had to be firm.

Unfortunately, the harling was no less adamant in the morning.

'I never looked at his feet,' he told me. 'I just went with him as he pulled on my hand. He was very cold, no mittens and surely outside for ages.'

'What did he say to you?'

'Nothing at all.'

I raked my hands through my hair. 'Go on.'

He took me up through the holly trees and out at the edge, by the field, we saw a har sitting on the snow crying. I'd think his tears would've turned to ice in that cold, but they were all running down his face.' Ailis' face brightened. 'But when he saw me, he smiled as if I were somehar he'd been waiting for and beckoned me over to sit on his knee. Which I did.'

'You did?' I murmured. 'And…?'

'I don't remember much except thinking how peaceful I felt suddenly. And then I must've fallen asleep.'

And this was the story the harling insisted on and from which he'd not be swayed. I brought him to tears trying but he simply wouldn't.

Finally telling him to get dressed, I went over to the kitchen to ask Dorlit about breakfast, which we'd been late for.

'Lorna wants you down as soon as you've eaten,' he told me, putting the kettle on. 'He wants to know what happened.'

I didn't spill the story then, I think because I didn't want to show Ailis as a liar. But a half hour later, I prepared myself to tell the head of the house. I was going to catch it. Although really, was it I who'd let a harling wander off?

I found Lorna alone in his dining room and told him the harling was now well. I then, with hesitation, went on to explain how Ailis had slipped out and why. At the mention of the supposed harling on the drive, he gasped, and when I told him how he'd followed this nameless harling out to the hollies and to this crying har, he shouted.

'No!'

Only moments later Innes flew into the room. 'What is it?'

Lorna beckoned him over and whispered into his ear. Innes suddenly turned on me. 'Ailis must not go near this harling again! Do you hear? He'll lure him to his death.'

Meanwhile Lorna sat with his hands over his face murmuring, nearly incomprehensibly, except for a few words, drawn out in his breathy voice. 'So long ago… impossible…'

I promised I'd keep an eye out and Innes said I'd best do more than that, for it was a matter of life and death. And with that, he sent me from the room, saying he was going to do his best to calm Lorna down from the shock.

I was given no further explanation.

I was very uneasy in my mind after that. Could it happen again? I began to watch over Ailis every moment he was awake, for fear he might slip off again. I wanted him to be able to spend time with just Dorlit in the kitchen or by himself in the library, but now I wouldn't trust anyone but myself with his welfare, nor could I trust him not to run off, wilfully or no. And there'd be no leaving him with Lorna and Innes – not after what had happened.

Meanwhile a battle waged in my head. On the one hand, it was possible that Lorna was attuned to forces I wasn't, from being tied into the very home and lands. On the other hand, what if he was simply going a bit mad, the way I'd heard humans used to? Could that happen to hara? As for Ailis, he too could be picking up on things unseen. Harlings' senses are very open, so it's possible he could have seen something. Had I been too harsh with him? Perhaps I had, but if so, it had only been from a sense of protectiveness. Which I would carry out by watching him closely.

And so a week went by like this, and I was exhausted from my diligence while at the same time feeling proud that I had staved off any further calamity. In fact, I'm ashamed to say, I had at the end of the week a growing hope that perhaps matters might return to normal sooner rather than later.

Then came the night that shattered me, the night I learned the truth.

Ailis and I were down in the salon where Lorna spent much of his time. He wasn't there, however. It was still light outside, partially from all the snow on the ground, but it was growing ever darker inside. I was thinking of going back upstairs rather than lighting the lamps, when suddenly…

'Struan! My little harling! Out in the snow!'

I turned to look and to assure the harling it wasn't so, but to my horror, I saw a harling at the window-door, beating his hands against the glass.

I was so shocked that I stood frozen, while Ailis rushed to the door to let the harling inside. But then I heard the racket as the locked door wouldn't budge and Ailis tore at it and cried. I rushed up to pull him away – and that's when I saw the creature outside had red hair, just as the harling has described. He was beating fiercely on the glass as suddenly the ghostly organ sounded, beginning a low moan and rising up nearly to a scream.

And suddenly I realised. There wasn't any sound coming from the harling banging on the window. If there were, it would have probably been drowned out by the music by then, but I hadn't heard any banging at all before. I'd *seen* it, but not *heard* it. Did my harling hear it?

I grabbed Ailis about the waist and tore him away from the windows and out of the room as he screamed and kicked.

'I have to let him in! He'll die!' He even shrieked that he hated me, which broke my heart, but I had to get us away.

By the time I made it upstairs Ailis had ceased his wild thrashing and was simply whimpering in my arms. Still, it was enough to draw Dorlit, who came to the hall to see what was going on.

'The harling is back,' I whispered.

My friend went white. After a moment, he leaned over and whispered to me, 'Leave Ailis in his room and I'll have Manus set a cantrip that'll tell him if he moves to leave. Then I'll come to your room and we can talk.'

A few minutes later I came straight out with what I planned to do. I was going to leave the manor and take Ailis with me, off to somewhere safe. 'There's something evil and wrong here,' I said, 'and I can't bear it.'

Dorlit shook his head and told me I couldn't take Lorna's ward; he wasn't mine to take.

Besides, he admitted, it was time he told me the truth about this cursed harling. The rest of the household already knew but it hadn't been an issue for some time, and so they had been hoping to spare me. But now I should know.

'I gathered the bits of this story from various neighbours back when I first came to work here,' he prefaced it. 'Back then, the hall was less isolated than it is today, and we had social events here. Lorna had a few local acquaintances – I won't say friends – and visitors, and down in the village people sometimes were willing to tell me things, whereas now they're as closed up as clams.'

He settled into my armchair while I listened, sitting at the end of my couch.

'You've seen the portraits, so you've a good idea of what the brothers looked like as young hara. And what Fingal looked like, too. All of three of them were haughty and proud. Not affectionate, but like nobles of old, I suppose.'

'Where was their other parent?' I interjected.

'Crane, who hosted them, had died even before their feybraiha,' he explained sadly. 'It was a freak accident, like with Ailis' parents, as a matter of fact. I can imagine that with Fingal being First Generation and not so understanding, focused on social standing, their coming of age wasn't all that pleasant. If it was, they never formed any bonds afterwards.'

I wanted to ask about the harling then, but I force myself to be patient, sensing there was a lengthy story ahead.

'Now I've told you how the brothers were tutored in music, but what I didn't mention is that music was Fingal's great love – his obsession really. I speculate it took off after his chesnari died. He could play a dozen musical instruments, and there was a whole room filled with them. In fact, there still is – but it's been locked up since before my time and I don't even go in there to dust. Manus told me not to bother, as Lorna doesn't touch the instruments.'

I thought of the organ and its broken innards.

'Eventually Fingal's love for music led him to hire a Ferike musician to come up to the house and play and teach for an entire month in the summer. Village hara told me a couple of different names, both starting with T, so I'll just call him Tranis. He and Fingal would spend days and days together, and there'd be concerts – the musician playing for Alpin and Lorna and, a few times, invited guests from town. One village har mentioned a concert at Cuttingtide. It started out as happy times.'

But did not remain so.

'By and by, Fingal got his heart set on a pipe organ. He located one in a church miles and miles away and had it relocated. I haven't the faintest idea how it got to be working, but I don't doubt some hara were well paid. And at last he had the organ up and running, and when Tranis came the summer after he spent most of the time having lessons to play.

'Thing was, Fingal became so obsessed with this organ, he failed to notice what Tranis was doing in his free time – seducing those young hara. Right under his nose, but all he could think of was that music. But you can bet Lorna and Alpin were interested. And I bet you can predict how things went.'

I didn't have to think long. 'If there was one har and two brothers, who I'd venture weren't amenable to sharing, it became a battle.'

'Oh, yes. The musician must've had a terrible time of it, having always to split his time between the two and placate each of them to alleviate their jealousy. And conceal it all from Fingal.

'But the situation that precipitated the tragedy came the following summer, when Tranis was persuaded to stay for two whole months. This was enough time for Alpin to gain the upper hand over his brother.

'The previous summer Tranis had played it coy, sharing breath and tempting them but not going very far, but finally he and Alpin shared aruna, somewhere hidden. And as the weeks went past, they intensified this affair. Tranis was, however, careful to spare time and affections on Lorna as well, for he didn't want to cause a dispute between the brothers. Yet in secret he pledged himself to Alpin, saying they were chesnari and should someday be blood bound.'

I now knew where this was going, in some part. 'Let me guess. After his lover left, Alpin discovered he was with pearl. And...' I considered what this vain har, in battle with his brother and apprehensive about his father, would do. 'He didn't tell anyhar, didn't let anyhar even guess he was with pearl, and dropped the pearl in secret.'

Dorlit nodded. 'In a little cottage no one was using, on the far side of the estate. He made up some story about where he was, visiting relatives I suppose. But then he came back again, beautiful and slim and haughty as ever, as if nothing had happened.'

'But what happened to the harling? Who cared for him?' I wondered. 'And what was his name?'

'Alpin visited several times a week I'm guessing. Left food for him. Maybe Alpin told people he'd grown a fondness for going on long walks. But otherwise he left the harling alone most of the time.'

I grimaced at the idea of this type of neglect. The harling must've been utterly dependent on his hostling.

'As for his name, I have it that it was Naoise, a very old name I think.' Despite the spelling, which I learned later in a book of names, it sounded like *Nee-shuh*, something one might say to soothe a harling.

'What Alpin was counting on was the musician returning that summer, which the har did. But the summer didn't turn out to be as happy as he'd expected. Tranis, wanting to avoid explosions of jealousy in the household, continued his flirtations with Lorna. I'd wager he was simply fickle. Because at the end of the summer, the relationship was still a secret and so was Naoise.

'Fall and winter of that year were dark days. Fingal seem to be going mad, playing the organ more than he paid attention to his estate or anyhar around him. This being the situation, Alpin, the older of the two and in line for the estate, stepped up and took charge of things, which is only right, but it infuriated Lorna. They were very close in age, so he felt the estate was every bit as much his right.

'By the time summer came around, the two of them were barely speaking and saw little of their father. But the musician arrived on schedule, giving both of them high hopes that soon there would be a resolution to their battle. That is, Lorna was hoping for that; Alpin knew that he had already won. But the tainted atmosphere in the house and the enmity between the brothers was such that Tranis announced that this was his last visit. He'd had enough of both of them.

'So off he went. Fingal continued off in his own world of madness in music, while the brothers were locked in battle, each living in their own separate wing and avoiding one another. Naoise, now two years old, remained out at the cottage, although I suppose he must've been going outside off on his own by then. No harling that age would just sit inside.'

'No, I don't suppose they would.' The idea of a harling living such a lonely existence sickened me.

'Tranis didn't return that next summer, and the brothers fought over whose fault it was. But as Shadetide arrived, they simply grew sad. That is, until Alpin came up with a plan to solve his dilemma with the harling being stuck out in the cottage. He wasn't going to admit to being jilted – and now the wretched matter of hiding

Naoise three years – but he came up with a way to secretly bring the harling into the house. So temporarily, he'd give the harling a better home, more attention, but hide him until, to be frank, his father died. After than he could do as he wished.

'Indeed, he did manage to settle Naoise into his wing of the manor house. It was a secret known only to a couple of hara in town like the clothier who made the harling's clothes and the old cook of those years. And even to them he told a tale of coming across an orphan in a village many miles off with nohar in a position to take him in.

'All the village knew this, but what they don't know is the rest of the story. I got most of it from dear Manus, who was just starting to work here then, and a couple of other househara since gone.

'Alpin could have just let matters lie, raising the harling, not breathing a word about the secret affair. It seemed, after all, that he had meant to conceal it. But sometime late in the year, near Natalia, he couldn't resist crowing to Lorna over how he'd come out on top. Not only would he be getting the estate, but he'd been the real winner with Tranis. He'd pledged to bond with him. All the flirting and attention after that first summer had been merely a ruse. And Lorna had never guessed, the idiot!

'Now, even though Lorna had clearly ruined any chance of a relationship, he was so furious and humiliated he vowed revenge.'

By now I was tense with anticipation. The candle had burned half down as Dorlit told the tale.

'And then came a night a few days into the new year when the clouds were heavy with snow and a blizzard blew about the estate. Hours after dinner, the quiet was split with the sound of enraged cursing and yelling, the slamming of doors, and against that the shouting of another har and the shrill sobs of a harling. Every househar heard but nohar came to investigate, as it was clearly a family matter. It was a few minutes that the voices continued, but then there came an unearthly sound, together with a shudder as if the air and earth together cracked. There followed a dead silence of some seconds, before the air was filled with terrible moans and wailing which, everyhar noticed, left the house and trailed off into the blizzard.

'All the househara were summoned afterwards and Fingal announced to all of them how Alpin was no longer his son. How could he conceal such weighty matters from his father as a potential blood bond? And a harling? A harling who had been living right in the house, and Alpin supposed his father would never know. (And he probably wouldn't have, but for Lorna sending Innes to spy. Innes had discovered the harling by listening through a wall and peeking in a window.) So the two, hostling and harling, had been thrown out of doors. Fingal announced that any har in the house who lent them aid would be let go.

'The next morning shepherds arrived at the house with a sledge. On it were the frozen bodies of Alpin and Naoise. The hostling's ice-covered arms were stiff about the harling's shoulders. The young one's face was a grimace of terror.'

Dorlit was staring up at the ceiling. Perhaps he was imagining the scene, just as I was.

I pressed my palms against my eyes to stem the tears.

'Fingal stopped playing his organ after that and was dead by year's end. I arrived about ten years later and by then, almost all the old househara had gone. The house was never the same and grew emptier and emptier. If not for Manus, I might have left myself, but with him here, life has been fair enough.'

I was still pressing back tears when Dorlit offered to bring us back some firewhisky. Afterwards both of us drank until our eyes crossed.

From that day on I wanted out of that house, but more than ever, I knew I needed to protect Ailis.

I watched over him even more carefully and began taking security measures. I checked the doors to the outside to make sure they were locked, and an hour before dark I'd shut the windows and pull shut the drapes. No ghostly harling was going to press his pale, frozen face against the window panes and lure my child out his death.

In the evening, downstairs and up, Ailis told me how he still heard the harling's mournful cries. I considered myself lucky to be deaf to this, but unlucky because I had to restrain the harling from going out to him. No matter what I said, the compulsion was strong.

Meanwhile I avoided Lorna as much as I dared, although of course he still wished to see his sori. But knowing what I knew, I wouldn't leave Ailis alone with him.

And so it was that a few days into the new year I was knitting in the harling's room as he slept when the bell by the door rang three times. This was Lorna's signal for me to come downstairs. He didn't use it often.

I scooped Ailis up and when halfway down the stairs he woke groggily, I hushed him and explained where we were going. I didn't mention to him that he was coming with me because I wasn't about to leave him alone. The organ music was wild that night and the trees outside were making a racket as wind and snow raged about the estate. Ailis wasn't so heavy that I couldn't carry him.

'Why have you brought Ailis?' Lorna asked as I came into the sitting room. 'I only rang for you and clearly he's asleep.'

I ducked my head. 'Sorry, but I won't leave him alone with that other... *harling*... crying and wailing.' At this Lorna's face filled with horror. Had he forgotten? 'He hasn't left Ailis alone in weeks. Keeps pleading with him to come outside.'

'He mustn't!' Lorna gasped.

Innes quickly leaned his charge back into the armchair and stroked his arm. 'It's alright, dear. Struan is keeping Ailis safe. Rest easy.'

Lorna did not look comforted, but Innes went on to say that he'd wanted help on some embroidery. There was a bit all knotted and neither of them could pick it out. Perhaps I could have a try?

Despite my wariness, I wasn't about to disobey an order, so I set Ailis down on the sofa and sat down on a stool to examine the embroidery. Innes moved the lamp closer, so I'd have the advantage of the light.

But the organ music was picking up, well above normal volume, and I heard a sound like ice pelting against the windows. I was picking ineffectually at the threads when all of a sudden Lorna got to his feet.

'There's screaming!' He put his hands to his ears. 'My father! Fingal! He's shouting!'

Before I could even sort out the meaning of this, Ailis started out of sleep and began crying out. 'My harling! He's in the house, not far away, crying. Something horrible is happening. We have to save him!'

I caught Innes' eye. 'Do you hear anything?' I mouthed.

'Just the storm and the... music.'

Each of our charges were now hysterical. Lorna was still holding his hands to his ears. I was forced to grab Ailis and hold him in my lap to keep him from running off.

But then Lorna rushed to his feet and out the door. Suddenly I too could hear the screams and howls. I even thought I heard a harling's voice, under the rising and falling wails of the organ. Taking Ailis hard by the hand, I ran down the hall with Innes and caught up with Lorna in the great hall.

Here we stopped dead in our tracks. We all stared at the door to the closed off rooms beside the fireplace – Alpin's rooms. The terrible noises seemed to be coming from the room just behind it.

But that wasn't all. The great chandelier was ablaze, although oddly it didn't seem to be giving off much light. The fire burned in the enormous hearth, but the room was icy cold.

Ailis resumed his pleas and I had to grab him by the shoulders to restrain him. Lorna stood still as a statue, just listening. Innes looked troubled but uncertain what to do.

At last the suite door flew open and out rushed a tall har with curly black hair, pushing before him a har and harling – Alpin and Naoise. The black-haired har was Fingal. He carried a thick, black walking stick with a brass handle.

'It's the har from the hollies!' Ailis cried, when he saw Alpin. 'See, I told you. And that's his harling. They've been in the house.'

Alpin stepped through the hall towards the great doors holding Naoise's hand. (I meanwhile had crouched to the ground to hold back Ailis, now more desperate than ever.) I thought Alpin would leave, but a few feet from the door he turned and faced his father. He looked just as in the portrait on the wall, gleaming red ringlets, but without the grand robe and furs. He wore only a lounge top and pants – and no shoes.

'You have never loved me,' he accused. 'I never knew until now, when you say you want to rob my Naoise of his life. I love him!'

The organ music seemed to answer for the long-dead Fingal, offering a clash of discordant notes and high-pitched whines.

'Spare us, I'm begging you!'

But Fingal stepped forward holding his walking stick before him, up off the ground, aiming it Naoise.

'No, Father!' cried Lorna. 'Don't do it! Spare the harling.'

Fingal didn't even acknowledge this, instead glancing over at a new figure, another ghost, this one with straight red hair and resembling a certain portrait I'd seen. Young Lorna's face was composed; he did not plead for the harling's life but instead displayed a look of triumph.

Fingal took a step forward and narrowed his eyes. The music

flared as a spark like lightening shot from the rod to Naoise, who convulsed and screamed before going limp.

All at once, the spectres vanished, along with the hearth fire. The illusion of lights on the chandelier faded. And the organ was quiet.

At my feet Ailis lay crumpled, having swooned straight away. Lorna was worse off, shuddering, gasping and murmuring. 'Spare him... spare him...'

After this, Lorna took to bed and never rose again. He spoke no more of the present but only of the past and to those long dead.

When he passed, Leven Manor went to Ailis, though held in trust by an older relative. It's taken years, but it's been remade now and is growing, living.

The organ is gone and so am I. Now I'm down in the village, on my own but hoping one day for a chesnari. And though I'm not certain I want a harling, of my own, I'd be happy to help raise one up at the manor. Ghosts or no ghosts, harlings need protecting.

> *'Alas, what is done in youth can never be undone in age.'*
> — 'The Old Nurse's Story' (Elizabeth Gaskell, 1852)

Glossary of Terms

Aghama – the first of all Wraeththu, regarded as a dehar.

Alba Caledon – the country formerly known as Scotland.

Alba Phorlakhan – the land adjoining Alba Sulh: the north and west portion of Alba Caledon, above the Great Glen.

Alba Sulh – the country formerly known as England.

Almagabra – lands corresponding roughly to what was once Mediterranean Europe.

Aruna – sexual union between hara that is both spiritual and physical.

Arunic – pertaining to aruna.

Bloomtide – a harish festival celebrated at the Spring equinox.

Chesna – (chez-nah) a close physical, emotional and spiritual relationship.

Chesnari – a partner in a chesna-bond.

Cuttingtide – a harish festival celebrated at the Summer equinox.

Dehar – a Wraeththu deity (pl. Dehara).

Devastation, the – one of many terms used to describe the final days of humanity, when the world was in turmoil, and there was catastrophic conflict between hara and humans. The days of change.

Fallsend – a city in northern Thaine known for musendsas and Garridan

Ferelithia – a town in Almagabra.

Ferike – a tribe of Jaddayoth.

Feybraiha – a period of time equating to puberty in humans when a har matures sexually. The term also refers to a day of celebration for this. At the end of his feybraiha, when he is physically ready, a har will take aruna with another for the first time. This is regarded as an important rite of passage.

First Generation – hara who became Wraeththu by being incepted as humans.

Fulminir – a fortress of the Varrs in Megalithica, often held in dread.

Garridan – a tribe of Jaddayoth, renowned for their expertise with poisons.

Gebaddon – an area of enchanted forest where Thiede imprisoned the vanquished Varrs and their leader, Ponclast.

Gelaming – the most influential tribe of Wraeththu, whose tribal home is Almagabra.

Girdle of Tiamat – what was formerly the Atlantic Ocean.

Har – a Wraeththu individual (pl. hara).

Harakin – a term used by a har to describe members of his family, or within small phyles, other phyle members. Also *kinshara*.

Harling – a young har not yet at feybraiha.

Hienama – equivalent of a priest/teacher/healer.

High-father – harish equivalent of a grandsire.

High-harling – harish equivalent of a grand-child

High-hostling – harish equivalent of a grandmother.

Hostling – the harish equivalent of a mother, a har who hosts and carries the egg, or pearl, in which harlings grow.

Hura – uncle (brother of father or hostling).

Immanion – principle city of Almagabra, founded by the Gelaming tribe, regarded as a centre of culture and learning.

Inception – the process by which a human becomes har, involving a transfusion of blood.

Jaddayoth – a country corresponding roughly to what was formerly northeast Europe and parts of Asia.

Kalamah – a tribe of Jaddayoth.

Kanene – hara more than usually adept in the arts of aruna, especially of a darker nature, who sell their services to other hara. Kanene are regarded with contempt by the majority of hara, since aruna is viewed as a sacred act, and the practices of kanene as profane or sacrilegious.

Kinshara – members of a phyle, sometimes bloody family

Kyme – a city of Alba Sulh, famous for its archives and libraries.

Lund – a territory in Alba Sulh, formerly known as the city of London.

Lyris, The – the phylarch of the Sahale, which see.

Majhahn – a magical ritual.

Megalithica – the landmass once known as North America.

Musenda – an establishment where hara can buy unusual forms of aruna.

Natalia – harish festival celebrated at the Winter solstice.

Nayati – a temple or sacred space for spiritual work

Ouana – the masculine aspect of Wraeththu

Pearl – the egg or sac within which a harling forms. Hara carry pearls within their bodies, which are expelled or 'born' some weeks before the harling reaches to state to emerge. Pearl is also a term of affection used by harish parents for their offspring. (*With pearl* – a har who is carrying a pearl.)

Phylarch – leader of a phyle

Phyle – a distinct community within a tribe, a sub tribe

Ponclast – former leader of the Varrs.

Pureborn – a har who has been born to harish parents rather than inception from human. A second-generation har and beyond.

Nahir Nuri – a har of high spiritual rank, who has undergone all caste training.

Roon (v) – slang word for taking aruna with somehar.

Roselane – a tribe of Jaddayoth.

Sahale – a tribe of Jaddayoth, who live underground.

Shilalama – capital of Roselane, a tribe of Jaddayoth.

Smoketide – a harish festival celebrated at the Autumn equinox.

Sori – nephew (harling of hura).

Soume – the feminine aspect of Wraeththu

Surakin – harish term equivalent to a cousin.

Thiede – influential har who founded the Gelaming tribe.

Tiahaar – a polite form of address (as in Sir, Madam)

Tuaththua – A tribe known for their scientific endeavours, hailing from Alba Phorlakhan and the surrounding islands (which see).

Uigenna -the proto-tribe of Wraeththu.

Unneah – a Wraeththu tribe of Megalithica.

Varrs – a Wraeththu tribe of Megalithica that controlled a large portion of the country – oppressively – until they were vanquished by the Gelaming.

Wraeththu – (ray-thoo) androgynous race that came to replace humanity.

Zigane – a nomadic tribe of hara and humans.

Map of Alba Sulh

About the Contributors

Storm Constantine has written stories since she was a small child and first went to school. Before that, she made them up in her head. Her first novel – the initial Wraeththu book, *The Enchantments of Flesh and Spirit* – was published in 1987, and has been followed by over 30 other books, both fiction and non-fiction, as well as nearly a 100 short stories. In 2003, she founded Immanion Press, in order to bring her back-catalogue novels (and those of writing friends) back into print, but it has since grown and thrived to publish new works, and – enjoying the freedom of publishing her work through her own company – Storm now releases her work exclusively through Immanion Press, although the first two Wraeththu trilogies, and her epic fantasy *The Magravandias Chronicles* remain in print through TOR in the United States. She's currently working on a new novel and more non-fiction titles in an esoteric vein. Storm lives in the Midlands of England with her husband and four cats.

Wendy Darling is based in Atlanta, Georgia, USA, and is co-author of *Breeding Discontent*, published by Immanion Press in 2003 as the first Wraeththu Mythos novel. She has been involved with Wraeththu in many different capacities, including editing various Wraeththu novels, maintaining the Inception and Forever Wraeththu fan web sites, and staffing several Wraeththu conventions. With Storm she also co-edits the Wraeththu Mythos story collections. Her full-time job is as a digital projects manager at Emory University, but she

engages in many side projects and hobbies, including photography, historic preservation, and fan fiction. She has also forged relationships with Wraeththu fans around the world and has been fortunate to meet several authors whose work is included in this collection. At home she is ruled by two cats, cats she did not have in her life until she met and visited with Storm, who as usual had a strong influence on her. Wendy enjoys international travel and tries to visit Storm and her husband Jim as often as she can. Connect with Wendy online at about.me/wdarling.

Martina Bellovičová is a professional translator, copywriter and language teacher, who resides in Brno, Czech Republic. Her first published short story, "A Piece of Meat", appeared in the fantasy collection "Rytiny". Since then, she published several fantasy/science-fiction stories in both Czech and English, one of which has been adapted for a comic, and is currently working on a steampunk novel. Next to fiction, she enjoys writing lyrics for a variety of bands. Prior to focusing more on writing, Martina devoted years of her life to theatre, music and dance, and some of these passions remained with her. A jack of all trades, she is the lead singer of the steampunk band Clockwork Animals, spins CDs at subculture parties under the pseudonym DJ Zlyhad and dances Irish and tribal styles. She considers herself a lifestyle goth/steampunk and does her best to revive the dying community in her country by organising a number of alternative events, most notably the regular goth party Clubbers Die Younger and the gothic bellydance festival Danse Macabre. Refusing to become a crazy cat lady, she decided to get a small collection of snakes instead.

Nerine Dorman is a South African author and editor of SFF currently residing in Cape Town. Her short fiction has been published in an assortment of anthologies, including the *Midian Unmade: Tales of Clive Barker's Nightbreed* (Tor Books); *The Endless Ages Anthology for Vampire: The Masquerade* (Onyx Path Publishing); Storm Constantine's Wraeththu Mythos (Immanion Press); fiction commissions for the role-playing game company Storm Bunny Studios; and *War Stories: New*

Military Science Fiction (Apex Publications), among others. Her YA fantasy novel *Dragon Forged* was a finalist in the South African 2017 Sanlam Youth Literature Prize, and she is the curator of the South African Horrorfest Bloody Parchment event and short story competition. Her short story "On the Other Side of the Sea" (Omenana, 2017) was nominated for a Hugo by Nerds of a Feather and shortlisted for a 2018 Nommo award. In addition, she is a founding member of the SFF authors' co-operative Skolion, that has assisted authors such as Masha du Toit, Suzanne van Rooyen, Cristy Zinn and Cat Hellisen in their publishing endeavours.

Zane Marc Gentis is the mild-mannered alter-ego of an even more mild-mannered real person, sitting at a computer and writing this bio in the 3rd person. He grew up on a wine farm in South Africa surrounded by a loving family but didn't let the lack of a tragic back-story prevent him from avoiding normality. His (deeply mysterious) past includes many social experiments, such as a bit part in which he acted as a pair of  hands in a short film, two occasions where he officiated at wedding ceremonies, and a short-lived stint spent as a burlesque show narrator. To date he has sold a horror screenplay and published several short stories but is still battling to complete his novel's second draft. If he spent less time designing a computer game about love or running table-top RPGs he might have finished a trilogy by now. Somehow Zane still manages to work a day job as a programmer, have a respectable social life and study for a degree part-time. Yes, he is just as surprised as you are.

 **Christiane Gertz** wrote her first book at the age of four, about two squirrels from outer space. Fortunately, it never got published, but still exists on some slowly-decaying pages hidden deep inside a cupboard somewhere in Wuppertal, Germany. As a teenager, she wore her mother's black skiing trousers because black jeans hadn't been invented yet (at least in Wuppertal), and made a music fanzine called "Torch" about several singers with the same taste in clothing. She became a photographer, and later studied to become a translator to earn some money for a change. Christiane is the author of a non-fiction book about the historical quarter she's living in, entitled "Der Ölberg, mein Kiez", and spends her free time organising rock concerts, walking and travelling with her husband, acquiring domains for just another website, collecting Mexican silver bracelets, cooking and thinking about the next projects. She's a firm Wraeththu fan and would love to do the casting for a TV series. Meanwhile, she's writing a fiction book in German, guaranteed to include mysteries, historical towns, singers and squirrels. She feels very honoured to be part of the Wraeththu world now.

Amanda Kear was born in a small town in the north-east of Scotland, where the bookshops all closed down long before the internet was even a twinkle in the universe's eye. Fortunately, she had fellow small-town geeks to keep her sane by introducing her to the concept of fanfic, fanzines and tabletop roleplaying games. She fled to Aberdeen University to study zoology, then to Bristol University to spent three years watching deceased sea creatures rot or – when the experiments went right – turn into fossils. Strangely, her expertise with decaying squid and rotting ragworms turned out not to have long term career prospects! She worked for 23 years at the BBC's Natural History Unit on series such as The Natural History of an Alien, Predators, Fossil Detectives, Deadly 360, Andy's Dinosaur Adventures and Nature's Weirdest Events. Finally, she ran away from telly to join the circus, but the jobcentre must have misheard her, as she is now a civil servant. In her spare time, she still messes about with fanfic, runs RPGs, self-publishes RPG scenarios (Squaddies military science fiction), paints miniatures and helps to run Bristolcon, a small science fiction convention.

Fiona Lane was born and brought up near Glasgow during the Time of The Flared Trouser and Unfeasibly High Platform Shoes. By the time we all came to our senses, she had relocated to Aberdeen, and spent several years waiting for a number six bus, in a horrible collision involving the nature of time and the Aberdeen weather. During the eighties, while she was waiting for the Internet to be invented, she acquired a husband and a couple of replacement units, and they all now live in a field full of sheep in Aberdeenshire, along with the odd cat or two

and Fiona's posse of obsolete computers, many of which she has single-handedly restored to a completely non-functioning condition. She once kept chickens, but they were messy, and she couldn't use them to buy vintage shoes from eBay. The eggs were good though. She likes gin and hats and dislikes the oppression of the proletariat. Her hobbies include cooking, gardening, and staring into the abyss.

Maria J. Leel is now enjoying early retirement after a varied career, which included everything from Urban Ecologist, Braille Transcriber, First Aid Trainer and Reflexologist. She lives in Shropshire with her husband, Malcolm, three cats and a varying number of chickens. They are turning their large garden into a permaculture paradise, complete with veggie beds and a food forest. Maria has travelled widely volunteering on many projects such as the California Condor Recovery Program, the Australian railway Puffing Billy and the

Fiji Pine reforestation scheme. For a time she lived on a Kibbutz near Jerusalem, and as a result has an abiding interest in alternative living styles and communal living. She has been writing plays and stories almost all her life and has contributed to several Wraeththu Mythos projects including her first novel 'Song of the Sulh'. She is now working on her second entitled *Last Ride to Lyonis*.

Ruby is the official artist for the Wraeththu Mythos, who creates all the covers for the Immanion Press editions. She started drawing from her imagination long before she could or indeed would talk. Still heavily influenced by the fairy tales and myths absorbed from her childhood, Ruby has grown into a multimedia illustrator interested in exploring the darkly sensual, symbolic and surreal undercurrents of life. Ruby's illustrations blend perfectly the mythological, the classical and the future fantastic and are also evocative of Beardsley and Mucha. She is now a much sought-after cover artist and interior illustrator for books across many genres, and is the creator of the ongoing Wraeththu Tarot project.

Ruby is up for designing anything as long as it fits in with her bohemian aesthetic and animal-loving ethos (her dream is to run a combined cat sanctuary and art gallery by the sea). On any one day she might be fleshing out a tattoo design and then the next sketching concept art for a theatre set or perhaps sourcing unusual props for a photo-shoot.

E. S. Wynn is the author of over seventy books in print and is the chief editor of Thunderune Publishing. In his spare time, he spins stories, builds board games, stitches together battle jackets, runs a pair of magazines and encourages people to create new art constantly. He's openly transgender and does what he can to pursue acceptance and love for and within the trans community. During the last decade, he's worked with hundreds of authors and edited thousands of manuscripts for nearly a dozen different magazines. His stories and articles have been published in dozens of journals, e-zines and anthologies. He's taught classes in literature, marketing, math, spirituality, energetic healing and guided meditation. He's also worked as a voice-over artist for several different horror and sci-fi podcasts, albums and eBooks. E.S. Wynn has written a Wraeththu Mythos trilogy, entitled *The Gold Country Series*, available through Immanion Press.

Books by Storm Constantine

The Wraeththu Chronicles
The Enchantments of Flesh and Spirit
The Bewitchments of Love and Hate
The Fulfilments of Fate and Desire
The Wraeththu Chronicles (omnibus of trilogy)

The Wraeththu Histories
The Wraiths of Will and Pleasure
The Shades of Time and Memory
The Ghosts of Blood and Innocence

The Alba Sulh Sequence (Wraeththu Mythos)
The Hienama
Student of Kyme
The Moonshawl

Other Wraeththu Books
Blood, The Phoenix and a Rose (triptych of novellas)
A Raven Bound with Lilies (short stories)

The Artemis Cycle
The Monstrous Regiment
Aleph

The Grigori Books
Stalking Tender Prey
Scenting Hallowed Blood
Stealing Sacred Fire

The Magravandias Chronicles:
Sea Dragon Heir
Crown of Silence
The Way of Light

Hermetech
Burying the Shadow
Sign for the Sacred
*Calenture
Thin Air
*Silverheart (with Michael Moorcock)

Short Story Collections:
The Thorn Boy and Other Dreams of Dark Desire
Mythangelus
Mythophidia
Mytholumina
Mythanimus
Mythumbra (forthcoming 2018)
*Splinters of Truth (NewCon Press)

Wraeththu Mythos Collections
(co-edited with Wendy Darling, including stories by the editors and other writers)
Paragenesis
Para Imminence
Para Kindred
Para Animalia
Para Spectral

Songs to Earth and Sky
(Stories of the Seasons, including a novella, a novelette and a short story by Storm Constantine, and six other stories by Mythos writers)

Non-Fiction
Sekhem Heka
Grimoire Dehara: Kaimana
Grimoire Dehara: Ulani (with Taylor Ellwood)
Grimoire Dehara: Nahir Nuri (with Taylor Ellwood)
*The Inward Revolution (with Deborah Benstead)
*Egyptian Birth Signs (with Graham Phillips)
*Bast and Sekhmet: Eyes of Ra (with Eloise Coquio)
Whatnots and Curios (essays and reviews)

(All titles available through Immanion Press, except for those marked with *)

IMMANION PRESS

Purveyors of Speculative Fiction

A Raven Bound with Lilies by Storm Constantine

The Wraeththu have captivated readers for three decades. This anthology of 15 tales collects all the published Wraeththu short stories into one volume, and also includes extra material, including the author's first explorations of these beings. The tales range from the 'creation story' *Paragenesis*, through the bloody, brutal rise of the earliest tribes, and on into a future, where strange mutations are starting to emerge from hidden corners of the earth. ISBN: 978-1-907737-80-0 £11.99, $15.50 pbk

Blood, the Phoenix and a Rose by Storm Constantine

This triptych of novellas begins with an enigma: Gavensel, who appears unearthly. He has been hidden away in Sallow Gandaloi by Melisander, an alchemist, but is this seclusion to protect Gavensel from the world or the world from him? As his story unfolds, the shadow of the dark fortress Fulminir falls over him, and memories of his past slowly return. The only way to find the truth is to go back through the layers of time, to when the blood was fresh. ISBN: 978-1-907737-75-6 £11.99, $18.99 pbk

Songs to Earth and Sky by Storm Constantine and Others

Six writers explore the seasonal festivals of the year, dreaming up new beliefs and customs, new myths, new dehara – the gods of Wraeththu. From the silent, snow-heavy forests of Megalithican mountains, through the lush summer fields of Alba Sulh, into the hot, shimmering continent of Olathe, this book explores the Wheel of the Year, bringing its powerful spirits and landscapes to vivid life. 9 new tales, including 3 from Storm herself, also *Wendy Darling, Nerine Dorman, Suzanne Gabriel, Fiona Lane* and *E. S. Wynn*. ISBN 978-1-907737-84-8 £11.99 $15.50 pbk

Madame Two Swords by Tanith Lee

An unnamed narrator, in the French city of Troy, finds an old book of the writings of the revolutionary, Lucien de Ceppays, who lived and died in the city two centuries before. She feels a strange bond to the life and thoughts of this long-dead man, and finds herself inexorably guided to meet the peculiar and unnerving Madame Two Swords, an old woman with a history, and her own enduring bonds to Lucien – as well as the book.
ISBN 978-1-907737-81-7 £11.99, $15.50 pbk

The Weird Tales of Tanith Lee

This anthology of 28 tales comprises all of Tanith's stories published in the seminal magazine *Weird Tales* during her lifetime. Some of them are previously uncollected, and appeared in print only in the magazine, so will be new to many of Tanith's fans. Her highly-respected and influential work spanned every genre, and this sumptuous collection demonstrates the range of her versatility. This collection showcases the myriad styles of the writer rightly known as the High Priestess of Fantasy.
ISBN: 978-1-907737-73-2, £11.99 $18.99

Venus Burning: Realms by Tanith Lee

Tanith Lee wrote 15 stories for the acclaimed *Realms of Fantasy* magazine. This book collects all the stories in one volume for the first time, some of which only ever appeared in the magazine so will be new to some of Tanith's fans. These tales are among her best work, in which she takes myth and fairy tale tropes and turns them on their heads. Lush and lyrical, deep and literary, Tanith Lee created fresh poignant tales from familiar archetypes. ISBN 978-1-907737-88-6, £11.99, $17.50 pbk

All these and more on our web site
Immanion Press
http://www.immanion-press.com
info@immanion-press.com

Wraeththu Mythos Novels

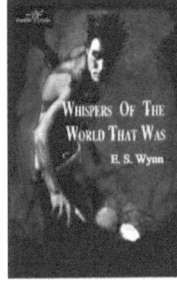 

Breeding Discontent by Wendy Darling & Bridgette Parker
Terzah's Sons by Victoria Copus
Song of the Sulh by Maria J. Leel
Whispers of the World That Was by E. S. Wynn
Echoes of Light and Static by E. S. Wynn
Voices of the Silicon Beyond by E. S. Wynn (forthcoming 2018)

Further details of Wraeththu Mythos and other fiction
can be found on our web site

Immanion Press
http://www.immanion-press.com
info@immanion-press.com

NEWCON PRESS

http://newconpress.co.uk/

The very best in fantasy, science fiction, and horror

Learning How to Drown, by Cat Hellisen

Cat Hellisen is a South African writer of dark fantasy. She has the ability to conjure a sense of 'otherness' that most writers can only envy, casting grounded characters driven by passions and ambitions we can all recognise in situations that take a step away from the reality we know. Her stories have already featured in such venues as Fantasy & Science Fiction and Tor.com, and she is the winner of the Short Story Day Africa Prize. This collection represents her best work to date, gathering together seventeen fabulous stories, two of which appear for the first time and all of which showcase why Cat Hellisen is being tipped as an author to watch. Available as a numbered limited-edition hardback, each copy signed by the author, and an A5 paperback. ISBN pbk: 978-1-910935-82-8 £12.99 pbk, £24.99 hbk

For Love of Distant Shores: Tales of the Apt by Adrian Tchaikovsky

In a narrative reminiscent of Phileas Fogg meets Professor Challenger, *For Love of Distant Shores* features the exploits of scientist-cum-adventurer Doctor Ludweg Phinagler, as recorded by his (semi-)faithful assistant, Fosse. Maverick academic Phinagler is able to charm almost everyone he meets... except for his fellow academics at Collegium. He mounts expeditions to the far-flung corners of the world during which he confronts ancient mysteries and deadly dangers. Includes 4 separate adventures. Tales of the Apt provides a companion to the best-selling *Shadows of the Apt* decalogy. Available as an A5 paperback and a signed hardback edition, limited to 100 numbered copies ISBN pbk: 978-1-910935-71-2 £12.99 pbk, £24.99 hbk

www.ingramcontent.com/pod-product-compliance
Lightning Source LLC
Chambersburg PA
CBHW020417260626
47156CB00007B/2435